RIKER'S APOCALYPSE

The Promise (Book 1)

SHAWN CHESSER

CONTENTS

ACKNOWLEDGEMENTS

For Steve P. You are missed, friend. Maureen, Raven, and Caden ... I couldn't have done this without your support. Thanks to our military, LE and first responders for all you do. To the people in the U.K. and elsewhere around the world who have been in touch, thanks for reading! Lieutenant Colonel Michael Offe, thanks for your service as well as your friendship. Larry Eckels, thank you for helping me with some of the military technical stuff. Any missing facts or errors are solely my fault. Beta readers, you rock, and you know who you are. Special shoutout to the master of continuity: Giles Batchelor. You helped make this novel a better read. Thanks to Joseph Fleischman for your help with the NY transit system. Thanks George Romero for introducing me to zombies. To my friends and fellows at S@N and Monday Steps On Steele, thanks as well. Lastly, thanks to Bill W. and Dr. Bob ... you helped make this possible. I am going to sign up for another 24.

Special thanks to John O'Brien, Mark Tufo, Joe McKinney, Craig DiLouie, Armand Rosamilia, Heath Stallcup, Saul Tanpepper, Eric A. Shelman, and David P. Forsyth. I truly appreciate your continued friendship and always invaluable advice. Thanks to Jason Swarr and Straight 8 Custom Photography for another awesome cover. I'm grateful to Marine veteran Buck Doyle of Follow Through Consulting for portraying Lee Riker on the cover. Once again, extra special thanks to Monique Happy for her work editing "The Promise." Mo, as always, you kicked butt and took names in getting this MS polished up! Working with you over the years has been nothing but a pleasure. I truly appreciate having a confidante I can trust. If I have accidentally left anyone out ... I am truly sorry.

***

Edited by Monique Happy Editorial Services
www.moniquehappy.com

Prologue

October 8th 2016 - Atlanta, Georgia – Zero Dark Thirty

Lee Riker, or *Leland* as it said on his birth certificate, awoke with a start. Acting against his initial instinct to sit up and take a visual recon of his surroundings, he kept his eyes shut, unclenched his fists, and relaxed all the muscles in a body suddenly and involuntarily gone rigid. Slowly releasing the trapped breath, he relied on his other senses to paint the picture for him.

The air inside the low-ceilinged building was still and smelled of farts, dirty socks, and fear-laced sweat. Until a week ago, when Riker's sister had called with good news long in the making, he imagined he had been a major contributor in the latter column. The years following the financial meltdown and subsequent housing collapse, during which the services of an expert finish carpenter were unneeded by speculators snapping up distressed properties and throwing lipstick on their pigs, the only constants in Riker's life were the weekly calls from his sister up north and the rising and setting of the sun.

Someone nearby on his right was snoring. Not the harsh sawing of logs kind of disturbance. This was more of a low rumble interspersed with a subtle yet very annoying whistle. And judging by the sour stink of alcohol riding the acrid breath being exhaled in Riker's general direction, the man who had stumbled in late under the bored gaze of the administrator was likely enjoying his last night. A bad thing considering that the moniker *Hotlanta* didn't apply after dark in October when the temperatures routinely dropped into the forties and continued a southbound slide all the way through the fall and winter months.

1

Closer still, the man to his left was talking in his sleep. Though muffled by a thin Army-surplus blanket identical to the one stretched across Riker's sternum, the plea for air support was sincere, the words bearing the weight of the conflict the man was reliving in his nightmare.

When Riker finally opened his eyes, he was greeted by the sight of dozens of unmoving forms lying atop cots like his and swathed in gray blankets like his. Awash in the diffuse light of early morning and reminding him of so many hillocks on a three-dimensional topo map, the uneven outlines of sleeping veterans impeded his line of sight across the spartanly appointed room.

Lancing in through the half-dozen opaque windows set high up on the east wall to Riker's right, blurry golden bars of light spilled across the soon-to-be-homeless Marine who called himself Snuffy. A decorated veteran of the war in Vietnam, the sixty-something had recently told Riker he had lost it all after hitting the bottle hard following the Veterans Administration's failure to get him in to see about abdominal pain. Cancer of the pancreas had spread and metastasized while his name languished on a secret waiting list created by civilians looking for a bonus based on keeping wait times respectable. After being put on hold too many times to count and then given the okey doke when he stormed the desks of the VA hospital pencil pushers unannounced, he had simply given up and resorted to augmenting the prescribed pain pills with Wild Turkey. Failed by a country he'd spent his youth serving and nearly died for, Snuffy had thrown in the metaphorical towel.

Riker sat up and planted his right foot on the cool, tiled floor. He glanced over his shoulder at the former Army staff sergeant now calling for *danger close* fire in his sleep. He imagined the young man coveted a C-130 gunship or a pair of A-10s to turn the tide of battle currently raging in his at-rest subconscious mind.

Riker shook his head as he worked his left leg off the cot. The same indifference that was adversely affecting the warfighters of Snuffy's era was now failing many of the young men and women coming home from the ongoing wars in the Middle East,

Africa, and various other hotbeds of terrorist activity across the planet.

As Riker sat up and folded the blanket into a neat square, he watched with sadness as a few bunks away, Staff Sergeant Justin Nunez drew his legs to his chest, clasped both hands behind his head, and pressed forehead to knees in the fetal position. As the man's whispered words became indistinguishable from Snuffy's snoring, the blanket fell away and Riker saw that the man's body was wracked by tremors.

Blanket in hand, Riker crept over to the prostrate Nunez. Keeping his distance, he scooped the fallen blanket off the floor and draped it along with his own atop the shivering man.

Choosing a spot on the floor between cots, Riker planted his hands a shoulder's width apart, extended his legs, and began knocking out pushups, allocating the first twenty-two as a tribute to the number of veterans lost daily to suicide, then finishing the set for Murphy, Grayson, and Kincaid, all fallen buddies of his. Though nothing close to the number of pushups he'd performed while still a cog in the Big Green Machine, he never did more than twenty-five, thinking to do so would somehow jinx his buddies who still resided on the good side of the dirt.

Since Riker always wore pants and a shirt to bed when sleeping in the shelter he'd been calling home for the last thirteen months, he only had to don a single sock and his scuffed tan work boots.

The gatekeeper of the Atlanta Mission was a grizzled veteran of the first war in the Gulf. A tank commander who got in his share of the shit against crack elements of Hussein's Republican Guard corps during the battle of 73 Easting, Jack Ross spoke rapid-fire as if he was still atop an M1A1 Abrams and issuing orders to a crew sitting unseen in its bowels.

"What's eating you, Riker?" he asked, setting his coffee cup aside and throwing his combat-boot-clad feet off the desktop as he sat up.

The desk took up most of the small, one-windowed room plastered with posters full of uplifting messages. The door to the room was a split item, the bottom half-closed.

Riker leaned against the door jamb and locked eyes with the man everyone called "Koss" — a bastardized pronunciation of *Chaos*, his Desert Storm call sign.

Exhaling, Riker said, "What time do you plan on showing Snuffy the sidewalk?"

"Why do you care?" asked Koss. "Snuff came in drunk last night. Made his bed, so to speak."

"I just want to speak with him before he moves on. That's all."

Koss looked Riker up and down. "You got your coat on. Going out?"

Riker nodded. "To get coffee and a newspaper. Back in ten." He studied Koss's face and detected a hint of approval.

"If he wakes up while you're gone," Koss said with a grimace, "I'll stay his execution a few minutes for you."

"He's fighting more than just the bottle. You can't cut him some slack?"

Silver brows hitching an inch, Koss said, "Rules are rules, Riker. If you fell off, I'd be showing you the door, too."

Riker thought, *I'll be showing myself the door later, anyway.* "Thank you," he said. "I appreciate the courtesy."

Koss extended a hand. "Where ya goin' *after* your jaw session with Snuffy?"

Riker adjusted his Atlanta Braves ball cap. "North," he admitted, adding a brief summary of his mother's recent passing and the promise he had made to her.

"How are you going to honor that promise with your means?"

Keeping his hole card close to his vest, Riker said, "I'll figure something out."

Koss opened a drawer and came out with a business card. "This kid is good people. Saved my son's life in the Sandbox. Give him a call if you scrape some cash together. Mention my name and he'll likely give you a friends and family discount."

Riker took the card. Looked it over on both sides, then tucked it in his wallet. Head cocked to one side, he said, "What tipped you off that I was going to move on?"

"You packed your bag last night. Then, a few minutes ago, I witnessed you bequeath your only blanket to Nunez."

Riker eyed the thin computer monitor atop the desk. On it were four separate panes displaying moving images beamed in from cameras mounted high on the walls in the bunkroom. In one panel, he recognized rows of cots standing out starkly against the white tiles. Awash in dim light, a few of the blanketed forms were stirring.

"Nothing gets past you, Chaos." Riker rapped his knuckles on the jamb he'd been leaning against and turned toward the door to the street. Two strides and he was through the door and standing on the trash-strewn sidewalk and squinting against the low-hanging sun.

Chapter 1

Middletown University - 7:15 AM

Third time's the charm, thought Charlie Noble when the red light above the door handle flashed to green. Acting quickly, lest he have to punch in the six-digit code again, he shouldered open the heavy oak door, trapped it midway through its backswing with his butt, and scooted his belongings inside with a forceful nudge of his boot.

There was an audible hiss overhead as a sensor on the fluorescent lights detected his movement and flared to life, bathing the entire forty-by-sixty-foot room in brilliant white light. Just as the door was closing behind him, a voice from down the hall called out for Professor Sylvester Fuentes.

Not expecting Fuentes in the lab for another ninety minutes or so, Noble figured he'd see what the caller wanted. Still clutching a pumpkin spice latte in one hand, he crabbed around his book bag and backpack, still on the floor where he'd dropped them, and poked his head into the hall.

He looked right. The hall was empty all the way to the T at the far end.

Craning around the door's edge, he cast his gaze down the hall in the other direction and spotted a man in a cobalt blue uniform walking toward him, slow and deliberate. Maybe a rent-a-cop or an armored car driver, the man was mid-thirties, a little overweight, and full in the face. Straw-colored hair peeked from under a patrolman's cap snugged down low over a heavy brow. From under the cap's highly polished black brim, searching eyes roved the hallway.

"Professor Fuentes?" asked the man, his gait slowing even further as he looked at the clipboard balanced atop the shoebox-sized package in his hands.

Still peering out from behind the door, Noble's eyes did a mad dance between the boxy black pistol hanging from the officer's thick leather belt and the parcel he was carrying.

The man stopped on the carpet an arm's reach from Noble, locked eyes with the TA and slowly, while enunciating every word, asked, "Are you Professor Sylvester Fuentes?"

Noble shot a quick glance at the badge riding above the man's left breast pocket. It looked like a kid's toy, chrome-plated, with the words *Secure Package Delivery* arching over a cluster of stars. Pinned below the badge was a thin plastic nametag with *Special Courier Butters* embossed on it.

"I'm not Professor Fuentes," answered Noble. "Name's Charlie Noble. I'm Professor Fuentes' teaching assistant." He switched the latte to his left hand and extended his right. "How can I help you?"

Butters ignored the offered hand. "The package is for the professor," he said. "It's got this radiation symbol on it. You sure you're high enough a pay grade to sign for it?"

Suppressing a chuckle, Noble said, "That's not a *trefoil,* that's the international biohazard warning. Just means there's something biological and of a sensitive nature inside. *Contagion* is probably a better description."

"Like the plague?"

"Not really," said Noble, shaking his head. "In addition to the professor's teaching duties here, he's also involved in a consortium. A far-ranging group of academics who research different strains of influenza for the CDC and other branches of government. 'There can never be too many cooks in the kitchen,' the professor is fond of saying. You know, different sets of eyes and all. So to answer your question, Officer Butters, whatever's inside there *is* viral like the plague and *might* give us the sniffles if we were exposed, but *the* Black Death plague—" Charlie chuckled again "—I'm pretty sure the professor would never receive samples of something that virulent here at MU."

7

Replaying in his head his fumble of the package in the parking lot and wanting nothing more than to rid himself of the mysterious item and all the perceived responsibility and dangers associated with it, Special Courier Butters handed over a ballpoint pen and a bulky metal box containing a clipboard and what seemed like half a ream of paper. Stabbing a finger on the manifest, he said, "Sign for it then … Mr. Noble. Right here on this line that says MU Biology."

Noble set his latte on a nearby table and took the clipboard from Butters.

Pen hovering over the form, clipboard heavy in his hand, Noble walked his gaze along the line, left to right, reading the different entries. He learned the package had been forwarded here from the Centers for Disease Control and Prevention in Atlanta by none other than John Halverson, *the* Director of Infectious Diseases. Then he read the fine print detailing its origin of birth, an acronym followed by a string of letters that were all foreign to him. Brow furrowing, he bounced the entry *DOD USAMRIID Ft. Det., Md.*, around in his brain. Drawing a blank on its significance, he signed his name, handed the clipboard over, and took possession of the delivery along with a copy of the document he'd just signed. Holding the door open with his body, he watched Special Courier Butters hustle down the hall with a sense of urgency missing on his initial approach. Once the guard was lost from sight, Noble shifted his attention to the parcel. It was wrapped tightly in brown shipping paper, all four corners reinforced with clear tape. Other than the white label containing the red biohazard sticker and a black barcode, there were no other clues as to what was inside. Interest piqued, Noble pored over the document and found that even it relayed nothing specific about the parcel's contents.

As if sizing up a present, he bounced the package in his hands gently, finding it much lighter than he'd anticipated.

Forgetting about his bags on the floor behind the door, Noble turned to enter the lab and caught one of the shoulder straps with the toe of his boot. Thrown off balance, he pitched forward, legs pistoning the air with his own words *Contagion is probably a better description* jumping to the forefront of his mind.

Miraculously, after doing a crazy midair dance with the box cradled in the crook of one arm like a football, he came back down, upright, with the sensitive delivery still in his possession. Heart hammering, trying to escape his chest, he set the box on the table by his latte. After stowing his bags in the professor's closet, he hung his winter jacket on a hook and donned a white knee-length lab coat.

Not completely convinced the box contained something as benign as this season's strain of influenza, Noble retrieved the package and paperwork from the table. Carrying it in a firm two-handed grip, he made his way carefully to the back of the room, deposited it on the professor's desk, and plopped down on the chair.

Chapter 2

Feeling the sun warm on his face, Riker walked past the shadowy recesses of doorways occupied by men whom the night before had arrived too late to secure a cot in the shelter. Off of his left shoulder was a lightly travelled four-lane boulevard. Empty airline liquor bottles and scraps of paper littered the gutter and grass strip paralleling the boulevard.

A block from the shelter Riker was getting ready to step off the curb when a rust bucket of a pickup with no turn signal flashing hung a sharp right and cut the air less than a yard in front of him.

Having already looked to all points of the compass and noticed the truck barreling down the boulevard from behind, he was aware of its proximity but not ready for the two-ton object to do what it did.

Gritting his teeth against the nails-on-a-chalkboard keen of worn brake pads grabbing bare metal, Riker froze mid-step and tracked the truck with his gaze until it ground to a halt a dozen feet to his right.

At least the backup lights work, thought Riker as they flared white and the old Chevy began to reel in the distance between them.

With another squawk from the brakes, the truck stopped broadside to Riker.

"Look before you leap, *dickhead*," barked the driver through his half-open window.

Riker felt his ears go hot as a familiar tension began to build between his shoulder blades.

Ignore him, said Riker's inner voice.

The driver ripped the pair of wraparound sunglasses from his head onehanded and tossed them on the dash. He leaned across the seat and cranked the passenger window down the rest of the way. "Big fucker like you should be able to see all the way to Olympic Park from here. Yet you had to step out in front of me anyway."

Riker was staring holes in the man's narrow face. That he was wearing a Chicago Cub's ball cap made ignoring the verbal barrage next to impossible. However, instead of opening his mouth and letting loose on the guy with both barrels, Riker drew in a deep breath and began to make his way around the front of the idling truck.

Last thing he needed was to lose his cool, beat the guy senseless, then end up in jail due to an injury sustained well over a decade ago and thousands of miles from here.

Disaster averted, he thought, proud of himself for channeling a little of Martin Luther King Jr.'s philosophy and truly 'turning the other cheek.'

The driver gunned the engine as Riker made the turn around the right front fender. The truck began a slow roll forward when Riker was fully committed.

All was still well with Riker until he heard the clink of the front bumper hitting his leg.

The heat manifesting in his ears and neck and cheeks was already burning hotter than ever when the vibration from what was little more than a tap coursed through his stump, setting the usually docile nerves there afire.

Back to back, as the driver rolled the transmission to Park and stomped on the emergency brake, there came a heavy clunk and metallic twang of a spring going under tension. In reaction to the sudden stop, the load of scrap metal in the truck's bed shifted and an old water heater clanged against the bedrails.

The truck was still lurching on its tired suspension when the driver's door creaked open and the noise of boots hitting the pavement reached Riker's ears. Instantly advice learned in anger management classes came to him: *Diffuse the situation with humor.* As he rounded the truck, arms at his sides, Riker locked eyes with the driver. "Listen, fella," he said calmly. "There's no sport in fighting a one-legged man."

In his early thirties, the man was wiry and well-muscled. He slammed his door and squared up with Riker who, at six-three and two-thirty, was a good head and a half taller and carried at least a seventy-five-pound weight advantage.

"There's no sport in running over a one-legged prick with a truck, either," shot the man, eyes narrowing as he assumed the classic Jack Dempsey-esque boxer's pose—fists at half-mast and legs splayed and planted a shoulder's width apart.

By now the heat had spread north to the crown of Riker's head and the Calypso beat of his heart was throbbing behind his eyes and in his temples.

"The bigger they are, the harder they fall," said the man.

Cars continued on their way, the drivers at the wheels with things to do and places to be mostly ignoring the lopsided standoff.

Sticking with humor, Riker said, "At least the Cubbies might win a pennant in your lifetime."

"Fuck you and the Braves," said the man, his breathing now coming rapidly. "We owned you this year. Makes me happy even if we don't win it all."

As a last resort, Riker resorted to honesty. After all, Mom always said it was the best policy.

"Hate my Braves all you want. But know that if you swing on me, I'll parry it. Next I'll be seeing red and you'll be down for the count. Cards always fall that way when someone gets my ire up. And I'd call running into a man's fake leg an applicable offense."

Eye twitch giving him away, the man Riker had decided henceforth would be referred to as Napoleon launched off his back foot and unloaded the right cross he'd had coiled and waiting.

Left forearm absorbing the blow, likely breaking a few of Napoleon's fingers as a result, Riker said, "I told you so," through gritted teeth and brought his closed fist down hammer-like on the blue button atop Napoleon's Cubs hat.

As if his power switch had been thrown to *Off,* Napoleon crashed vertically to the sun-warmed asphalt, legs and arms all akimbo.

Riker bent at the waist and grabbed the smaller man two-handed. Palms cupping the man's underarms, he easily lifted him off the ground and put him back behind the wheel of his truck.

After reaching across the slumped-over man to kill the engine, Riker pocketed the keys and cast a glance through the rear window. Seeing what he was looking for, he reached his right arm into the bed and came out with a Budweiser can. He shook the empty and was pleased to hear a sloshing noise telling him it truly was not a dead soldier. He dumped the can's contents down the front of Napoleon's shirt and closed him inside with the skunky odor of stale, day-old beer.

Riker looped around back of the static pickup, and mounted the curb with a faked look of worry on his face. Waving one arm in the air while pointing at the pickup, he successfully flagged down a woman in a shiny black BMW.

Dressed for business in a navy blue pantsuit, hair tucked nicely into a bun atop her head, the woman snatched her phone from the console and leaned over. Meeting Riker's gaze, she mouthed, "What's wrong?"

"Drunk driver," said Riker. He made a fist and pantomimed rolling a window down. Which the woman did, but only a fist width.

"Want me to call 911?"

Nodding, Riker said, "He hit me as I was walking across the street, then passed out right there." Sticking his hand inside the window, he dropped the keys on her passenger seat.

The businesswoman's mouth formed a silent "O." She cast a furtive glance at the keys then regarded the pale blue truck still blocking the side street. "He *hit* you?"

"Just my *prosthetic* leg. Lost the real one in the war."

Face full of empathy, the woman pounded out a three-digit number on her phone. Mouthing, "I'm sorry," she pulsed her window down all the way.

13

Though the traffic noise mingling with the steady, ever-present ringing of tinnitus kept Riker from hearing everything she was saying, her body language and the few words he picked up told him she was grateful for his service and was pissed at the disrespect shown him by the drunk.

Riker merely nodded—his go-to when the tinnitus was acting up. Then, without warning, the woman sat upright in her seat and ran the window up. Seeing her talking animatedly into the phone, free arm waving around the sedan's interior, Riker rose and scanned his surroundings.

No witnesses.

Good.

The rage-induced heat all but subsided—having retreated down his collar and exited his body through his extremities—Riker resumed his original course and double-timed it down the block.

Up ahead on the right was an electrical substation. A long line of thirty-foot-tall metal towers dangling insulators and sprouting wires rose gantry-like above a cement wall and strategically planted trees mostly failing at shielding its existence to passersby. As Riker reached the center of the block, the subliminal crackle-hiss of millions of out-of-sight volts had the hairs on his arms and neck standing to attention. Though nothing like the similar, albeit in your face sonic crackle-hiss of bullets fired in anger cutting the air nearby, the noise, though diminishing at his back as he strode east, still had his nerves jangling. Maybe the prospect of reuniting with his sister before day's end was the true culprit, he thought. The business they had to attend to was serious stuff. Then there was the impending encounter with a very proud Marine. He figured should Snuffy rebuff his offer, either the Marine would fix him with a cold stare and abruptly about face, never to talk to him again, or the old Devil Dog would listen to reason and accept his proposition without condition.

Riker hoped for the latter. He truly liked Snuffy. And as of yet, the cancer hadn't sapped the man of his strength nor drained an ounce of the piss and vinegar that was known to flow through his veins.

Before slipping around the corner, Riker stole a final look over his shoulder. Two blocks distant, the business lady was now out on the sidewalk and waving down an arriving patrol car. As the officers stepped from their Charger, she turned and pointed up the street in his direction.

Before the officers had a chance to react to the woman's gesture, Riker was already around the corner and out of sight.

***

Eschewing the multitude of chain locations bordering Centennial Park on all sides, Riker chose a little shop off the main drag called COMMON GROUNDS. The ten-table establishment had the look and feel of an owner/operator-run enterprise. A bell above the door signaled his entrance, causing a few of the patrons to look up from their laptop screens or peer over their splayed-open newspapers. The aroma of fresh brewed coffee hit Riker in the face and the twenty-something behind the high counter greeted him by name. As he approached the counter she was going through the ritual of slipping a paper sleeve on the cup and readying a lid.

"The usual?" she asked.

Riker nodded and smiled. A creature of habit, he always took his coffee black. Grounds or no grounds, he didn't care. The inkier the color and higher the viscosity the better.

The small flat-panel television atop the counter was tuned to CNN. The female anchor's lips were moving but no sound was coming out of the speakers. It was the words on the crawl at the bottom of the screen that caught his eye. As he read the tail-end of a story about a big pharma company and the new batch of performance-enhancing drugs they were set to test on military volunteers, the woman he knew as Kylie pushed his coffee forward and quietly said, "Two dollars, please," which was the initial reason he bypassed the corporate entities in the first place. After all, service-connected-disability bump on his monthly check or not, two bucks was a lot less than the big boys wanted for basically the same product. Soon all that wouldn't matter, he mused, as he slid a five across the counter and instructed Kylie to keep the change.

Chapter 3

Ten minutes into grading a stack of technically correct, yet awfully put-together early semester research papers, Noble's gaze settled on a desktop stationary set—a gift Professor Fuentes had received from the World Health Organization—recognizing his efforts in the ongoing fight against Ebola. In fact, one particular component of the set was calling his name.

He plucked the gilded letter opener from its indented resting place. Wasting no time, like a kid attacking a gift on Christmas morning, he corralled the parcel and made quick work stripping it of the clear tape and brown paper. He sliced the tape sealing the top of the box and began to pry it open. Rationalizing the action, he thought, *Just going to open it up so the professor doesn't have to be bothered with it.*

He replaced the letter opener on the tray and carefully lifted the brushed-aluminum box from within the cardboard shipping container. Feeling a touch of guilt creeping into the equation, he pushed the aluminum box to the top corner of the desk blotter, where he stared at it and sipped his drink for three long minutes.

What could one little peek inside hurt?

He looked over the top of the chest-high tables, fixed his gaze on the door to the hallway, and tried to guess where Fuentes was at this very moment.

At home, and likely still in bed.

The aluminum box had no markings. Its lid was secured with latches equidistant from each corner, four in total, all dogged down tightly.

Just a glance inside.

Noble clicked the catches into the up position and cast a furtive glance at the classroom door.

Clear.

He wiped a bead of sweat from his brow and lifted the lid free. It wasn't an easy endeavor, and once or twice he thought about turning back. But as the old idiom went: *In for a penny, in for a pound.* There was no turning back for Noble. He had already lost the penny, might as well wager the pound. Wanting badly to see what DOD USAMRIID at Ft. Det., Md. had sent little old MU Biology by way of the CDC DID for the professor—and hopefully his TA—to analyze, Noble gently rocked the lid back-and-forth to separate the rubber gasket from the box's tooled metal lip.

The lid came off with a soft hiss as trapped air leaked out. He placed the lid where the box had been and peered inside. The box was fitted with a hard plastic insert drilled through with half a dozen dime-sized holes meant to hold test tubes upright and separate from one another. All six holes held stoppered glass vials, one of them much shorter than the others.

Noble reached in and, with thumb and forefinger, removed the shorter vial from its sleeve, finding instantly that it had shattered and was empty, its milky contents now coating the bottom of the box.

In a bit of a panic and with hands tremoring from the hot mess he had just gotten himself into, Noble lowered the broken vial back into its slot. With unsteady hands, he tried to mate the two pieces back together so that the vial again sat level with the others. Satisfied it would pass a cursory inspection, he grabbed a handful of absorbent towels from a nearby drawer, wadded one into a ball, and soaked up the spilled agent. Lastly, he policed up the tiny shards of broken glass from the bottom of the box and placed them on the original wrapper, suffering a series of microscopic cuts in the process.

In the first half of his next heartbeat, Noble had replaced the lid and dogged down the latches. In the latter half of the same beat, he had convinced himself that getting rid of the damning evidence was the smart—albeit not necessarily most ethical—

thing to do. He quickly hid the glass and the parcel's original packaging in the soiled napkins and stuffed the tightly wadded biohazard ball into the one-way neck of a wall-mounted *Sharps* container.

With beads of sweat erupting on his forehead and upper lip, and less than an hour to go until the professor was due, Noble began drafting the first lines of a grand lie in his head.

Atlanta

Confident his unlikely antagonist was out of his hair for good, Riker retraced his steps from Common Grounds back to the shelter.

Sure enough, when he rounded the corner by the electrical substation and paused there to take a sip of his coffee, Napoleon, his rattletrap truck, the lady and her shiny black BMW, and the bored-looking Atlanta P.D. officers were no longer there.

Putting the substation and its angry white noise behind him, he stepped onto Lovejoy Street and noticed a cluster of men standing near the mission door.

Twenty feet from the mission door Riker was met by the expectant looks of three men who were regulars of the Shepherd's Inn. After halving the distance from the curb to the entry, the three men parted to reveal Koss standing back to the door with retired United States Marine Corps Gunnery Sergeant, Snuff Wilburn—all five-foot-six of him—stationed on the sidewalk, fists clenched and squaring up to him.

Tucking the newspaper into his waistband near the small of his back, Riker raised his arms in mock surrender. Careful to keep the paper cup level lest he lose some of its precious liquid cargo, he stopped a yard short and looked down on the grizzled Marine combat veteran.

"If you've got something to say to me," said Snuff, a touch of red creeping up his neck, "you better say it here and now."

Wily move, Gunny, thought Riker. *Take the conflict outside where a streetfighter had the advantage. Could range around and grapple a bigger opponent in order to bring him down. Maybe even pick him up by the legs and deliver him head first to the cement. Let gravity and his own weight do him in. The boots to the head and neck would come next.*

"I'm not spoiling for a fight," declared Riker. He flicked his gaze to the ground near Koss's boots. Saw his desert-tan NRA gym bag sitting by one side of the doorway.

Snuffy's worldly possessions—two small gym bags and a fully stuffed olive-drab military duffel—sat opposite Riker's lone bag.

Seeing the briefest shift of attention on Riker's part, Koss indicated that he'd taken the liberty of policing up Riker's toothbrush and shower shoes and stuffing them into the bag prior to bringing it outside for him.

Riker nodded. He scanned the faces left to right, pausing long enough to lock eyes with each of the three men. "Nothing to see here, gents. Best move along."

The men hung around until Koss shooed them away with threats of assigning them KP duty. Koss watched the trio shuffle off, then parked his gaze on Snuff. "You fellas need a referee?"

Scowling, Snuff nodded toward the doorway. Said, "I survived Khe Sanh."

That was all Koss needed to hear. He turned and followed the three lookie-loos inside.

Riker regarded the spry sixty-something for a long three-count without saying a word. Finally, he said, "There's something in the bag I want to give you. Then I'll be on my way."

A quizzical look replaced Snuff's scowl. "What could you possibly give me?"

"Freedom. I've been thinking about what you told me yesterday."

Snuff swallowed hard. His gaze ranged to the cars trickling by on the boulevard. He said, "My last wishes?"

"Affirmative," said Riker.

Now looking directly at Riker with eyes misted over, Snuff went on, "Those were just the mumblings of an old leatherneck with a lifetime of regrets."

Riker scooped his bag up. Unzipped it and came out with some keys on a Ford fob and a worn slip of paper with official-looking seals and some kind of hologram on it. "My old F-150 is in the side lot. She ain't much and her radio don't work, but she runs like a champ. Take her and see your son and daughter. Pretty sure she'll get you all the way to Chicago without anything breakin' on you."

"Why in the name of Christ are you showing empathy toward an old jarhead? You're Army. We're like oil and water, you and me."

Riker said, "Although it happened to me much sooner in life, I've been where you are right now. Someone lent their hand when I was down. I'm just paying it forward ... as corny as that may sound."

Snuff accepted the offered items. Choking back tears, he said, "Why?"

"Don't need it where I'm going. Don't need the tools in the bed box, either. Key for the box is on the ring, too. If Koss will let you back in, you might see if the kid on the cot opposite mine can use them."

"Nunez needs a diversion," agreed Snuff. "Anything to get his mind away from Helmand Province. I'll do both. Hell, all three. I'm done with the bottle, too. Going to be clear-eyed when I get to Chiraq."

The men shared a laugh, then embraced, Army and the Corp enjoying a brief moment of harmony.

Riker threw the retired gunnery sergeant a crisp salute, hitched the NRA bag over one shoulder, and wove between a pair of beat-up imports lining the curb. Without so much as a glance over his shoulder, he crossed the street diagonally to his left toward Williams Street which eventually merged with, of all things, Ted Turner Drive. From there the Greyhound bus terminal was a short ten-minute walk south by west.

Chapter 4

Not long after deciding Special Courier Butters would be the perfect fall guy for the specimen breach, Noble's salivary glands went into overdrive. Mouth filling with bitter saliva and feeling the first tickle of bile rising in his throat, he put Chastity Jones's paper, titled *Cell Phone Radiofrequency Energy and Its Effect on the Human Body*, aside and clamped a hand over his mouth.

With the courier's words, *Like the plague?* playing on a loop in his head, Noble rose shakily from the professor's desk and staggered toward the eye-washing basin. He made it less than five feet, half of the way there, before the vomit surged up his throat and sprayed between his fingers. A torrent of bile and pumpkin spice latte painted the floor and walls surrounding the alcove containing the waist-high stainless steel sink.

Heaving and sweating, Noble made it to the sink and emptied everything from his stomach—or so he thought—then reached up and knocked the receiver off the wall-mounted phone. Vision gone double, he reached for the keypad and managed to punch *9* the requisite two times.

With long streamers of snot making the slow journey from his nose to the gray tiled floor, Noble kept his forehead pressed against the cool steel lip of the sink and brought the receiver up to his ear.

After four rings that each seemed to drone on for half a lifetime, there was a click and a raspy smoker's voice said, "Custodial department."

As if his intestines were stuck in a taffy stretcher, Noble felt a pain in his gut like he had never experienced. Though he wanted to speak into the mouthpiece, the pressure behind his eyes was making him see the floor and the mucous pooling there in Technicolor—pulsing and expanding and contracting—like some kind of an acid trip flashback. Then he felt his body spasm and again he heard the disembodied male voice say, "Custodial department ... this is Hal."

Noble swiped away the spittle and snot and flicked it at the floor, where it hit with a sloppy, wet smack. Composing himself, he took a deep breath and managed to choke out four words: "*Requesting cleanup in bio.*"

A floor down and on the opposite side of the six-story building from the biology labs, the barista who had made what would prove to be Charlie Noble's final pumpkin spice latte was busy preparing yet another. And while the steam wand did its thing, frothing the milk in the metal cup that would top what seemed to Tara Riker like the thirtieth pain-in-the-ass specialty coffee of the morning, she cast her gaze up and watched the clouds scudding by through the glass panes making up the all-encompassing atrium.

As the machine hissed and spit, the thirty-two-year-old watched students and teachers taking advantage of the weekend day file through the main doors and then board the pair of elevators directly across the lobby from her tiny kiosk. Once the milk in the cup was light and fluffy, she turned back to Dean Kurtz, looked him in the eye and, while coaxing the topping onto the latte with a metal spoon, asked in as cheerful a manner as the early hour allowed, "Cinnamon? Nutmeg? Or both?"

The Dean swiped his card and exhaled sharply as he keyed in his PIN. "Nutmeg will suffice," he said curtly, as if such an inconsequential decision was beneath him. Without putting a dime in Tara's tip jar or even faking a half-smile, the miserable little man snatched up his drink and stalked off toward the nearby bank of elevators, briefcase in hand, presumably on his way to go do whatever it was that university Deans did at the butt crack of dawn.

Watching the Dean's wavy reflection in the stainless steel, Tara gave her espresso machine a thorough wipe-down, all the while envisioning the man as a kid pulling the wings off flies.

Catching her own reflection, she realized that her sleeves were hiked up to mid-bicep, which left the majority of the black thorny runners and flowers tattooed from wrist to shoulder in plain view. Muttering an expletive and cursing the Dean's rules-and-regs, she reluctantly pulled the sleeves down to conceal the forbidden ink.

Staring out at the cars beginning to line up for the parking lot and knowing that her morning was just about to go from zero to sixty, a flash of yellow and the squeak of rusty bearings caught Tara's attention. Focusing on the highly polished pane of glass to her fore, she saw reflected there an overall-clad custodian pushing a wheeled yellow bucket and mop into one of the elevators at her back.

Chapter 5

Riker was rudely awakened when the Greyhound bus he'd boarded in Atlanta came to a complete and lurching stop. Opening his eyes a crack, he peeked at his neighbor's watch, saw that it was twenty of eight, then closed them again.

"Fucking dumbass drivers," crowed the sixty-something woman with the timepiece. "Where do they get their licenses … out of a *Gawd damn* Cracker Jack box?"

Through parted lids, Riker watched the woman, who smelled like he imagined a house full of cats might, stand up and walk her gaze a near three-sixty over the other passengers. Showing no regard for anyone on the bus with her, she started stabbing an arthritic finger at the driver, screaming shrilly, "If I wanted to see the *entire* Indiana countryside at a snail's pace I'd have rented a clown car and driven myself."

Doubtful, thought Riker, trying to tune out the woman who was obviously enjoying playing to her captive audience. In fact, she had been bitching about one thing or another since boarding the bus at the Cincinnati depot. And though he wanted more than anything to open his window and show her the road face-first, he instead shifted his large frame to face the window and tried to get comfortable in the seat designed with the average-sized traveler in mind. Feeling the conjoined seats vibrate when the woman plopped down, he closed his eyes and visualized palm trees and softly crashing surf and basked in the momentary silence.

Riker's moment of bliss was cut short when the pneumatic hiss of air brakes engaging erased any chance of him falling back to sleep. *Sweat dries, blood clots, and bones heal. Suck it up, buttercup.* Acting on the words pounded into his gray matter by a frothing-at-the-mouth drill instructor years ago, he sat up straight and stretched his arms to full extension. Next, he rolled his shoulders and popped every vertebra in his neck, prompting the woman to start bitching about how *certain sounds* make her skin crawl. *Join the club*, thought Riker. Pretending the woman *was* that drill instructor barking in his face, he completely ignored her and stared out the window at the hectares of brown dirt stretching away to the distant horizon. He saw the raised railroad tracks the bus was sitting atop cutting between level parcels of fenced-in dirt, home to rows of scraggly vegetation, presumably cornfields left to go fallow for winter. He let his gaze follow the two parallel razor-straight lines of polished steel all the way east until they disappeared into a pewter smudge of clouds far off in the distance.

The motor coach was still rocking slightly from the abrupt stop when the brakes hissed a second time and Riker felt it lurch forward again. Body swaying to-and-fro as the bus bumped sloppily over the tracks, Riker leaned forward, stole a look past his cat-lady captor, and spied a rundown four-pump filling station complete with the obligatory attached quickie mart, its red and white paint chipped and faded with age. Sitting on a sea of dull gray asphalt and ringed by a dozen late-model cars in various states of disrepair, the only thing new and shiny about the place was the red-and-black Texaco sign rising above its flat roof.

Wondering why the bus had left the interstate, Riker watched the station slip from view, then returned his attention to the landscape scrolling by outside his window.

As if the driver had been privy to Riker's thoughts, the overhead speaker came alive with a hiss of white noise and she announced that a fatal accident on the interstate would require a detour and add an extra thirty minutes of travel time to the trip.

While Cat Lady spewed another string of expletives, the driver went on in a cheerful voice about how sorry she was and that the delay would be noted on the arrival boards for anyone awaiting them at their final destination. Which was information that did very little to placate Riker, whose final destination was some distance from Muncie, south by west if his memory served.

And that Greyhound didn't see fit to service Middletown—a town of roughly two thousand—the insult added to that injury meant he faced a cramped taxi ride in the not-too-distant future.

Resigned to the fact that reaching Middletown was another ninety minutes or so in the future, Riker closed his eyes and, with Cat Lady still going on, reluctantly revisited boot camp.

Chapter 6

Middletown University

The bell dinged at the second floor. All alone in the elevator, Hal Crawford, acting head of MU's custodial staff, waited patiently as the car slowed and settled with a slight bounce. Once the doors parted, he pushed the industrial-sized wheeled bucket out ahead of him. With gentle course corrections delivered via the mop handle gripped in calloused hands, he shoved off to the right. Hearing the *ding* and grating sounds of the elevator doors closing a dozen feet behind, he negotiated the ninety-degree right and set out on the long walk down the orange-carpeted hallway. Pushing the bucket carefully lest he slop the bleach water and risk the ugly carpet being replaced by something even more repulsive, Hal's attention was drawn to the window and the queue of cars pulling into the secured parking a story below. By the time he reached the far end of the biology wing and was unclipping the key ring from his belt, the yellow-and-black-striped bar had opened and closed a dozen times, yet the line of cars snaking along the west side of the building had only grown longer.

Working his fingers over the ring, Hal found the oversized passkey by feel, pushed it into the lock, and opened the door. As he backed into the darkened room, pulling the bucket after, simultaneously the bitter reek of vomit hit him full on and the automatic overhead lights flared to life.

After recoiling from the stench, Hal covered his nose with his T-shirt, fished a rubber stop from his back pocket, and used it to trap the door partway open. Breathing through his mouth, he traversed the room, pushing the bucket before him. Nearing the professor's desk, he wheeled the bucket expertly around a lake of yellow vomit and spotted the party responsible.

Revealed in little slices—like degrees cut off a compass— he first saw the waffle-patterned lug soles on a pair of well-oiled leather hiking boots. One more half-step past the professor's wide desk let him see that the person wore a white lab coat over brown corduroy pants and was kneeling before the emergency eye-wash sink. The puker's head was parked inside the shadowy alcove. There was more vomit here than Hal had ever seen. It coated the floor and walls yellow, and tendrils of it were still making the lazy journey from the front of the sink to the gray floor tiles.

Based on the man's size, Hal knew at first glance it wasn't Professor Fuentes. *Much too big.* His best guess was that he was looking at a student teaching assistant trying to ride out the mother of all hangovers.

"You called me for this?" Hal said, a trace of indignation in his voice.

The man was unresponsive.

Hal upped the ante by moving closer and tapping the man on the back. Three jabs between the shoulder blades and still nothing.

So Hal gripped the man's shoulder and shook him gently. Zilch. Zip. Nada.

Finally, at the top of his voice, Hal bellowed, "One too many Irish Car Bombs at Horse Feathers?" Which was a place Hal had never been, but knew from eavesdropping on student conversation was a popular after-class hangout.

Bingo.

The assistant moaned. The harsh sound, amplified by where his head was resting, lasted a couple of seconds, during which every hair on Hal's arms stood to attention. The guttural growl continued as the man hauled himself up, then lessened in volume somewhat as he took a drunken step away from the sink.

Hal hustled to the oak desk and pulled the sturdy wooden chair to the sink, the legs etching a pair of lines in the vomit.

"You better sit, buddy," he ordered.

Now wavering on shaky legs, the slightly overweight fella turned and emitted a sound kind of like a cornered animal's worried yelp. Which was wholly inappropriate considering the second Hal saw the man's bared teeth and lifeless, glazed-over eyes, it was he who felt trapped.

There was a split second where Hal entertained the idea of talking the younger man into splashing cold water on his pallid face and telling him to go home and sleep it off. But that thought was edged out a nanosecond later when the primeval lizard part of Hal's brain screamed *fight or flight* and, of course, flight won out. However, as synapses were firing impulses to get his arms and legs pumping, the leaden extremities weren't processing the signals in any kind of organized manner.

Instead of making a hasty retreat, Hal looked like a drunken break-dancer as he back-pedaled away from the growling student. Finally, a couple of things went right for Hal and he got his torso turned around, but still his feet and legs were a half-beat late in responding. Which didn't matter, because the soles of his outdoor boots were no kind of answer to the saffron-yellow mix of bile and half-digested four-dollar coffee slickening the floor.

In the end, Hal fell flat on his face and his momentum carried him through the morass in a slide that would have made Charlie Hustle proud. Still in flight mode and only two seconds removed from looking a monster from his nightmares straight in the face, Hal willed himself up on all fours. Feeling like a water bug on an oil slick, he got his hands and knees moving but only managed to get himself winded before, once again, pancaking to the floor.

Excited by all of the motion and spurred on by deeply buried memories of the thrill of the hunt, the shell of a human who used to be Charlie Noble found a second gear and rapidly cut the short distance to its prey.

Seeing the monster's shadow—complete with outstretched arms and claw-like fingers—darkening the floor around him, Hal's will to survive trumped his first reaction. Simultaneously he found purchase with the toe of his left boot, pushed off with his left hand and, in a strange display of muscle memory from his high school wrestling days, finished the move by whipping his head around to the left. And just like he had been taught two decades before by a coach whose name he failed to recall, those three actions, when combined, had him rolling away from the puddle and the overarching feeling of impending doom.

But Hal was no longer seventeen. He was thirty-seven and his fast-twitch muscles were that in name only. Plus, as he rolled over onto his back, the overhead fluorescents blinded him long enough, literally and figuratively, to be ignorant of the fact that he was dead meat.

Upon leaving the realm of the living, Charlie Noble had lost all ability to reason or think or strategize. But that was no kind of advantage to the fresh meat writhing on the floor a yard away. The undead creature currently locked onto Hal like a heat-seeking missile had three things working in its favor: forward momentum, gravity, and inertia. When put behind a hundred and eighty pounds of dead weight and delivered in the form of an unintentional head butt, it was more than enough to mercifully render the janitor unconscious. Which then left the door wide open for Patient Zero's first kill of the day.

Chapter 7

Nearing Muncie, Indiana

Riker opened his eyes and wiped a gossamer thread of drool from his chin. He stole another look at Cat Lady's watch, did the math, and found he'd only been asleep for thirty minutes. Glancing out the window, he saw that the bus was still creeping along the back road behind a long line of vehicles full of people all in the same boat as him—almost.

"Why in the fuck is this *cunt* driving so slow?" said his seemingly Tourette's afflicted neighbor.

Riker said nothing. He aimed his muscled back at the annoyance and stared uncomfortably out the window at Middle America. There were farmhouses set back on large tracts of land. Behind gnarled post-and-beam fences he saw rusted farm implements, hand-painted sandwich boards hawking farm-fresh goods, and old cars sitting on half-filled tires, most of them adorned with handwritten *For Sale* signs.

"At this snail's pace, we're never going to get to Muncie for my connection," said the same woman, her voice several octaves higher this time.

Riker felt a twinge between his shoulder blades as a muscle spasmed. On the heels of that, the ringing was back in his ears.

When the lady stopped her bawling, a murmur went through the half-filled bus. Then someone in back implored the woman to *Shut her pie hole.*

Which only added fuel to the fire.

Her voice becoming shrill, nearly unintelligible, the woman asked, "Do you know who *I* am?"

There was silence. Not even the initial heckler added to his *pie hole* comment.

Which only emboldened Riker's miserable seatmate. "I bet the *black* bitch up there gets paid by the hour and is driving like *Miss Daisy* just to make sure she gets her bonus."

To that, Riker turned away from the window, looked down on the woman, and said sardonically, "Actually, in the movie, *Daisy* didn't drive. And I *bet* your friend the driver gets paid whether you're happy or not. And I'd bet she doesn't know you from Adam. In fact"—he dragged out his wallet and extracted a crisp Andrew Jackson—"twenty dollars says you're a nobody to her." Riker pulled his Braves cap low over his face, concealing a wicked smile, and waited for Vesuvius to erupt. And she did. The woman spewed words that'd cause a merchant marine to blush as she told Riker to do things to himself in positions he doubted could be found in the *Kama Sutra*.

Eventually the driver could take no more of the woman's ranting and the bus drifted to the shoulder, where it lurched to a stop amidst a grinding of gears and squealing of brakes.

Mission accomplished. Riker tilted his cap back to normal, gripped the armrests, and rose up from his seat. Over the other passengers' heads, he saw the driver talking into a handheld microphone. He watched her for a short while under the white-hot glare from the waste of skin to his left, then sat back down and stared out the window. A couple of seconds after fixing his gaze on the distant clouds, the bus began moving again. It wasn't long before another burst of static emanated from the overhead speakers and, in a singsong voice, the driver was promising to have whoever was acting up yanked from the bus and delivered to the Muncie jail in the back of a squad car.

The threat seemed to do the trick.

The woman's lips pursed into a thin white line and she slammed her slight frame into the seatback.

Checkmate, Riker thought triumphantly. Doing his best to ignore the holes being burned into him by the woman's hate-filled glare, he kept his gaze fixed on the gray strip of asphalt scrolling by outside his window, where soon a long string of military vehicles, of which he possessed intimate knowledge, began passing them by. He saw a trio of camouflaged deuce-and-a-half troop transports painted in a black, green, and brown woodland scheme. Used mainly for moving soldiers and supplies, these vehicles were at the head of the column. Next came a half-dozen desert-brown Humvees: squat, slab-sided vehicles, the first four sprouting whip antennas and turret-mounted heavy machine guns. The two bringing up the rear had camper-like shells out back with large red crosses on the top and sides. Filled with specialized lifesaving equipment, the top-heavy-looking rigs were used mostly for transferring gravely wounded soldiers from casualty evacuation helicopters just arriving on a flight line to the trauma surgeons awaiting them in a nearby field hospital. Or, as in Riker's case a decade or so ago, to a waiting Air Force C-17 Globemaster III that delivered him to Ramstein Air Base in Germany where he was immediately delivered by ambulance to Landstuhl Regional Medical Center for skin grafts and other unspeakable operations. Just seeing the vehicles tooling the road right outside his large tinted window started a knot twisting slowly in his stomach and got him to rooting in his pocket for the roll of antacids.

He stared at his visage reflected back at him in the window. The Braves cap failed to completely conceal the evidence of that day. Stretched tight on his forehead, the pink scarring was but one reminder of how close he'd come to meeting the Reaper.

Pushing the sounds of imagined screams from his thoughts, he popped three chalky Rolaids into his mouth and stuffed the remainder in his pocket. In the process, his left elbow brushed his neighbor's leg, starting a chain reaction he should have seen coming.

The vibration from the kick delivered by the woman coursed up Riker's leg but barely resonated in his stump. However, the flurry of expletives she spewed following the loud clunk was heard round the bus and likely in the next county.

What happened next was mildly amusing to Riker. Cat Lady lifted her right foot off the ground, removed her canvas shoe, and with the sleeve of her cat-hair-covered sweater, staunched the blood flowing from a split big toe.

Suppressing a smile, Riker removed his ball cap, rubbed his bald head, and uttered the words, "Bitch's toe, meet prosthetic leg. Prosthetic leg, meet bitch's toe." Then, before she could answer, he was on his feet and pushing past her on a mission to find a seat as far away as possible.

Having seen the altercation as it happened, and clearly aware of the outcome, the man two rows back and to the left who had shouted the *pie hole* comment, bellowed, "We have a bleeder."

Settled into his new seat a couple of rows behind the driver, Riker closed his eyes and cracked a sly smile.

Chapter 8

Middletown University

Attuned to the constant ding and whoosh of the doors on the distant elevator opening and closing, the thing that used to be called Charlie Noble placed one bloody hand on the janitor's slack face, clumsily planted both feet in the growing pool of blood, and rose on shaky legs.

It stood there for a few seconds, listening to conversations between students on their way to the journalism wing a couple of hundred yards west across a glass skybridge. Driven by a primal urge to feed, and moaning softly, it staggered to the open door, bulling into the bucket and mop and sending it rolling across the hall to the far wall where it stopped, sloshing foul-smelling water onto the carpet.

As Charlie's husk stood wavering in the hall, the brain propelling it was bombarded by stimuli. The jerking movements of the cars trickling into the lot below drew his gaze. Then, the elevator bell dinged again far down the hall, causing his head to swivel slowly left. But it wasn't until the high falsetto of someone singing filtered down the hall to his right that signals were sent from deep in his brain to the limbs that started him moving toward the sound.

Jamming out to Bruno Mars, Savion Jones emerged from the stairwell, pleased with himself for having avoided a ride in an elevator potentially filled with a dozen of his highly caffeinated peers. Head bobbing to the beat and causing the white wires attached to his earbuds to sway to-and-fro, he continued on down the back hall toward the media center, where he hoped the October issue of *Filmmaker Magazine* awaited him on the shelf.

With the last few bars of the peppy dance song fading, he retrieved his iPhone from his coat pocket, thumbed it to life, and searched for something moody to carry him the rest of the way.

He selected the Music icon, scrolled down through the available artists, and started an Imagine Dragons tune playing. *One hundred percent moody*, he thought, cracking a smile. How could a song called "Radioactive" not be? He slipped the phone into his pocket and looked up to see the backlit silhouette of a person cutting the corner ahead.

The first jangling guitar chords were starting up when the overhead lights illuminated the form from the front and it registered to Savion that the lab coat on the cat didn't come crimson off the rack but was instead thoroughly soaked in blood that, at the moment, was dripping steadily onto the carpet.

As Savion jammed to a halt, his Adidas made a soft squelch on the carpet. Conversely, the pallid, hunched-over figure to his fore let out a soft moan and took a stilted step closer. In the ensuing split-second during which Savion was deciding which way he was going to run, the lead singer of Imagine Dragons drew a deep breath and the music rose to a crescendo. As the vocals rode over the bass-heavy track, a switch was seemingly flicked in Savion's brain and his smile returned when good old normalcy bias shoved the primal urge to run aside and convinced him the monstrosity was merely someone making a dry run at Halloween in one hell of a kickass costume.

The apocalypse, indeed, thought Savion as he yanked the buds from his ears and fumbled for his phone.

"*Duuude*. That is some sick ass makeup," Savion said, looking the groaning man up and down. "But if you're gonna prank some fools and put it on YouTube … you had better be *recording* that shit." He raised his phone and flicked through three pages of apps until he found the one with the cartoonish-looking black camera. Finally, with the zombified student trudging steadily closer, he started the video rolling and zoomed in on the dude's pasty-white mug.

The shell that was Charlie Noble saw the meat moving and making sounds but was no longer able to comprehend the words. The inflection and nuances meant nothing. The hunger pangs, however, were back with a vengeance and something deep down in its brain told it that eating the noisy thing was the only way to numb them.

With the thoroughly made-up guy inexplicably remaining in character and his faux moans getting louder and carrying down the hall, Savion decided to go with the flow. Playing along for the camera, he backed up until he was adjacent to the stairwell he'd just exited. Then, placing a palm up, universal semaphore for halt, he said, "Stop there for a just a sec and be quiet."

The dude kept moaning.

"Shhh," Savion said. *Are you a freakin' exchange student?* was what he was thinking as he tucked a stray dreadlock behind his ear, reached blindly behind his back, and took ahold of the door handle. "Shhh …" He smiled big. "You hear those footsteps? Someone's about to be coming out."

You're a natural, thought Savion as the guy advanced on him and the hollow-sounding footsteps at his back drew nearer and grew louder, resonating in the stairwell behind the closed door.

In a perfect moment of cinematic confluence—*timing is everything*, as Savion's thespian father liked to say—the dude in zombie makeup was nearly even with the stairwell door and the footsteps echoing behind it had just ceased. So Savion did what any aspiring filmmaker coveting a clip worthy of a million social media hits would do—he flung the door open and stepped aside, hoping for both an Oscar-winning performance out of Zombie Dude and an *epic* reaction from the unsuspecting mark poised to emerge from behind the door.

Chapter 9

Coming down from the fifth floor, expecting nothing more than to burn a few calories by descending the three flights of stairs, Tiffany Jensen paused behind the second-floor door, hitched her pack higher on one shoulder, and reached for the handle. But someone had beaten her to it and it turned freely in her hand. Then, on its own accord, the door was ripped away from her outstretched arm and a form half a head taller than her was darkening the doorway.

Pissed at the prospect of having to step aside so that some asshat in a hurry could barge past her, Tiffany was about to give the offender a piece of her mind when she found herself trapped in the embrace of a snarling madman.

"You're laying it on a little too thick, my man," said Savion, standing on his toes and jostling for a better camera angle. Wishing he was filming with the Blackmagic video cam instead of his effin iPhone, he edged partway into the stairwell, keeping the door propped open with his hip.

The would-be actor snarled, gutturally, like an animal—an altogether too realistic a sound that started a ripple of gooseflesh coursing up Savion's ribcage.

Struggling to break free from the man's cold grip, Tiffany held her breath against his awful, vomit-tinged breath and brought her knee up viciously between his legs, connecting solidly with no noticeable effect.

"You're pushing the envelope, man!" shouted Savion. Still filming, he put a hand on the guy's shoulder and pulled back just in time to see him sink a picket of obviously brace-straightened teeth into the co-ed's ivory-hued neck, causing a spritz of hot blood to splash the tiny camera lens and continue across Savion's face and into his mouth. It smelled to him like a jar full of ancient pennies, metallic and strangely chemical. It tasted bitter and salty on his tongue. Spitting the sticky warm glob onto the carpet, Savion dropped his phone on the landing. Incredulous, he shouted, "This is *not* gonna fly with YouTube's TOS."

As the statement echoed inside the stairway, three things happened. Tiffany fell backward onto the unforgiving cement landing, her head impacting with a sharp *crack*. Savion leaped onto the crazy guy's back, trying to wrap him up in a WWF headlock. And the door leading out to the deserted hallway swung shut, sealing them all inside behind an audible *snick*.

With a scream stuck in her throat and a flat fan of dark crimson pulsating rhythmically onto the wall and stairs all around her, Tiffany struggled to breathe with what seemed like a ton of cold flesh crushing down on her.

For all intents and purposes, Savion Jones died the second he caught the mouthful of saliva-tainted blood. But seeing as how he was oblivious to his fate, plus feeling like a massive douche for setting the girl up like he did, he fought tooth and nail to pry the silent dude away until she stopped struggling and the blood-drenched freak turned on him.

Flicking his gaze from the girl's wildly fluttering eyelids to the crazy man now easily overpowering him, Savion felt a flare of white-hot pain as his supposed *actor's* teeth plunged into his neck. Then, seeing his blood mingling with the girl's on the landing, darkness began to close in on the periphery of his vision and the overhead lights danced violently back-and-forth in front of his eyes. Drawing a final breath, Savion Jones witnessed through tearing eyes the freak rearing back and coming away with a mouthful of his flesh. Trailing ribbons of tattered dermis, the glistening plug of meat jiggled as his killer worked it into his maw with both hands. The last sensations received by Savion's brain before it switched off was the soft little patters of his own lifeblood raining down on his upturned face.

***

Less than a minute after dying the first time, Tiffany Jensen's hands opened and closed, the recently manicured nails raking the concrete and sending ripples across the warm, sticky pool. A tick later, her body began to twitch and shake as the prehistoric part of her brain rebooted. In the next instant, her eyelids snapped open and the glassy vacant eyes started their never-ending search for prey.

Teeth grinding and clicking, Tiffany Jensen's reanimated corpse rolled over onto its stomach and rose to all fours. With the lake of blood now encompassing the entire landing, the monster shuffled forward on hands and knees, starting a mini crimson waterfall cascading over the top stair. The nerve-jangling noise of its teeth coming together ceased only when it nudged undead Charlie Noble aside and dove face-first into Savion Jones's guts.

Feeding next to its killer, the ravenous creature shook its head side-to-side doglike and came away with a greasy rope of intestine clutched two-handed, working one end greedily into its mouth, the other dribbling partially digested Egg McMuffin onto the dead kid's khakis.

Chapter 10

Tara knew her day had just rocketed from bad to worse the instant the young male student with blood sluicing from a gaping neck wound stumbled from the elevator and landed face-first on the floor not thirty feet in front of her. Acting on muscle memory, while gaping past her customer at the gory spectacle, she popped the lid onto the cup with practiced ease and pushed the coffee forward.

"You're *welcome*," said the fortysomething rather snottily as she took her coffee in hand and slam-dunked the two quarters change into Tara's tip jar.

Without meeting the woman's gaze or catching the sarcasm dripping from her words, Tara muttered, "Thanks," and felt her limbs stiffen.

Shaking her head, the woman adjusted her pack on her shoulder, turned and took her first tentative steps toward the elevators—the one on the left now buzzing angrily and opening and closing continuously on the prostrate body in its path.

While the lady with the backpack hustled across the lobby toward the fallen man, the rest of the people present seemed to gravitate to the coffee kiosk, their nervous chatter rising as blood pooled around the fallen man's head and upper body.

With the noise of the gathering crowd matching the level of the elevator's warning peal, Tara's last customer reached the body and dropped her pack to the floor. Gripping her short skirt with one hand, she set her coffee by her pack and, completing a sort of slow-motion curtsy, knelt primly next to the body. While she went to all fours, in what looked like a very uncomfortable position for one wearing high heels, Tara felt a sudden pang of guilt for not following the woman's lead. Not wanting to be lumped in with the gawking bystanders, Tara willed herself back to work. In an effort to detach from what was transpiring, she began dragging a white towel in big lazy circles across the kiosk's stainless steel counter.

The busywork distracted Tara for a second, but when she finally looked up, she saw that the elevator had gone silent with the doors locked open, and an older bearded man, presumably a professor, had emerged from the other. As the man skirted the rapidly growing lake of blood, the Good Samaritan shuffled around on hands and knees until she was parallel with the body. Then, as if trying to seize a charmed cobra, she slowly reached out and pressed three fingers gently to the man's neck.

"An ambulance is on the way!" called a man, a phone pressed to one ear.

Voice wavering, a woman on the periphery asked, "Is he alive?"

Grimacing, the middle-aged woman drew her hand back. She regarded the young student who'd posed the question and shook her head.

"He's gone. Most of his neck on the right side ... where the carotid runs ... it's torn wide open."

Grateful that it was the woman she'd just served coffee to and not her who had touched the dead body, Tara tossed the towel into a bleach bucket and walked out from behind her kiosk. Without uttering so much as an *excuse me* or *coming through* or *make way*, she elbowed a passage through the throng of people, some of them snapping photos or taking videos with their phones. Just as she found a better vantage point and was absentmindedly rolling up her sleeves, the woman rocketed out of her crouch as if she had just received an electric shock. With the clicking of her high heels the only sound in the atrium, the woman took two steps back just as the body convulsed and began to twitch strangely, like a fish out of water. As if checking to see that she was not the only witness to the dead student seemingly come back to life, the woman turned mechanically toward the crowd and accidentally kicked her Venti cup, sending a torrent of steaming brown liquid across the floor tiles.

Meanwhile, on the opposite side of the building, aided by the unfortunate placement of a panic bar meant to allow breathing humans a quick escape from the north stairwell in the event of fire or other calamity, an oblivious undead Charlie Noble stumbled off the last step, hit the waist-high metal bar with a full head of steam, and staggered into daylight.

With the door closing at its back, the ashen-faced abomination took a single lurching step forward and made a wild, slow-motion grab for the fresh meat strolling the sidewalk an arm's length away.

Reacting much faster than one would think a person with their eyes glued to a handheld device would, the co-ed passerby performed a quick stutter-step that caused undead Charlie to miss horribly, perform a clumsy pirouette off the curb, and collapse in a vertical heap directly in front of an approaching city bus.

There was a squeal of brakes as fifteen tons of Detroit metal bled speed. Riding the blast of air ahead of the bus, a drift of red and orange and yellow oak leaves was sent skittering along the ground ahead of it. A fraction of a second later, Newton's Law kicked in as the shocks and brakes working in unison reeled in the kinetic energy and the bus ground to a noisy halt, its right front tire three inches from the fallen monster's skull, and the act that may have altered the course of history sadly averted.

Chapter 11

Inside the university's main entrance, illuminated by bars of sunlight infiltrating the glass atrium, the student who had fled after receiving the mortal wound from undead Janitor Hal was now reanimating in front of Tara, the fortysomething Good Samaritan, and nearly two dozen witnesses—a just-arrived and under-caffeinated Professor Sylvester Fuentes counted among them.

People gasped and a murmur rippled around the lobby as the man, whom the woman in high heels had just pronounced dead, flopped around in the pool of his own blood.

With everyone frozen in place, the pallid corpse suddenly lay flat, turned its head to the left, and fixed a lifeless gaze on the woman in heels.

Feeling a cold chill rip up her spine, Tara put her hand on a stranger's shoulder and stood on her toes. Through a sliver of daylight between the people in front, she watched her last paying customer stand and inexplicably take a couple of steps toward the thing writhing away on the floor.

No, Tara thought as the lady again knelt next to the prostrate man.

In the next beat, two things happened near simultaneously. First, speaking softly, the woman urged the man to remain still. Then she turned to the crowd and at the top of her voice said, "Somebody give me a hand here." But before anyone could react, and with the bellowed plea still echoing off the high ceiling, the man sat up straight and grabbed two fistfuls of blonde hair. Already off balance, the high heels doing her no favors, the woman pitched over backward with her straining neck angling straight for the thing's gaping maw.

At first sight of the supposedly *dead* man sitting up, every instinct in Tara's body urged her to run. Yet like a passerby at a fatal car wreck, she couldn't tear her eyes from the sight her mind was having difficulty processing. And it wasn't until the woman screamed and crimson blood was gushing from a puckered wound behind her right ear that Tara decided she had seen enough.

As more screams rang out and echoed about the atrium, the man Tara had been using for support doubled over and emptied the contents of his stomach all over his shoes. Then, like a school of fish parted by a predator, half of the people who had been rooted in place dashed toward the entry, and the rest rushed forward and dragged the bloody attacker from the woman's unmoving body.

Through the dissipating crowd, Tara caught a glimpse of the crazy guy's eyes and threw a visible shudder. There was almost no white to them. Where she expected to see rage, she only saw two dime-sized pools of black conveying no emotion whatsoever.

As electrical impulses jumped synapses in Tara's head one word came to mind: *Zombie?*

In that instant, closing the store, counting the till, and calling her boss to tell him what had happened and that she was leaving as a result ranked in importance just below whatever her last asshole boyfriend was doing at this very moment. Flight instinct activated, Tara grabbed her pack and, without a second glance at the kiosk, made a beeline for the front entrance, thumbing her phone alive on the run. Once outside, she squeezed past a clutch of people talking excitedly into phones of their own. Body-checking slow movers out of her way, she ran down the wide walkway, past a phalanx of cement planters, and turned right at the sidewalk, head down and sprinting for the distant student parking lot opposite the glass skybridge. Backpack threatening to slip off her shoulder, she turned the next corner, crossed the street, and zippered between a pair of cars on their way into the lot.

Slowing to a trot three rows in, she brought the phone to her mouth and instructed her phone's AI helper to call, *"Bro."*

"No match found," replied the semi-robotic female voice.

Breathing hard, Tara said, "Eff you," and tapped the green phone icon, selected *Contacts*, and scrolled down until she found the correct one.

Nearly running headlong into her little red car, she selected the number with the 678 Atlanta area code, hit *Speaker*, and took a knee next to the car door. As the first ring drifted from the tiny speaker, she set the phone on the ground by her knee, ripped open her pack, and started rooting around inside for her keys.

Before she was wrist-deep into her pack, the first ring had dissipated and a connection was made, going straight to voicemail. She heard a beep and a digital recording of her brother, sounding uncomfortable and out-of-sorts, emanated from the speaker: *"This is Leland Riker and you have penetrated his cellular phone's defenses. So um ... please ... um, leave a message"*—there was a pregnant pause and then his voice went on—*"and if I can remember my passcode"*—another second or two of dead air—*"I will call you back A-sap."*

Not likely, thought Tara. And it didn't surprise her he hadn't picked up. It was par for the course for typically tech-challenged Lee to accidentally leave the ringer off and then play dumb when called out for it later. So she cursed again and jammed her arm elbow-deep into the pack. She grimaced and rooted around then pursed her lips as she dragged her keys out. Wasting no time, she tucked her phone into the bag and stood up straight. Grimace returning, she watched a pair of black SUVs nose in hard against the curb adjacent to the front entry where people were now surging out in twos and threes, half of them screaming, the rest wearing incredulous looks, their mouths frozen into silent O's.

Emblazoned on the SUVs' doors were silver shield-shaped decals sporting the words *Middletown Campus Security*. In unison the driver and passenger doors on each vehicle flew open and uniformed security guards spilled out. Leaving their doors opened wide, the quartet put their heads down and ran toward the action, blissfully unaware of the scale of carnage they were about to encounter inside.

Chapter 12

Tara punched the button on the fob, popping the door locks. In one fluid movement she yanked her door open and tossed the pack onto the small shelf behind her seat. Casting an expectant glance toward the lot's secure exit, she slid in behind the wheel and closed and locked the door. Breathing hard, hands visibly shaking, she guided the key into the ignition.

Pausing momentarily to get her breath, Tara was caught off-guard when a woman roughly her age staggered up, stopped outside her door, and bent at the waist. Eyes glazed and mouth agape, the stranger looked Tara in the eye, spread her arms like a pair of wings, and mouthed the words, *What the fuck?*

WTF indeed, thought Tara as the woman continued on her way and the little three-banger under the hood turned over with nary a sound. She slipped the transmission into Reverse, then flicked her eyes to the rearview mirror, where she saw the woman at her own car working a key in the door.

Coast clear, Tara tromped the gas and J-turned out of the spot. She negotiated the lot at twice the posted speed, dodging a couple of cars reversing from their spaces, and arrived at the exit chute third in line. Thankfully for her, whoever was driving the cars ahead of hers had likely seen the same thing she had and wasted no time getting through the gate. The first sped off to the left, nearly colliding head on with a Middletown P.D. Crown Victoria. The second, however—some kind of modern muscle car painted lime green with twin stripes on the hood—sped off to the right, past the arriving officers, leaving a pair of long, black burnout marks on the pavement and the street clouded with a low-hanging blue haze.

With the green car already out of sight, Tara swiped her key card in front of the reader. It always took a second to register. While she waited for the arm to rise, she looked to the atrium and saw that her kiosk had been pushed up against the glass. Outside the building, the guards were struggling mightily to advance toward the entrance against the river of bodies streaming through the double doors.

About the time Tara was swiping her card at the gate, Patient Zero was back on his feet two blocks away. As Tara waited for the gate to open, Patient Zero made its way up onto the curb and wavered before the closed bus door. And by the time the gate was opening to let Tara drive her car out, Patient Zero was hungrily eyeing the oblivious bus driver bouncing rhythmically in his air-ride seat and talking rapid-fire into a hand-held microphone.

Seeing the man whom he had already written off as street pizza pressing up against the bi-fold doors, the ashen-faced driver, suddenly realizing a coroner wasn't necessary, called off the meat wagon and stowed the sweat-slickened handset. Suffering from a welling state of shock, the portly driver opened the door and started to babble at Patient Zero. "Thank God you're alive," he said, tears welling in his eyes. Choking back a sob, he covered his face with one hand, bowed his head, and exhaled sharply.

A smattering of applause started among the passengers up front and continued to the rear of the bus, rising to a crescendo like a stadium wave until everyone was clapping.

Head down and scrutinizing the stairwell, the beast stepped over the threshold. Acting on a flash of buried memory, it gripped the brushed metal railing and took a tentative step up.

With the clapping slowly giving way to the low hum of conversation, the driver drew a deep breath, shook his head, and said, "Oh *nelly*. I was sure you were my *first* ... I've seen what one of these tires will do to a person's head. And it's not pretty ... not by a longshot. No, siree." Calming down a touch, the driver shifted in his seat to wipe his eyes on his uniform sleeve, causing his chair to hiss as it bounced up and down.

While the driver was preoccupied, the corpse conquered another step.

"Come on in," the driver said, looking up and forcing a smile. "You gonna need one zone or two today?"

Patient Zero made it to the landing and paused. Sounding like a person who had been dealt a lifetime's worth of misfortune and was having the mother of all bad days, the dead thing emitted a thick guttural groan that resonated throughout the bus.

Seeing the fella's wobbly legs and awful pallor, and thinking maybe he'd tied on an early one, the driver, who had suffered similar battles of his own with the bottle, made a quick and fatal decision. Intent on letting the day's luckiest man in the world ride for free, the driver extricated himself from behind the wheel, covered the fare box with one meaty hand, and gently grasped the drunk's elbow with the other—a move that left him defenseless as he unwittingly became Patient Zero's next victim.

Losing most of his left ear when the drunk bit down on it, the driver emitted a high-pitched warble and reflexively released his grip on his attacker's elbow. Hopelessly off balance, the driver fell backward, becoming wedged in the small space between the seat and the horizontally oriented steering wheel.

As Patient Zero ground the bloody hunk of skin-covered gristle between its teeth, the kids immediately to its left started screaming, and the kicking and flailing bus driver instantly lost all appeal.

Chapter 13

Thirty silence-filled minutes after Riker escaped his seat next to Tourette's Lady, the bus was nearing the Muncie exit and he could see what looked like a half-dozen Day-Glo yellow emergency vehicles, red lights strobing hypnotically and sirens blaring, barreling down a side road paralleling the interstate the Greyhound had finally gotten back to. As the driver braked and pulled the bus hard to the shoulder to heed right-of-way, Riker saw the emergency vehicles curl around the adjacent on-ramp, nose to bumper, and enter the six-lane heading the same direction as the bus and in quite a bit of a hurry.

Thinking nothing more of the first responders who appeared to be doing what they were supposed to—responding first—Riker slipped his four-year-old flip-phone from his pocket and flicked it open. The numeric keypad flared green and he punched *1* followed by the # key and pressed the speaker to his ear.

He listened to the sound of his phone automatically dialing the ten-digits for him, and then endured six drawn-out, warbling rings. Not a message guy, preferring to actually converse—whether over the air, on a landline, or in an honest to goodness face-to-face tête-à-tête—Riker was about to fold his phone and try again later when he heard a beep and, distant and tinny-sounding, his sister's greeting started playing. He put the phone back to his ear and listened to the pertinent information, after which another tone sounded and the urge to close the phone hit him broadside. Having already come this far, he sucked it up and left a message telling her he'd be at her apartment within the hour. Ending the call a little pissed off at himself for giving in to technology, he folded the Motorola away and recalled that he was about to be let off in *Muncie, Indiana.* Way different from Atlanta, where one could be in a cab and pulling from the curb nearly as fast as the legendary Scotty of Trek fame could beam up a four-person away party. And without a smartphone, he conceded, the time he was going to burn trying to find a taxi in the college town was likely going to make a liar out of him. Mulling over the idea of calling Tara back and amending his message, he subconsciously started thumbing the phone's thin earpiece open and closed repeatedly in one hand. Staring out the window at the squat, appropriately hued battleship-gray Greyhound depot, Riker stowed his phone in a pocket, deciding to let fate run its course on the taxi issue.

As the bus bumped over the curb cut and slipped into a brightly lit bay, Riker saw a second bus offloading passengers, a dozen of whom were already gathered around its rectangular luggage compartment door. Without waiting for his bus to stop completely, he was out of his seat, single gym bag in hand, and edging for the front door.

Riker caught a dose of stink eye from the driver due to his premature approach. Out of respect for her, he stopped behind the line, smiled, and in a low voice said, "The racist pottymouth back there—" He paused while the driver engaged the brakes.

As if saying *go on,* the driver looked at him in the mirror with one brow arched.

Riker said, "She has a *gun* in her bag." He said *gun* real slow and with menace. Then he lifted his left pants leg, showing off his gleaming metal and carbon fiber prosthesis. "I'm a veteran. I know a Beretta semi-auto when I see one."

The driver killed the engine. Looking Riker straight in the face, she smiled wide and winked. "Thank you, sir," she said, throwing the door open.

Riker grabbed the rails and let his muscled upper body do the work as he swung his legs down to the landing. Gathering himself there, he took the final step in one bound, hitting the ground running, prosthetic leg be damned. On his way toward the door to the overly lit waiting room, he peered over his shoulder and saw the bi-fold door closing and the driver with the microphone to her lips.

Riker went sideways through the door as a burly security guard with a fresh high-and-tight haircut bulled past him. Smiling at the cat lady's sudden misfortune, Riker transited the lobby whistling the theme from *Mission Impossible*. Exiting onto a dirty sidewalk fronting a two-lane street, he set his bag between his feet and did his best to look like someone who needed a taxi.

***

Securing a taxi driven by someone willing to take him to Middletown wasn't as hard as Riker had imagined. In fact, it took less than five minutes. However, understanding the man behind the wheel, who must have started the meter running about the time the Greyhound driver was calling the heat on his former seatmate, was another story altogether. Settling into the back seat and glumly regarding the $6.75 fare already on the meter, Riker retrieved a scrap of paper from his pocket and read aloud to the driver his sister's Middletown address.

Speaking with the same tone and inflection as the people manning seemingly every call center Riker had ever called for tech help, the severely hunchbacked man repeated the address. Though it came out sounding to Riker like *blah, blah, blah,* followed up with a *Milton*, the weary traveler merely nodded, sat back on the lumpy seat, and closed his eyes.

Chapter 14

Atlanta, Georgia

Nearly six hundred miles south of Muncie, Indiana, deep in the bowels of the Centers for Disease Control in Atlanta, Georgia, the personal cell phone in Director of Infectious Diseases John Halverson's lab coat pocket emitted a steady electronic trill. He fished it out and saw the incoming call was from his colleague at Middletown University. Thumbing the *Talk* button, he smiled and greeted his old friend enthusiastically. He listened for a brief second, the smile melting from his face. Without so much as uttering a "goodbye" or "talk to you later," Halverson ended the call—and his plans for lunch.

Face suddenly hot as the surface of the sun and a nervous tick taking root in one eye, the CDC DID extracted a secure satellite phone from the opposite pocket and hit a single key that connected him instantly to his direct superior at the newly christened super-secure USAMRIID (United States Army Medical Research Institute of Infectious Diseases) facility at Fort Detrick, Maryland.

The second conversation lasted much longer than the first. Halverson said his piece and then was interrogated for two minutes straight, during which he uttered more than a few "I don't knows" and half a dozen "maybes" followed up by one line whispered in the lowest of tones, "Someone swapped samples." He listened for twenty seconds and when the big sweeping hand on the clock on the far wall made it to twenty-one, he drew a deep breath and, as if he actually thought his mistake could ever be rectified, said, "The genie is out of the bottle ... I get that. But you can rest assured, General Purnell, we have a protocol for this." He pinched the bridge of his nose and took a deep breath. "I *will* get a handle on this."

Halverson waited for the general to end the call and then thumbed in another number from memory.

Five hundred seventy-seven miles away by crow, in Kent, Ohio, a person in a nondescript building near the Kent State campus picked up.

Without letting the person on the end of the line get out more than a *Hello*, Halverson barked that he wanted to speak with Dirge. When Dirge came on the line a moment later, Halverson, again eschewing pleasantries, said, "This is John Halverson, DID of the CDC."

"Yes?" said Dirge. "What can I do for you?"

Halverson relayed everything he knew so far based on what Professor Fuentes had told him.

Silence on the other end.

Halverson drew a deep breath. "Are you still there?"

Another moment of silence, then Dirge asked, "Is this a drill?"

"No. This is not a drill," said Halverson calmly. "We have an event in your jurisdiction. Just keep it quiet and start the process."

"On it," said Dirge, his voice cold as ice.

Halverson ended the call. There was nothing more to say. And a whole lot to do before the day was done.

Kent, Ohio

Dirge stood there, holding the handset to his ear, and stared out the window for a long moment. The sense of urgency in Halverson's voice hadn't been lost on him. Having decided on the exact course of action and the players necessary to see it set into motion, Dirge made a series of calls. Five minutes after his chilling conversation with the Director of the CDC, he thumbed off his phone for good and tossed it in a burn bag.

Confident the biological "genie" would soon be back in the bottle and all evidence of its existence scrubbed from the face of the earth, Dirge sat down behind the empty desk, turned on the television, and settled in to wait for the inevitable.

Spring Valley Campground, Middletown, Indiana

Four hundred and eighty miles north of the CDC, Indiana National Guard Staff Sergeant James Morrison was swinging the ten-pound sledge, driving steel tent poles into the ground with all the fury of John Henry working the railroad.

Stopping for a moment to sip from his Camelbak, Morrison heard the low growl of a 6.2-liter GM Hummer engine approaching and turned in time to see the squat tan vehicle grind to a halt. Wondering what all the hurry was for and where the fire was, he clamped down again on the flexible stalk, took another pull, and watched as a corporal dismounted the vehicle and ran at him full bore, one arm extended and a cell phone held face high.

No words passed between sergeant and corporal as the phone changed hands. Sergeant Morrison immediately pressed it to his ear, announced himself, and listened intently.

***

Three minutes after taking the call, and acting on orders from someone several paygrades above his, the perplexed sergeant barked orders of his own to the eighty-eight man-and-woman guard detachment. Soldiers stopped what they were doing and sprang into action. One baby-faced corporal ran by with a ruck still on his back. "We just got here, Sarge. And we're leaving now without setting up the gear?"

Another soldier screwed up her face. Hands on hips, she said, "We can't be going back to Mansfield already … we just started setting up the med tents."

The sergeant nodded affirmative to the first question. He looked an order at the nurse and she went scurrying away. The sergeant put his hands on his hips and surveyed the assemblage of uniformed troops. They were all sizes and colors and genders. All came from different backgrounds and most held civilian jobs. Only a handful, he realized, were actual combat veterans. To set things straight once and for all, he raised his voice, saying, "That's right, people. The drill is over." He bellowed to be heard across the clearing. "Drop everything. We have a new mission. We will *not* be returning to Mansfield nor will we be returning to our garrison. We will, however, be asses in seats and Oscar Mike in two minutes."

A minute later, sledgehammers were left lying in the grass next to partially driven tent stakes, and a dozen diesel engines were throbbing to life. Gray-black exhaust hung low to the ground as the men and women mounted up, the latter of which were mostly Medical Corp personnel recently attached to the unit for this weekend of training and driving their own specialized M997 ambulance Humvees—slab-sided vehicles emblazoned with the universally recognized Red Cross symbol.

At the two-minute mark, as per Sergeant Morrison's orders, two six-wheeled deuce and a half troop transports and ten Humvees lined up bumper-to-bumper on the swath of crushed grass. They pulled out one at a time, inexplicably leaving tens of thousands of dollars' worth of gear sitting in a clearing smack-dab in the middle of Spring Valley Campground's ring of group sites.

Chapter 15

During the short drive from Muncie to Middletown, fighting sleep, Riker passed the time watching the scenery glide by, which helped little as most of it was nothing like the modern architecture dominating the skyline of the city he'd left behind hours ago. Watching the old one- and two-story brick structures flit by—along with the occasional glass-and-metal gas stations erected where crumbling examples of the former had been razed—was no more stimulating to Riker than listening to the liars on C-SPAN. And still holding onto a good deal of their leaves, the trees lining State Road 67 were nothing more than a multicolored wall blurring by that only helped deepen the funk he was in.

Between the two towns he found much more to look at. There was the occasional pasture full of grazing cows. He saw a big sign that had been erected in a farmer's field decrying the current sitting president while also bemoaning the senate sitting in opposition. *A man of his own mindset*, thought Riker. *Eff 'em all, and let God sort them out.* This got him thinking about the election just weeks away. It would be more of the same: different names beholden to the same ruling class. Nearing a north-south-running two-lane intersecting 67, a roadside vendor was setting up a stand. *Probably hawking Blu Blockers or some other crappy Chinese-made fad item du jour*, thought Riker. And serving as a backdrop to it all, rising up from bigger plats of land and hemmed in by rusted barbed wire, were sturdy old houses and swaybacked outbuildings lorded over by gargantuan barns and silos, all of them fighting gallantly the ongoing effects of gravity and the forward march of time.

In no time, the thin belt of countryside gave way to Chesterfield, Indiana, an unchanged little blip of a community, no more stimulating than the scenery Riker had already absorbed.

Without warning, still glistening with dew and awash in the flat light of late morning, the State Road plunged south. Shortly after entering the laser-straight stretch of blacktop, simultaneous to Riker glancing out his window and seeing a sign reading *Middletown Pop. 2,278*, the driver announced in a singsong voice, "*Almoss dair.*"

And he wasn't lying. Tara lived near the university on the west side of town. A couple of minutes after entering the town proper and one turn down a narrow tree-lined street, the cabbie pulled to the curb, put the car in park, and with a flourish turned and said, "*Vee are ear. Dis your stop, mista.*"

Riker nodded and smiled as he passed the man two crisp twenties. To show his appreciation to the cabbie for picking up a fare of his stature dressed in rumpled clothes and carrying a minuscule bag, Riker had the man keep the eight dollars and change that was left over. With something sounding distinctly like *Tank you berry mulch* coming from the driver and seeing a toothy smile directed his way via the rearview, Riker shoved open his door and planted his *bionic* leg onto the street. Clutching the NRA gym bag he'd received for donating a year's subscription to a soldier still toiling away over there under the hot desert sun, he grabbed the handle near his head and hauled his oversized frame from the backseat.

Bag in hand, Riker closed the door and waited in the street while the cabbie completed a crisp U-turn around him. After watching the taillights flare and the yellow Crown Vic slide around the corner on a tack due north, presumably taking it back to Muncie, Riker crossed the street and paused on the frost-heaved driveway.

There was no sidewalk, only a trampled brown path cutting through the grass parking strip. Riker stood with the deserted street at his back and stared at the two-story apartment building his sister currently called home.

Obviously built in the sixties or early seventies, when architects were smoking grass and designing things the old-fashioned way—not on a computer—the cedar-shingled twelve-unit building had all the charm of a Kleenex box and the powder blue exterior to match.

Riker scanned the parking lot for Tara's car but saw only econoboxes—foreign and domestic vehicles bigger than a coffin yet still small enough to be buried in if the Jaws of Life couldn't pry you out. His gaze reached the far end of the rectangular lot, and still no Chevy Impala. As he made tracks in the dew-laden grass, in his side vision he saw an emergency vehicle blaze by the end of the street, left to right, heading south, its flashing lights but a Technicolor blur.

With the noise from the warbling siren fading, Riker crossed the parking lot and edged between a pair of parked cars. Back and legs still stiff from all the sitting, he scaled the run of cement steps leading up to the door to his sister's apartment.

Chapter 16

Riker let himself into Tara's apartment using the key left for him under the welcome mat.

With the shades drawn and lights extinguished, the interior was gloomy. All he could make out at first as he set his bag on the floor and shrugged off his coat were the indistinct shapes of a sofa, a coffee table, and perched on the stand across from it, the large matte-black rectangle he knew to be Tara's prized television.

When his eyes adjusted to the dark, he realized the lump on the couch was Tara. She was wrapped in a blanket, legs drawn up under her and arms hidden inside.

When their eyes met she didn't smile or speak. The lack of expression on her face made Riker's stomach drop. The flat affect suggested to him something awful had happened to her or perhaps she'd seen something recently she wouldn't soon forget.

Before Riker could take a step toward Tara, she sprang from the couch, crossed the distance, and was squeezing the life from him.

"What happened?"

"You wouldn't believe me if I told you," she answered, releasing her arms from around his waist.

Riker's jaw took on a hard set. He looked down at her and said, "Try me."

She wavered.

Fearing the worst—an abusive boyfriend, maybe a rape that resulted in her becoming pregnant—he insisted she tell him what was the matter.

All of it.

Every last detail.

Tara sat on the worn couch and started her story from the first pumpkin spice latte of the day. When she was finished, Riker was relieved his first assumptions were off base. However, thinking back to the part about the fella she had called a "zombie," who supposedly bled every drop of his blood out onto the lobby tiles and came back to life a minute later, he began to wonder if she had started taking drugs. Maybe a boyfriend started her on some stuff and she was having flashbacks. After Mom died and she started telling him about all of her new tattoos, the fear had been planted that she was hanging with the wrong crowd. So, taking the initiative, he broached the subject.

"We do not say the *Z* word again."

"Zombie? That's what the eff he looked like to me."

Riker looked to the ceiling. "Is the *bath salts* thing up here yet?"

Tara made a face. "The what?"

"That *drug*"—he enunciated the word drug—"that kids are doing down in Florida. One guy ... *thinking* he was a zombie or something, ate that homeless guy's face right off. It was caught on surveillance tape. I watched it ... three times. That. Was. A. Guy. On. Drugs. Not a Z word."

She stared blankly at him.

"Maybe that kid was on *bath salts*," Riker said, stressing the last two words.

Tara took a step closer, looked up, and locked eyes with him. "You think *I'm* on drugs, don't you?" Tara pissed off was not a good thing—pacifist or not—this Riker had learned the hard way growing up with the hothead.

"I. Saw. What. I. Saw," she said slowly, taking a cue from him and also enunciating each word. Then, all business, she added, "The CDC has a plan for them. So does the military. This I'm not making up. And I'm not crazy either, *Lee*."

Riker had been studying her face, close enough that he could smell the stale coffee on her breath. He picked up none of the telltale micro expressions indicating deception. He had read about the subject in *Popular Science Magazine* or something. Tara didn't look away. She never crossed her arms or shifted from foot-to-foot. She was solid and he was beginning to believe her version of what she saw. Then he recalled the National Guard convoy that passed his window earlier, the emergency vehicles screaming out of Muncie, and the ambulance that had just roared by the end of the street heading south, and suddenly all of his doubts were thrown into a complete one-eighty. He continued looking at her and cocked his head as the obvious dawned on him. He paced to the coffee table, grabbed the remote off of it, and pressed the *Power* button while pointing the brick of a thing at the cable box.

"Let's see what's on the news," he said practically.

The television flared to life. Realizing he didn't know the channel lineup, he handed over the remote.

"Doesn't matter what they're saying on the television," she said. "In the car I had the radio on and heard the deejay say there was an active shooter at the university. Then down by the Dairy Queen what looked like a SWAT van blazed by going the opposite direction."

"Heading towards MU?"

Tara nodded. She began surfing through the channels, skipping the fluff on the lower end and going straight for the big numbers, where CNN, FOX, and MSNBC were parked. She found nothing but the same drivel spewing from all of the perfectly coiffed and credentialed anchors.

"Local news, Sis." Riker removed his ball cap and mechanically rubbed his bald pate. Feeling the first hint of stubble rough against his palm, he made a mental note to get a fresh razor and shaving lotion. *First the head, then this thicket on my face.*

Punching in a lower number brought up a local station and, sure enough, a mousy little reporter Tara recognized was in front of the camera describing a whole lot of nothing. She looked to be standing on the far southwest corner of the student parking lot where she might be able to see a sliver of the front of the building if she was lucky. However, when the brunette reporter turned and pointed, she wasn't pointing in the direction of the atrium where Tara had witnessed the unthinkable. Instead, she was hooking her arm, trying to indicate the area behind the university. A street was back there. It ran west to east. And though she didn't find herself back there often, Tara knew that was where the city bus stops were located. The reporter said: "Back behind MU's main building … out of sight of our cameras, is where the gunman boarded the MTS eastbound Number 9 and unleashed two of his thirty-bullet *clips* from his *assault* rifle."

"Bullshit," Riker said at once.

Not sold on the story, but wanting badly to see the building behind the reporter, Tara set the remote on the coffee table. She ran a hand over her tight braids, rose, and approached the thirty-two-inch flat screen.

"If there were an active shooter, the dumbass reporters would already have a chopper up from Muncie and giving the SWAT team's positions away for all to see … shooter included," insisted Riker.

"Look here. And here." Tara pointed to the walk in front of the building. Then she put a finger on the windows fronting the walk and tapped. "Here's my kiosk pushed into the windows"—she traced her finger down the screen, zigzagging between little splashes of yellow—"and these are bodies draped over the planters. These are, too … the ones sprawled on the walk here and here." When the camera pulled out, she counted them and ended up with nearly two dozen tarp-covered bodies, quite a few of them leaking blood, the shiny black trails meandering across the cement squares.

"All of that shooting and none of the glass is starred or blown out," Riker said. He finally lowered his frame to the low-slung second-hand sofa.

"Still think I'm on drugs?"

He shook his head. "Not at all, Tara. And I'm sorry I even went there."

"Then what do you think happened?"

"My gut says something went sideways in the microbiology part of the school. Where's it located?"

Tara gave him a quick tour of MU, pointing out areas of interest on the image frozen on the screen.

"He could have come from the lab area upstairs."

"I think so, too," said Tara agreeably. "What should we do now?"

"Wait until dark and go anywhere but there," he said. "We should probably stay indoors until we move out just in case whatever affected the kid is airborne."

"If it is," Tara said, grimacing, "then we're both already dead. I was so close I could smell the blood … it was like, like … metallic, or something."

Recalling the sight and stench of his own blood and soiled fatigues from the day he'd died the first time, Riker crinkled his nose. "We're alive now," he said. "We need to gather as much information as we can before dark."

"Then?"

"Then we get the hell out of Dodge."

Tara gestured at the television with the remote. "Let's keep it here and see what the mayor has to say."

"That's a problem right there," said Riker. "He … or she should have been on already … with a prepared speech, calming the community. What time is it?"

Tara said, "Mayor's a he. Bill Weston." She poked her head in the kitchen and glanced at the green numbers on the microwave. "A little after noon."

"So it's been ninety minutes and still there's no mention of any measures being taken by the higher-ups. Nothing from the chief of police. Not a peep out of the mayor. Governor must be under a rock up there in Indianapolis to not have heard about this. Hell, that school shooting in Dover … the bodies weren't even cold yet and the entire anti-gun crowd and the President were on in record time and blaming everything but the crazy drugged-up kid who did it. Why the silence now?"

Tara said nothing. She thought: *You're ranting now, Bro.* So to spare him—and her ears—the anguish, she muted the news lady and made her way to the tiny galley-style kitchen.

"Got any coffee?" Riker called.

"Hardy har har," she countered. "You want soy milk? An extra shot?"

"Oh duh," he called sheepishly. "Of course you have coffee. I'll take a cup of whatever fell off the truck."

"My moral compass doesn't swing that way, Bro. This coffee is paid for."

The shrill whirring of a machine grinding beans started up. It lasted a few seconds. Once it subsided, Riker said, "You've got a degree in design, Tara. Why are you still working the coffee stand?"

She briefly poked her head out of the kitchen. "Because somebody had to go off and play war and get himself blown up. Which meant somebody had to stay close to the aging mother. Who was already a widow. And who also was fighting the big C for the first time."

"I'm sorry," said Riker. "You sacrificed a lot for her. For me, too."

Tara made no reply.

Just the sounds of coffee being poured.

"I saw you got some new ink," he called. "Looks nice. Girly, too."

"Thanks," she called back. "I got the inspiration for them from Mom's urn."

Chapter 17

Tara came back with two mugs full of steaming, inky-black Arabica. Voice soft and low, she said, "Why don't you ever answer your phone, Lee?" She offered him one of the mugs. Tone taking a quick one-eighty, exasperation clearly evident, she asked, "Which begs the question why the *eff* do you even lug one around with you in the first place if you're not going to answer it?"

He shrugged, accepted the mug, and sniffed the steam. "Good brew."

"Phone?" she pressed.

"Check yours, smarty. I *did* call you."

She dug her phone from her bag and checked the call log. Seeing the missed call, she noted the time, did the math in her head, and then stuck her tongue out.

Riker arched a brow and shot her a look as if saying, *I told you so.*

"My bag was behind my seat. Phone was in the bag. Twenty minute drive home took forty-five minutes because the police were setting up a cordon." She feigned a smile. "So bugger off, *Bro.*"

"Cordon? Were they checking cars for the shooter? They check yours?"

She snickered. "My car has no back seat."

He said, "It used to. And why aren't you parking in your usual space?"

Tara opened a bag of Double Stuf Oreos, her favorite, which up until now had had no ill effect on her athletic figure. She took two for herself and passed the package.

"My car *is* out there," she answered, taking a bite. "My *new* car"—crumbs rained on the coffee table as she spoke—"named her *Tee.*"

The Type A personality in him coming out, Riker brushed the black crumbs into his hand. "You finally broke down and bought a new car?"

She smiled. "Just getting a little bit ahead of the inheritance curve. You'll see it when we leave." She cast a glance at the gym bag that looked more like a lunch sack in proportion to him. "Good thing you packed light."

Riker wolfed down an Oreo, wiping the crumbs on his Levis. When he looked over at Tara, she was fiddling with her phone. Then he felt his eyes, heavy from lack of sleep, no thanks to the Cat Lady, begin to flutter. He glanced at his half-empty mug and decided to stop fighting it. He rolled his pants leg up and removed his prosthesis and the damp sleeve covering the six-inch stump protruding below his knee. He stuffed the sleeve in the prosthetic and set the aluminum-and-carbon-fiber number on the floor by the table. He massaged the aching nub of fibula, pressing the thick slab of reddish-pink scar tissue for a couple of minutes.

"Why don't you lie down. Just rest your eyes for a bit," Tara suggested. "I'll keep tabs on what's happening on the tube."

Riker said nothing. Simply stretched out across the sofa and closed his eyes.

***

Six miles northwest of Tara's apartment, a root-beer-brown Chevy Volt was pulling into the drive of a single-level ranch-style house. The brake lights flared then went dark as the driver cut the motor.

Seeing this, a man in black coveralls and wearing a like-colored hardhat stepped from a white van parked on the curb across the cul-de-sac. A canvas satchel was slung over one shoulder and he carried a clipboard in his left hand. While the Volt's driver was exiting his car with a briefcase in one hand and a porkpie hat in the other, the man with the clipboard had crossed the oval of asphalt and took up station on the sidewalk bordering the curb cut.

Holding the clipboard before him, the man from the van called out from a dozen feet away to get the Volt driver's attention.

No inflection in his voice. "Are you Professor Fuentes?"

"That's me," replied the bespectacled man. He shifted the hat from his right hand to his left and turned to face his caller. "How can I help you?"

The man from the van said nothing, Nor did he look left or right or behind him. He was focused only on the professor's face as he reached inside the satchel and came back with a suppressed black pistol clutched in his gloved right hand.

Though his eyes were hidden behind dark glasses, the man from the van didn't flinch when he aimed for the professor's left eye and pulled the trigger. He stood there still as a statue as his victim crashed vertically to the sloped driveway, the glasses he had worn now a yard away and twisted like a pretzel.

The shooter's mouth retained the same grim set as he approached the fallen body and calmly pumped another round from the pistol into the other eye.

Expression unchanged, the shooter knelt and yanked the wallet from the corpse's pants pocket. Opened it up and quickly confirmed the dead man's identity. Satisfied, he rose and policed up the spent shell casings.

The shooter's retreat was made in the same manner as his approach: slow and measured as if he answered to nobody. Which in a sense was true.

Along the way, the shooter jammed the suppressed pistol into the satchel and dumped the casings in a pocket.

At the van he opened the door, tossed the satchel across the seat, and climbed inside.

As he wheeled around the cul-de-sac and nosed the van toward the single egress, he thumbed his secure satellite phone alive and dialed a number from memory. Once the hand shake was complete and encryption enabled, the man said, "It's done," then promptly ended the call.

***

Thinking the thick comforter draping his body was a piece of flaming wreckage from the destroyed Land Cruiser he'd just been thrown from, Riker came to, swinging. As the latent memories jumped synapses, he sat up straight, breathing hard, sweat beading heavily on his forehead. Still acting on the supposition gleaned from the nightmare, he swung his good leg hard off the couch with the stub following and knocked his mug over with it, sending the cold coffee cascading off the tabletop and onto the carpet.

"You okay, bro?" Tara looked up, the soft glow from her phone lighting her face.

Groggily, Riker asked, "What time is it?"

"You've been out for hours."

He pointed at his bare wrist. "Time?"

"Quarter to seven."

"PM?"

Tara nodded. "Looked like you needed the sleep. So I let you."

"Was I ...?"

She nodded. "Yep. Fighting a whole damn army in your sleep." Her chair clattered as she rose from the kitchen table. Her tennis shoes chirped on the linoleum as she approached the couch, phone in hand.

"Take a look," she said. "Told you I knew what I saw."

"What is it?" Riker asked, rubbing sleep from his eyes. He looked up to take the phone and saw Tara's eyes locked onto what was left of his left leg.

"Sorry," she said, quickly looking away. "It's just that ... I've never really seen it up close."

"Just a hunk of tough skin, that's all," he said, patting the mottled pink nub contrasting greatly with his mahogany-hued skin. Then, without checking for a reaction from her, he grabbed his fake lower leg off the floor and deftly snugged it on. Looking up and smiling, he smoothed down his pant leg and added, "Besides, you've seen one, you've seen them all."

Changing the subject, Tara pointed at the phone, saying, "While you were out I was going over what I saw in my head. Walking myself through it like I was on the stand and Matlock was grilling me."

Riker thought: *She likes Matlock.* In that moment, he realized he didn't know his grown little sister as well as he'd thought he did. He said, "And?"

"At first, not one of the arriving students or teachers stepped forward to help the guy I told you about."

Finished lacing his boot, Riker hinged up and asked, "What did they do?"

"They watched … gawked is more like it. But so did I. However …" She pointed a finger at Riker. "I didn't stoop so low as to record the guy as he was dying"—she tapped her chest—"and it didn't even cross my mind once he started to come back to life."

"But everyone else was?"

"Some of them. Most … actually."

Riker looked toward the door where his bag was sitting next to a daypack bulging with who knew what. "Human nature sucks," he said, nodding. He cast his gaze back to Tara. "Did it make the news yet?"

She shook her head side-to-side and extended her arm, phone in hand. "And that's the weird thing. Just hit the play button. It's the opaque arrow."

Taking the phone from her, he said, "This isn't my first rodeo, Sis."

Chapter 18

Riker swiped the iPhone's glass screen, cradled the thing in his palm, and watched through a few different clips, the audio especially chilling. The screams started a skin crawl near his scrotum that worked its way up his back until his chest was going tight. "How did *this* get on your phone?"

"Once the television screen locked up with a gray 'stand by' message, I did a search on YouTube. People load ... never mind. That footage was what people in the lobby were recording when I abandoned my kiosk." She shook her head. "YouTube already took them all down. And the news channels are just now dropping their original lone shooter story and speculating some strain of rabies or a released virus is responsible for the 'shooter' and the guy I saw in the lobby. The Number 9 bus I saw from a distance when I was getting away——." She went quiet.

"Yes," said Riker, standing and cupping her shoulder. "Go on."

"It was nearly full. Twenty or thirty people on it ... a handful of kids among them. Most of them are unaccounted for as of the last report. Channel Six showed the blood on the windows. They zoomed in on these"—her voice cracked and she paused—"tiny, really tiny hand prints on the glass. And they just had to show a little body, one shoe sticking out from under a yellow tarp."

Speaking softly, Riker asked, "Were there any survivors?"

She nodded. Swallowed hard and said, "One. A teenager who hid in the back of the bus. He blabbered on for a second to the reporter about dead people getting back up and walking away *after* dying in pools of their own blood. The reporter finally calmed him down and when he started going on crazily about a drunken cannibal starting it all—"

Riker finished it for her. "They cut him off."

"Not the reporter. She was hanging onto every word. Some soldiers in black uniforms whisked him away. They just came up and grabbed him while he was still talking." She took a deep breath. Took the remote from the table. Pointing it at the television, she said, "We have a decision to make."

Riker watched the screen light up and saw a man in a navy Brooks-Brothers-type of suit speaking straight into the camera. As the frazzled, middle-aged guy gesticulated with his arms, making the official-looking badge on a lanyard around his neck bob up and down in front of his loosened tie, Riker stopped listening to the words and keyed in on the body language. The man was scared. Petrified, actually. Something was keeping him from bolting from in front of the camera, of that Riker was certain.

The less-than-convincing man in the suit breathlessly urged anyone who had been in or around MU during the events of the day to relocate to one of three locations in Middletown, where witness statements would be taken and proper inoculations administered. The feed ended abruptly and the gray screen Tara had mentioned was back. It was frozen in place and loaded with all kinds of information fully endorsed by FEMA. It stayed unchanged while a crawl moving slowly along the bottom of the screen listed addresses to Middletown's largest hospital, the city's only mental health facility, and a local high school.

Riker shook his head. "Run right into the lion's den. Seems pretty smart to me."

"Sarcasm, much?" she said.

The windows rattled and a bass-heavy chopping sound filled the room. The noise increased and then its source moved off to the northeast, taking the cacophony with it.

Riker snugged his cap down tight. Shrugging into his parka he said, "Black Hawk."

"A what?"

"A helicopter. Probably National Guard—." Riker's voice trailed off.

"What makes you think that?"

Riker told Tara about the Guard convoy that passed the bus on the interstate. The sight of which took him back to his last day in the Sandbox. Then he detailed how the roadside IED stole his leg. He talked about lying on his back on the ochre sand, the remains of his shattered leg taped to his chest during that fifteen-minute wait for the dust-off bird to arrive. He stressed how his life was saved that day by a crew of Air Force aviators and a trio of Air Force Pararescue men who worked on him and a fellow soldier during the entire flight to the field hospital. "So that others may live," he said solemnly.

"Their motto?" she asked, her voice low.

"Yep. And that sound you just heard. To me ... that sound represents survival."

On cue, another chopper passed overhead. Much louder, and more than one, judging by how long it took for the vintage aluminum window behind the sofa to stop banging around in its channel.

"Chinooks," he said, "followed by more Black Hawks." He rose from the sofa. "Let's go."

"I already packed."

"I noticed," said Riker. "Where's Mom's urn?"

"We're going to take *it* with us?"

"*Her*," he corrected. "The same *her* that put Band-Aids on our boo boos. The same wonderful woman who stuck up for me in fifth grade when some of the boys were calling me King Kong and Sasquatch."

"I don't remember that. I was six or so. But I get it, Lee. Sorry." She went quiet and let her gaze roam the room. "We'll be coming back here eventually ... won't we?"

"With all that's already happened, we can't afford to take anything for granted. I have a *promise* to keep."

Tara looked at him quizzically.

He closed his eyes and went silent for a second. Finally, when he reopened them he said, "I didn't want to bring this up until after the inheritance was distributed." He paused and took a deep breath. "I have to tell you something that Mom told me that last day."

"She told you something on her deathbed? Like a confession, or … ?" Her face took on the same set as when Riker arrived. Then her hands went to her knees and she gripped them tightly.

He shook his head. "Nothing serious like that. She told me where she wants her ashes spread. It was more of an order, actually."

Tara relaxed her grip and made a face. "Where?"

"I can't tell you that. I can tell you, however, that we have to get out of Middletown to make it happen." He looked in the direction the helicopters had been heading. "Gotta admit … the timing to do so couldn't be better."

Tara stood and left the room as Riker rose from the couch and shouldered his bag.

His sister returned with the urn. It was polished bronze and the size of a cantaloupe. The lid was adorned with silver roses. Delicately etched on the fluted base was baby's breath and more roses and stems complete with pronounced thorns. On the front was a silver tag. Etched on the tag was: *Rita Marlene Riker 12-12-1955 —7-7-2016.*

Tara went to her tiptoes. Looked Riker in the eye. "Come on," she begged. "Tell me where we're taking her."

Riker pursed his lips and shook his head. "Any idea what kind of financial windfall we're looking at?"

Mimicking him, Tara pursed her lips and shook her head. "Mom's effin with me twofold. I'm just glad you're in the dark about *something*."

Riker forced a smile. "Misery loves company, huh?"

Cradling the urn like a football, Tara stalked out the door, keys in hand. Remaining tightlipped, she led Riker down the stairs and through the lot, stopping behind a tiny red car.

Riker looked at the car. It was dwarfed by the empty parking spaces bracketing it. He took a step toward the rear bumper and looked in the back window. Tara wasn't exaggerating. The car had no backseat. Hell, its roof barely reached Riker's sternum.

"What is this *thing?*" he asked.

"This is Tee. Short for *Thumbelina*," Tara said.

Riker heard the soft hiss as the door locks popped. "What is it?"

"It's a Smart Car."

"Hardly," said Riker. "On both accounts." He stooped and sized up the interior—or lack thereof.

Tara placed the urn on the shelf behind her seat. She put her pack on one side to keep it from sliding around. Riker bookended the urn with his bag, then pulled the lever and put his seat all the way back. It stopped after traveling less than six inches.

Starting the motor, Tara said, "Lease is seventy-nine bucks a month. That souped-up cop engine in Mom's old Impala sucked that down in unleaded every two weeks."

Riker winced when he remembered the final trip to the hospital in that Impala. Mom's battle with cancer was long and drawn out. Truth was, three months removed from her finally succumbing, he was still numb from all of the ups and downs of her valiant struggle. And now that they were finally going to have some closure, the whole ordeal was back, the memories rattling his bones as if he'd just stepped off an unseen curb.

Tara closed her door. "Get in," she said, revving the near-silent motor.

Chapter 19

Somehow Riker wedged himself into the car seemingly designed for Keebler Elves. Even with his seat at maximum extension, his shins pressed twin divots into the horizontal padding below the glove compartment. He grinned as he was struck with the thought of the car's designers trolling the dolly department at Toys R Us in search of Lilliputian-sized dolls to use as crash test dummies. And as he reached back for his shoulder belt, his gaze fell to the sliver of dash where the airbag that would be kneecapping him would deploy from should Sis pile them up.

"I don't think I've ever sat in a smaller car," grumbled Riker.

"It's not small to me."

"Master of the obvious."

Tara reversed while Riker clicked his seatbelt home. "Which site do you want to … what'd you call it … *recon?*" she asked.

His answer came with no hesitation. "The high school."

Tara made the turn at the end of her street and nosed *Tee* east. As houses and trees flashed by, she looked over and said exactly what her brother was thinking: "So we can make a quick getaway if it's a shit show."

"Bingo," he said.

"I figured you would say the high school would be our best bet. It's got an open campus. We can approach from a couple of different directions if need be. Take a quick peek and carry on"

"Great minds," he said. And though he doubted they could win a pink-slip race against a moped, he added, "Step on it.

Just don't get us in a wreck. I don't want to have to explain to the ER doctor how my bionic leg ended up lodged in my ass."

Tara turned right off of Earl Avenue and onto 8th Street. Planning on riding the two-lane all the way south—almost a straight shot to Shenandoah High—she pinned the pedal and regarded her brother with a sidelong glance. "Thanks for the stunning visual, by the way. You have no need to worry about that scenario coming to fruition. My driving record is spotless."

Riker didn't respond. He was busy taking in the surroundings. Judging by how deserted 8th was, he concluded someone with major pull had ordered Middletown to roll up its sidewalks and go home. *Nothing to see here.* All along the blink-and-you-miss-it town center, the windows were dark and nothing moved. Riker expected to at least see a couple of bars open with seats full and people lamenting the state of the world. But he was sadly mistaken.

As they neared the south edge of the downtown core, the thin purple band of dusk gave way to night and the street lights began to flicker to life. A block removed from the darkened city center, the Smart Car's headlights washed over a pair of tangled vehicles. It didn't take a crash reconstruction expert to conclude that one of them had blown a red at the intersection. They had come to rest in an inverted "V" and blocked most of both lanes. If one of the twisted hunks of unmoving metal could have been declared a winner, thought Riker, the SUV facing them with its driver's door hanging open was it. Churned under the rig's high-clearance front end was a Volvo station wagon, the driver and passenger just shadowy forms, their unmoving bodies draped by a number of deployed airbags. There was nobody inside the SUV. On the ground by its open door was an empty liquor bottle. Drawing Riker's eye to the nearby sidewalk was a glistening trail of blood that ended in the shadowy alcove fronting a pharmacy with a CLOSED sign positioned prominently behind one of its huge plate glass windows.

"You're going to try and shoot the gap, aren't you?"

Tara nodded, tapped the brakes and aimed the car's stunted nose for the meager opening between the pileup on the left and the light pole on the right.

Having squeezed an Army deuce-and-a-half through many a tight spot in his day, Riker was first to realize that, though tiny was being kind when describing their ride, there would be no threading this needle.

Simultaneously, he leaned away from the looming pole, braced for impact, and hollered for Tara to stop.

Too late.

The warning had barely crossed Riker's lips when a bang and the follow-on keening of metal being reshaped sounded from the rear quarter panel on his side. All forward motion ceased abruptly and the equal and opposite part of Newton's Law was in effect as they were both being thrown hard against their shoulder belts.

Relieved that he wasn't the recipient of a face full of deploying airbag, Riker looked to Tara and said mockingly, "My driving record is spotless,"

Tara slammed the shifter into Reverse. Then she applied a healthy dose of pedal to no effect. Throwing her hands up in mock surrender, she put the transmission into Neutral and looked a question her brother's way.

Riker craned around to see their bags mashed against his headrest with the urn still wedged between them. Then he sat back in his seat muttering something about his first mistake having been getting in the rolling sardine can in the first place. He looked past Tara and saw that the corner of the high-centered SUV's chromed bumper was blocking her door. He looked out his window and saw a bank of newspaper boxes chained to the steel light standard responsible for all of the noise prior to their abrupt stop. Opposite the curb was a check cashing place, its windows dark and uninviting. Expecting to be trapped in what to him amounted to nothing more than a rolling casket, he clicked out of his shoulder belt and worked the door handle with his little finger. Success! The door opened with ease, but when he finally extricated himself from the car's cramped confines, he saw that the car was hung up on the light standard, its halide lights now fully lit and bathing the intersection and crash scene in an eerie orange hue.

Inside the car, Tara felt a tremor transit her seat. Looking over her shoulder, she saw her brother crouched behind his open door, face screwed up with exertion, and just starting to rock the car side-to-side. After a few seconds of this and uttering some choice expletives, he gave up, looped around the light pole, and stopped behind the car. For a second she saw the top of his blue ball cap through the rear window as he bent at the waist. In the next beat his barrel chest was pressing against the window. A violent shudder rolled through the car from back-to-front and she heard through her open window her brother grunting and breathing hard. Shifting her gaze to the Volvo, she saw the driver snap to attention. Then, like some kind of parade automaton gone haywire, its misshapen head lolled around in a lazy circle until its wildly roving eyes found her brother. The steering wheel airbag fluttered and a horribly broken arm snaked over the window sill, causing the remaining pebbled glass to break free and cascade to the road. The driver's shredded appendage hinged mid-forearm and there was a resonant *thump* when its bloodied hand impacted the outside of the door. As a result of the failed swipe at Riker, the soiled cotton bandage wrapping the driver's forearm slipped to its wrist, revealing a crater with raised purple ridges where an oval plug of flesh had been excised.

Someone had taken one hell of a bite out of him, that was clear. Wondering what led up to the injury, she regarded its stark white face again and saw reflected in those unblinking eyes the blurry movement of her brother working to get their car moving again. And as she continued to stare into those shark-like black orbs, she came to realize there was no life in them. Nothing whatsoever. Not even a fleeting glimmer. This sudden revelation sent a shudder racing up her spine. Then she was choking back bitter bile as a wave of revulsion churned her guts.

Mercifully, the car stopped rocking.

Words coming between labored breaths, Tara heard her brother say, "I'm going to try something different."

"Whatever it is, make it quick," she called. "I'm about to lose my Oreos."

With a million unanswered questions concerning the thing pinned in the car chiseling away at the normalcy bias keeping her somewhat calm, Tara craned around to see what her brother meant by "something different." However, instead of seeing his hulking frame by the car's rear quarter, she witnessed an indistinct form dart from the darkness, disappear for a split second behind the light pole, then launch off the curb.

Time seemed to slow and the orange wash from the streetlight revealed to Tara a man, arms outstretched and seemingly frozen mid-stride.

Behind the car, Riker was crouched down with his hands hooked under the rear bumper and trying to lift it up and over the light standard's fluted base. Though he was certain Tara's new ride was barely heavier than a Harley Davidson, he couldn't do more than lift the body up a couple of inches before having to let it back down. Defeated again, he was about to tell Tara to put it into drive and mat the pedal when he detected an out-of-place sound.

Leather on cement, perhaps?

In response to the phantom noise, the leering Volvo driver reared back, wagged his head side to side, and emitted a mournful moan through a picket of broken teeth.

Simultaneously, a low growl reached Riker's ears and he detected in his right side vision a flash of movement. But before he could rise up, let alone take his eyes from the Volvo driver, a hundred-some-odd pounds of attacker letting out a hair-standing snarl hit him broadside. In the next beat, as Riker instinctively braced against the car to keep from being bowled over, his assailant's cold hands were going for his neck.

A tick too late to shout a warning, Tara watched in horror as the twenty-something man, a full head shorter than her brother, opened his mouth and dropped from view.

Acting on long-dormant training, Riker transferred the majority of his weight to his good leg. Then, as if surrendering to the unseen threat flailing against him from behind, he thrust both arms up and reached back over his shoulders. Expecting to feel hot breath on his neck, he felt nothing. Inexplicably, he heard no breathing going on back there, either. Blindly grabbing two handfuls of wispy hair, Riker locked his elbows and stood up quickly, a move that dragged his assailant off its feet. Standing straight-legged yet bent slightly at the waist, Riker twisted his hips counter-clockwise and hurled the dead weight onto the roof of his sister's tiny ride.

With the driver now hanging half out of the Volvo's window, and her brother's attacker laid out on her roof and mashing his pallid face against the windshield, Tara put the car into Drive, stood on the accelerator, and hollered, "Do something, Lee!"

When he allowed it, the heat of battle became a real thing for Riker. The instant the adrenaline dump hit his system, the tinnitus was back full bore, the tightness was gripping his neck and shoulders, and he was graced momentarily with a burst of superhuman strength.

Ignoring the tennis-shoe-clad feet scissoring the air near his face, Riker grabbed ahold of the bumper and clean-jerked the car a foot off the ground. With Tara's admonition spurring him on and a slow burn taking root in his shoulders and trapezius muscles, he slow-walked the car forward a foot and a half and then dropped the rear end down hard just beyond the light standard's base. The moment the wildly spinning rear tires contacted the road, the car lurched and sped forward. It continued on for a dozen feet before the brake lights flared and it came to a juddering halt, relocating the man from the roof to the road, where he hit face first and came to rest spread-eagle and spasming.

Inside the car, Tara was busy shifting gears when a distant fusillade of pops she guessed to be firecrackers sounded off to her left. A half-beat later, drawing both her and the Volvo driver's attention skyward, a tiny egg-shaped helicopter with a pair of uniformed soldiers positioned on either side roared overhead. It had buzzed so close to the ground while banking directly over the intersection that she saw clearly the silhouette of the helmeted pilot through the canopy glass.

Multitasking, Tara backed the car away from the twitching body and leaned over to open the passenger door. Stopping just shy of kneecapping her brother with Thumbelina's rear bumper, she let the door swing open and returned her attention to the stricken man struggling to rise up from the road.

There was a clatter of metal striking metal and the car dipped to the right when Riker thrust his prosthetic-clad leg inside the car and sat down hard on the seat. Gripping the handle by his head two-handed, he dragged his good leg inside as a wild-eyed Tara accelerated and steered around the kneeling attacker.

With the debris-strewn road flicking by just inches from his right thigh, Riker slammed the door closed and let out the breath trapped in his lungs.

"Did you hear that back there?" he asked.

"The fireworks?"

"The *gunshots*," he corrected. "That was automatic rifle fire."

"And the helicopter?"

"I didn't see it clearly," admitted Riker. "It sounded like one of the Little Birds that drop special ops shooters onto rooftops."

Nodding, Tara said, "There were guys with guns sitting *outside* of the cockpit."

"Then it's worse than what we saw on the tube," said Riker somberly. "Much worse."

Eyes on the road and knuckles going white from her death grip on the wheel, Tara said, "You know, I was thinking." She let the statement hang.

He regarded her with a sidelong look and removed his hat. "What?" he asked as he went about probing scratches on the sides and back of his neck.

"That guy in the car and the one that jumped you were acting just like the kid who died and woke back up in the lobby." She went quiet as they blew an intersection on the yellow.

"Like zombies?"

She nodded.

Grimacing, Riker flipped down the visor and examined his neck in the vanity mirror there.

Voice wavering, she added, "It *almost* had you, Lee."

Riker grabbed the bar near his head as Tara threw the car into a hard left off of 8th and accelerated along Fall Creek Boulevard, heading east and seemingly on a collision course with the low-hanging moon.

"'*Almost*' and '*did*' are miles apart in my book, Tara." He put his hat on and pulled it low to cover the scarring. "All it did was scratch my neck a bit. No blood,"—he showed her his hands—"no foul."

Tara went silent, her lips pursed into a thin white line as her eyes roved the mirrors.

A quarter of a mile later, Tara stopped briefly at the intersection with North Raider Road, then hooked a right.

Tara kept Tee to the far right of her lane, now and again having to dodge erratically driven cars coming at them. Twice over the three miles they travelled on North Raider Road, her stellar peripheral vision and quick reflexes saved them from getting T-boned by drivers disregarding traffic controls at crossings.

"I don't think you're in danger of being arrested for that hit and run back there," said Riker, his head on a swivel, scanning the crossings and road ahead. "You can probably back off the speed a bit."

Tara said nothing. Knowing they were nearing their destination, she slowed. Picking up on the soft glow at their ten o'clock, she turned toward it, taking a side street whose sign she failed to get a glimpse of. Halfway down the tree-lined drive, silhouetted against the harsh white light of hundreds of bulbs ensconced in the phalanx of rectangular standards ringing Shenandoah High's football field, were three people moving with a slow, unnatural gait.

"What do you want me to do?" she asked, already applying the brakes.

"Stop right here," Riker ordered. Wishing he had a pair of binoculars, he resorted to squinting to try and make out the details. Once his eyes adjusted to the Klieg lights, he saw that the bleachers and press box were empty. He regarded the steadily advancing trio and saw slack faces on all three. No affect whatsoever. They looked like they were dead. And if he hadn't already seen a pair of them up close and personal, he would have thought himself crazy for even thinking it.

Chapter 20

"I've seen enough," said Riker as he toured the mirrors with his gaze.

Tara pointed at the advancing figures. "What about those?"

Shifting in his seat, Riker said, "Avoid them."

Tara tromped the gas and steered Tee in a crazy arc around what looked to her like walking cadavers. After avoiding the clumsy swipe of the pale-faced teenager that had tracked her with the same kind of dead stare as the Volvo driver, Tara turned right and sped along the west side of the field. Soon the parking lot and more of the surreal sight they had seen from afar was unfolding before them. They saw that, despite the lights burning and the hundred or so passenger cars, trucks, and SUVs parked helter-skelter in both the main lot and the overflow parking area, the Raiders' scoreboard was darkened, and the field empty.

"Where is everyone?" Tara asked, slowing and pulling over to the right beside a row of Jersey barriers left in place to block entry to the field.

"No idea," he answered. "After seeing that guy in the Volvo ... coming back to life or whatever that's called, I'm glad we're alone here."

Tara hooked a thumb over her shoulder. "That kid back there had those same unblinking shark eyes as the Volvo dude and the faster one that jumped you back there."

"Faster?"

She nodded and described the attack the way she saw it.

Riker nodded. Pinching the bridge of his nose, he said, "I want to know how that whatever it was survived the head-butt with the asphalt back there." He paused to collect his thoughts.

"A normal person would've been out cold or dead the way his face was caved in."

Tara's eyes were now moving between Riker and the rearview mirror where she saw the trio ranging down the middle of the street.

Riker gestured at the lots on the left and swept his hand toward the deserted field. "And now this. This is the straw that broke this camel's back."

"What are you saying?"

"There's no witness statements being taken here. You see any medical vans that'd cause you to believe any inoculating is going on in there?"

Tara shrugged. "What do you want to do, Lee?"

"I want to head for the hills and stay there until we know what the hell is really going on."

"What hills?" said Tara, her voice strained. "We're in *Indiana*. Nothing but cornfields and mole hills here."

"You know what I mean. Let's get our road trip started tonight."

"We're supposed to meet with the lawyer on Monday for the big inheritance reveal."

"What's Mom having him do, present it to us in cash?"

"No," said Tara. "Since Mom named me executor of estate and bestowed power of attorney on me, all I had to do was sign a few forms electronically."

"How do we get the money?"

"It's set to be disbursed electronically by Monday."

He shot her a skeptical look. "You sure about that?"

She nodded.

"And you can't tell me how much?"

She shook her head. "I don't know how much, Lee. You know how Mom always wanted us to make our own way in the world. She could have given all the patent money to the United Negro College Fund for all I know."

"Wouldn't be such a bad thing," said Riker. Exasperation showing in his tone, he asked, "So you going to tell me why we're meeting with the lawyer?"

"To hear the reading of the will. It's mainly symbolic. Plus we'll receive the deeds to the houses. I'm guessing we'll each get one."

Riker was back to rubbing his shoulders and neck.

"The concussion thing back?"

Riker nodded. "Never left. Docs call it Chronic Traumatic Encephalopathy. Or CTE, for short. What that Will Smith movie Concussion was all about."

Tara nodded, then looked over her shoulder. Seeing the creepers still coming like they were on some kind of mission, she tromped the gas again, nosing Tee in the same direction they'd been travelling, only backing off once they were moving double the posted twenty-miles-per-hour speed limit.

At the end of the side street was a T where a right turn would see them onto the high school campus, and a left would get them back to Raider Boulevard where they could continue north to the interstate. Nearing the junction, Tara began to slow and then threw on her left turn signal.

"Good call, Sis," said Riker, just as an intense beam of light, at least a million candlepower, he figured, hit them full in the face.

Momentarily blinded and acting out of self-preservation, Tara braked hard.

A half-beat after the miniature sun lit up everything inside of the car and out, it flicked off and Riker was left with blue tracers darting in front of his eyes.

"I can't see shit," said Tara, her voice an octave or two higher than normal.

Riker lowered his hand and slowly his vision returned. Blocking their way was a trio of vehicles. Judging by the squared-off forms, he pegged them as Humvees. Confirmation came when their widely spaced headlights flicked on.

"What should I do?" whispered Tara.

Because he was focused on the half-dozen forms emerging from the squat Humvees, Riker said nothing. With carbines in hand, muzzles trained on the ground near their feet, they advanced cautiously through the weak beams of light. *Low ready* is what Riker's first drill instructor called how they carried their rifles, and by the way the men were comported, moving slow and steady and confident, he figured no hills or cornfields were going to be visited by him or Sis anytime soon.

Staring straight ahead and speaking from the corner of his mouth, Riker said, "Stay calm and let me do the talking."

Five of the forms halted just beyond the blue-white spill of the Smart Car's headlights. One man continued, stopping and training his rifle on the car once he was an arm's reach from the driver's side door. A bright beam lanced from a tiny flashlight attached to his weapon. Without saying a word, he tilted his head and peered inside.

Momentarily blinded yet again, Tara kept her hands on the wheel and squinted hard against the light.

"Stay calm," said Riker, his mitt-sized hands now splayed out on the near-vertical dash where the uniformed man could see them.

Tara nodded and said, "Easy for you to say, he's not aiming that thing at you." She opened her eyes slowly to see that the soldier had extinguished the light and was reaching out with one gloved hand. The glove she saw curling into a fist was a high-tech item featuring some kind of molded material for knuckle protection. She jumped and yelped as a series of raps vibrated the glass by her face. The soldier bent at the waist, stared in at her from behind clear-lensed wraparound Oakleys, and rotated the fist in a tight clockwise circle—the universal sign for *roll down your window*.

And she did, blurting, "We were just looking for a through road to see us east … Officer?"

What part of let me do the talking did you not understand? thought Riker as he craned and looked at the five uniformed men who had stayed back. Nothing about them save for their bearing—which screamed highly trained and likely special operations shooters—pointed to what outfit they hailed from. He looked back at the man talking to his sis. He was ruddy-faced. Hard eyes looked out from underneath bushy red eyebrows. The black beret on his shaved head was cocked so far over that it seemed in danger of falling off. He looked to be fortyish, prime age for a top dog spot in the teams. The uniform they all wore was a standard MultiCam pattern, mostly browns with some black and green. Adaptable to all environments, the DOD bean counters claimed. There was no visible name tape. Nothing pointing to his rank, branch of service, or unit. Save for the fact that the point man spoke perfect Midwest English, the soldiers could have been UN peacekeepers for all Riker knew.

"State Road is closed," said the man in an authoritative tone. "As of 1500, per the governor's orders, Middletown is under martial law."

"May I back up and go home?"

The soldier stepped two paces closer. Raised his black carbine. *All business*, thought Riker as the man padded left and then right, eyeballing the inside of the vehicle. "Do you have any weapons in the car?"

They both shook their heads, slowly, side-to-side.

"Bites?"

Caught off guard, Tara screwed up her face and asked, "Bites?"

"Have either of you been bitten? Or scratched?" He paused in thought. "Or ingested anybody's blood or saliva?"

"What have you *effin* been smoking?" shot Tara.

With his right hand, Riker surreptitiously zipped his jacket up to his chin. While doing so, he had put his left on Tara's arm and leaned forward to meet the soldier's steely glare. "We're good. Been in all day," he lied. "What do you want us to do, sir?"

Gesturing with a nod to the patch of street lit up by the headlights, he said, "Showing us your hands first, open your door using the outside handle. Keeping your hands where we can see them, shoulder open your door." He paused and regarded Riker. "You first. After placing your hands over your head, get out and go to your knees, keeping your fingers interlaced."

Riker saw Tara shoot him a worried look. Her hands were kneading the wheel as he reached over, turned the car off, and pocketed the keys.

"This is going to take a me a bit," said Riker as he completed the first part of the orders. Struggling to swing his legs around without using his hands, he added, "I'm wearing a prosthesis on my left. Knee down is VA-issued hardware."

The man in the beret said nothing.

Under Tara's watchful gaze, Riker used the toe of his right boot to hook and lift his bionic over the narrow rocker panel. Standing up sans hands was a bitch and strained to the limits abdominal muscles that hadn't benefitted from a sit-up since January 1st when Riker's resolution to get back in fighting shape was edged out by the need to rise at dawn and hit up job sites to find daily carpentry work.

Breathing hard from the exertion, Riker went to his knees, the resultant metallic clink drawing stares from the soldiers assembled nearby. "Just my bionic," he quipped.

The man in charge lowered his weapon and rifled through Riker's pockets, turning them inside out and leaving them that way.

"I'm mostly broke and unarmed, as you can see," said Riker.

The soldier with the eyebrows and black beret simply nodded and took a step back.

"You," he said, gesturing toward Tara with the carbine. "Same routine."

Riker met Tara's gaze and saw fear in her eyes. He mouthed, "Don't worry. Do as he says."

Eyebrows patted Tara down once she was on her knees in the street. He backed away and had her turn her own pockets inside out. Seeing nothing of interest in the coins and small amount of folding money the order produced, the soldier motioned his comrades forward.

While five of the six men trained their carbines on Tara and Riker, Eyebrows slipped a pair of rigid plastic flex cuffs over Riker's wrists and cinched them down. Not pain-inducing tight. But tight, nevertheless. As the point man flex-cuffed Tara, who happened to be shooting a pissed-off look Riker's way, Riker shifted his body slightly so he could see past the Humvees. About a hundred feet behind the static vehicles was a sea of body bags, all of them glossy black and reflecting the ambient light from the standards illuminating the distant football field. And as he heard the *zipping* noise of his sister's hands being bound, he realized that the contents in many of the bags were causing them to undulate slowly. Now and then one would tent up for a second and then go back to lying mostly flat.

Without warning, the only man to have spoken to them thus far pulled a pair of black hoods from a cargo pocket. "For *our* safety," he said.

"If this is a vaccination facility," said Riker, "where're the doctors? The medical tents? At the least, shouldn't there be an ambulance or two here?" He was staring into the man's eyes as he posed the questions. And he definitely saw a softening in them, however subtle.

Tara set her brown eyes on the hood and then regarded Riker with a look that could only be construed as a silent plea for him to go into big brother mode and get them out of this alive.

Though Riker didn't quite believe the words as he thought them, he locked eyes with Tara and gave voice to them anyway. "It's going to be all right, Sis. I promise."

A tear flowed down Tara's cheek as the stony-faced soldier hooded her up.

Riker looked up at the lead man. "Can you at least say where you're taking us?"

As everything went dark and he found it difficult to breathe, he heard the scraping of shoes on cement and rustle of fabric of Tara being helped to her feet. Then, whispered by his right ear: "The high school bunker, where you'll spend some time in quarantine."

"How long? And why?"

There was no answer. Instead, gloved hands grabbed Riker's biceps and his captors silently helped him to stand.

***

Riker was propelled forward and steered forcibly for a minute or so across what he guessed was the sidewalk ringing the school parking lot. When his forward momentum was halted, he

93

heard the sound of keys being worked in a lock. Then there came a subtle squeak of hinges as a door somewhere to his fore was opened.

Once again he was prodded forward. Ten steps later the temperature of the air hitting his face dropped by a couple of degrees.

During the long walk through what he guessed was a subterranean catacomb of sorts, the only thing Riker heard was the sound of footfalls echoing all around him.

Feeling himself being guided around a corner, then hearing yet another door open, Riker immediately noticed a radical change in temperature. Whereas the air behind him had been stale and cool and damp, the air hitting his exposed arms and hands and neck here was warm and dry. All in all, absent the aroma of hewn timber and crackle of seasoned wood burning in a stone fireplace, the sensation reminded him of stepping into a hunting lodge on a cold fall day.

Without warning, the pressure on Riker's biceps loosened and the hood was yanked from his head. Squinting against the light thrown from overhead fluorescents, he let his gaze roam the room. The walls were clad with subway tiles arranged in a staggered pattern, gleaming white as if laid yesterday. The wall beside the door he had just entered was home to a host of posters with frayed corners and featuring motivational quotes and cautionary words. A waist-high doctor's-office-style examination bed was on his right. Its gray vinyl upholstery was cracked in places and held together with generous strips of silver duct tape.

A soldier clipped Riker's cuffs with a multi-tool and asked him to strip naked. Seeing as how the other soldiers in the room as well as the pair stationed outside the door were all armed with carbines and Beretta pistols, resisting the thinly veiled order was out of the question.

Seeing a space heater humming along in a corner, Riker looked a question at Eyebrows.

"Go ahead," said the soldier, nodding toward the heater.

Wearing only the metal and carbon fiber prosthetic, Riker edged around the training table and stood facing the heater.

"How'd you get the scratches on your back?"

Without missing a beat, Riker said, "Rough sex."

"You must know what you're doing."

"What I lack in the lower leg department—"

Interrupting, the soldier said, "Clearly the old 'size of the boat and motion of the ocean' thing didn't come into play."

Riker said nothing.

A long silence-filled minute passed before the door opened and a female soldier wearing a white lab coat entered.

Riker turned away from the heater and saw in Eyebrow's gaze that the brief moment of male camaraderie just shared was gone. The dull stare and set of the soldier's jaw conveyed clearly to Riker that the levity on his end was not to be construed as weakness.

The female soldier visually inspected Riker from afar, saying, "Turn around for me." She had him stop with his back facing her and said "Lift and cough" as if she was conducting some kind of prison in-processing.

A no-nonsense tone to her voice, the woman asked, "How do you explain the fresh wounds on your back and neck?"

Riker repeated the two-word response he'd given to Eyebrows.

Disgust in her voice: "The *much* younger woman you were processed in with?"

"That's his sister," replied Eyebrows.

"Keeping it in the family, huh?" She stood with hands on hips. "I'd much rather have heard you say you were attacked by crazed cannibals."

Eyebrows shot the soldier a murderous look that did not go unnoticed by Riker.

"That's wrong on so many levels," said Riker. "This was inflicted by a lady I met at the Greyhound station in Muncie."

Under Eyebrow's watchful stare, the female soldier used a tongue depressor and looked inside Riker's mouth.

Indicating the poster near the door admonishing bullying of any kind, Riker said, "Isn't denying me my due process a form of bullying? When do I get to make my phone call?"

"Circuits are overloaded," said Eyebrows.

The woman soldier said nothing as she tossed the depressor into an overflowing garbage can.

"When do I get my shots, Nurse Ratchet? It's what we came here for."

"That may not be necessary," she answered. "The facts of the *event* are still being sorted." She took his temperature at the temple with a handheld device and jotted something on a sheet of paper.

Riker's neck and shoulder went tight and the ringing in his ears was back. He looked to Eyebrows. "Is this a chemical, nuclear, or biological *event?*"

"Need to know," replied Eyebrows, shifting from foot to foot.

The female soldier donned a stethoscope and strapped a blood pressure cuff on Riker. As she went through the motions while staring at the wall-mounted clock, Riker saw that her hands were shaking. Drawing in a deep breath, he asked, "Am I going to live to see another sunrise?"

The question went unanswered.

Nodding toward the other poster beside the door, Riker tried the comedy route on the stoic pair. "So if there's no *I* in TEAM … what does that make me? *I* don't feel like a citizen of the United States at the moment. And *I* am no longer a member of the Big Green Machine." He stared hard at Eyebrows. "So where exactly do *I* stand in all of this?"

Carbine still at a low-ready, Eyebrows made no reply.

The female soldier removed the cuff, and her demeanor instantly changed. The sharp edge to her voice gone, she told Riker to hold still, adding a "please" prior to issuing the order. She took a syringe from its sterile wrapping and drew several mils of a clear liquid from a stoppered bottle. "This is just an inoculation."

"Against what?" asked Riker.

"All kinds of things," she said. "Everyone receives it." She cleaned the injection site on his shoulder with an alcohol swab, then wasted no time sticking the needle in him and pushing the plunger.

Riker tensed as he received the inoculation. Part of him wanted to fight. To bash Eyebrows in the face and escape the room. Run naked down the hall in search of the exit. But he couldn't. There were men with guns outside the door. And he had no idea where Tara was.

Whatever she was administering stung as it entered Riker's body. As the soldier tossed the used syringe in a plastic receptacle with a one-way opening, he asked, "So I can leave now with my sister?"

"Not how it works," said the female soldier. "You may get dressed now."

Riker dressed slowly and then presented his hands to Eyebrows to be cuffed.

"They're not necessary for quarantine."

"What about my sister?"

"Follow me."

Riker asked, "What's your name?"

Eyebrows paused at the door. "Logan."

"Branch and unit?"

Logan said nothing.

"We have somewhere we need to be," said Riker. "We've really done nothing wrong. Why don't you just let us go?"

Logan shook his head slowly side to side. "I'm Army ... like you used to be. Fourth Infantry Division out of Carson at first. I'm now running 10th Group."

Deploying Special Forces for a simple quarantine? Bullshit, thought Riker. "What's this all about?" he asked.

"Trust me," said Logan over his shoulder. He paused to usher Riker into the hall, then added, "You don't want to go out there right now."

"Can you do me a solid?"

Logan didn't respond as he started off down the hall at a leisurely pace.

"Get my NRA bag from that little ass car?" called Riker. "The clean sleeves I line my bionic with are in it."

Logan kept walking.

"You'll find it on the package tray next to my *mom*."

Logan slowed and turned around and walked backwards down the wide hall. His rifle barrel dropped vertical with his leg. One brow arched up, the unruly red hairs crowding the black beret.

Your *mom*?" said Logan. "I'm not following."

"She's in the urn next to my bag. It's a bronze number with silver roses on it. Can't leave her out there all night with those things creeping around."

Logan nodded, then spun around on his heel and continued on down the hall, his pace quickening with each step.

With the female soldier beginning to crowd him from behind, Riker double-timed it to catch up with the SF shooter he guessed to be at least a captain in rank. He followed in silence and pulled up when the soldier paused to use a key to unlock a set of double doors. Once they pushed through the doors, Riker was struck by the eye-opening scale of the facility. He was standing in a Cold-War-era fallout shelter that before being put into service by FEMA or whoever the soldiers answered to looked to have been used only as storage for old desks and worn gym equipment. It was currently home to at least three hundred people. Some were lounging on cots with their kids. Others were sitting on folding chairs, solo or in small groups, talking quietly amongst themselves.

An Indiana National Guard soldier approached Riker and offered him a bottled water, which he politely declined, for a dozen feet in front of him was Tara. No hood. No cuffs. And a smile spreading on her face at the realization that everything was in fact going to be all right—for now.

Chapter 21

"For now" ended at six in the morning when a commotion kicked up at the far end of the near dark room Riker guessed still held at least a hundred people—down from the three hundred he estimated were being held there when he and Tara had been brought in a handful of hours ago.

The slow trickle of people being removed had begun around midnight.

Since being led into the facility, Riker hadn't seen the SF soldier, Logan, the female soldier in the lab coat, or any of the cheerful National Guard soldiers who were present earlier. Instead, a dozen soldiers clad in black and armed with high-dollar carbines were running the show. Like the Special Forces contingent Riker and Tara had encountered outside, the soldiers' uniforms bore nothing that spoke of their rank, unit, or branch of service. What troubled Riker most was the bare hook-and-loop field on their shoulders where an American Flag patch should be.

A six-footer with a full black beard and hard eyes seemed to be calling the shots, leading twenty men out in the first wave. Their ages ranged from twentysomething to upper sixties. Some were coughing into handkerchiefs. Others were hanging their heads in defeat. A couple of the older men grumbled for a bit but finally acquiesced and moved out willingly when Black Beard raised his voice and threatened to have them flex-cuffed. Amazingly, not a man among the group had put up a real fight. Not even those leaving loved ones behind. *Sheep to the slaughter*, thought Riker at the time.

The room Riker and Tara had spent the night in was nearly identical in its accoutrements to the Atlanta Mission. Out of the pan and into the fire was a good way to describe how his previous day had begun and ended.

Thanks to Riker insisting to Logan upon entering the room that he had been waging a lifelong battle with claustrophobia—a lie made up and told on the fly—Logan had a National Guard soldier procure cots for them and set them up on the periphery of the room near the doors Riker had initially entered through.

The floor was a sea of pale green vinyl tiles on which sat roughly twenty rows of folding cots. The canvas and aluminum numbers looked to be Army-issue and stretched the entire length of the building. More of the same were pushed against the walls beneath a row of opaque windows. Inset into the cement wall several feet overhead, the windows ran the entire length of the subterranean facility. At first blush it looked to Riker that even if he could get close and manage to pry one open, no way was his head fitting through, let alone his wide shoulders and barrel chest.

At the far end of the room, where rolled-up wrestling mats and an assortment of gymnastic equipment was being stored, were clusters of pushed-together cots where entire families awaited their fate.

Riker estimated the cement ceiling to be at least twelve feet overhead. The walls were poured cement, the horizontal lines where each batch had settled and cured clearly visible. Though measurement and distance had never been Riker's strong suits, he figured the room had the same footprint as the gymnasium above them. In his mind's eye, he saw the brick gym abutting the football field. Gleaming aluminum bleachers ran away to the west from the makeshift quarantine building. In his head he was seeing those damn glossy black body bags again. Only now the neat rows from the night before were buried under a shifting mound of bags conjured up by his imagination. His jaw took a hard set and his gut did a back flip as he realized it may not be far from the truth. After all, where had all the people gone? Were there busses waiting topside? At thirty passengers a bus, it would take a half-dozen of them to relocate all of those now missing to the post quarantine depository he had overheard Black Beard mention.

Busses?

He hadn't seen a single one on the way in—Shenandoah High, Middletown city bus like the one the shooter allegedly slaughtered the people on, or otherwise.

"What are you thinking about, Bro?"

Riker caught himself looking right through Tara. He blinked once and stared her hard in the face. She was still on her cot, but now her head was propped up on one hand.

"Our current predicament is what's on my mind," he whispered. "Did you sleep?"

She shook her head. Just a subtle side to side wag.

"Me neither."

From the direction of the cot islands, someone called out for water. When the request wasn't immediately acknowledged, an expletive-laden threat was directed at the soldiers in general, then Black Beard specifically.

The room was quiet for half a beat, then more shouted demands echoed from the periphery of the room.

Someone screaming "I'm an American!" threw one of the metal bedpans provided earlier by the National Guard soldiers.

The person splashed by the bedpan's contents turned on the person who had thrown it.

Riker looked away from the mayhem unfolding a hundred feet beyond the foot of his cot. Locked eyes with Tara and asked, "What time do you have?"

She shrugged and showed him both bare wrists. "They took it along with my phone and wallet."

"Same here," conceded Riker. Looking away from the growing throng of people, the pair and their meteorically rising tempers at the center, he let his gaze land on the set of double doors leading to the long hall he and Tara had been marched down after their medical check.

Nothing.

The squad of uniformed men and women he expected to burst through by now weren't coming.

Or, more than likely, they were being rousted from their sleep and gunning up.

The hall behind the windows in the door was black as night. Meaning the lights in the hall were extinguished. Meaning he had a decision to make: What do I do when the inevitable happens?

The ruckus was now a full-blown shoving match between two men in their forties.

Tara nodded toward the cot nosed perpendicular to the nearest pillar. On it was a small form curled up underneath a blanket. On the floor by the cot was a stuffed kangaroo, its orange and white coat matted and worn.

"The toy," she said. "Get it."

He shot her a quizzical look.

"Just do it," she hissed.

Riker rolled over onto his right side, planted his right hand on the floor for stability, and reached out for the plush toy with his left. Straining mightily, arm at full extension, he trapped one stub ear against the polished floor. Applying pressure with his index finger, he slowly drew his arm back, bringing the well-loved kangaroo along for the ride.

Someone screamed. A woman. Her voice was shrill and full of worry.

The boy stirred and then sat bolt upright. As the blanket slithered to the floor, the kid panned his head toward the growing commotion.

Beckoning with one hand, Tara leaned forward to accept the toy.

Sitting up, kangaroo in hand, Riker said, "What do you want with this?" He turned it over, inspecting its appendages and long, tapered tail.

"It's in the pouch, Lee," she said, still gesturing for him to hand it over.

The kid two cots away was now scratching his head and scanning his surroundings. He was calm. Which told Tara he was no stranger to drama. The shouting and shoving seemed to have already slipped off his radar.

Riker probed the kangaroo's belly. He found the slit and reached inside. His fingers brushed something slim and cool and smooth. When he introduced the mystery item to the light of day, he had what looked to him like an iPhone pinched between thumb and forefinger.

"What's a kid his age doing with a phone?" he asked.

Again with the gimme hands, Tara said, "It's an iPod Touch. Give it here."

Handing over the sleek black device, Riker said, "And what good is an iPod to us?" He felt foolish sitting there on the cot in a room that now smelled just like the one he left behind the day before. The stink of fear-laced sweat hanging in the air now had a tinge of urine to it. *Perfect*, he thought. *Should have stayed in Atlanta.*

Tara's fingers were already dancing across the shiny glass screen. She spoke as she tapped. "It's good for playing Angry Birds, which is what little Johnny there was playing."

The screen flared to life.

"How'd you know his password?" asked Riker as he tightened his boot laces.

"Watched him tap it out. One, two, three across the top—"

"And five in the middle," finished Riker.

She nodded.

Riker ran his hands through his beard. Then he cracked his neck, saying, "So what … you going to play Angry Birds while the folks play WWE wrestling down there?"

Now the kid was actively searching for his kangaroo. Mouth agape, he whipped his head around one final time before falling to his knees beside his cot and rifling through the blanket's many folds.

Focused only on the screen and swiping and tapping away furiously, Tara said, "Most of these things have Wi-Fi connectivity and a web browser of some sort."

"Boob Tube?"

"Yeah … *YouTube*, too."

While Riker was shooting Tara a questioning look, the kid had gotten back on his feet and was turning to face them.

Seeing the movement in his side vision, Riker turned toward the kid. The kid locked eyes with him momentarily, then dropped his gaze to the kangaroo still sitting on his lap. Fighting hard to keep a sheepish grin at bay, Riker spoke out of the side of his mouth. "What are you doing, Sis?"

Just as the kid opened his mouth to say something—or scream bloody murder—a whole bunch of things happened.

Down at the end of the room the sharp reports of skin slapping skin were interspersed by hollow thuds of punches finding their mark.

Nearby, the windows on the entry door lit up with a soft yellow glow. The light was ranging around, which told Riker it was likely the beam from someone's flashlight. A second or two passed, then the clunk of the door lock being thrown sounded in Riker's right ear and the doors blasted inward.

Riker stayed seated and watched as a half-dozen armed soldiers clad in black body armor charged in from the hallway.

Looking up from the glowing screen, Tara's face was a mask of worry bathed in color thrown from the bright display. "No service," she said, her eyes tracking the soldiers as they fanned out and wove serpentine patterns between the support columns and folding cots full of bleary-eyed citizens.

The twin gunshot-like bang of the doors hitting the stops woke everyone who had been able to sleep through the altercation, the kid's mother counted among them. She hinged up and regarded the boy, who was just voicing his displeasure at seeing one stranger holding his stuffed animal hostage and another playing with his iPod.

Just as the woman swung her gaze Riker's way and he got a good look into eyes that were red and glassy from what he guessed was an Ambien-induced slumber, he was casting the kangaroo toward the double doors and saying a silent prayer. On the heels of the whispered words, he stood, leaned forward, and hauled Tara up onto her bare feet.

"My shoes," she protested as he pulled her along with him. *My jacket,* he thought, seeing it crumpled in a ball on the floor underneath the cot.

There were squeaks of rubber on the slick flooring. The soldiers were now shouting orders to the disgruntled masses crowding in to see what was happening.

On the move, Riker tracked the kangaroo's travel with his eyes. After sliding the first six or seven feet face down and rump up, the toy went flat and began to spin in lazy counterclockwise circles all the while heading straight for the rapidly shrinking gap between the closing entry doors.

Still a yard from the door and picking up a head of steam, Riker witnessed the kangaroo reach the threshold and stop mid-spin, instantly becoming wedged between the closing doors.

Slipping his fingers into the vertical gap and dropping his shoulder, Riker yanked the right side door toward him.

"Left or right?" he bellowed.

"Ramp to outside is to the left," said Tara. "But our stuff is in the coach's office to the right."

Can't leave without Mom, thought Riker. Without giving the matter a second's thought, he struck off right, the subtle creak of his ankle joint and steady slap of Tara's feet in direct competition with the rasp of his labored breathing.

Chapter 22

Zen Pharmaceuticals' CEO James Merkur stood before the floor-to-ceiling windows in his corner office atop Four World Trade Center surveying all of Lower Manhattan spread out before him. Two blocks by crow, and casting a long, narrow shadow on the Hudson River, One World Trade Center—all glass and steel and beveled edges—spiraled gracefully 1,776 feet into the brilliant blue October sky.

Sunday traffic on Greenwich Street, seventy-three floors below where Merkur stood, was moving at a decent pace. Darting in and out of traffic, toy-like taxis sporting garish colors delivered tourists to the curbs near the North and South 9/11 Memorial pools—somber monuments to that awful day in September when the two towers once standing there fell to box-cutter-wielding fanatics aboard two hijacked commercial jetliners.

Shifting his gaze to the orange and yellow trees dotting distant Battery Park, Merkur addressed COO Martin Underhill, the man responsible for ZP's day-to-day operations.

"How the hell does a sensitive package from the CDC in Atlanta that's destined for a biosafety Level-4 Army base in Maryland find its way to a university biology lab in Middletown, Indiana?"

Swallowing hard, Underhill ran a hand through his close-cropped gray hair. "Somebody in the chain of custody dropped the ball."

"That *somebody* dropped more than that!" Merkur barked. "Have you caught the news?" He went on before Underhill had a chance to answer. "It's really hitting the fan. Zone Five's Regional Response Team was scrambled. They set up mandatory evac centers and are administering 'inoculations' of saline solution."

He took a deep breath and turned to face his old friend. "My contacts in Washington say the first responders are stretched so thin that there's high probability of Romero jumping the fence. The Middletown quarantine is just hours old and already video shot by MU students and others is showing up on YouTube. They're being scrubbed as fast as they appear ... but that's not enough. There's no way established protocol is going to fly. Nobody will believe this is an act of homegrown terrorism."

"The local fixers tried that angle?"

"No," conceded Merkur. "They kind of reverse engineered the whole thing. Twisted the facts and embellished where necessary to make it look as if the bus attack was the work of a lone wolf shooter. To explain the escaped virus and casualties in and around the university they're saying the shooter continued his rampage there."

"I'm guessing this fairytale started with a nudge from higher ups at Detrick."

Merkur nodded. "Hell," he said, planting one hand high up on the window, "I've lost track of who all is involved. As far as enacting protocol? We're so far down the rabbit hole now we couldn't sell *protocol* even if we had access to a hundred more crisis actors and Middletown's chief of police on our payroll. Everything that's being done now is proving to be no more effective than treating a malignant brain tumor with aspirin."

"So it's on us to get rid of the evidence on our end."

Merkur shook his head, the vein snaking his temple pronounced and throbbing. "Affirmative. Dollars to donuts," he replied, "like a bag of dog shit on fire, the blame will eventually land on our doorstep and we'll be the ones stomping it out."

Underhill made a face. "At least it wasn't the aerosol model."

"Thank God for small miracles," Merkur conceded, throwing his hands up in mock surrender. "Still, the genie is out of the bottle and far from contained."

"What about the Department of Defense? Or the folks at AMRIID? Won't they acknowledge their culpability in *all* of this if we point to them?"

Shaking his head, Merkur said, "They have firewalls of plausible deniability to hide behind."

"You're right," Underhill said, the sweat from his underarms creating dark half-circles on his maroon Polo. "There's no way they'll fall on the sword let alone take some of the blame to help keep us from being dragged before a House Select Committee."

"I've watched some of those YouTube videos," said Merkur, nervously adjusting his tie. "Those soldiers manning the checkpoints are *not* Indiana National Guard. Those hard-eyed men are off the books contractors molded in the same vein as the CIA's SOG."

"SOG?"

Merkur unbuttoned his navy blazer and shrugged it off. "Special Operations Group," he said.

"Like their SAD, only more clandestine, right?"

Merkur shook his head side to side. "Not the same animal, Martin. SOG operates under the Special Activities Division. SOG's made up of Tier One operators drawn mainly from Delta, Seal Team 6, and Marines who've served as Force Recon or MARSOC." He tossed his blazer on a chair and began to roll up his sleeves. "Those soldiers on the videos are not SOG."

"Who are they?" asked Underhill.

Merkur poured Scotch from a crystal decanter into matching high ball glasses. Passing one to Underhill, he went on, "I've heard them called *Omega Teams.* Usually only whispered. They're the bad apples who've been busted doing things unbecoming to their oath to flag and country. They're basically an army of bad hombres with outstanding skillsets. And to avoid being sent to Leavenworth, they're willing to do anything that's asked of them. No questions."

Underhill took a sip of Scotch. "Does Congress know about them?"

Merkur shook his head. "Best kept secret in Washington. Hell, in the whole world." He drained his Scotch and reached for the decanter. "The simple fact that the powers that be brought them on line to cauterize this wound means it's burn bag time for us. Only a matter of time before you, me, and the entire *Romero* project disappears from the face of the earth."

"Burn bag?"

"It's a metaphor, Martin." Merkur sat down hard on the chair behind his desk. Steepling his fingers, he flicked his eyes to the wall-mounted television. The crawl below the senator droning on about the upcoming election was still attributing the attack on a city bus in Indiana to a lone, drugged-up gunman. Merkur was shocked to see that the handful of follow-on stories made no mention of the MU biology department, or, for that matter, anything to make him think ZP's escaped virus was doing damage beyond that already reported. Furthermore, speaking to how tight the lid was being shoved down on all of this, there was no mention of the civilian detention centers or alphabet agencies likely on their way to further lock down Middletown.

All was well in the world of James Merkur until he read on the crawl a mention of an agency-wide operation along the lines of Jade Helm 15—the multi-branch special-operations drill that had conspiracy theorists and right wing radio all abuzz the summer before.

Underhill was reading along. Once the words had cycled off the screen, he exhaled sharply and said, "Statewide drills in Indiana *and* Ohio? That's no coincidence."

"It's out of control," said Merkur in a funereal voice.

Underhill planted both hands on Merkur's desk. "What do we do about the stockpiles here?"

Rapid-fire, Merkur said, "Get Victoria in an Uber. Then call Carson and see how far out he is."

Underhill's face was flushed bright red. "If the phony drill fails to contain Romero"—he paused and drained his second Scotch in as many minutes.

Merkur finished his thought. "Then all of the aboveboard government research money is gone. And we can expect to kiss the backroom briefcases full of cash goodbye as well."

Underhill began pacing the carpet. "What if it does boomerang back to us?"

"If we get fingered for this, ZP stock will be worthless come opening bell tomorrow." Merkur pounded his fist on the desk blotter and let fly a few expletives.

Underhill stopped pacing. "We were sunk the second Romero got out, weren't we?"

"Damn it, Martin. I need you to have a little faith. And grow some balls."

"You're betting on the bad apples?"

"They'll play a big part in the drill. It'll do two things: provide them cover. And keep the media at bay. I have a strong feeling they're going to corral Romero."

"You had to name it that, didn't you, James?"

"If the shoe fits," Merkur said, reaching for the phone on his desk. He punched the key connecting him directly to the security desk in the lobby below.

Underhill's hands shook as he extracted his smartphone and placed a call to Carson Peet, personal head of security to James Merkur.

While Underhill was setting the in-house cleanse in motion, Merkur got the lone guard on the line and ordered him to disable all pass cards of ZP employees not already in the building. He finished by asking the guard to personally escort his administrative assistant, Victoria Davis, upstairs when she finally arrived.

Seeing his boss return the handset to its cradle, Underhill muted his phone. "Carson is briefed and just a couple of minutes out. Victoria is balking at coming in on her day off. Says she's on the verge of throwing up. What do you want me to tell her?"

"Brown bottle flu is no excuse," Merkur said. "Put her on speaker."

Underhill fumbled with his phone for a second before finally locating the microphone icon on the glass screen and giving it a tap. "You're on speaker with me and Mr. Merkur."

There was no immediate reply.

"This is James," said Merkur, sounding annoyed. "Cut the crap, Miss Davis. If you want to remain the highest-paid person in this company without a doctorate, I expect you to board your ride when it arrives. Leave your pass card at home. You won't be needing it. The guard will let you in."

Underhill looked on, lips pursed and losing color.

Voice filled with defeat, Victoria capitulated and broke the connection.

"Alert the Uber driver that there's one hundred dollars extra in it if the fare gets here within the hour. Time is *not* on our side."

As Underhill contacted the Uber driver, Merkur's eyes were drawn to the television where a live shot was now gracing the screen. The network's field reporter was standing sideways and gesturing at the long line of military vehicles rolling by behind him. His mouth was moving but the television was muted. Still, Merkur got the gist and was convinced more now than ever that things had just gotten way more complicated.

The camera panned from the reporter to show a wide open field where a helicopter was just landing. "That's being broadcast nationally. Only a matter of time before the cat is officially out of the bag," Underhill declared, his face blanching. "I'll have the chemists begin destroying the stockpiles."

Merkur tore his eyes from the television and fixed a stare on his number two man. "I pulled the trigger on that hours ago. But we're saving some as insurance. Just in case we have to remind some people that we're all in this together."

"What about the ambulatory specimens?" asked Underhill.

"They're already on it downstairs," answered Merkur. "We're keeping the freshest one."

"You're having the lab personnel bag them without Carson's supervision?" His Adam's apple bobbed as he swallowed hard. "It didn't end well last time."

"That's a risk we have to take," Merkur replied icily. "Have Carson start moving them to the garage when he gets here."

Underhill nodded. "How many chemists are on hand?"

"Skeleton crew of six."

"Thank God this isn't a normal workday," said Underhill. "No way we could keep this quiet with a full floor shift."

Merkur paced to the south-facing windows. Settling his gaze on an L-shaped landing pad jutting out into the East River where a black and gold helicopter was landing, he said, "Carson and his team just touched down."

Chapter 23

The hallway went dark as the inside of a coffin the second the doors sealed shut behind Tara and Riker.

"Up ahead and on the left," she said, thumbing on the iPod and activating the flashlight feature to light their way.

"I remember," said Riker, slowing his gait and letting go of her hand. "Let's hope it isn't locked or—."

"Occupied," said Tara, finishing the thought for him just as a shaft of light lanced from the nearby room and the door sucked inward.

The siblings came to a complete halt and pressed their backs to the wall.

Holding the iPod to her chest to extinguish the light, Tara whispered ahead. "What now, Mister *Let's Go Right?*"

Wanting nothing more than to remind her that Mom's urn was likely in one of the nearby rooms, Riker instead pressed a finger to his lips, then splayed two fingers and with them made a stabbing motion toward his eyes.

Wait and watch.

Message received. Tara knelt and craned to see past her brother's slightly bent knees.

From a dozen feet away, ensconced in a modicum of shadow, the sibling duo watched a male soldier step into the hallway and spin back around toward the door. The stocky thirty-something held a flashlight in one hand and keys in the other. As he struggled to get a key in the lock, a radio came alive with a hiss of white noise and a harried male voice said, "Hall ... we *really* need those extra flex cuffs."

Trying rather unsuccessfully to become one with the cool cement wall, Riker noted that the soldier's sidearm—likely a

Beretta M9—was still snugged into its drop thigh holster. Then the soldier turned his way slightly and he caught a glimpse of the rank insignia affixed to his camouflage fatigues. The twin black vertical bars sewn into the removable patch were hard to miss against the mostly muted green and light beige of the Army's latest permutation of its combat uniform.

An officer?

Captain, no less.

This sudden revelation took some of the sting out of what he was about to do.

Thanks to two of Riker's strides being equal to three or four of a normal man's, he was at the captain's side the exact moment the shorter man was turning his way and bringing the radio up to his lips.

From her spot down the hall, Tara observed her brother's near silent approach. Halfway to the soldier, she saw his arms rise up vertically over his head. As absurd as it was considering what her brother was about to do to the soldier, Tara pictured a referee signaling a touchdown.

Like a bird of prey swooping in for the kill, he surged forward. There was a rustle of denim and, barely audible over the din from the room behind her, a creak of protest from the prosthesis.

Arms sweeping down and inward, he dipped slightly and wrapped the soldier in a bear hug. Plucking the shorter man off the floor, he looked her way, saying, "Take the gun, then empty his left thigh pocket."

Finding his arms suddenly trapped to his sides and his feet no longer on terra firma, the soldier let go of the radio. There was a clatter as the plastic item bounced on the floor. A tick later, the jangle of metal on cement echoed in the hall as the keys slipped from his hands and joined the radio on the floor. Hearing a voice by his ear issue the order that would lead to him being disarmed, he swung for the man's shins with the heel of a combat boot. Just as he was about to yell for help, one of the captor's arms slipped down to encircle his waist, and a calloused hand clamped down hard over his mouth.

Acting on her brother's whispered order, Tara sprinted from the shadows. Without a word, she unsnapped the strap and worked the black semiautomatic pistol from its holster. After stuffing the Beretta into her waist band—a move that was as foreign to her as anything she'd ever done—she plunged her hand into the bulging side pocket and came out with a handful of pre-looped nylon zip ties.

She quickly got one separated from the tangle and looked a question to her brother.

"Secure his wrists with one of them."

Easier said than done, thought Tara. While the soldier's left arm was still pinned to his side, his right was ranging around wildly, alternating between trying to pry Riker's hand away from his mouth and reaching back and up and raking blindly for his eyes.

Tara slipped down, her back against the door, worked one loop of the makeshift cuffs over the hand on the soldier's trapped arm and cinched it down to where it couldn't slip off.

"Your body is in the way," she said. "I'm going to have to cuff his hands in front."

"Just do it," said Riker. "He's a squirmy little effer."

When the opportunity presented itself, Tara grabbed the soldier's right wrist and muscled the other open end of the cuffs over his scrabbling fingers. Fighting off a rising wave of panic brought on by the realization of what she and her brother were doing, she cinched the second cuff tight.

"Get the keys and radio," said Riker as he lowered their captive to the ground and held him close so that the sharp edges of his boots could no longer find his shin.

Drawing in a much needed breath, Tara plucked the keys and radio off the floor and rose from her crouch. Facing the soldier, whose struggles were beginning to subside, she said, "You messed with the wrong people, dude. Rikers don't take kindly to unlawful search and seizure."

Riker craned toward the set of double doors down the hall. Whatever was happening behind them was not good. The shouts and angry words ringing out moments ago had been supplanted by piercing screams of what sounded like women and children under extreme duress.

"No more talk, Tara," said Riker. "Get the door open."

Working by the light of the kid's iPod, the simple act of finding the correct key and inserting it into the cylinder took a few seconds. Hands shaking, she threw the lock and led them all inside.

This therapy room was much larger than the ones they had been processed in. It was twenty deep by thirty long and branched off to the right. Illuminated by the faint beam Tara was sweeping around the room, the pair of waist-high tables in the center threw long shadows across the gray floor. Atop one of the tables were several boxes of syringes and dozens of bottles labeled SALINE SOLUTION. A rolling trashcan overflowing with various articles of blood-soaked clothing was positioned equidistant between the tables. And wafting from the industrial-sized vessel was the coppery tang of freshly spilt blood Riker was no stranger to.

"Ewwww," exclaimed Tara, the beam frozen on the brimming bio hazard.

"On the table," said Riker. "The syringes and saline solution. That's what we were *inoculated* with last night. Placebo to keep the prisoners calm through the night." Tightening the bear hug on the captain, Riker walked him to the counter at the head of the nearest training table. "We're not going to hurt you," he said directly into his ear. "I just want to know what the hell is going on out there. Black Beard and the others … who are they? Military contractors?" He paused, then added, "If I release you, take my hand away, will you cooperate?"

The captain nodded and stopped struggling.

Riker loosened his grip and slowly dragged his hand from the man's mouth. As he spun the captain (whose nametape read HALL) around to face them, a knee rocketed toward his family jewels and the man's bound hands shot up towards his neck.

Riker easily parried the knee with one hand, then lashed out with the other, his enormous fist impacting Hall below the solar plexus.

All fight left the captain and he started a slow fall to the floor, doubled up and wheezing.

Riker grabbed a handful of collar, yanked Hall to his feet, and wrapped one arm around his neck.

Voice barely rising above Riker's labored breathing, Hall called out for help.

Riker took a soiled scrap of fabric from the trashcan and force fed the makeshift gag into Hall's mouth. "That's *not* what we call cooperation where I come from," he hissed, standing Hall up straight.

Already one step ahead of her brother, Tara had snatched a roll of training tape from a nearby shelf and was tearing a long strip from it when Riker spun the soldier around to face them. Staring daggers at the captain, she lashed the tape twice around his head, securing the gag in place.

Pointing at the pouch on Hall's belt, Riker said, "Take the spare mags. And then check his pockets."

While Tara was doing her thing, Hall's gaze went to the trashcan, lingered there for a beat, then flicked to Riker. Eyes wide and terror-filled, he twisted free of Riker's grip and slumped limply onto the training table as if he'd just taken a right cross to the chin.

Tara placed the items on the counter, lining the pair of magazines for the pistol side by side. Then she leaned over and looked Hall in the eye. "Where's *our* stuff? Phones, wallets, keys?"

Hall's gaze swung toward the door and his head jerked to the left a couple of times.

Riker made eye contact. "Down the hall away from the *dorm?*"

Hall nodded emphatically.

Tara said, "The coach's room?"

Again with the enthusiastic head bob.

"I hate to do this to you," said Riker, extracting another pair of nylon cuffs. "Can you breathe okay?"

Hall nodded.

"Good. Cause we're not bad people." He lifted Hall up, sat him on the table facing them, then proceeded to cuff his ankles together. "Not too tight, is it, sir?"

A muffled, "Uh, uh," from Hall.

"Good," said Riker. He held a hand out to Tara, palm up. "Gimme the gun."

"You're going to shoot him?"

Hall's eyes bulged from his head. His breathing intensified and he began to moan.

"Don't worry, Captain," said Riker. "I once walked in your boots. I just want to make sure you can't use it against us after we leave."

Tara shook her head side to side. "No Lee, we *need* it. What if we come across more of those things?"

Fingers beckoning, Riker repeated himself. "Gimme the gun."

And she did, reaching to her waistband and bringing it around butt first. "You sure about this?"

"Hand me the magazines," he said, again with the hand gesture. "We're not bad people, Captain. Want you to remember that." He pocketed the spare magazines. After a cursory glance at the semiautomatic, he ejected the magazine and racked the slide. He caught the single 9mm shell in his free hand and tossed it into the trashcan. Working fast, he thumbed the remaining nine rounds in after. As the bullets made their way to the bottom of the can in quiet little spurts, he quickly disassembled the weapon and placed the slide and empty magazine on a shelf with the tape and other supplies. The rest went in his pocket with the spare magazines. As he turned from the garbage can, his eye was drawn to a scrap of paper torn from a yellow legal pad. It was laying flat on a shelf to his left, its edges rippled from getting wet and drying again. On the sheet, scrawled in black Sharpie, in all caps, were the words **DO NOT LET THEM BITE YOU!!**

Whoever had written the warning had taken the trouble to underscore each word twice. The note was succinct and to the point and grabbed Riker by the short hairs, that was for sure.

Tara jangled the keys and cracked the door.

Eyeing the eerily quiet radio on the counter below the shelf, Riker cocked his head toward the door and listened hard. From somewhere down the hallway he heard the squeaks of sneakers on freshly polished tiles. Looking back to the Army captain, Riker said, "Remember ... we're not bad people," and stepped into the hall.

Chapter 24

Head still throbbing from overindulging at the Misfits' show the night before, Victoria Davis stepped from the Prius and thrust a five-dollar bill through the open passenger side window.

Flashing a palm at his fare, the college-aged Uber driver spilled about the hundred-dollar tip a man named Underhill promised to post to his PayPal account if he got the "pretty brunette" to 4WTC in record time.

"Mission accomplished," said Victoria, stuffing the Lincoln into her jean's pocket. "I don't know about the 'pretty' part." A little pissed at being upstaged by her boss on her day off, she slammed the door and stepped onto the sidewalk bordering Church Street. Wincing from the dual attack of glaring sunlight to her optic nerves and the incessant pounding of wood on plastic coming from the trio of street drummers camped under the glass portico angling out over the entrance to 4WTC, she clutched her courier's bag tight to her body and wove between the throng of tourists watching the show.

With no pass to gain entry, she resorted to pressing the Call button on the intercom.

As she watched the teenagers punishing the makeshift drums in the reflection on the glass to her left, she saw the silver-painted cowboy arrive and drop his like-colored wooden pedestal a few feet from the drummers. In the two minutes she spent waiting for the weekend watchman, Tony, to arrive to let her in, the crowd had nearly doubled in size and a mime complete with white-painted face and ruby lips had taken up station opposite the drummers and started performing the old "invisible wall" routine.

There's a mint to be made today, she thought as a sharp rap drew her attention back to the glass door where she saw a large uniformed man peering back at her from within.

The door hinged inward and the keys rattled on Tony's belt as he stepped aside to allow Victoria entry to 4WTC's marble-clad grand foyer. The ceiling fifty feet overhead was lost in shadow and she could see oak trees and snippets of the south reflecting pool mirrored in the polished black granite gracing the far wall.

"Morning," the watchman said, glancing nonchalantly up and down the street, one hand resting on the pistol-shaped TASER holstered on his patrolman's belt.

"I should still be asleep, Tony."

"Long night?" he asked as the door shut behind them with a metallic *click*.

"Bright lights, big city."

"Live fast, die young, and leave a beautiful corpse," Tony said, chuckling. "Oh to be young again." He sighed. "Even if I could pull a *Cher* and turn back time ... I'd be rubbing shoulders again with stinky hippies instead of a beauty such as yourself."

Three compliments in twenty minutes, Victoria thought to herself. *Maybe I should come in hungover more often.* "Stop it, Tony," she said, cheeks flushing red. "You're old enough to be my father."

Tony worked his pass card in the slide to call the elevator. "I'm harmless," he said, hitching up his pants. "You want the Executive Level?"

Nodding, she said, "I sense a shred party coming on." She stepped into the car first and quickly spun around to face him. "Between you and me?"

Tony nodded, eyes wide behind his thick glasses.

"I bet Mr. Merkur's scientists went afoul of some FDA rule and I'm here to help hide that fact."

"Maybe ZP has got something to do with what's going on in Indiana." He pressed *74* and, when the doors closed, added, "You didn't catch the news about the Middletown, Indiana shooter? Guy was hopped up on *pharmaceuticals*. That's what ZP is pushing, right? Oxy and the like?"

On the wall display above the lighted buttons the red digital number denoting each floor ticked by rapidly as the elevator picked up speed.

Victoria shook her head. "I didn't see it. My boss didn't mention it, either. No news is good news for this girl. I punch out at five on Friday and avoid all of that shit until seven on Monday. I want to live life, not cower in fear."

Fair enough. Tony tipped his ball cap and stared at the ceiling as the express car rocketed by half a billion dollars' worth of prime real estate located on the high-rise floors.

Suddenly, shattering the quiet, Victoria's stomach growled.

"You going to be all right?"

"One too many bourbons last night, is all."

As the elevator began to slow, Tony pointed to the skull face logo on her black tee shirt, then read the squiggly font above it. "Misfits … is that the band you were listening to while drinking said bourbons?"

The display on the wall showed 69. Then 70. Finally, Victoria said, "Yep. I've seen them a dozen times."

The number 74 showed up on the display and turned green as the elevator decelerated and came to a gentle halt.

"Here we are," said Tony, removing his mesh ball cap. "Hope you get to feeling better."

Me too, she thought, swallowing hard against the sharp, acid tang of rising bile tickling her throat. "Thanks for the escort."

As the doors began to part, Tony winked and donned his hat. "Hail me if you need *anything*. I'm all alone downstairs until four o'clock."

Martin Underhill's puffed-out chest and pasty round face were the first things Victoria saw when she turned back to face the parting elevator doors.

"I'll remember that," she said to Tony over a shoulder as she grimaced and brushed past her immediate supervisor.

Chapter 25

After a quick turkey peek, Riker stepped into the hall, leaving Tara in the trainer's room with the bound and gagged Army captain. Looking right, he saw people streaming from the room he and Tara had been forced to spend the night in. Swinging his gaze left, he saw mostly a dark void. The scant amount of ambient light coming in from the opening and closing of the double doors behind him reflected strobe-like off a trio of evenly spaced windows on the left wall.

Exiting the room behind her brother, Tara took a final look back at Captain Hall and mouthed, "We're sorry."

Hearing the door seat with a soft click, she overtook her brother and stopped in front of the first of three doors all accessing rooms on the same side of the hall as the trainer's room. A placard inset above the pane of wire-reinforced glass read: *Coach Grant Phillips*. PAIN IS JUST WEAKNESS LEAVING YOUR BODY was emblazoned on a sign affixed to the inside of the window.

A key on the ring opened the door. Again using the iPod's flashlight feature, Tara went in first. The room was six by six at best. Just a desk and filing cabinet. Posters were pinned to corkboards affixed to the walls.

"This is the room they brought me to," said Riker.

"Mine is one door down," she replied.

Tara illuminated a trio of large Rubbermaid bins sitting atop the desk. Bin number one was nearly full to the top with men's and women's wallets. Various loose pieces of identification were mixed in with the leather and nylon and fabric items.

Bin number two was half full and held nothing but cell phones. Not a sound was coming from the box, which meant they were likely all powered down or there was no service.

The third box held nothing but keys on rings and dozens of the electronic fobs that passed for keys in today's modern automobiles.

Peering over Tara's shoulder, Riker said, "You find our wallets. I'll go through the keys." He closed the door then dumped the wallets onto the desktop. Next, he upended the keys beside the wallets and stacked the empty bins atop the filing cabinet.

A shouted order drifted down from the direction of the quarantine room.

Tara set the iPod on the desk with its face resting against the wall so that its rear-mounted beam fell across the piles of personal effects. "What's your wallet look like?"

Already working through the pile of keys and fobs, Riker paused and looked sidelong at his sister. Speaking from the corner of his mouth, he said, "It's green nylon, secured with Velcro, and damn near empty."

Tara spotted her black anodized aluminum card keeper right away. Pocketing it, she asked, "Any other distinguishing marks on yours?"

"It's an Izod," said Riker. "Got a little alligator patch on it."

"Isn't that cute," she replied, fanning the small mound out before her.

"Got it for cheap at the discount store in Atlanta."

"I bet you did," she answered. "Never knew you were a closet preppie."

Riker pocketed a handful of the electronic fobs. "Now that I know you're keeping tabs," he said, "I'll pay more attention to my fashion choices."

"Found it." She passed it over to him then swept the rest of the wallets and billfolds onto the floor.

Riker did the same with the keys and fobs. Finished, he slowly poured the phones and tablets from the third bin onto the desk top.

His archaic flip phone stood out like a sore thumb. He pocketed it and began inspecting the high tech items, choosing any that he thought resembled Tara's iPhone.

"This it?"

"Nope."

"This one?"

"Look for a scratched-up face," she said, pawing through the shifting pile on her side.

There were several loud pops out in the hall.

"Gunshots," said Riker.

"One more minute," Tara insisted. "*Everything* is in my phone."

"Pictures of Mom?"

Simultaneously, she nodded and dragged her phone from the pile.

Riker said, "Light up the screen and illuminate the walls over the desk."

Tara activated the flashlight feature on her phone and aimed it at the walls. With both phones lit up in the enclosed space, a lot more was revealed.

There were trophies for wrestling and various gymnastic and track and field events on a shelf above the desk. Mostly second and third place finishes—or Silver and Bronze—Riker wasn't sure what they called them these days. Sitting front and center amongst the trophies and propped-up plaques was their mother's urn.

Thank you, Logan.

Seeing the light glint off of brass and her mother's name spelled out in cursive lettering, Tara let out a sigh of relief.

Without a word, Riker took the urn down from the shelf and snatched his NRA bag from a peg behind the door. It was empty, his clothes and spare sleeves for his stump nowhere to be found.

"Logan came through for us with Mom," he said as he put the urn inside and zipped the bag shut. "But, damn it, someone swiped my *only* change of clothes."

Another fusillade of gunshots echoed loudly outside the door.

"Least of our worries," remarked Tara.

"You're right," said Riker agreeably. "Let's go."

Again he cracked the door a few inches.

Again with the turkey peek.

And once again he filed out ahead of Tara. But instead of going right toward the light where the long string of gunshots had sounded, he went left, into the dark, Mom safe and sound in the bag and the promise he'd made to her on her deathbed much closer to becoming reality.

The puny bulbs on the pair of Apple devices clutched in Tara's hands splashed weak pools of light ahead of them as they passed the doors to two small rooms assigned to different coaches. The motivational signs on the windows here were nothing like the ones on the walls in the recruiter's office on 9/12/2001 when Riker joined the Army. The signs on these windows were aimed at a slightly younger crowd. Nobody in these colorful placards was armed to the hilt and wearing night vision goggles. None of them were pouring from the back of a tracked Bradley in full battle rattle and brimming with swagger and determination. And most notable of all to Riker, none of them were driving high-level brass in and out of the Green Zone in an armored Land Cruiser or Rover—the job he'd inherited upon finishing basic and arriving at his overseas deployment brimming with swagger and determination and eager to "get some."

After leaving the beaming faces of the teens in the PSAs behind, they came to the end of the hall and found their choices limited.

"What's it going to be, Mister Right?" asked Tara. "Right, or … *right?*"

Riker ignored the quip, about faced right, and led them deeper into the darkened tunnel.

Pipes and electrical conduits snaking overhead reflected light from the iPhones back down on the siblings. Doors on their left opened into dressing rooms and equipment closets. On the right were banks of orange lockers stretching all the way down the hall to what Riker guessed was a pair of doors players and coaches used to access the football field. The faint slivers of light around the doors grew brighter the nearer they got to them.

"You know where this is taking us, right?" said Tara.

Knowing the answer, Riker responded with a grunt.

More gunshots followed by shouts and screams sounded down the hall from the direction they had come. It was all followed by an animalistic grunting noise. Then the staccato slapping of what could only be the bare feet of someone running their way was echoing down the tunnel at their back.

Riker slowed and came to a stop at the doors.

Tara pulled up, too. Voice full of concern, she said, "That wasn't you. And it sure as heck wasn't me." She turned a slow one-eighty in the widening tunnel.

"I know."

"Then why are we stopping?"

"Because I don't like bursting into the unknown." He reached down and wrapped a hand around each of the horizontal crash bars. Finding them secured with a thick chain and government-issue padlock, he added, "Besides, they're chained."

"Like I said earlier, Lee. You and I both know what we're going to find out there."

Again, in his mind's eye, Riker was seeing the piles of undulating body bags on the football field he knew lay just beyond those doors at the end of a short walk down yet another tunnel. He was imagining this must be how the prisoners entering the Roman Coliseum felt on one level or another when Tara's shrill scream snapped him back to reality.

Chapter 26

Victoria walked down the darkened hall toward her office with Underhill hot on her heels and spouting everything he needed her to accomplish in the next thirty minutes. Taking a seat at her desk, she accepted the sheet of paper he'd been waving at her all the way from elevator to office doorway. Quickly determining the tasks he'd already verbalized amounted to about a ten-minute job, she waved Underhill off, powered on the desktop computer, and entered the password to access the main ZP server.

After using the password written on the sheet to access Merkur's personal Zen email account, she began by pulling up every correspondence he had made to the half-dozen institutions scribbled in Underhill's hand on the yellow sheet. All of the contacts were acronyms of the individual entities' titles, CDC—Centers for Disease Control and Prevention in Atlanta, Georgia—being the only one instantly recognizable to her.

After retrieving all of the emails to and from the various organizations, she started filtering out individual pages that contained the flagged keywords.

At first glance, the long list of words Underhill had written on the sheet below the acronyms amounted to nothing more than a high school biology spelling quiz. But when Victoria noted the standouts—**Romero, Virility, Mortality, Reanimation, Cutaneous, Aerosol, Weaponized**—and correlated them with one another, she drew in a deep breath. *What the eff are Underhill and Merkur covering up?* In the next beat, a dull ache started in her gut as her conscience and curiosity got the better of her—the latter being the stronger pull of the two.

As she stroked the keys, she heard Merkur in her head: *If you want to remain the highest-paid person in this company without a doctorate* …

Screw you, J.M. Acting on impulse, she scrolled over the header of an email sent by Merkur to a General Lawrence Purnell at Fort Detrick, Maryland. Let the pointer hover over the words Operation Peasant Overlord. *Always with the crazy random names*, she thought, clicking on the Open tab.

After a quick glance over her shoulder, she scanned the body of the email, noting the particular paragraph that contained calculations pertaining to the amount of an aerated version of a specific ZP bioagent code named *Romero Bravo* necessary to render a standing enemy army inert. The words *low altitude spray dispersal* and *unmanned aerial vehicles* leapt out and were enough to compel her to print a paper copy before backing out of the email.

As the printer churned out the hard copy, she scrolled to another email carrying the header: **UNINTENDED CONSEQUENCES.** The information contained in the body of the second email was almost too much for her to swallow. Something called Romero Alpha had recently been tested on willing participants. The "treatment" as it was referred to in the communication did indeed prolong a soldier's life after suffering a mortal wound and being treated for it on the battlefield. Some of the "specimens" exhibited augmented strength and stamina but lost cognitive abilities. However, the consequence if they died as a result was horrifying to her. And apparently, if she was to believe the percentage of cases deemed to be a success—it was no wonder they decided to go the Bravo route and weaponize the agent. Use it or lose it was the government's doctrine in case of a nuclear attack. She only knew that because Merkur had gone on a rant about it a couple of times. Once when the Russians invaded Crimea where he had a vacation home, and again when the little leader in North Korea was threatening the United States with his rubber sabre. *Might as well just use them now*, he had shouted at the television in his office on both occasions.

Feeling the hairs on her neck stand to attention, she looked over her shoulder.

Nothing there except the always-present specter of Underhill placing one of his clammy hands on her bare skin.

"Are they effin with me?" she said under her breath. For a brief second, remembering that Halloween was just around the corner, she thought that maybe she was on the receiving end of some kind of interoffice prank. While Merkur had been known to surprise staff with outings and such, never, in the five years she had worked for ZP, had he shown any kind of a humorous streak. Which was why she quickly dismissed the notion and continued reading as the Army general from Fort Detrick went on to describe in chilling detail how an early version of Romero Bravo had been used on enemy combatants somewhere in Northern Africa and the unbelievable side effects that came after its use.

To make certain she wasn't seeing things, she read the next paragraph out loud: "Aerosol transmission one hundred percent lethality. Time lapse between flatline and reanimation varies by host. All hosts will eventually reanimate, becoming ambulatory at once and at varying speeds. Coorelation not yet conclusive. Once aware, host will immediately seek out the flesh of the living."

This is no kind of a prank. And this is definitely not the usual cover-Merkur's-ass shred fest.

Victoria reclined in her chair, head back, gaze locked on the dropdown ceiling tiles. She kept that pose for a long five-count as she thought through her options.

"Boom," she finally said under her breath. Hinging forward, she cracked her knuckles in front of the screen and exhaled sharply.

Opening a new window in which her search history wouldn't be recorded, she typed "Fiscal years 2014, 2015, 2016 federal whistleblower awards" in the Google Search Box and hit Enter. Right off the bat, she got thousands of hits. Without a second's thought, she skimmed the first ten headings, eyes widening upon seeing the size of the most recent monetary awards. There was one to the tune of one hundred million levied against the pharma company peddling boner pills. Another whistleblower secured a large percentage of a nearly seventy-million-dollar fine assigned against an overseas group that defrauded the DoD by providing sub-par food service to U.S. soldiers fighting in Afghanistan.

The thick carpet having masked Underhill's approach, his large frame suddenly filled up the doorway a yard from Victoria's desk. "Almost done?" he asked, making her jump.

"Yes," she lied, quickly closing out the open window.

"Good," he said. "I have another task for you."

Like going home and sleeping the Makers Mark from my system?

As if Underhill had read her mind, he produced a roll of Tums from a pocket and offered to get her some Extra Strength Tylenol from his office.

Victoria chewed a few Tums but declined the Tylenol.

"Suit yourself," said Underhill. "When you're finished shredding the files, I need you to go to 73 and pull the hard drives from all the chemists' computers. By the time you're done there, Carson should be in the building."

"Then I'm free to go home, right?"

Underhill made a face, his brow, nose and upper lip coming together in one fleshy mass. "Not quite," he said. "I need you to help Carson on the bio floor."

Victoria sighed. "Not that, Mr. Underhill. Not today. Besides, you know that is *not* my domain," she stated forcefully, her anxiety rising at the mere thought of donning one of those yellow, full-body bunny suits while still nursing a hangover of epic proportions.

"Mask only today," he said, again with the gassy face. "Even if we had the luxury of time to get you suited up, it'd be a waste."

Do I get hazard pay like Uber Boy? she thought, regarding her boss with narrowed eyes.

"You'll be performing the same task on the bio floor computer that you're doing here."

"Can't you just give me their password so I can perform the task remotely?"

Underhill shook his head, then grimaced for the third time in a minute.

Upon reflection, Victoria pegged the expressions as quite theatrical. *This is no FDA fuck up,* she told herself. Coinciding with that realization, a full-blown anxiety attack hit her solar plexus with the force of a mule kick. Every breath harder to draw than the previous, she merely smiled and nodded, all the while willing Underhill to leave her office.

These are not the droids you're looking for was the mantra looping in her head as her boss fielded a call and disappeared as quietly as he'd arrived, slim smartphone pressed to his ear.

Once Underhill was gone, Victoria printed out a few more choice emails, folded them hastily, and secreted them in her courier bag. Then, without e-shredding a single damning file, she powered the computer down and rose from her chair.

A lifelong subway rider who didn't bother with a purse, Victoria instinctively turned back for her bag before leaving to get a pass card.

Chapter 27

The grunting and staccato slaps of bare feet echoing down the dark hall behind them had caused Tara to spin on her heel. The subsequent bang as the man-shaped silhouette hit the wall at the bend prompted her to bring the iPhones' lights to bear. The twin beams revealed a gaunt, blood-slickened face, making her heart skip a beat. The wild guttural snarl overriding the slaps of its bare feet on the tile floor was the final straw for a woman who thought herself mostly unflappable.

As Tara's piercing scream plateaued and began to roll the length of the tunnel, Riker turned to see the man-sized form carom off the wall, take a few stilted steps, and crash vertically to the floor.

"Light," he bellowed, turning his attention back to the lock at the end of the length of chain still clutched in his hand.

Tara brought one of the lights to bear but kept the other on the shirtless, prostrate man.

"Hurry," she hissed.

"I'm trying," he shot. "Give me the keys."

The jangling of the keys echoed off the cement walls as she blindly handed them over her shoulder. Seeing the figure rise from the floor in a series of herky jerky movements, she whispered, "I think it's one of them."

"I've a feeling you're on to something," said Riker. Working by the dim light, he jammed key after key into the lock, all the while ignoring his sister's elevated breathing.

"Hurry," she pleaded.

The steadily rising sound of flesh slapping tile momentarily dragged Riker's attention back down the long hall. And though illuminated by the lone beam of light coming from the iPhone, it was clear to him Tara was right: The grunting and snarling form almost upon them was no longer human.

Turning back and selecting another key, Riker said, "Hold the light steady."

"I'm doing my best," replied Tara, voice wavering, the last of her already compromised facade crumbling as the thing approaching broke into a full-on sprint.

Riker cursed as yet another key failed to open the lock.

The slaps were now echoing loudly at *their* end of the hall. "Where is it now?"

"Halfway, maybe," reported Tara. "Sure would be nice to have that gun right about now."

"Can't change the past," said Riker as he ripped what seemed like the hundredth dud key from the lock and quickly jammed in the next on the ring. "We can only affect the future."

That key wasn't the one. So he tried the next and got the same result.

Voice gone child-like, Tara said, "You've got ten seconds, tops."

Head down and concentrating hard, Riker began a silent countdown from ten.

At *nine* he fingered the last two keys on the ring, selecting the shinier of the two. *You're the one*, he thought as he slammed it home and was crushed instantly with disappointment when it failed.

By *seven* he had inserted the last key in the lock and had his hopes dashed one final time.

At *five* he dropped the worthless ring full of keys on the floor and spit a couple of choice expletives.

By *four* the combined stress from the creature stalking them, Tara's incessant needling, and the failure of every single key on the ring to open the lock was producing a hydrogen-bomb-about-to-blow pressure behind Riker's eyes. Breathing also became a chore and it seemed as if his neck and face were suddenly ablaze. His countdown was disrupted at *three* when the mental dam developed over numerous sessions of court-ordered anger management classes let flow a year's worth of pent-up rage.

Letting out a primal scream, Riker took hold of the left-side crash bar two-handed and dropped into a deep crouch.

Caught off guard, Tara fell to her knees, holding the electronic devices in front of her as if they possessed some kind of magical power to ward off the thing bearing down on them.

Spittle flew from Riker's mouth as he rocketed out of the crouch.

The muscles in his neck were corded and stood out against his skin. His head snapped back as he went straight-legged. There was a rattle of chains and a gunshot-like *crack* when the stanchions holding the push bar in place sheared cleanly from the door.

Gripping one end of the bar two-handed, Riker dipped his shoulder, braced the hollow length of steel against the door, and brought the other around and up so that it was directly in line with the charging man's chest.

Riker felt the urn pressing through the slung nylon bag as he braced for impact and the light from Tara's devices swung away.

Mom literally had Riker's back when the man hit the bar at full speed. The urn grated on his spine and there was a sharp report of what had to be the attacker's ribs snapping. Then came a crunch as what Riker guessed was the man's sternum breaking in two. In the next instant the attacker's feet were leaving the floor as Riker hauled up on the bar. A wet squelch came next and the body shuddered as the bar found a path of least resistance through muscle and organs. At the very least the man's lungs were punctured, though there had been no rush of expelled air to confirm Riker's theory. And strangely, through it all, the man did not cry out. Not at the initial impact, nor when he came to rest against Riker's fists, fully impaled on the steel handle.

"Get us out of here," cried Tara. She had scooted on her butt to the nearby wall and was pointing one of the devices at the man and one at Riker.

The man's face was a foot away and aglow in the soft light when Riker learned two things. First, the man was still alive. Second, the clicking noise that started up when the slapping of feet and snarls ceased was coming from the teeth snapping the airspace dangerously close to his neck.

No way this guy should be alive, let alone squirming like this, thought Riker. The idea that the bar had glanced off of bone and missed everything vital—beating heart included—was a far-fetched possibility. Trying to remember what side the heart was situated in one's chest with cold fingers raking his face and neck wasn't working for Riker. So he pushed the thoughts of the man's mortality from his mind and jerked the bar to his right with all the strength he could muster. As he watched the man slip off the bar and go spinning away into the dark, he spied on his back a pair of gaping bullet wounds.

Dumbfounded by the revelation, Riker turned and pulled Tara to her feet.

A series of hollow pops sounded around the corner at the far end of the long hall. Then shouts and a long burst of automatic rifle fire.

"Let's go," said Tara as she brought the beams to bear on Riker, illuminating the bloody bar in his hand.

There was a scrabbling sound in the dark to their fore. Then the clicking was back. It was all too soon joined by a moan that caromed around the hall, causing gooseflesh to break out on Riker's ribs. *How are you still alive?* he thought. As the unchecked rage began to ebb to but a dull throb in his head, a wave of fear rushed in to replace it. At that moment, as he hiked the bag with his mom in it higher up on his shoulder, he wanted nothing more than to get as far away as possible from a man who by all accounts should be dead.

Bloody bar in hand, Riker shouldered open the door and hustled Tara outside ahead of him.

Chapter 28

Manhattan

After taking a shortcut through a couple of darkened executive floor offices to avoid running into Merkur or Underhill, Victoria found herself inside the main elevator and wrestling with a career ending decision. *Press 73 and keep your job, or 72 and roll the dice on what you might find there.*

The ride to 72 lasted a handful of seconds. When the elevator doors parted, Victoria was hammered by what seemed like a million watts of overhead fluorescent. As soon as her eyes adjusted, she saw that things were not right here. It was quiet—more so than usual—and what looked like a bloody handprint stood out starkly on a dividing wall far away to her fore.

While the executive floor on 74 with its bird's eye maple paneling and high-end art gracing every wall and flat surface smacked of a Vegas Presidential suite, the bio floor was sterile and odorless and bright—extremely bright. With its white walls, floors, and ceiling, the space seemed more like a set from a sci-fi movie than a fully operational Level-4 lab.

The bio lab took up the entire seventy-second floor and was made up of three separate glassed-in areas. The true Bio Level-4 containment facility—all twelve hundred square feet of it—was a glass cube tucked out of sight on the far southeast corner. Beyond the glassed-in corridor Victoria was standing in was the "pit," which contained numerous chest-high stainless-steel work stations. To her left, partially blocking the already heavily tinted windows, was an entire wall of head-high shelves housing plastic storage containers filled with all manner of medical supplies. The floor space on the far side of the pit was set up like an office cube farm, but instead of computers at every station, inert centrifuges, expensive-looking microscopes, and exotic scientific monitoring equipment could be seen. This was where the hand-shaped red streak graced one of the low walls.

Beyond the pit was a corridor splitting the center of the farm. The narrow windowless hall led back to the Bio Level-4 room the chemists and biologists called the "fishbowl." Moving toward the outer door to her left, Victoria detected a brief flash of something red and yellow at the end of the hall leading to the distant fishbowl.

Curiosity trumping the urge to return to the elevator and ride it up to 73 where the hard drive removal job awaited her, she got a slim oxygen bottle and mask from a closet off the hall. After donning the mask, she connected its thin clear hose to the bottle, making sure the metal coupling was secure and the full-face mask snugged tight. Finished drawing a few test breaths, she shouldered the bottle and swiped the borrowed card to gain access to the pit.

You sure of this, Vicky? she asked herself as the door sucked in behind her. *No going back now, future millionaire.*

As she padded past the chest-high tables on her way to the cube farm, two things caught her eye. First, behind and to her left on the floor near the entry, she spied six aluminum boxes stacked in two columns of three. Rugged-looking and sporting brushed-metal snaps, the out-of-place items could have passed for tackle boxes full of lures and bobbers and lead sinkers if it weren't for the blaze-orange biohazard symbols adorning their sides. Then, as she panned back and got an unobstructed look at the end of the corridor, she realized the flash of yellow and red she'd spotted moving in the vicinity of the fishbowl was a bloodied Racal safety suit *inside* the fishbowl.

Continuing on down the middle aisle, more was revealed. Standing in the center of the Bio Level-4 cube was one of the chemists. She couldn't determine whether it was a man or woman due to the glare off the face shield, but one look at the limp form told her that the person was hosed—literally and figuratively. The former due to the fact that their only source to scrubbed and conditioned outside air—a twenty-foot-length of blue hose attached to the ceiling by a metal coupling—was around the person's neck and stretched to its limit like a tightrope full of Flying Wallendas. And the latter, which had likely signed the chemist's death warrant prior to the—presumably—accidental lynching, was the foot-long gash in the yellow suit, which was currently flapping noiselessly like semaphore on a ghost ship and a clear indicator the taut hose was still delivering air.

Victoria groaned at the sight, her breath causing a sheen of condensation to form on the inside of her mask. Taking a few more steps forward afforded her a view of the floor inside the bio cube where another suited chemist lay on her back, her blue eyes bereft of life and staring at the ceiling. The floor around the body was spattered with pinhead-sized droplets of drying blood.

In that quick snapshot in time, Victoria picked up several clues that instantly jumpstarted her flight instinct. On the chemist's left hand, several fingers were missing from the glove. In their stead were stumps oozing blackish blood and trailing ribbon-like strands of dermis and sinew. One pale finger lay on the ground by her side; the other two were clutched in her other gloved hand as if she had expected to have them reattached at a later date. Strangely, a hose wasn't connected to her suit, which prompted Victoria to edge around to the left, the need to put the puzzle pieces together overwhelming the kick of adrenaline that first glance inside the cube of death had triggered.

The viewing angle from the left side of the cube let her see a bigger slice of the room beyond the hanged person in the Racal suit. The interior door leading to the airlock on the cube's far right corner was being held open by the dead woman's leg, which was stripped of flesh from calf to ankle. Just outside the door was a body bag. It was tented up in places and undulating ever so slightly. Whatever was inside and causing the movement, she decided, was no bigger than a grade-school-aged child.

Shattering the silence, her iPhone came alive. Muffled just a bit because of the phone's location—tucked away inside the bag slung over her shoulder—a driving guitar solo kicked in and then the Ramones were singing about wanting to be sedated.

In response to the blaring ringtone, Victoria started visibly and issued a girlish squeal, which in turn produced the fresh film of fog inside the mask that caused her to miss seeing the body suspended in the cube convulse. And due to her side vision being limited by the clouded facemask, she failed to detect the figure to her right, nor did she see its shadow creeping slowly across the floor near her feet.

Executive Floor

"Underhill!" bellowed Merkur. "Where is Carson? His Town Car pulled off the pier and into traffic five minutes ago."

Calling back from his east-facing office a dozen yards down the hall, Underhill replied, "I see tourist busses lining up on Liberty. Just a traffic problem, I suppose."

"Call him. If he's stuck in traffic, order him and his team to get out and sprint the rest of the way here."

Merkur walked his gaze over the maze of streets below. In just a handful of minutes the vehicles had seemingly ground to a halt. Flicking his eyes to the helicopter, its rotor blades still spinning lazily, he formulated a plan that would cost ZP a sizeable fine but ultimately see the company live to see another day.

Chapter 29

Riker first noticed the overwhelming stench as he and Tara burst through the doors to outside. The air in the covered exit was heavy with an odor he hadn't encountered in a very long while. It was the sickly sweet stink of death, only on a grand scale. The kind of thing that one never forgets once exposed to. Only difference between what was enveloping him and Tara now and the air over Baghdad when the war was in full swing was the absence of the sour nose of rotting garbage and the ever-present haze that was a combination of diesel exhaust and burning tires.

As Riker met Tara's wild-eyed gaze, he pressed his back hard against the door to hasten its closing. Handing the bloody bar to her clean end first, he said, "Slip this through the handles."

She took the bar and was edging around Riker when something crashed heavily against the doors, bowing them out slightly in the center.

The bar was shaking subtly in her hands now. Patters of congealed blood dripped from one end as she took a knee.

Hands tremoring mightily, Tara asked, "How did he survive this thing running through his guts?"

"Chest," corrected Riker. "Though it looked to have missed both heart *and* lungs, it still broke some bones and left behind a hole. Through and through is what it's called." He went quiet for a second and watched her work the bar through the handles. Finally he drew a deep breath and said, "No way in hell he should have even been hunting us in the first place with the wounds he already had."

Head listing a degree or two, Tara let go of the bar and looked Riker in the eyes. "What wounds?" she asked. "I only saw the blood on his face and neck. Looked like he'd been French kissing a cherry snow cone."

Riker shook his head. "That wasn't syrup, Sis. That *was* blood. Same as what was on his back. And soaking his jeans. It all came from a pair of gunshot wounds bracketing his spine about the same level as his heart. I've seen men die from lesser wounds."

Incredulous, Tara said, "Gunshot wounds?"

He nodded and raised one hand, pointer finger and thumb extended to form a make-believe gun.

As if the thing knew they were talking about it, it hit the door again, creating a tremendous thud and rattling both doors in their frames. Threatening to work loose and fall out altogether, the brass bar clanked against the door pulls and started to wriggle free.

"No you don't," said Tara as she repositioned the bar. Finished, she turned around, hands atop her head. Now facing her brother, who was a head and a half taller, she said, "*Two* gunshot wounds?"

Riker nodded. "It's what killed him."

The man who should be dead hit the door again.

The bar jangled but stayed in place.

"So it's true. They do die and come back." She screwed up her face. "Like *zombies*."

Riker made no comment. He stared at her for a second then looked away.

Tara placed a hand on his shoulder. "So tell me this, Bro."

Riker was studying the phalanx of body bags stacked three-high in the red zone. Bringing his gaze back around, he shot Tara a questioning look.

Dropping her hands to her sides, she said, "If the guy I saw in the lobby, and those other ones we saw last night were slow and lethargic in their movements, why in all that's holy did the gunshot victim have moves like freaking Usain Bolt?"

Riker raised a hand and cocked his head toward the mouth of the tunnel.

"What?" she asked.

"Hear that?"

"Hear what?"

"A helicopter. And it's coming this way."

Craning toward the oval of light a dozen feet distant, she said, "I don't hear a thing."

"I'm still attuned to the sound," he said, "It's a Black Hawk. I'm guessing it's coming to extract their skeleton crew."

"The guys in black?"

Riker nodded.

"Who do they work for?"

"Some kind of contractors," he replied, starting a slow walk toward the tunnel entrance. "There were thousands of them making big bucks over there."

Brow furrowed, she asked, "Then what happened to the real soldiers?"

The man hit the barred door again, sending a sonorous gong-like sound crashing about the tunnel.

Riker winced but kept walking. "They probably got called away to take care of more pressing matters."

Peering over her shoulder, Tara asked, "What's more pressing than ridding the streets of Middletown of those things?"

"Ridding another part of the state of those things," he replied soberly.

They reached the mouth of the tunnel where Riker stopped abruptly and planted a splayed hand on the cement wall to steady himself.

Reacting to what she was seeing, Tara drew a sharp breath and took a half-step backward.

The football field stretched off to their left on a shallow angle. Also to their left, the bleachers rose up mostly out of sight. The near end zone shot off on a diagonal to their right. Opposite it was the beginning of a vehicle-choked parking lot. Though the scene didn't quite live up to the picture Riker had imagined earlier, the all-encompassing maze of body bags spread from goal post to goal post before him was enough of a shock to start the bony fingers of dread scratching at his insides.

"Oh my God!" blurted Tara.

143

Amplified by the tunnel's natural acoustics, the nerve-jangling report of the man hitting the door yet again all but drowned out her shock-filled exclamation.

"God had nothing to do with this," said Riker. "This is man's doing. And if I had to venture a guess, my money would be on the Department of Defense, specifically."

"It looks like they have a handle on things."

Riker took three long strides forward and stopped on the edge of the field where he noticed a bit of give to the grass under his boots. "I think this, Tara"—he swept one arm in the direction of the body bags—"is only the beginning." Before Tara could reply, a half-dozen hollow-sounding gunshots rang out and a whole bunch of people surged from the opposing tunnel.

"We need to go," insisted Riker.

More gunfire filled the air, drawing a yelp from Tara. "You're not scared?"

Riker shook his head. "Nope," he said. "I'm terrified." Wishing he had blinders on to shield him from the stuff of his nightmares, he put his head down and struck off through the maze. Wouldn't have helped if he did. For the low moans and constant raking of nails against slick neoprene coming from within the tenting bags was enough to make him want to bolt. Rounding a misshapen mound of bags somewhere near the twenty yard line, Riker regarded Tara over his shoulder. "This Hussein Bolt guy ... who is he?"

"*Usain* Bolt. Not *Hussein*," she answered, still on the move. "The guy's a Jamaican track star. They call him"—she made air quotes with her fingers—"Fastest Man on the Planet."

Riker turned a corner near the fifty yard line and struck a diagonal tack toward the parking lot. On the turf at his feet the high school's mascot was nearly obliterated. Chevron patterns were pressed into the bottom of the deep furrows splitting the logo in two. That they were closely spaced and easily sixteen inches across told him the tires on an Army deuce and a half had likely done the damage.

When he looked up he got a clearer view of the parking lot. Behind a low chain-link fence, windshields sparkled with light thrown by a low-hanging watery sun. The people who had emerged from the other tunnel were distancing themselves from something. Heads bobbed between the parked vehicles as the crowd fanned out and continued moving right to left toward where the Humvees had been parked the night before.

Tara stepped around the muddy ruts, then went on. "Bolt does that move with his arms that *all* the kids are mimicking. My former boss said his nephew calls it *dabbing*." The moment the word *former* had rolled off her tongue the indisputable fact that her work relationship with Middletown University was forever changed hit her. No more pumpkin spice lattes in her future added a little bit of a silver lining to the horrific events that led up to her being here—embroiled dead center in another rapidly unfolding event.

There was a sound like a long, drawn-out fart as without warning a pile of rubber body bags to their fore shifted and a slow-motion avalanche ensued, spilling a half-dozen bags in her brother's path.

Reacting to the movement, Riker planted the booted prosthesis on the field and pushed off hard, deftly sidestepping the glossy black drift. While the bags from the top of the pile remained still as they settled on the grass, a trio making up the bottom row—likely the cause of the entire stack shifting in the first place—had very active contents. The filled-out bag near Riker's boots snapped taut as the thing inside went rigid. At the zipper stop near the top of the bag, a single pinky finger thrust through an inch-long opening left there and seemed to probe the air.

"You have got to be effin kidding me," said Tara as the zipper moved and the entire hand made an appearance. It was pale and blood-streaked and glistening where the light hit it. Due to the fact that the three fingers between the thumb and pinky had been reduced to nubs trailing ragged strips of pale skin, the impression it was flashing the "hang loose" sign at them was impossible to ignore.

Stepping over the bag and keeping his distance from the unreal sight, Riker said, "Think he knew Jeff Spicoli?"

Following in her brother's footsteps, Tara picked her way through the bags on tip toes without looking back. Once clear of the blockage, she said, "Who the eff is Jeff Spicoli?"

"You haven't seen Fast Times at Ridgemont High?"

"Nope. Before my time, Lee."

"Before my time, too. Caught it on the television in one shelter or another. It's got a young Forest Whitaker."

***

Riker reached the far sideline near the opposing thirty yard line with Tara trailing a few feet behind him. The helicopter was out of sight and orbiting something other than the high school. The gunshots were replaced by shouts and screams coming from the vicinity of the parking lot. Standing on his toes, Riker saw that the Humvees and transport trucks were no longer blocking the driveway that looped behind the squat building abutting the opposite end zone.

Having seen enough to know they should scoot from here as soon as possible, he threaded his way through a few more bags whose contents were far from full sized and not entirely dead. Sickened at the prospect he was likely in the company of a dozen kids who would never see another birthday, or their parents again for that matter, he trudged ahead to the parking lot fence where he stopped, bent at the waist, and planted his hands on his knees.

The first tell-tale tingle arriving in the back of Riker's throat coincided with his sister's bare feet entering his limited field of view. With nothing more than bile and water in his gut, the initial surge of vomit came without further warning, forming a yellow-green puddle near his boots and Tara's left foot the victim of a fair amount of collateral damage.

The dry heaves that followed wracked his body for a few seconds.

"I don't like this," said Tara as she surveyed the parking lot. "I'm standing here with puke-splattered bare feet and freezing my tits off." She pulled her arms inside her shirt and bent over to catch her brother's eye.

The thwop of rotor blades from another helicopter drawing near caused the activity inside the body bags to ramp up.

Ignoring the noise, she said, "Now what?"

Riker wiped his mouth with his hand and dragged his hand through the grass. Hinging up, he said, "We find some wheels."

"You mean we find *my* wheels," she said. "You got the key, right?"

Shaking his head side to side, he said, "I got *some* keys. Not sure if Thumbelina's is among them."

Grumbling something about "Carl" having "one job," Tara stuck her arms back through her sleeves. Lips pursed, she stuffed the Apple devices into her back pockets and grabbed the top of the fence two-handed. Jamming her bare toes into the diamond-shaped openings, she hauled herself up and over with little effort.

Scaling fences not his strong suit—even before losing the leg—Riker walked the length of the fence until he found the entrance to the lot. Eyes locked on Tara standing a dozen yards to his right, he dragged the liberated key fobs from his pants pocket and began punching buttons.

Chapter 30

Realizing she'd already been exposed to air tainted with whatever microbe may or may not have been inside the breached cube, and coming to the conclusion that she was not keeling over anytime soon, Victoria tore off the stuffy mask and let it and the attached oxygen tank fall to the floor. Instantly, in her right side vision, she detected something coming straight for her head.

Caught flatfooted, she was unable to completely avoid the incoming blow. Instead, as the clumsy right-cross glanced off her shoulder, she got a look at something that at once baffled and terrified her in equal measures.

The bearded attacker was familiar to her. His unusual pallor was not. She'd seen the gray-haired vagrant panhandling on Church and Greenwich as recently as last Monday. Only then there had been no blood in his unkempt beard, his cheeks had been rosy and his eyes full of life. Now, however, it looked as if he'd been bobbing for apples in a vat of blood. The windows to his soul were glazed over and he was moving as if he had in fact been sedated.

After instinctively backpedaling and dropping to the floor to avoid the incoming left, Victoria made a mad dash for the outer ring door, scurrying down the hall like a dog—on all fours.

Seeing the boxes stacked by the door gave her an idea. With the Ramones still serenading her from within her bag, she came to a stop and twisted around to a sitting position in front of the boxes.

After an over the shoulder glance told her the milky-eyed man's pursuit was anything but high speed, she began working the latches on the box labeled B: ROMERO. Inside were a half-dozen aluminum cylinders roughly the size of a twelve-ounce soda can. Stuck into foam padding two across and three deep, only an inch or so of the top of each remained visible. She plucked one from the foam and slipped it into her bag. Then she shoved the open box aside and attacked the latches on the box labeled A: ROMERO.

A soft shuffling rising over the hum of the fluorescent lighting drew Victoria's attention from the glass vials inside the second case. Looking over her shoulder, she saw that Milky Eyes had halved the distance to the pit, his paper slippers and hospital gown responsible for the out of place sound. And just when she lifted a vial from the snug padding, the man opened his toothless maw and emitted a low, throaty moan that stood the hairs on her arms at attention.

Victoria added the lone glass vial to her whistleblower cache, closed both boxes, and then replaced them at the bottom of each stack. Rising, she saw that the pair of chemists she had thought dead were now up and struggling to navigate the breached airlock. The woman, even with one leg reduced to mostly bone and cartilage, was attempting to push through the door. The hanged chemist was still being held back by the oxygen hose encircling his neck. However, he was now facing her from a slightly different angle, giving her a clear look at a masculine face complete with five o'clock shadow and black, horn-rimmed glasses. And like the street person weaving through the pit and knocking things on the floor with his wildly swinging arms, the chemist's eyes were lifeless and dull and fixed on her.

Hands shaking, she swiped the pass card through the reader and exited the pit through the glass door. Without a backward glance, she sprinted to the elevator bank and tapped the card on the call panel. The doors opened right away. Ecstatic to learn that the car hadn't been recalled to another floor—another weekend blessing that may have just spared her from a second attack by the moaning, blood-soaked juggernaut—she stepped inside and stabbed a black-painted nail at the Door Close button.

"Close, close, close," she chanted, pummeling the button repeatedly.

Milky Eyes had just begun to bang against the glass door when her prayer was answered. Her new mantra, "Move, move, move," echoed off the elevator walls as she pressed 73 repeatedly to get the car moving. She had no idea if the man had the strength to break the glass door, let alone the faculties to press the elevator call button, and she surely didn't want to be here if that were the case.

The ride to 73 was brief. Victoria pressed her back to the mirrored wall as the doors opened, relaxing only when she saw that the dimly lit reception area was empty. She stared at the milled metal, three-dimensional ZP logo affixed to the walnut-paneled wall to her fore. Pausing for a second, she listened hard for any out of the ordinary sounds.

Nothing.

She heard only the soft whoosh of air transiting hidden overhead ducts.

The carpet here wasn't deep pile like that on the executive floor. It was utilitarian and gray. Good enough for middle management, she supposed.

Using the master pass card, she moved swiftly between glassed-in offices, removing the hard drives from each computer and stacking them on a wheeled cart she had pulled from a janitorial closet.

Fifteen minutes into the operation she had collected seven hard drives, leaving seven open computer cases and even more tangled wires in her wake.

The sun glinting off the east-facing flank of One World Trade drew her gaze to the windows. Burning a few seconds on one last look from her favorite vantage wouldn't hurt, she figured. Fantasizing about the kind of views one hundred million dollars was going to buy her, Victoria stood before the windows and watched the ant-like people as they slowly milled about near the shimmering reflecting pools.

"What do you see?" asked Carson, causing Victoria to nearly jump out of her skin. Like Underhill earlier, Merkur's head of security had skulked up behind her unannounced. Unlike Underhill, the five-foot-eight ball of coiled muscle named Carson

Peet was trained in some kind of deadly arts Victoria had heard rumors about, but had never seen put to use—until now.

He was all alone, yet still filled the room with his presence.

"Just the scars where the towers were," she stammered, her eyes wandering his pale scar which ran from under his left ear all the way to his Adam's apple. "Just taking a break from pulling the manager's hard drives, that's all." She made a face and motioned toward the cart.

Looking her straight in the eye, Carson asked, "Have you been downstairs yet?"

"No," she lied. "It's my next stop on the grand cover-Merkur's-ass—"

"It's more than that," he said, cutting her off. "Finish up." He looked at the floor. "And come downstairs when you're done. I have a myriad set of skills … unfortunately, navigating an egghead's computer is not one of them."

Victoria swallowed hard. Hoping there were no outward signs pointing to the fact that her heart was battering her ribcage like a trapped animal, she nodded and said, "Be there as soon as I deliver these to Underhill." A lie. Because, possessing all the proof she needed to burn ZP and retire rich, she had zero intention of ever again setting foot anywhere near Underhill's office, let alone the creepy cube of death.

Barbados, here I come.

She watched Carson board the elevator. Once the doors were closed, she pressed the Down button to call for an elevator of her own.

The doors on the second elevator bank opened and she quickly stepped inside. *You're really doing this*, she thought, as she pressed the button labeled Ground Level.

A few seconds passed and nothing happened. So she tried the button again. Still no movement.

Sensing her flight instinct ramping up, she exited the car, hustled around the corner, and tried the pass card to access the stairwell.

Nothing. No green light. Thus no soft click telling her she was free to go.

The light on the slide-through remained red as she tried the card in it several more times.

Resigned to the fact there was nowhere for her to go but up, she reboarded the elevator and pressed 74.

Chapter 31

The first fob Riker selected was emblazoned with the blue Ford oval. The owner had also added a brass tag to the key ring. It was heavy and a couple of inches long with RAPTOR engraved down the middle.

Riker pressed the button imprinted with the open-lock icon.

Nothing.

He turned the fob over and punched the red panic button.

Still nothing.

Out of range.

He tossed the useless fob to the ground and began trying the rest.

The second and third fobs made the alarms chirp and lights flash on two distant vehicles. Seeing the cars clearly from his vantage, he quickly deduced they were barely larger than his sister's joke of a car and pocketed the fobs.

The rattle of chain-link preceded Tara as she threaded her way between the front row of vehicles facing the field.

"The helicopter is almost here," she said. "What kind do you think it is?"

"From the sound of it, Chinook transport," he said confidently.

Eyes roving the parked cars, he pressed buttons on fob number four, which brought the same result as fob number one: silence.

As Riker turned the last fob over in his hand, he sensed eyes on him.

Tara was now standing on one leg with her hip and thigh pressed against the front end of a black four-door SUV. As she wiped gravel from the sole of her foot, she said, "I saw the lights flash back there. You think you're too cool to be seen in a Civic or Prius, eh?"

"I'm too damn *big* to drive either one of those econoboxes, Tara." Still looking her in the eye, he made a show of pressing the unlock button on the fob in his hand.

The chirp of the horn tucked somewhere behind the bumper touching Tara's right knee made her let go of her foot and visibly start.

Grabbing ahold of the mirror to keep from falling, she blurted, "Asshole."

"Sorry," said Riker sheepishly. "I promise I didn't plan that."

Tara smirked and turned to face the full-size Suburban LT 4x4 towering over her. "Looks like we found your shoe, Cinderella."

Riker hit the unlock button again. There was another thunk and flash of lights as the rest of the locks were actuated. "Get in," he said, looping around front of the boxy rig.

The second chopper was drawing nearer, the thump of its rotors startling a murder of crows waiting patiently on the goalpost crossbar. As the corvids gave flight, cawing in displeasure, Tara scrabbled up onto the SUV and stood on the hood, causing it to buckle slightly.

"What do you see?" called Riker as he shrugged off the NRA bag and threw open his door.

"More people pouring out of the building. Some are heading this way. Most are splitting up and hoofing it for the neighborhood, though."

The truck settled slightly on its suspension as Riker took the driver's seat and fumbled to get the correct key into the ignition. He noticed straight away that the interior still had the new-car smell. Which was a good thing, seeing as how it was in direct competition with the faint odor of decay following him inside.

Hollering to be heard through the windshield and over the thrum and whine of the descending helicopter, Tara said, "I see a few of the slow slogging ones like we saw last night, too. People are avoiding them pretty good."

"Any Usains?" bellowed Riker.

"Thank God, no," she called. "But it looks like your Chinook is going to land somewhere close."

All business, Riker asked, "What about the first helo?"

She looked to the sky. Pointing toward a spot over the faraway goal post, she said, "It's still way up high and circling."

They're surveilling us, thought Riker as he started the Chevy. He imagined the Black Hawk's nose-mounted optics suite swiveling in its gimbal as the copilot glassed the surroundings for a landing spot suitable to accommodate the monstrous CH-47 Chinook en route from the north. As he was adjusting the rearview mirror, he saw a ghostly pale form moving right to left behind them. From two rows away and mostly viewed through the tinted windows of an imported minivan, he couldn't decide if he'd spotted an elderly person just walking slow and hunched over or another reanimated corpse trying to get the jump on them.

Better safe than sorry.

He threw the locks and hit the button starting the moonroof rolling back. Once it seated and the wind deflector popped into place, he hollered, "We have company, Tara. Climb in through the moonroof."

She must have mistaken "climb through" for "dive through," because just as the rotor downwash from the descending twin-rotor behemoth was curling the corners of the nearest body bags, and dirt and debris were being sucked airborne, she was coming in hot, head first and blabbering about seeing a walking dead thing that resembled their cancer-riddled mother on her last days.

After seeing his petite sister handle the unorthodox entry and get turned around and seated with all of the grace of a Vegas circus performer, Riker punched the button to close the moonroof and threw the transmission into Reverse. But instead of peeling out and pulling an impressive J-turn, he just sat there, arms encircling the wheel and looking skyward through the windshield.

"You're wasting gas letting it idle," chided Tara. "And Bro, something has been bugging me."

Eyes never leaving the inbound Chinook, he said, "What's that?"

Tara made a face. "Usains doesn't work for me. Let's call them *Bolts* from here on out."

"Deal," said Riker, sounding more than a little annoyed. He glanced at the gauge cluster. Saw that the fuel needle was just north of half full. He also learned that the Chevy had just over a hundred miles on the digital odometer. Spying the temporary paper license affixed to the back window made him fairly confident the rig was also still wearing dealership promo plates.

Brand spanking new and on her first tank of gas.

Flicking her eyes to her wing mirror and picking up movement there, Tara said, "Are you going to drive, or what?"

Still focused on the airspace over the football field, he said, "I want to see what happens here."

"The soldiers hanging out the back are going to jump out with machineguns at the ready and round everyone up again," she said, glaring at the slowing chopper through the moonroof glass. "That's exactly what the eff they're about to do, Lee. And if we're still sitting in this stolen truck when they do, no telling where we'll be spending tonight. And that's assuming they let us live after escaping and tying up one of their own."

Rows of bags toppled as the Chinook came in hot, flared hard, and then settled on the distant twenty-yard line where the bags were mostly stacked knee-high. Its landing gear found footing and compressed and the chopper leveled out. Seeing the rear wheels crushing down atop a long row of bags showing definite movement—compressing some flat, popping others as the bags failed when the air inside collected at the ends with nowhere to go—told Riker this was a quick reaction force called in to exfil the soldiers left behind. They didn't care about the evidence on the field at this point. And it was highly unlikely the trucks that made the tracks on the field would be back anytime soon, either. Their mission was over. Things were out of hand. All of this was borderline speculation on Riker's part. But it was what he was going to run with until he saw something to change his mind.

"The thing I saw *really* looked like Mom did in the end," was coming out of Tara's mouth at about the same instant the cadaverous-looking woman slapped her dainty white palms against the liftgate window.

"Looks nothing like how I remember her," said Riker as he tromped the gas and spun the steering wheel clockwise one-handed.

The sudden acceleration knocked the elderly woman from the Suburban, sending her to the ground where she performed a reverse somersault, arms and legs flailing.

Grimacing from the hollow thud and seeing the tail end of the encounter which was little more than a flash of floral print fabric and a split-second glimpse of furry slippers crossing the side mirror, Riker threw the still shimmying truck's transmission into Drive.

Tara was looking in her mirror now and astonished to see the woman she thought resembled their dying mom snap her head around and fix an unblinking stare on the idling truck.

"Go, Leland," she said, still focused on the mirror where the woman was already on her hands and knees. Inexplicably, the long nightgown she'd been wearing had worked up on her body, leaving only her forearms poking out of the arm holes. And as she rose and lurched after the speeding truck with her mouth full of blood-stained teeth snapping open and closed, all Tara could think of was how she looked like the Tyrannosaurus Rex from *Jurassic Park*.

Riker made a quick visual sweep of the mirrors. In Tara's he saw virtually the same thing as she. Only instead of seeing the woman as a T-Rex on the hunt, he saw something escaped from an old-time sanitarium. Coupled with the encounters from the night before and, more recently witnessing an already dead man get impaled and come back for more, the sight of the frail woman getting up after suffering a vehicular hockey check didn't really surprise him. In fact, backing into her was a kind of test whose result would either be empirical evidence bolstering what he'd already experienced, or a hit-and-run charge as the cherry on the sundae that, up to now, consisted of escape from federal detention, kidnapping an officer of the United States Army, and grand theft auto.

As Riker tooled through the lot with the freedom of a nearby side street in his sights, he saw men in black disgorging from the back of the Chinook. Passing by the long row of vehicles nosed in against the fence bordering the football field, he caught glimpses through Tara's window of the contractors fanning out, rifles raised and aimed toward the dozen or so civilians vectoring toward the helicopter.

"Could have been us," said Tara.

"It isn't, though," replied Riker, a hard edge to his voice. "We're still alive." He reached across the seat and palmed Tara's head. "Get down so you don't catch a stray bullet if they decide to engage those things."

Chapter 32

Victoria felt the elevator spool down and saw the scrolling digital numbers slow and freeze at 74. Once again Underhill was waiting by the elevator bank when the doors parted. Thankfully, Merkur wasn't there as well to scrutinize her with his hawk-like gaze. He'd see right through the thinly held facade. Detect the subterfuge straight away. Hell, she mused, the old fucker would probably be able to smell the fear on her, too.

They didn't call Merkur "Shark" for no reason. Word around the water cooler was that the man cared only about Zen Pharma. Everything and everybody was expendable, and the proof of that was clearly evident by what she had seen on 72. The suited duo had been far enough away that she couldn't quite be certain what she had actually seen. However, the vagrant and whatever was convulsing inside the body bag sealed the deal for her. Then there was the cryptic information on the printed-out pages secreted in her bag. Whether she learned the truth of it all now or later certainly wouldn't affect a whistleblower award.

Underhill stood rooted in place. "Carson said there's something he wants you to see on 72. C'mon, let's ride together."

Pausing in the path of the elevator doors, Victoria shook the bag containing the hard drives, making them clunk and rattle as they settled to the bottom. "Where do you want these?"

"Anywhere is good," answered Underhill, a knowing smile curling his lip.

Fuck. She'd been hoping to get away from Underhill long enough to try the pass card in the nearby stairwell. Even a ride to Church Street on the window washer's platform sounded better to her than revisiting the bio lab. She tossed the bag unceremoniously on the carpet. "That going to work for you?"

"Perfect. And don't worry, you're almost done," Underhill said, wagging his sausage-like fingers at her. "Unless I don't like what I see downstairs."

***

Carson and two of his men were inside the pit when Victoria and Underhill stepped from the elevator on 72. Carson was holding Milky Eyes at bay with what looked like a dog catcher's tool. Gripping the long aluminum pole two-handed, he maneuvered the uncoordinated man into a cubicle while, to Victoria's horror, another man slid a long, thin knife directly into its temple.

"This is how it should have been done," barked Carson, staring at the new arrivals. "I just replayed the holding cell video feed showing the transfer. The eggheads tried bagging the specimens without using the leash. That's how they got bit. Apparently, if you want a job done right … you gotta do it yourself."

Stomach reeling, Victoria averted her eyes, noticing at once that the six boxes containing the Romero agent had been moved and were sitting on the floor beside the outer security ring door.

Seeing the biohazard symbol, Underhill gave them a wide berth and called out to Carson. "What are these doing *outside* of the cube?"

Carson made no reply as he transited the pit dragging the limp body. Along the way its head banged against chair and table legs, the leaking wound leaving behind a trail of brackish liquid. When Carson paused to open the door, both Victoria and Underhill got an eyeful of the trio of bodies lying on the floor just inside the pit. There was a dark-haired boy of about ten who Victoria guessed had been the one inhabiting the body bag. The blue-eyed female chemist, sans hood and facemask, lay beside the boy. On her right was the male chemist, also stripped of his hood and black-rimmed glasses.

Victoria's mouth formed a silent "O" when she saw the neat, dime-sized bullet holes in each of their foreheads.

Pretending not to notice what amounted to a triple homicide practically lying at her feet, she said matter-of-factly, "Let's wipe the server and all go get a drink, shall we?"

Carson removed the leash and positioned Milky Eyes by the others. He shook his head and fixed his gaze on Victoria. "Were you aware of these things already?"

Eyes wide and earning an Oscar, Victoria indicated she had gone straight to 73 and had been there for the duration.

"What's on your knees, then? he asked. "Looks like smeared blood to me."

Underhill was tracking the conversation, head moving from Victoria to Carson and back again.

Shaking her head no, Victoria steered the questioning to the corpses. "What are *those?*"

"*Those* are Merkur's failed attempts at creating a super soldier serum to be used for a DoD black project."

Victoria backed away from the leaking corpse and stood close to Underhill. Lesser of the evils at this point, she figured.

"The man your guy just knifed to death is a fixture of the neighborhood, Carson. And what about the kid?"

"Neither one of them will be missed by anyone. The kid's a runaway. And the panhandler here, he was already a zombie. Only it was booze driving him, not Romero. Stupid name for a drug meant to extend battlefield longevity."

"I concur," said Underhill. "I take it, save for Indiana, the damage here has been contained?"

Victoria felt a chill run through her upon hearing Carson say "save for Indiana." What the eff did that mean? Did they set Operation Peasant Overlord in motion?

"Afraid not," said Carson. "After the ambulatory specimen transfer went wrong, four of your lab workers fled the building."

Victoria swallowed hard. A sheen of sweat was forming on her forehead and upper lip.

Underhill said, "So we're enacting Protocol Red?"

"There's no other way to maintain plausible deniability," replied Carson. "My men have already dogged down the main sprinkler valves on 40. The accelerant is spread there and on 73. I had them place timed explosives on both floors. Our tracks *will* be covered here when we leave. Both the hard copies"—he nodded to the shelves full of notebooks—"and the server next to the bio lab will burn before the fire crews leave their houses."

Underhill arched a brow. "And the missing employees?"

"Good news and bad," stated Carson as his men looked on, apparently awaiting orders. "One has already met the Seventh Avenue Express head on falling off the Franklin Street/Varick platform. Real messy, I hear. I have a team surveilling another at a Midtown bar. They're just waiting for him to leave or visit the john."

Victoria's head moved subtly as she followed the conversation.

"What's the bad?" asked Underhill, craning to get a better look at the ashen corpses.

Carson grimaced. "We lost the other two," he conceded. "However, we have their residences under surveillance."

In a wavering voice, Victoria asked, "What about me?" She gripped her chin with one hand and snugged her bag tight with the other. "Can I go home now?"

"Afraid not," Carson said. "Merkur wants you to come back upstairs with us." He thumbed the elevator's Down call button and, once the doors parted, helped his men move the tackle-box-looking things inside. Then Carson held the door while his men lugged the bodies of the kid and the bearded vagrant into the elevator. Once all of the incriminating evidence was loaded, Carson nodded to his men, then struck off down the hall. "Follow me," he called over a shoulder, "we're taking the stairs."

Victoria caught herself staring at her co-workers' corpses. Letting her gaze linger on the tear in the male chemist's suit, she spotted a bite wound partially concealed by the flimsy-looking yellow material. The apple-sized, raised oval was purple-rimmed and crusted with dried blood. Throwing a visible shiver, she tore her eyes from the dead and fell in between Carson and Underhill, where she remained until the former led them up six flights and through a door sporting the warning: ROOFTOP ACCESS - AUTHORIZED PERSONNEL ONLY.

The high-decibel humming from the head-high stacks of HVAC equipment crowding the door caught Victoria by surprise as she crossed the threshold. After a brief moment of hesitation, Carson was gripping her shoulder and steering her one-handed through the warren of roof-mounted mechanicals.

Turning the corner near the east edge of the building, the group was met by the steady blast of rotor wash coming from a helicopter waiting nearby.

Merkur had changed into jeans and hidden his sparse head of graying hair under a black ball cap. In place of the navy blazer, silk tie, and Oxford button-down was a khaki jacket and hunter-green Polo. To round out the L.L. Bean look, he had traded the black Bruno Magli shoes for a pair of sensible brown wingtips. He was standing near the helicopter's right-side cabin door and motioning Underhill forward.

Chapter 33

Ducking low in the seat, Riker wheeled the Suburban forward at a walking speed until he neared a small throng of people milling about the mouth of the tunnel he guessed he and Tara were taken through the night before. A quick glance over his right shoulder told him the soldiers were still negotiating the body bag maze. So he stopped a yard short of the group and pulsed down his window.

Voice wavering, Tara said, "What the eff are you doing, Lee?"

Ignoring the query, Riker called out to a man who seemed as if he still had it together.

Balding, maybe in his fifties, and of average height, the man approached the Suburban on the driver's side.

"Need a ride?" asked Riker as a rolling gust of wind—likely augmented by the Chinook's rotor wash—lifted the man's threadbare tee-shirt, exposing the substantial beer gut hanging over his beltless waistband.

"No, no, no," chanted Tara, her head still below the crest of the dash.

Face a mixture of confusion and relief, the man stopped an arm's length from Riker.

"Hell yes," he said. "I'll go wherever you're going as long as it's far away from here."

Riker jangled the set of keys out the window. "I'm not offering you a ride. I'm offering you and the others rides of your own. These unlock the coach's offices. Inside you'll find the keys, identification, and cell phones they took from us."

Moving slowly, the man took the keys from Riker's outstretched arm. "There's things in there. Weird things I can't wrap my head around." He shook his head rapidly back and forth. "I can't go back in there."

A younger woman standing nearby with the kid Riker had lifted the iPod from stepped forward. "Effin coward." She snatched the keys from the man's open palm. "I put a mop handle through the door pulls. Whatever those things were, they're locked inside with the soldiers." Without another word, she turned and hustled toward the sports facility entrance, kid in tow.

A tick later a man and woman standing with the group of people blocking the Suburban peeled away to follow the woman with the keys. That was all it took to turn the exodus around. Just a lone woman with a young kid showing bravery in the face of the unknown. In a handful of seconds the driveway was clear and Riker was turning onto the street fronting Shenandoah High.

Hinging up, Tara said, "You just encouraged them to go back into what sounded to me like hell on earth." She looked over her shoulder and saw a half-dozen escapees split from the group and take down the trio of slow-moving zombies, pinning them to the ground with hands and knees. She missed what happened next as Riker drove the Suburban over the curb and cut the wheels hard left. Half a block later, Riker turned right. He proceeded slowly to the far end of the block where he pulled hard to the curb in front of a row of homes whose curtains were all shut tight. It was real quiet here. No sirens. No gunshots drifting from the bowels of the high school athletics building. Only thing to suggest this partly cloudy morning was shaping up to be anything but a normal Sunday in Middle America was the faint drumming of the helicopters a few blocks away.

Tara put her bare feet on the dash and drew in a deep breath. "You're okay with what you did back there? Seems to me that move was just so we could get out of the parking lot."

"That was done solely out of empathy for their plight, Tara." He reached into the center console. Rooted around in there for a second.

"Sending them into the belly of the beast?"

He slammed the console, then regarded Tara with a serious look. "Going back in and getting their belongings means they have a better chance of getting to safety than just standing there waiting for the soldiers to come and let out whoever or *whatever* that woman trapped inside the equipment room when she barred the doors."

"So why are we here"—she wiggled her toes on the dash—"and where am I going to get some new shoes?"

"Shoes can wait." He gestured toward the dash. "Try the radio."

Tara powered it on and cycled through the dial, finding mostly stations playing music. Once or twice she came upon a snippet of news, weather, and sports, but nothing about MU or the quarantine.

A gust rattled the branches of the trees lining the street. Red and orange leaves broke free and fluttered to the ground. Finally, Riker rolled the volume down and proffered an answer to Tara's first question. "I stopped us here to give those folks enough time to get in and out and find a set of wheels." He cocked his head toward his open window. "No gunshots so far. That's a good thing."

She shot him a questioning look.

"Would a cat have a harder time catching one mouse or multiple mouses?"

"Mice," she said. "And I see your point. Give the helicopters a bunch of targets to chase."

Riker said, "That is, if they're in the chasing mood."

She thumped the center console lid with her palm. "What were you looking for in here?"

"A map."

Tara leaned over and pressed a virtual button on the touch screen in the dash. The image cycled from the *Audio* screen to one labeled *Navigation*. Showing on the display was a mostly tan map marred by a tangle of solid red lines. It was obvious from the scale that the image of the general vicinity was zoomed way out.

"Not good," said Tara. "Anything solid red means traffic is at a standstill. Or pretty damn close to a standstill."

"Can you zoom in?"

A pickup with a hemi engine and loud pipes roared by on the street behind them. It was followed close behind by a compact import and a shiny red minivan.

Turning her attention back to the multifunction display, Tara pressed repeatedly on the digitally rendered button labeled with a black minus symbol.

Nothing happened.

She tried cycling back and forth. Pressed the minus button again.

Nothing.

Just the web of red representing nowhere Riker wanted to be near or stuck travelling along in a stolen vehicle.

"Check the glovebox for an old-fashioned paper map."

She popped the glove box open. All it contained was an owner's manual, Department of Motor Vehicle documents, and an ice scraper complete with a red fur-trimmed mitt.

"How cold does it get here at night?"

Tara closed the glovebox.

She looked at the headliner, obviously crunching some kind of numbers in her head. After a bit, she said, "This time of year, mid-forties. That's a give or take pulled-it-outta-my-butt figure. I'm not a Farmer's Almanac, Lee."

"Why don't you do what everyone else your age does?"

"Elaborate, Lee."

"Google it."

Tara dragged the pair of devices from her pants pockets. Thumbed the iPhone to life.

After a minute or two of swiping and then cycling the device through a hard reboot, she said, "No service."

"Same here," said Riker, flipping his phone closed. "We better get to brainstorming."

Chapter 34

Victoria was taken aback by how small the black and gold helicopter appeared up close. Then it struck her that at most the thing could accommodate six. Counting heads, including the pilots and herself, she came to the conclusion she'd have a place to park her butt. However, based on the iron grip Carson still had on her shoulder, she had an awful feeling she was going to be left on the roof with two choices: either burn to death, or escape the flames by jumping as so many had fifteen short years ago.

The Shark is bolting for the Hamptons, she thought to herself as Carson stopped her advance just outside the reach of the spinning rotors. In the next beat she was being led to her left. Twenty yards from the helicopter and within spitting distance of the waist-high parapet ringing 4WTC's sizable roof, Carson turned her around to face him.

"Mr. Merkur tells me you've been drinking a lot lately."

"Me? No way," she lied.

"He says you're no longer a team player."

Knowing where this was going, she said nothing. Instead, she took one step back and covertly loosened the clasp on her bag.

"You've seen too much," Carson stated, his lips parting into a Cheshire-Cat-like grin. Instantly, the inches-long facial scar was stretched, taking the form of a lightning bolt and going stark white against his tanned skin.

"I won't say a thing." She took one half-step back, turning sideways in the process.

"Bullshit," said Carson. "Underhill saw you printing some of Mr. Merkur's emails. Don't you know who I am? What I do for Zen?"

She had already snaked one hand into the courier's bag and was coming out with the smooth glass vial when Carson began to advance on her.

"Yes I do," she said through clenched teeth as she brought her right hand up so he could see the glass vial. "You're the asshole murderer who's going to give me back the pass card and turn a blind eye while I go back to the stairwell and mosey on home."

Carson chuckled. "You think what's in that vial gives you leverage? What do you plan on doing with that? You going to break it on the ground like a beer bottle and try to stick me with it?"

"You take another step and I will infect me and you and your masters."

He took a step forward.

She took another backward.

"I'll do it," she said, making a show of throwing the vial to the ground between their feet.

Carson took one more long stride, cutting the distance between them and forcing her back so that her calves were pressed against the low wall. Then, performing one of those Jason Bourne disarm-the-bad-guy-type maneuvers, his hand shot out, the strong fingers wrapping vice-tight around her wrist.

Suddenly the tendons in Victoria's wrist felt as if they were on fire, and she was losing her balance. The two sensations working together caused her to relax her grip on the vial. What had seemed like the perfect plan evaporated before her eyes when Carson's free hand came away holding the vial full of Romero virus. Then, to add insult to injury, the wide expanse of nothing at her back brought on a paralyzing bout of vertigo that trumped all of the lingering hangover symptoms.

"You know what?" Carson said, throwing the vial to the ground by her feet where it shattered into tiny shards. Horrified at the ramification of the virus doing to her what it had already done to the bio lab workers, she shrank away, putting herself in a near seated position on the building's edge. Smiling, Carson finished the thought, "You chose the wrong Romero strain. You'd have to introduce this into my blood stream directly. Or *you* could become infected and bite me. Those are the *only* ways this nasty little bug at our feet can hurt either one of us."

Victoria was sitting on the edge now, her legs instinctively drawing up from the spreading puddle. Her lip was quivering and her breathing rapid.

"You know something else?"

Victoria said nothing. Tears were streaming down her face. A gust of wind screaming up the building's sheer facade moved her long brunette hair.

"You have been exhibiting suicidal tendencies, Victoria."

As Victoria lifted her gaze and opened her mouth to rebut Carson's claim, he let go of her wrist, leaned in, and tapped her lightly on the shoulder.

There was no mad scrabble to find purchase on Victoria's part. Her eyes simply went wide with recognition as the unstoppable effects of Newton's Third Law were set into motion. Like a diver entering the water off a boat's gunwale, she simply rocked back and disappeared heels over head.

There one second, gone the next.

Strange, thought Carson. She didn't scream or curse like nearly every other person he had sent to their death. The trivial thought fading, he turned and loped to the awaiting helicopter.

Victoria knew she was dead the moment the vial was no longer in her possession. With nothing to use as leverage, she had simply given up hope then and there. The tap on the shoulder, however, had come as a complete surprise. And as she tumbled over the edge, time seemed to slow. She caught a fleeting glimpse of herself in 4WTC's mirrored glass. Then, inexplicably, she saw a streak of movement on the adjoining building's mirrored surface that she knew also had to be her own fast-moving reflection. And as absurd a thought as there could be, she wondered if someone was taping her plunging to her death. She remembered seeing the desperate businessman hanging off one of the original towers. She vividly recalled how he'd performed the sign of the cross on his chest before releasing his tenuous purchase on the tower's mangled metal skin. The sight of his sooty shirt and tattered pants flapping in the wind was indelibly burned into her memory as he let go and rocketed to the ground head first in a seated position. The same image had been captured by a photographer and broadcast over the news and plastered on the pages of every periodical and gossip mag for weeks after the horrific attack. That was definitely *not* how Victoria wanted to be remembered.

As she approached terminal velocity on her way to the inevitable rendezvous with Church Street, she heard the heavy percussion of the street performer's makeshift drums riding the wind opposite her trajectory. A wave of sadness then washed over her as she thought about how badly her aging parents and old buddy Tony the security guard were going to take it when she was wrongly labeled a jumper.

Victoria didn't feel a thing when her hurtling body knifed through the canted glass portico. Mercifully, the air was gone from her lungs and she was on the verge of blacking out when she struck the sidewalk spread-eagled and facedown.

The impact with the ground when coupled with one hundred and twenty pounds of flesh and bone coming down on top of it caused the spun-metal canister inside of her bag to implode. No longer structurally sound, the lid came off, and the aerosolized Romero virus was no longer contained.

The sound of the impact was like nothing the crowd watching the street performers had ever heard before. Kids were screaming. Mouths hinged open as men and women gaped at the destroyed body.

Even the mime screamed.

And Silver Cowboy Guy went out of character, moving for the first time in several minutes in order to step off his pedestal and search the sky for more falling bodies.

***

Tony had heard the impact from his post. Eighteen seconds after the first sound of breaking glass reached his ears, he was through the doors and traversing the sidewalk. "Make a hole," he bellowed as he swam his way through the growing crowd. Finally parting the sea of humanity, half of whom were newly arriving tourists who had just spilled out of a double-decker sightseeing bus, Tony got his first look at what snippets of everyone's harried conversation told him was a jumper.

The ripped-open yellow and black satchel was his first clue that he knew who the jumper was. The splayed-out head of jet-black-dyed hair was the second. Going to his knees involuntarily, he looked to the sky, pressed his radio to his lips, and made the call. "This is Officer Anthony De Luca at 4WTC. We have a fatality at the Church Street entrance." Seeing a column of black smoke begin to pour from venting near the top of the building, he added, "Send Fire, too. Looks like a multi-alarm."

Chapter 35

Riker was pressing his thumbs hard into his temples and staring into space through the Suburban's glass moonroof when an open hand impacted his window. Caught entirely by surprise, he let out a string of expletives and raised his fists to the threat.

Caught head down and fiddling with her phone, Tara sat bolt upright and screamed. Not a long, drawn-out affair. More of a piercing yelp that preceded her pressing her back against her door and drawing her legs up defensively.

Having recovered somewhat from the sudden interruption, Riker craned around and caught sight of a man dressed in Wrangler's, a Western-themed button-up shirt, and sporting a white Stetson. Even shod in cowboy boots that looked to have two-inch heels on them, when the man leaned in again, hand poised to deliver a closed-fist rap on the window, looking upward was necessary for him to meet Riker's gaze.

Expecting to see the same hungry look the Bolt had fixed him with, instead Riker found himself staring into the bluest eyes he'd ever seen. They were watery and had a certain spark in them. It was as if they were asking him a million questions all at once. He looked the man up and down, searching for anything to suggest he may have been the victim of an attack and his unorthodox approach was just the calm before the proverbial storm.

The man's blue jeans were stiff and new, not a spot of blood on them. Riker figured they'd probably stand on their own if they hit the floor cuffs first. They were held up by a wide leather belt with a silver and turquoise buckle big enough to give Captain America's shield a run for its money. The tucked-in denim shirt was pressed and clean and several shades lighter blue than the pants. With pearl snap buttons and intricate threadwork on the yolk front and back, it looked like something Porter Wagoner might have worn on stage at the Grand Ol' Opry.

Seeing nothing threatening at all about the man, Riker powered down his window.

"Hello," said the man, the syntax perfect though his voice had a nasal quality to it. "I'm Steve-O."

Riker looked away for half a beat and met Tara's gaze. Shrugging, he turned back and said, "I'm Lee and"—he hooked a thumb over his right shoulder—"she's Tara. Is your first name Steve and last name Oh? Or is O the initial your last name begins with?"

Though it didn't appear physically possible, the man's smile widened, revealing a mouthful of perfectly straight teeth. He said, "Just Steve-O. My last name is Piontek."

A block distant the turbine whine rose to a howl and the thwopping of the rotors increased in tempo exponentially. Riker didn't have to look to know the Chinook was launching from the football field.

"Where'd you come from?"

"The high school," he said, going to his tiptoes and craning to see Tara. "The Army men were being mean so I left."

"I don't remember seeing you there, Steve-O," said Tara. She regarded Riker. "Do you remember seeing him?"

Riker shook his head. "I didn't exactly tour the place," he admitted. Regarding Steve-O, he asked, "Were you underground with a bunch of people and trampolines and balance beams?"

Steve-O tipped his hat and his smile faded. "Lots of people in there. Monsters, too. The Army men killed some of them. Then one of the monsters attacked the Army men. Biting and scratching them. One of the Army men told me to run. To go home."

Riker was trying to gauge Steve's age when the man divulged the last bit of information. The red stubble on his chin and upper lip and the beginnings of sideburns creeping down from his ears made Riker think he was somewhere in his late thirties. If he was any older than that, he sure didn't have the accumulated wrinkles and gray hairs to show for it.

Wondering where "home" was, Riker asked, "Were you alone?"

Steve-O's hat brim cut the air left to right and back again as he shook his head. "Darren and Marcy were there. Marcy said the man on television ordered everyone close to our house to go to the school to get medicine. She brought us in the van last night."

Tara asked, "Who's us? And where are they now?"

Steve smiled again. Real wide. Then he stepped up on the running board. Invading Riker's personal space, eyes locked on Tara, he said, "You are pretty, Tara. June Carter Cash, pretty." He laughed and clapped his hands, the latter action forcing him to lose his balance and step back down to the road.

"Darren and Marcy," said Riker. "Where are they now?"

Steve-O screwed up his face. He looked over his shoulder in the general direction of the school.

Riker again: "Are they still there?"

Nodding, Steve-O said, "They're probably monsters by now."

Tara put her hands on her face. Speaking through her fingers, she asked, "Were there any real fast monsters inside?"

Riker looked at the side mirror, then back to his sister once he saw that the road behind them was still clear.

"One inside and one in the hall," replied Steve, his voice nearly a whisper. "Can I have a ride home?"

"Where do you live?"

"By the school."

Riker said, "But you said you came to the school in a van."

Again with the cherubic smile. "The older people school. Where the man shot people on the bus yesterday."

Riker looked at Tara. "We can't go anywhere near there."

Whispering, Tara said, "He has Down Syndrome, Lee."

Under his breath, Riker said, "What's that got to do with anything?"

"Technically speaking, if he goes with us and we don't tell anyone, wouldn't we be"—she went silent for a second—"*kidnapping* him?"

"What does it matter? We've already scoffed enough laws to earn us jail time. Might as well up the ante to a trip to the Big House."

"You sure he'll even come with us if asked?"

Seeing a stream of vehicles begin flitting by the end of the street in twos and threes, Riker said, "He's a grown ass man, Tara. We can't leave him here. Worst case scenario, we find a sheriff to leave him with."

Tara gestured to the mirror.

In response, Riker flicked his eyes there. He saw the woman Tara thought resembled their mother. Her nightshirt was dirty and ripped down the front. Arms now free of the sleeve holes, they hung at her sides until she rounded the corner and caught sight of the idling SUV.

As if a switch was flicked somewhere deep inside the woman's lolling head, both bruised and bloodied arms went horizontal to the road and her gnarled fingers started kneading the air.

"That's a monster," said Steve-O matter-of-factly.

Eyes tracking the lurching figure, Tara said, "Do you want a ride home, Steve?"

Smiling, he raised up on his toes and caught Tara's gaze. "It's Steve ... O, pretty lady."

Riker said, "Can we give you a lift, *Steve-O?*"

Totally fixated on Tara, Steve-O didn't move a muscle. It was as if Riker wasn't sitting there a couple of feet from him. Seemingly, the approaching "monster" didn't exist, either.

Riker popped the locks.

The solid *thunk* made Steve-O blink. Then, looking as if he was slowly deflating, he went flat-footed and regarded Riker.

In the side mirror, Riker saw that the woman was nearly to the Suburban's bumper. She emitted a guttural growl just as the helicopter circling high and tight overhead broke away and thundered off to the north.

If Steve-O had heard the change in pitch of the turbines, let alone the animal-like noises made by the thing homing in from his right, he didn't let on.

Adopting a fake drawl, Riker said, "It's your lucky day, Steve-O. This is the last stagecoach to Deadwood. Hop aboard, *pahdna.*"

Riker's improvisation drew an even bigger smile out of the man. It also got him to board the Suburban just as the woman's growling morphed into a long, drawn-out moan.

The hair on Riker's arms and neck snapped to attention when the moaning reached his ears. By the time fingernails were raking the SUV's flat side, he was pulling slowly from the curb, wondering with a bit of trepidation what other horrors would be thrown at them before the young day was done.

Chapter 36

Tony covered Vicky's leaking body with his windbreaker, then pushed the gawkers back a few feet and waited for the first responders to show. A handful of minutes after he had secured a perimeter with the help of the double-decker tour bus operator, his supervisor had arrived from a nearby property and mercifully released him early.

With the image of the broken and twisted body of the forty-something Zen Pharmaceuticals employee he had just spoken to an hour prior to her jumping haunting his every thought, Tony trudged to the nearest subway platform. He just didn't have the energy to go back inside the building and retrieve his lunchbox, thermos and watch coat.

Old Crow and his well-worn leather recliner was calling.

Middletown, Indiana

Riker zippered the Suburban through the residential neighborhood bordering the high school for a couple of minutes then steered onto a county road that eventually spit them out on a deserted arterial connecting Chesterfield and Daleville. From there they drove in silence north toward Chesterfield until Riker pulled the Chevy hard to the curb a few blocks east of where Commerce crossed over Interstate 69.

Along the way they had passed only a handful of vehicles moving slowly in the opposite direction. Riker's first instinct had been to stop and ask the driver of a large 4x4 pickup what he knew about the situation in Middletown. However, that move was quickly dashed when he saw the rack full of guns behind the driver's head and detected in the man's bugged-out eyes the look of a trapped animal.

Riker threw the transmission into Park and scanned the street and sidewalks. *All clear.* He turned his attention to the reason he pulled over in the first place. Situated smack-dab between a nail salon and a dry cleaning business was a lawyer's office featuring a rather nondescript façade. As if the goings on inside the place weren't meant for public scrutiny, the windows were mirrored and displaying the Suburban's reflection back at them.

The building was one level. Rising up from the flat roof was a parapet designed to hide the heating and ventilation apparatus. Darkened signage adorned the parapet above each business. Sandwiched between signs emblazoned with *Dee Dee's Beauty Salon* and *Im-Press-Ive Dry Cleaning* was a vacuum-formed plastic number that read *Saul McGill — Attorney at Law.* Below the lawyer's name and title was his business tag line which Riker felt was lifted directly from the Ghost Busters movie.

"Who ya' gonna' call?" Riker clucked his tongue then paused for a second.

"Stay Puft Marshmallow man was the worst villain ever," commented Steve-O, punctuating the statement with a raspberry.

Tara chuckled. "Say it don't spray it, Steve-O."

Eyes roaming the mirrors again, Riker said, "We already called *you*, Saul. And you didn't pick up."

Stating the obvious, Tara said, "It's Sunday, Lee. Doesn't look like *anyone* is in."

"But I'd bet there's a pair of envelopes with a check in each one made out to us just sitting inside there on Jimmy's desk."

Tara shook her head. "That's not how it works. We were supposed to get together tomorrow, cross T's and dot I's. Mainly the reading of the will. Our funds are going to be transferred electronically by Mom's bank directly into each of our accounts. If we're lucky, that'll happen at midnight tonight."

"Probably going to happen at midnight Zurich Mean Time. I think they call that Zulu hour." Truth was Riker preferred his checks and cash how he liked his books—good old-fashioned papyrus. It was tangible. He could feel it and smell. He could also fold it and tuck it away for a rainy day. Or, God forbid, dogear a page to come back to when he was ready. The latter example, however, being a near capital offense worthy of a solid tongue-lashing from his late mother.

Tara whispered, "Let's adjust our plan, Lee. Get out of Middletown and take Mom wherever it is you promised to take her. We can reschedule with Jimmy."

Riker peered over the seatback. First he saw the NRA bag, its front bulging out unnaturally. Then his attention was drawn to the nearby strip mall where a person was emerging from around the corner of the furthest darkened establishment. Looked to be a man. Late twenties or maybe mid-thirties. Just jeans and a tee shirt and a mop of red hair bouncing with each stilted step. *Still a little drunk from a wild Saturday night out?* If the fella *was* walking home at this early hour, he surely wasn't dressed for it.

"Is that a partier going home? Or is it one of those things you're calling a *zombie?*" he whispered.

Tara pressed her face to the glass. "Can't tell," she answered.

As if the redhead had somehow heard the whispered query through window glass and from across the forty-some-odd foot divide, he halted mid-stride and his head commenced a slow swivel toward the idling SUV. He stood rooted for a beat. Glaring. Seemingly in thought. Then he simply jerked into action. Stepping off the short walk fronting the dry cleaning enterprise, his jaw dropped and arms rose until they were near horizontal to the pocked and pitted parking lot.

There had been no flash of recognition on his face. He was still one moment, then in full locomotion the next, the stilted steps quickly becoming a semi-stumbling shuffle. Once momentum was established, the flail of arms and legs found a bit of rhythm and the stumbling shuffle became a stilted half-sprint.

Bolt! was the first thing that popped into Riker's mind.

Tara, however, was the one who voiced it. "It's a *Bolt!* Let's go, Lee!"

"Seems to be the ongoing theme," replied Riker. He turned back and regarded Steve-O. Locked eyes with the man. "Hang on, buddy. I'm getting us out of here."

Hearing that, Steve-O broke out in a near perfect rendition of *We Gotta Get Out of This Place*, the Animals' hit song from 1965. And just as he was finishing up the refrain in which the ultimatum was declared, the force from the SUV's rapid acceleration threw him back in his seat and he stopped singing.

Turning and cutting across the four-lane in the direction of the I-69 overpass, Riker looked to Tara. "I've got a bad feeling that Chesterfield and Daleville are caught up in a widening perimeter."

"Why?" she asked.

"Because their first attempt at quarantine has failed," answered Riker.

"What do we do now? Where do we go?" She drew a breath and exhaled sharply. "And how are we supposed to get there if all of the roads are blocked?"

"Calm down, Sis. What's your navigation gizmo have to say?"

Tara pressed buttons below the eight-inch color touch screen, causing it to come to life. The word *MyLink* appeared dead center on the display. The digitally rendered logo remained frozen there for a tick as the thing booted up. When the home screen finally replaced the logo, she tapped a virtual button and brought up a detailed map of Middletown. Though it was zoomed out so far that individual city blocks were the size of a Tic-Tac, the spider web of red lines representing the surrounding streets and nearby freeway were clearly evident.

She zoomed in so that only their immediate vicinity filled the screen. Apparently the navigation unit wasn't communicating with the global positioning satellites orbiting overhead. Whereas the solid red lines overlaid on both the interstate and four-lane bisecting it were indicative of a traffic jam to be avoided at all costs, as Riker slowed the SUV to a walking speed dead center on the cement span, the scene on I-69 below totally contradicted this.

Tara gripped the grab bar near her head and lifted herself up in order to get a better look at her surroundings. "Where is everybody?" she said to no one in particular.

"At church?" joked Riker as he made a quick visual recon of all four points of the compass.

Sitting on corners diagonal from each other and nearly casting their shadows on the interstate's ramps, both the Travel Inn and Budget Inn's yellow-lined parking lots were mostly devoid of vehicles. Off Tara's right shoulder he saw the distinctive towering red roof of a Pizza Hut rising up from the center of a lot that *was* totally empty. The darkened sign came across as mostly dull red in the flat light of morning. The store's usually tinted windows were darker than normal.

No one home, he thought.

Panning left, he saw a completely empty I-69 stretching away to the south. Craning to see around the left side A-pillar, he followed the six strips of oil-stained gray asphalt with his eyes as they disappeared underneath the overpass and then picked them up off the right front fender and continued walking his gaze down their laser-straight length as they spooled off to an eventual rendezvous with the horizon far off to the north. Strangely, there were no vehicles approaching from either direction. More importantly, contrary to what the navigation unit indicated, there were no static vehicles anywhere to be seen. Nothing was parked in the breakdown lanes. Nothing took up space on the shoulders or ramps. There was nothing keeping him from reversing to the entry-ramp and taking them all north toward what he guessed would be a military checkpoint somewhere out there beyond Middletown's city limits.

A cold chill wracked Tara's body. "This is damn eerie," she said, looking directly at her brother. "I never remember seeing the I-69 so desolate. Even at three in the morning coming back from the clubs in Fort Wayne there was *some* traffic."

Riker said, "I'm guessing the governor sent the National Guard to block the interstates and state routes last night while the contractors were doing their thing at the so-called inoculation centers." He made a sweeping motion left to right. "That would explain this."

"That's what I was afraid of," said Tara. "Means we'll have to find a road they're not monitoring."

Steve-O appeared between the seats, forearms framing his face, elbows planted on the seatbacks.

Voice full of innocence, he asked, "What's up?"

"We're just trying to figure out where to take you," replied Riker. Turning his attention to Tara, he added, "There's got to be someone with authority left in Middletown. A church might work. Or maybe the VFW. They don't close for anything. That'd be as safe a place as any to leave him."

Tara shot Riker an incredulous look. She opened her mouth to speak, but Steve-O beat her to the punch by voicing exactly what she was thinking.

Looking directly at Riker, head starting a slow side-to-side wag, Steve-O said, "Hellooo ... I'm sitting right here. And I don't want to go to either of those places." Head still shaking slowly, he asked, "Can we go to the Opry instead?"

Tara made a face. She wanted nothing to do with country music at the moment. After a brief pause, she said, "We're going north, Steve-O. Lee promised our mom we'd take her someplace special."

Three minutes had already slipped into the past with the Chevy's big V8 idling and burning gas. Though Riker couldn't see the needle moving, he imagined the fuel level in the tank dropping steadily as they sat there jawing.

Steve-O thrust his arm horizontal between the seats, pointer finger extended. "Fire," he said. "Down, down, down into a burning ring of fire ..."

Riker pulled from the curb, sped past a darkened *Wendy's* fast food joint, and then stopped the SUV at an intersection below a nonfunctioning traffic control light.

"There," said Steve-O insistently.

"I may need glasses," said Riker. "Tara?"

Again with the one-armed pullup on the grab bar to gain a better vantage, Tara stared over the hood. Sure enough, up ahead and on the right, she saw a plume of smoke rising from the roof of a two-story home. It looked pencil-thin from this distance and was dissipating quickly. She had no idea how their new friend saw the smoke from two blocks back looking through the near pop-bottle-lenses of his glasses.

The longer she looked, the less she knew. Sure there was smoke, but she couldn't immediately tell if it was wafting from the chimney or somewhere on the far side of the house.

There were no firetrucks with flashing red and orange lights on scene.

"I can't tell if it's on fire or that's smoke from the chimney," she conceded.

"No telling if our names were logged into some database last night. Which means we should at all costs avoid contact with the authorities," said Riker just as two people emerged from the home, descended the short stack of stairs, and shuffled across their lawn. A half-beat after they made the sidewalk, licks of flame rose above the roofline at the rear of the structure.

Sounding satisfied, Steve-O said, "Told you. Burning ring of fire." He punctuated the statement with a soft *harumph*.

"June and now Johnny," said Riker. "Can't leave those folks to fend for themselves." He eased off the brake and drove toward the worsening blaze. Save for a lone Humvee crossing an intersection a half-dozen blocks beyond the burning home, the streets all around were quiet and devoid of both foot and vehicular traffic.

As the Suburban crossed the intersection one block prior to the burning structure, Riker saw several things happening simultaneously. The elderly homeowners were both taking actions to save what he assumed to be their home. The woman, blue hair in a bun and wearing a long housecoat, was furiously stabbing a finger at the phone in her hand. Meanwhile, the man had unspooled a garden hose and was directing a weak stream of water toward the roof.

In his left side vision, Riker saw a flash of red and white. The sudden and unexpected burst of movement drew his attention from the couple half a block distant to his side mirror, where he saw a twenty-something man bounce off a parked car near the previous intersection. Though the mirror didn't translate everything, the clumsy loping strides and the way its arms didn't quite work in unison with its legs was all he needed to see to make up his mind.

He said, "We have another *Bolt!* It's on my side."

Chanting, "Monster, monster, monster," Steve-O planted a palm on his glasses and disappeared into the back seat.

Lowering her window a few inches, Tara said, "Run it over."

"Yeah, Sis. Brilliant idea," said Riker. "Then we can add vehicular manslaughter to the list of stuff they can already hang on us. I'd like to stay out of prison."

Tara looked away from the elderly couple long enough to say, "You were a soldier. An effin combat veteran, Lee."

Slowing the three-ton rig with a hard stab of the brakes, Riker said, "I was a glorified truck driver, Tara. Chauffeured brass here and there, basically. Hell, garbage guys in Chiraq have probably dodged more bullets than me."

"You lost a leg."

"And then some. Still doesn't make me a war hero."

The frail-looking elderly woman was now aware of the black vehicle jamming to a lurching halt at the curb a couple of yards from her. Mouth forming a silent O, the woman held the phone out in front of her and shrugged—age-old semaphore for *this thing is useless.*

And that's how Tara received it. Hanging her head out the window, she said, "No service. I know. It's not safe for you two out here ... "

Though its reflection was still small in the wing mirror, the Bolt was close enough that Riker could clearly see its pale face contorting. A guttural grunting and the swish of its red windbreaker reached Riker's ears at about the same time Tara was urging the couple to get in the station wagon in their driveway and leave Middletown.

Once fixated solely on the occupants of the big black SUV, as soon as the Bolt was behind the static Chevy and caught sight of the elderly couple on the passenger's side, all of its attention shifted to them.

The woman pursed her lips and dropped her phone. Her eyes did a sort of wild three-step, jerking from Tara to the growling man then to her husband, who was just realizing the seriousness of his situation.

Caught between the proverbial rock and hard place, the elderly man froze in place with the stream from the hose directed on the house and his eyes glued to the hundred and fifty some odd pounds of rage barreling down on his wife.

The takedown was instantaneous and full of violence like nothing Riker had ever seen. Like a clip from the NFL's greatest sacks, the Bolt had launched at the woman from a couple of yards out as if it were Lawrence Taylor and she a quarterback in his crosshairs.

The pair rolled head over heels, coming to rest with the Bolt atop the woman and a sizeable hunk of her flesh already in its maw and quivering as it chewed and shook its head side to side, animal-like. Blood sluiced from the severed veins and capillaries dangling from the meat rent from the woman's neck. It painted the beast's torn white tee shirt a color complimentary to the red windbreaker.

Tara said, "God no," under her breath, then yelled at the man, urging him with shaky hands and a wavering voice to get inside the Suburban.

After receiving the blow that would have leveled a fit adult, the elderly woman hadn't let out so much as a whimper. She had curled up into a fetal ball and remained still as her lifeblood formed a growing black pool around her head and shoulders.

In the Suburban's back seat, Steve-O had done the same, only upright, drawing his legs up to his chest and wrapping his arms around both shins.

Riker had his door halfway open and was negotiating his leg out of the footwell when the elderly man turned achingly slow to his right and did the unthinkable—turned the stream from the hose on the Bolt.

Before Riker could set foot on the pavement, the poorly thought-out move backfired horribly on the elderly man. Swallowing the last of its meaty *prize*, tee shirt now tie-dyed by the mix of blood and water, the Bolt rose and locked its shark-eyed gaze on the man. If the thing had any idea the man was pleading for his life, it didn't show. Hunched over slightly, it stalked toward the man with the hose. The advance was purposeful and without pause. Like a lion locked onto wounded prey, seemingly oblivious to the water stream, the Bolt walked against it, causing it to fan out in all directions before splashing down on the lawn. With a yard still to cover, the Bolt leaped, wrapped up the man in a bear hug and dragged him to ground. With the looming house groaning from heat-affected studs contracting and warping as they burned, the Bolt, totally oblivious to anything save for the flailing man making an angel in the ankle-high grass, bit down in nearly the same location on the neck as it had the woman and reared up with a similar-sized hunk of flesh clenched in its blood stained-teeth.

Smoke was now billowing from the street-facing windows.

Tara said, "Gonna leave behind the *next* gun you find?"

Stomach queasy from what he'd just witnessed, Riker drew his leg back inside the truck and slammed his door, throwing the locks as he did so.

Heart heavy from his inability to change the outcome of the situation, he slow-rolled past the ongoing scene of carnage, taking a quantum of solace from the soft warble of sirens approaching from afar.

Riker let his gaze roam the surrounding homes. Saw a man peeking through the parted curtains of the Tudor to the left of the elderly couple's burning home. That he didn't come to the couple's aid really pissed Riker off. So much so that the dull throb started up again behind his eyes and he actually contemplated slamming the transmission into Drive, marching up to the house, kicking in the door, and dragging the waste of skin out and beating him within an inch of his life. However, leaving the man broken on the lawn to be the Bolt's next course, as satisfying as it may be, would only add to his growing list of crimes and misdemeanors.

Searching for the source of the siren, Riker looked up and down the street one last time.

Nothing.

Though he despised people who stood on the sidelines rubbernecking when someone was in duress, he found it hard to believe that the blaze had drawn not a single person. Nor were there cars with lookie-loos at the wheel sliding up to the SUV and breathlessly asking questions to satisfy their morbid curiosities.

The Bolt was now ears deep into the old man's ribcage. Its blond hair was now blood-drenched and sticking to its head.

Causing Riker to start, Steve-O showed up between the seats unannounced. Eyeing the feeding Bolt, he asked, "Aren't you going to help them?"

"Nothing we can do for them now," answered Tara.

Spinning the steering wheel counterclockwise, Riker said, "She's right, Steve-O. We tried. They didn't listen." His hunch as he cut a U-turn and drove back toward the deserted freeway was that things in Middletown were going to get far worse before they got better.

If they got better.

Chapter 37

For Tony, the walk from 4WTC to the Broad Street Station where he always caught the Jamaican Line to Queens truly was a trudge. But not in the sense of the word where one is following a purposeful course with a clear terminus worth getting to. Not today. For Tony, who had just witnessed something no human should ever have to, this was the solemn slog variety of trudge. The type of leaden-footed trek that saw him navigating pedestrian-choked sidewalks, crossing streets teeming with tourists and people going to work on a weekend, and then boarding a subway car packed in like a sardine only to be delivered not to a mansion in the Hamptons but to a small one-bedroom apartment full of dust-covered mementos, ghosts of squandered opportunities, and solemn memories of days gone by.

What was in reality a two-minute walk covering all of four blocks ended up taking Tony fifteen minutes to complete. And when he made it to the bottom of the Broad Street Station stairs and was wrapped in the embrace of the cool air circulating the subterranean subway stop, his train arrived almost instantaneously.

Aboard the car were people coming home from jobs similar to his, only conducted during off hours, of which, in New York City, there were very few. There was only a small sliver of time during which he felt the city was idle. The time between when the bars closed and sunrise. Shadow workers is what he called the folks who kept the city alive while the majority of her nearly nine million citizens were snugged away in their beds.

He took a seat across from a woman dressed in khakis and a light-blue Polo shirt. She had a heavy winter coat slung over one arm. She was still wearing a plastic nametag that read

189

Charlotte. Below her name, emblazoned in red, was the name of the outfit she worked for. Merry Maids might have sounded good to a focus group; however, the bags under Charlotte's eyes, coupled with her downturned mouth, told a different story. Just when Tony had finished his quick recon of the car and parked his gaze dead ahead, Charlotte furrowed her brow and pointed at the air above his head.

Realizing he was still in uniform, armed with his Taser and sidearm and wearing a hat indoors—a no-no to the older set—Tony acknowledged her with a nod, concealed his weapons with his windbreaker, and removed the ball cap.

Peering down at the hat sitting in his lap, Tony saw the true source of Charlotte's dismay. There, stuck to the mesh portion of the ball cap, was a silver-dollar-sized shard of skull with several inches of his dead friend's brunette locks still attached to the pale flap of scalp clinging to it. He guessed it had hitched a ride there when he embraced the dead woman. It had been a spur of the moment gesture that came on the heels of him kneeling next to her body and seeing straightaway she was dead.

Repulsed, Tony concealed the human detritus by rolling it up inside the hat, an action that earned him a funny look from Charlotte and brought back the mental image of Victoria's broken and bent body he feared was indelibly burned into his memory. As a result of the instant recall, he caught a whiff of the coppery smell of her spilled blood. Then he was hearing again the murmurs and the sound of someone retching that filtered from the crowd as he took that knee near the body.

Tony was mentally back in the train car less than a second after experiencing the gut-wrenching flash of total recall. Hat still in hand, he stood on shaky legs and made his way to an empty bench near the side door. He sat down hard and leaned his upper body against the grimy beige wall. Feeling deep in his bones the subtle vibrations of the wheels passing over seams in the track, he tucked the balled-up hat in the gap between the wall and seat in front of him.

While Tony's aim with the sneaky move had been to get the hat and its cargo out of sight and out of mind—he had to settle for just one out of the two. For try as he might, he couldn't let go of poor Victoria.

So young and vibrant.

And now gone forever.

Tony was mostly alone during the second half of his trip. Tourists and locals came and went in Brooklyn and Queens. One rider, who'd been a constant fixture on the car since the Canal Street stop when Tony had switched seats, had had her face buried in her smartphone the entire ride.

Twenty minutes after leaving the Broad Street Station, the J Line rolled to a smooth stop at the Crescent Street platform, the doors slid open. and the familiar sights, sounds, and smells of a city just building a head of steam on an unseasonably warm and cloudless Sunday flooded inside the car.

As a smattering of riders collected belongings and moms drew their kids near to them, the twenty-something with the smartphone blurted an expletive and threw her head back. Thrusting an extended middle finger at the glossy screen she'd been fixated on for the duration of the ride, she opened the shoulder bag draped across her thighs and rather unceremoniously chucked the device inside.

Seeing this, Tony checked his phone and saw NO SERVICE displayed prominently across the top of the LCD screen. Remembering the first responders he'd called to 4WTC immediately after discovering Victoria, he shifted in his seat and looked toward Manhattan. In between the buildings flitting by he saw snippets of blue. Lifting his gaze by a degree revealed a sky marred by a drifting black smudge.

James Merkur drained his fourth tumbler of Johnny Walker Blue and went to pour himself another.

Voice filtering through the speakers, the pilot said, "Twenty minutes to Logan. It may take a couple of minutes to be cleared for landing."

"We pay a lot of money to keep the backup jet there," bellowed Underhill. Voice softening, he added, "We *should* have priority. Work on the controllers. Do what you can."

Cheeks flushed red and slurring a little, Merkur said, "I want that G6 spooling up and ready to receive us as soon as we land."

Underhill took his eyes off the countryside scrolling by and regarded Merkur. He'd found the colors of fall calming considering the circumstances. When he saw his boss's flushed face and hunched shoulders, the severity of what they were all caught up in came flooding back.

"Flight plan is set," said Underhill. "The crew and plane will be ready."

As Merkur slumped back in the plush leather seat, the Bell 429 made a slight course correction that presented a fine view of the Atlantic out the starboard-side windows.

Having taken in the conversation without comment, Carson shifted in his seat and locked eyes with Merkur, who seemed to be melting into the seat next to him.

Carson said, "We're *all* in the shit up to our eyeballs now. That's why I respectfully ask that you come clean with me, sir."

"What is it," grumbled Merkur.

In the aft-facing seat opposite Merkur, Underhill's head began to swing slowly side to side.

Ignoring this, Carson tapped the aluminum boxes at his feet and asked about the Bravo iteration of Romero.

"Don't," said Underhill.

Merkur raised a hand.

Underhill sat back and looked out his window.

"What is Romero B and why not just let the fire eat it all up? Then we'd have plausible deniability."

"Bravo is the failed Alpha strain weaponized." He went on to detail Operation Peasant Overlord. Finished, he tilted his head back and downed three fingers of Scotch in one gulp.

In the aft-facing seat opposite Carson, his right-hand man, Frederick Pavel, ran a gloved hand through his graying goatee and cast a thoughtful gaze toward Carson.

"Why infect North Korea?" asked Carson.

Underhill was squirming in his seat.

Bending forward, Merkur snatched up the box labeled Romero B and threw the latches. He opened the lid and spun the box to face Carson. "The contents of just one of those dispersed over their nuclear production facility will start a chain reaction of mayhem that the Hermit Nation will attribute to an attempted coup. The dispersal of Bravo over a select number of their bases will further add to the illusion and point the finger of guilt back a government known for dabbling in bio weapons. Hell, their leader lets them starve by the millions while he diverts money to the nuke and ICBM program. Ultimately China will come to this conclusion and seal their borders."

Carson looked to his man then back to Merkur. "What happens to Bravo, then. Will it burn out quickly?"

"It'll be contained in their bases. Eventually the North Korean people will have their country back."

"That'll denuclearize them for sure," quipped Carson. Tone in his voice taking a sharp edge, he went on, "You can't sell this as an *altruistic* venture. I don't believe it for one second. Neither will the judge before he sends us all to prison for life."

Merkur gripped the armrests and sat up straight in his seat. "You're not seeing the big picture, *Mr. Peet.* Who do you think they'll call on to provide the cure? Zen Pharma, that's who they'll call." A sloppy half-smile ghosted across his face.

"One problem," said Carson as he spun the box so the interior faced Merkur. "A canister is missing."

Chapter 38

Unable to do anything to change the outcome, Riker had taken one last long look at the Bolt ripping flesh and entrails from the splayed-out old man, then sped off to where the Suburban was now parked on the overpass bookended by motels and facing the Pizza Hut and strip mall. In the minutes since they'd last set eyes on the interstate, nothing had changed. Just the same ghostly silent stretch of blacktop spooling out north and south.

The furniture store across the parking lot from the Pizza Hut, however, was a different story. A panel van was now backed up to the glass front doors. The massive plate window left of the doors had been reduced to pebbled glass on the ground. Three younger-looking men were carting smaller pieces of furniture from the store to the van.

Ignoring the looting taking place what amounted to a couple of blocks away and in broad daylight, Tara regarded Riker. "That was effin murder back there." Body shaking subtly, she leaned forward against her shoulder belt and buried her face in her hands. "The way he moved was *nothing* like the others."

"You're wrong about that, Sis. That was *exactly* how the one inside the tunnel was moving. You were behind me and hugging the door by the time he saw us and hit that second gear. He, it, *Bolt* ... whatever you want to call the bastard, rushed me the same way the one rushed that elderly lady."

"Not *that* fast, though," said Tara. She was biting her lip when she took her hands away from her face. She directed her gaze to the side mirror and watched the plume of smoke roiling up from the distant house.

Looking to Tara, Riker said, "Cute nicknames for whatever that man had become aside, what we just witnessed back there was Ma Nature at work. Call it natural selection. Call it whatever you want. Simple fact of the matter is that *we* are no longer the only ones atop the food chain."

Steve-O reappeared in the empty space between the front seat headrests. Looking to Riker, he said with a put-on Native American baritone, "Who is 'we,' paleface?" He chuckled and glanced at Tara, who appeared unamused.

"Better be careful with that kind of talk around my sister, Steve-O. She can't take a joke."

Tara shot a frosty glare Riker's way. "We stole their land," she said. "Gave them blankets laced with smallpox. Shall I go on?"

Clearly expecting a different reaction than the one playing out before him, Steve-O said, "Who is 'we'? Do you have a mouse in your pocket?"

Riker looked away from the looting taking place and flicked his eyes to the rearview. Still no flashing blue and reds of a police cruiser, or red and yellows of emergency fire and medical.

Nothing.

Riker began to believe they were truly alone within Middletown's city limits. Tearing his eyes from the smoke marring the sky above the fully involved structure fire, he turned and met Steve-O's gaze.

"That's more like it, Steve-O," said Riker casually. "Tara ... she prefers jokes of the banal variety. Sanitized. Stripped of anything pointing to ethnicity, religious bent, or sexual orientation."

"*Sex*," said Steve-O as a smile creased his face. Drawing in a sharp breath, he melted back into the Suburban's cavernous interior.

Tara stared daggers at Riker. Whispering, she said, "I'm pretty sure people with Steve-O's condition don't understand nuance like we do. I bet he's just repeating something he heard someone else say."

Craning to see over his shoulder, Riker said, "The mouse in the pocket crack was real good, Steve-O. I'm stealing that one." Off his right shoulder he felt the heavy bass kick of rap music but couldn't see the source. Simultaneously, he heard the distinct metronomic *thwop* of rotor blades beating the air. Looking over the hood, he spotted far off in the distance a pair of dual rotor helicopters. The way they were moving, slow and low to the ground on a diagonal taking them away from the overpass, conveyed no sense of urgency. It struck Riker that this was all some kind of drill to them.

The reality of the situation was people had been lured into several makeshift evacuation sites scattered about the small city the night before. And even worse: Just blocks away, an elderly couple had been taken down, killed in the worst manner, their flesh consumed by a madman Riker had no clear explanation for.

"Stealing is bad," said Steve-O. "Did you steal this truck?"

Before Riker could answer, Steve-O was singing the lyrics to yet another Cash song in which an autoworker smuggled car parts home from an assembly line in a lunchbox. Halfway through the first chorus, Riker interrupted, saying, "I borrowed it, Steve-O. There's a big difference."

As the noise from the helicopters dissipated and they became specks merging with the ground clutter far off on the horizon, the thumping of music emanating from a high-powered stereo was becoming more pronounced.

There was a whirring noise and the window behind Tara began to open.

"Be alert with that window down," said Riker. "No telling when a Bolt might appear."

"Don't see a Bolt. But there's a car coming. A red one. Real fast from over there," said Steve-O. He had taken his hat off and was pointing south down I-69 with his head and upper body hanging outside the SUV.

With the bass heavy song infiltrating the Suburban's interior, Riker found the master switch to Steve-O's window by feel. "Watch yourself, Steve-O."

Seeing Steve-O pull his head and arm inside, Riker pulsed the window up.

Tara turned in her seat and picked up the red car tearing their way on the freeway below. She'd recently seen one like it peel out and leave rubber on the street in front of the MU biology building. Only this car was lipstick red and sporting dual black stripes that ran from hood to trunk.

But a red blur as it disappeared from view beyond the far overpass rail, the car emerged a split second later on Riker's side.

Even inside the Suburban with the windows closed, the engine roar echoing and rising from below easily overpowered the music that had preceded it.

Steve-O launched back into the Cash tune and soon was rattling off the makes and models of cars likely found only tucked away safely in a collector's garage or rotting away in a rural field or some farmer's barn.

Riker squinted and watched the car emerge from the shadows and seem to pick up speed—if that was at all possible considering its jet-plane-like rate of approach. Though he considered himself far from expert at calculating the speed of an object in motion, to him, it looked as if the muscle car was doubling the posted speed limit. *Damn*, he thought. *Pushing one-thirty, throttle wide open, and no* policia *in sight. What I wouldn't give to do that one day.*

The Dodge Challenger raced off north, shrinking to Hot-Wheels-scale before his eyes. In the couple of seconds he had eyes on the retreating vehicle, he noted the horizontal taillight cluster parked below an abbreviated trunk-mounted wing. As the car's big throaty V8 gulped air and the revs screamed up the power band, the glint of sun off the softball-sized chrome fuel cap caught his eye and confirmed his suspicion.

"That *was* a Hellcat," he said to nobody in particular. "One day …" The last part was uttered in a voice low and betraying a touch of longing.

"So let's see where she's going," chided Tara.

Riker slipped the Chevy into drive and cast a sidelong glance at her. "Who taught you it's proper to refer to a car with a female pronoun?"

"I was talking about the *driver*," shot Tara. "Had to be a woman. The color of the car is a dead giveaway."

Riker pulled away from the guardrail and drove down the center of the overpass as if he owned the road. Steve-O was still riffing about his Frankenstein automobile when Riker hooked a left and they entered the deserted freeway at a fraction of the speed of the car that had just blazed by. A car that, strangely, he had a burning desire to see up close.

Chapter 39

Near Logan International Airport – Boston, Massachusetts

"That fucking bitch," said Merkur, veins on his neck bulging. The box labeled Romero A was open on the cabin floor. "She stole one of each."

Having already spoken of what happened to the vial of Romero A, Carson asked Underhill what he thought about the missing canister.

"I think she put it in her bag," he answered. "She was acting strange. Wanting to go home. She asked me if she could leave on a couple of separate occasions."

"What are the ramifications if it was in her bag?"

Underhill looked to Merkur. The Zen CEO was slumped in his seat and snoring.

"If the canister was breached, anyone present is infected. All first responders are infected."

"A good deal of them will be dead or dying by now."

Underhill nodded. "In ten to twelve hours the first wave will have all turned." He swallowed hard. "If it was breached, all of Manhattan will be a no go zone by end of day tomorrow."

"It's an island," said Carson. "It'll be contained. Won't it?"

Pavel said, "Too many tunnels and bridges."

"Considering Alpha was released in Indiana this morning, at the first sign of infection the city will go on lockdown. You can bet they'll attribute it to a dirty bomb. Who they attribute it to is anyone's guess."

Carson looked at Pavel. "We're coming with you, Underhill. I don't think Merkur is in any shape to veto the motion."

"You're needed in New York. There's still ZP employees unaccounted for."

Carson merely smiled and shook his head.

"Stay onboard and get back to New York. We'll call with instructions."

Hand resting on the pistol on his hip, Carson said, "That's not how it's going to go down."

Without warning the helicopter shuddered and leaned hard left, obviously taking some kind of evasive maneuver.

Merkur jerked awake and demanded to know what was happening.

Already focused on something outside the starboard window, Underhill said, "We're being shadowed by a pair of black helicopters. No markings."

Looking out the port-side window, Pavel said, "There's another one about seven o' clock to us. She's hanging way back." One gloved hand went to his sidearm. With the other he cinched his lap belt tighter.

"Our clearance to land at general aviation has been rescinded," said the pilot over the shipboard comms. "We're being ordered to divert to Beverly Regional. It's a two-strip designated as a reliever. It's about five miles northeast of Logan."

"Ignore them," barked Merkur. "Going there with these helicopters dogging us would be akin to walking into a dark alley with muggers on your tail. I'm not a stupid man. Put us down as close to the Gulfstream as you can."

The pilot balked at first. Carson shoving a Sig Sauer semi-auto pistol in his face changed everything.

As the Bell banked to port and started to descend, the pair of helicopters closed in fast, taking station off the starboard side.

Gesturing out the window at the G6, Merkur said, "Right there by the fuel truck."

Still under duress of the lethal lead variety, the pilot nosed the Bell toward the open patch of tarmac.

All around the general aviation facility, ground support vehicles zipped back and forth. Close by, a trio of jumbo jets were lined up nose to tail with maybe a hundred feet separating them. The shades were up and there was movement behind the windows of all three. Judging by the colorful flash on their massive tails, they were all bound for international destinations.

Holding up the procession and turned with its nose aimed at the runway entrance was a stark white jumbo jet. Emblazoned on the tail in a deep red and floating above the letters *JAL* was a stylized crane. Painted above the row of windows in bold black lettering, the words *Japan Airlines* ran from the cockpit to the front edge of the wings—nearly two-thirds the length of the bird.

"I'm being reprimanded by the tower," shouted the pilot.

"Land," growled Carson, the boxy black pistol still menacing the man.

Just as the Bell side-slipped past the waiting jets, a third helicopter came roaring in from the right and alit in the only spot near the Gulfstream that would accommodate the larger Bell.

Words dripping with contempt, the pilot said, "What now, sir?"

Merkur said, "Put us down near the British Airways jet. We'll go the rest of the way on foot."

"You won't get there before security is on you," replied the pilot.

"We have an ace up our sleeve," said Merkur. He looked to Pavel, then met Carson's gaze. "You two deal with the helicopter when we're getting close to the G6."

Underhill lifted the aluminum boxes off the floor. Keeping hold of the handles, he balanced them on his knees and braced for landing.

The helicopter settled softly forty feet off the tip of the British Airways port-side wing.

As the door slid open, hot air tinged heavily with jet exhaust followed the howl of spooling engines into the cabin.

Undeterred, the two smaller helicopters landed side-by-side off the Bell's port side and men in black with automatic rifles spilled onto the tarmac. They ducked and sprinted toward the Bell, covering half the distance by the time Carson and Pavel were taking a knee on the tarmac near the nose of their helicopter.

Out of the corner of his eye, Carson saw the pair of executives angling away from the Bell's starboard-side. He saw the half-dozen muzzle flashes but didn't hear the reports. The air-robbing impacts of a trio of 62-grain hunks of lead entering his body center of mass confirmed what his eyes had detected. And as he fell face first to the tarmac, the energy behind the speeding projectiles started his upper torso spinning to the right. In turn, Carson's head followed. What he saw in the seconds before the pain caused him to curl up in a fetal position was at once satisfying and greatly disturbing.

Witnessing his boss and the morbidly overweight Underhill both take as many bullets to the body as he feared he had was the satisfying aspect. Seeing the case in the latter man's possession shredded by bullets and spill punctured canisters to the tarmac didn't sit well with him. For should he somehow survive and be whisked away for interrogation by whomever the shooters represented, he wouldn't be long for the world thanks to the Bravo agent being released.

Spread by the Bell's still spinning rotors, the Romero agent was dispersed to all points. In seconds the HVAC equipment atop the nearby concourses were sucking in microscopic particles and distributing them inside to be breathed in by untold numbers of workers and passengers. And unbeknownst to the aircrew and passengers aboard the four jetliners beginning to taxi toward the runway—nearly a thousand souls total—Merkur's criminal negligence had also doomed every single one of them.

Chapter 40

Tony exited the Jamaica Line one stop prior to his usual stop. After the morning he'd had, he felt the blocks' long walk to his brownstone through the neighborhood he had grown up in might help to purge his mind of the events of the day. Nothing doing. As he walked and dodged an inordinate amount of people stopped in place and fiddling with their smart phones, his mind was back at work. He imagined that the fire crews called from the four stations situated near 4WTC had already knocked the fire down and were trundling up the stairways in their heavy gear. While the attacks on 9/11 had occurred early enough on a workday that the number of lives lost were cut way short due to the thousands of workers still in transit to the towers, the opposite was true at 4WTC. However, though the events had occurred mid-morning, it *was* Sunday. Ninety-nine percent of the tower's workers were probably making plans for lunch at home, or attending a Knicks preseason game, or, what Tony was eager to do—drinking before noon. Then there was his insider knowledge: He had checked in less than a hundred workers prior to the tragedy and follow-on fire. The loss of life, if there was any beyond Victoria's, he guessed would be minimal. Could probably count on two hands how many were still on the upper floors when he had started his solemn walk to the subway platform.

The financial blow would be nothing compared to the towers falling. On the other hand, the blow to the builder's ego would be catastrophic. How in the hell does the fire suppression system in a brand-spanking-new building fail? As if privy to information Tony was not, his stomach broadcast a loud prolonged growl.

He patted his ample midsection. "Trying to tell me something, fella?"

The action drew a funny look from a passing couple likely headed to one of the dozens of Starbucks peppering Brooklyn and Queens. It seemed to Tony that if the company didn't slow their eastward expansion, they would be forced to open mini Starbucks *inside* of the already established stores.

Other than the long gone couple, people on the streets were carrying on as if nothing had happened on Manhattan. Sure, the fire wasn't being attributed to terrorism, yet. That it was not caused by hijacked jetliners screaming in fast and low off the Hudson was a big part of it. The rest Tony attributed to normalcy bias. New Yorkers had been there, done that. Multiple times, in fact. And once a person had watched the thing unfolding on their doorsteps in real life, nothing else quite compared.

Tony felt naked walking the last few blocks to his place without his lunchbox and thermos in hand. Stomach still making noises, he stopped in front of a local bakery and looked in the window at the pastries on display. There were pillowy sugar-coated donuts, plump muffins dotted with blueberries, croissants drizzled with chocolate, and rolls in all shapes and sizes. He went inside and stood in a long line that looked stalled out at the moment.

There was the throaty rush of steam as a young barista converted fifty cents worth of ingredients into a five-dollar drink. The aroma of the beans in use started a tingling in the back of his throat. The case before him held scones and custard-filled items. Out of the blue a cough wracked his body. It originated deep within his lungs, and before he could bring a hand up to cover his mouth, the length of glass chest-high to him had mostly done its job.

His gaze fell first to the spittle dotting the glass top to bottom. There were rivulets of the stuff running to the black and white tiled floor. In one place a thick rope of snot had caught on the top of the sneeze shield and somehow ended up on the back side of the glass where it was just now beginning a slow-motion crawl to the baked goods below. Tony focused on the pancake-like pastries spewing raspberry filling from slits in their sides. In the next beat he was seeing the crushed and leaking body again and none of what was laid out within arm's reach looked appetizing. *Why commit suicide?* he thought to himself. As he turned and walked past patrons wearing disgusted looks, what he wanted more than anything was in a bottle in his cupboard, which, thankfully, was in his apartment less than a hundred steps away.

***

Scaling the steps to the front door of his stoop was akin to what Tony imagined Sir Edmund Hillary had gone through to summit Everest. Collecting his breath on the landing, he stared through the door's windows at yet another run of stairs disappearing upward to the shadow-filled upper landing. Wishing he had a Sherpa to help him the rest of the way, he unclipped the keys from his wide patrolman's belt and worked them into the lock. Rent being lower than most of the places for blocks around solely because there was no elevator in the three-story brick building, Tony had no choice but to suck it up and tackle the twenty-four individual eight-inch high mountains rising before him.

The landing servicing his apartment and one other was dimly lit by a single sixty-watt bulb hanging on a frayed cord. Though nothing like outside this time of year, the still air was cool and welcoming.

Tony used three different keys to open three different locks and went inside. He shrugged off his windbreaker and hung it on the hook affixed to the back of the door. He left his soft-soled shoes in a jumble in the hall and padded to the kitchen, where he reached into the cupboard and retrieved the bottle of Old Crow that had invaded his thoughts in the bakery. He carried the bottle and a tumbler taken from the drain board to the living room with him and plopped down on his faithful La-Z-Boy recliner. The only thing that had remained faithful for the duration of a thirty-nine year marriage recently gone by the wayside.

Picturing his wife and her new husband in their new multimillion dollar apartment in the Flatiron District of

Manhattan, he switched on the television and tuned to WGN out of Chicago. Though there was no sporting event going on at that moment, a replay of one was better than the macabre images that had taken residence in his head. Along with the booze, the game whose outcome he already knew would serve to help him forget the disparity between his and his ex's lives.

The last thing Tony remembered after kicking the footrest up and downing the first three-finger pour of Old Crow was the game on the screen bracketed by his tube-sock-covered feet going to commercial and the sound of sirens kicking up outside his window.

Chapter 41

Shortly after entering I-69 northbound, Riker slid the Suburban into the center lane. It was where he preferred to be. Always had been. The center lane gave you options. Though not worried about an IED like the one that stole his leg and left him with anger issues and prone to phantom feelings in the nonexistent limb, he wanted to be able to choose from multiple routes of egress should another fast mover such as the Dodge fill up his rearview mirror.

He pressed the accelerator pedal to the floor and felt the Suburban's front end rear up subtly. He shot a quick glance at the gauge cluster. Saw the needle sweep past sixty. Six seconds, he figured, had elapsed since leaving the entry-ramp. Not bad for a Soccer-Mom-mobile. As the rig leveled out and the hiss of the radials on grooved pavement began to infiltrate the cab, Riker glanced at the fuel gauge and saw that in the span of just a few minutes—many of them sitting inert with the engine idling—the red needle had dropped from three-quarters full to half. Maybe it had been his mind playing tricks on him, but nonetheless, in the short blip in time his eyes were focused on the gauge, he could have sworn he saw the indicator take a substantial dip closer toward Empty.

He pounded a palm on the wheel and cursed under his breath.

"What is it?" asked Tara.

"What's gas cost these days? Three fifty or so?"

"About that. Why?"

"Because unless the attorney honors the digital signature thingy and puts the transfer through as promised, I've got less than a hundred bucks to my name."

"I'm broke," said Steve-O. "Payday is next Friday."

Tara smiled at that and leaned over the center console to peek at the gauges. "I see your point," she said. "Don't sweat it. I've got a big wad of tips in my pocket."

How much could a barista make in tips, thought Riker as he did some math in his head, concluding that every eleven or so miles this big beast sucked down the equivalent of one of those foo-foo coffee drinks she whipped up so expertly.

Not much, is what he came up with before grudgingly admitting that taking her clown car might not have been such a bad idea.

Tara said nothing. One hand went to the A-pillar grab bar. The other she planted on the dash as she lifted off of her seat.

"What is it?"

"The red car. You can't see it?"

Riker shook his head. "I've become a little nearsighted in my old age."

Tara tore her eyes from the distant scene. "Thirty-eight is *old?*"

"I'm forty-five," said Steve-O matter-of-factly. "Richard Millhouse Nixon was president when Mom had me." He went quiet for a beat. When he spoke again he was waving twin peace signs between the seats and saying, "I am *not* a crook," in a voice eerily similar to that of the long-dead president.

"Better slow down," said Tara, her voice now wavering. "This won't stop like my car."

It's not an up-armored Humvee or bloated Land Cruiser skinned in Kevlar and fitted with inches-thick ballistic glass, thought Riker. *It's a production vehicle and should perform as such.*

But it didn't. Because what he didn't know was that the SUV was closer in weight and maneuverability to what he had been tasked with driving over in the Sandbox. Still, he remained calm and stood hard on the brakes, which started the speedometer needle on a rapid plunge south from the hundred-mile-per-hour hash.

The Suburban's nose dipped and the rear end waggled a bit.

"The hot rod is mangled—" began Tara.

"It's a muscle car. And jersey barriers will do that," interrupted Riker. "Under the overpass. Those are Humvees. And that boxy thing is an MRAP, if my eyes don't deceive me."

The Suburban was still moving at seventy miles per hour when Riker figured there was less than a football field's length—give or take an end zone—for him to get her stopped.

Fearing the pedal might break off under his weight, he applied more brake. The pulsing from the hard at work ABS system caused the pedal to kick back against his boot sole like a miniature jackhammer.

Seemingly oblivious to the reality of what was rushing up at them, Tara asked, "What's an MRAP?"

"Stands for mine-resistant armor protected. That one's a Cougar, I think. Didn't have them yet when I was over there."

"Might have saved your leg."

He flicked his eyes to the speedometer. Saw the needle sweep through sixty miles per hour.

"Might have saved more than that," he proffered. "We lost lots of guys to roadside bombs before the up-armor program kicked in. I lost too many buddies to the effin things."

The needle was passing fifty and almost to forty when soldiers dismounted the Humvee, stepped from the shadow of the overpass, and fanned out left and right of the crumpled red hulk.

Knuckles on both hands gone white, Tara said, "I see bullet holes in the windshield."

"Usually happens to folks who don't stop for roadblocks," said Riker. He almost added *Especially in the Sandbox* but held his tongue for fear that voicing it would bring those particularly horrific nightmares back to life.

"Somebody is in big trouble," crowed Steve-O from the back seat.

"Don't think they'll be getting any kind of punishment," said Riker in a funereal voice. "If they didn't catch a round before hitting the barriers, they died from the collision." He saw where the floor pan had buckled near vertical to the front seats. He imagined that the big-block Hemi had punched through the firewall and come to rest deep inside the passenger compartment.

When Tara had initially hollered for Riker to stop, they were barely two miles north of the Commerce Street overpass and less than a mile south of the one currently filling up the windshield.

Now, just seconds later, as the soldiers were taking up positions behind the third layer of barriers, they were close enough to see the whites of their eyes. Riker glanced at the needle. Saw it creeping slowly downward toward thirty. "Stop, you big bastard," he said through clenched teeth.

Bringing a monster like the Suburban down from over a hundred-plus-miles-per-hour in the distance allotted when they rounded the bend and Tara's order rang out was akin to landing and stopping a Navy Hornet on an aircraft carrier's deck. Only the Chevy had four disc brakes for stopping, not a tailhook hanging out back, nor the waiting arrestor cable and deck pendant to catch if it did.

With less than a hundred feet separating the Suburban's front bumper and the Challenger's jutting rear end, the ABS feedback ceased, the big rig came to a complete halt, and, consequently, the scenery all around snapped into sharp focus.

When all was said and done, the Suburban ended up cocooned by a roiling cloud of blue-white tire smoke and rocking on its springs several hundred feet closer to the wrecked Challenger than Riker would have liked. In short, they had bypassed the nearby off-ramp and were trapped on a run of highway blocked by a contingent of soldiers and cement barriers to the fore and an impenetrable run of traffic dividers to their left. And adding insult to injury, the Humvees parked broadside behind the barriers sprouted top-mounted Ma Deuce heavy machine guns, the MRAP was training some type of heavy weapon on them, and the dozen soldiers clad in tan camouflage were brandishing black rifles—at least two of which were aimed at the thin pane of curved glass directly in front of Riker's slackening face.

Chapter 42

The cloud of blue-white smoke that had come from the Suburban's overtaxed radials was mostly dissipated when an artificially amplified voice said: *"Turn off the motor and put your hands where we can see them."*

Tara ran her window down partway. Crisp air carrying a hint of death wafted in as she thrust her hands through the opening.

While Tara was busy complying, Riker was yanking the keys from the ignition and spinning the ignition key off the keyring. When he was finished, he threw the fob and ring full of keys to the road beside the SUV and stuck his hands out the window for all to see.

Tara asked, "Who are they?"

There was a whirring noise behind Riker's head. Remaining rigid in his seat, he said, "Slow movements, Steve-O. We wouldn't want to fall victim to the Indiana National Guard."

"That's the National Guard?" said Tara.

"Yep," replied Riker as a female soldier in full battle rattle—Kevlar helmet, bullet-proof plate carrier, MOLLE rig bulging with extra magazines—skirted the red car and began a slow walk toward the Suburban. On the outside she was ready for war. That much was clear. Her movements, however, told a different story. She was light on her feet, footsteps tentative, almost as if she were ready to drop the rifle and run away should someone holler *"Boo!"*

Riker moved his head to the right to see past the advancing soldier. What he saw assembled on the road behind her cemented his next move. For barely visible next to the MRAP's front end where she had been stationed before the loudspeaker belched the amplified orders was a waist-high mound of corpses. As if the Guard soldiers were working with some kind of a system, the unmoving bodies had been arranged with their heads all facing east. From his viewing angle, Riker saw jutting from the mound the scuffed soles of a dozen types of footwear ranging in sizes from toddler to adult. There were even a few bare feet, all pale and waxy and protruding from the mix. The sheer number of bodies stacked like cordwood shocked Riker into a momentarily silence, during which the reptilian part of his brain began sending the first jolt of adrenaline surging into his system. With the age-old fight-or-flight mechanism ramping up, he turned and regarded Tara with a thoughtful look.

"You think their orders are to shoot unarmed civilians?" she asked, the words coming rapid-fire and laced with incredulity.

Riker swallowed hard. "We're about to find out."

"We're going to run?"

"We may have no choice," said Riker. "But don't worry, Sis. If they don't gun us down here on the interstate, we'll be okay."

A look of horror ghosted across Tara's face.

"Those rigs are meant for tackling difficult terrain at slow speeds, not for mounting any kind of a high-speed pursuit. Plus," he assured her, "they're *behind* the barriers."

The soldier was now a dozen feet away. One gloved hand was raised, the other clutching her rifle.

"Keep your hands where I can see them."

"No shit. You've got the gun," muttered Tara, a half-beat prior to shooting her brother an accusatory glare and saying aloud, "They *all* have *guns*, Leland."

The soldier halved the distance to the Suburban, raised the rifle, and began a deliberate crab walk—her body open wide to the SUV and the muzzle never wavering. After looping counterclockwise around the SUV and taking a quick turkey peek through the smoked rear glass, she stopped near the passenger-side front wheel where getting a shot off at her would be complicated by the A-pillar and oversized wing mirror blocking the way.

Speaking out of the side of her mouth, Tara said, "I don't want to get shot, Leland. I have an idea. Let me talk to her."

Riker said nothing. He had already slipped the single key back into the ignition. His mind was made up the second he saw the drift of death beside the MRAP. As his eyes roamed the roadblock and the soldiers manning it, he was transported back to Iraq. Sitting in the driver's seat of the armored Land Cruiser. Looking at the colonel next to him who was going ape shit because they were sandwiched between a pair of Humvees and going nowhere. Tension was building at the base of his skull. He sensed the muscles running up his neck constrict and go rock hard. It was as if high-tensile steel cables had been laid underneath skin already flushed and hot to the touch. In his subconscious he knew he had thirty seconds before the little white car squeezed up on the shoulder and the ordnance onboard was detonated.

Thirty seconds until his leg was gone forever.

Thirty seconds until the colonel was killed outright by the initial shockwave.

Thirty seconds until his friends Jo Jo and Ricky were torn apart in a hail of metal and glass shrapnel, leaving three kids fatherless and making widows of two young wives thousands of miles away.

Taking her brother's silence as tacit approval, Tara kept her hands in plain view and fixed the soldier with her best semi-confused *I'm sure we know each other from somewhere* smile. She had even narrowed her eyes and incorporated the head tilt. Finally, with an *aw shucks* shrug, she said, "You went to Shenandoah, didn't you? Go Raiders!"

As Tara was lying, Riker was sizing the soldier up. The black chevrons on the rank patch affixed above her sternum designated her as a staff sergeant. The nametape next to it read BURKHOFF. She looked to be around Tara's age: mid to late thirties. Something about her face struck him as odd, though. It was strangely symmetrical. Almost too perfect. Smooth forehead. Thin nose. Milky white skin under a squared-off jaw pulled in tight by a fully cinched chin strap. And to punctuate the *Barbie goes*

214

to war look, Burkhoff's tiny ears were framed by a hint of blonde hair snaking from under the desert-tan helmet.

Tara noted the look of confusion cross Burkhoff's face as the soldier's head began a slow side to side wag.

Riker was about to mention something about the blonde soldier's good looks when Steve-O beat him to the punch.

"She's too pretty to be in the Army," said Steve-O.

Riker looked over his shoulder and nodded an affirmative.

Trying hard to ignore the commentary going on around her, Tara said, "Oh shit. Forgive me. You didn't go to *Shenandoah*. You went to our rival *Daleville*." Then, fully utilizing the imaginary hip waders she had just donned, Tara jabbed a thumb over her shoulder and doubled down on the bullshit. "That's definitely where I know you from. I was being a little turd so Mom sent me there for eighth and ninth grade. Effin hated being a Bronco."

Burkhoff's blank stare moved from Tara to Riker then settled on Steve-O, who was now perched in the space between the seatbacks and eyeing her from afar.

Remembering an article she'd read about an English teacher who'd been boinking Daleville High students for the better part of a decade, Tara said, "We were both in Mr. Flack's intro to English lit class."

Burkhoff furrowed her brow, exposing the thin horizontal line made by her snugly fitting helmet.

Building on the lie, Tara took a wild stab at the timing of everything. "I think it was oh-three or oh-four when he made a bunch of passes at me. Freshman year, anyway."

Hearing this, Burkhoff's eyes widened in recognition. Whether it was because the woman thought Tara was being truthful and believed the crap she was spewing, or that simply hearing the dirt bag teacher's name uttered out loud stirred something in her memory, Tara had no way to gauge. Truth was, she didn't care either way. This was a means to an end. And it appeared some kind of credence had been established. Because after a long two-count, Burkhoff began to nod agreeably.

"Flack was a piece of work," pressed Tara.

"And then some," agreed Burkhoff, whose rifle was now aimed in a slightly less lethal direction.

Nodding at Riker, Tara said, "My brother, Lee, was in Iraq in oh-four and oh-five. If he'd have been here instead of in the Sandbox when that all went down, Andy Flack wouldn't be in New Castle Correctional." She paused for a second not only to let the mention of her brother's service to country sink in, but also to imbue a bit of high drama to her story. "If Lee hadn't been in Landstuhl recuperating from the IED that took his leg," she went on, "Flack's bones would be occupying a hole in a field somewhere."

Hearing this, Riker drew his arms back inside and made a show of closing a fist and pounding it against his palm, real slow and deliberate.

Burkhoff seemed to relax a bit more, her rifle now at a low-ready.

Voice hushed, Tara asked, "What's this all about? The living dead people? The cannibalism?"

Craning across the center console to make eye contact, Riker said, "What's with the roadblock?"

Before Burkhoff could answer, Steve-O said, "Why did we need to be locked up last night?"

Over his shoulder, Riker said, "Not the time or place, Steve-O." He turned the key, setting the seatbelt alarm chiming. Whispering, he added, "Better buckle up, my man."

Steve-O *harumphed* and disappeared from sight.

Riker heard the metallic *click* of a seatbelt clasp finding its home.

Tara felt the cold finger of dread tickle her spine. Subconsciously, she pushed her sleeves to her elbows, exposing the ink work there. Running with the first thought that came to mind, she stared into Burkhoff's narrowed eyes and said, "Steve's talking about the house he lives in. The director didn't have a nurse to consult so she decided against taking the residents to one of the shelters. So they stayed home. Hence the *locked in* part."

"Why is he with *you* now? And why didn't you follow the mandate and find a shelter?"

Lying his ass off, Riker said, "We were out of town last night and don't know a thing about any *mandate*. Steve-O's our brother ... by adoption, of course. Mom just died so we're all he has left. We picked him up a little while ago and were on our way to see the lakes when we hit your roadblock." His own eyes narrowing, he repeated his earlier query. "What's with all this, anyway?"

If the sergeant planned on answering Riker's question, she wasn't afforded the time. Because the second her lips parted, a dirt-streaked hunter-green delivery van roared up to the Jersey barriers denying east/west passage atop the overpass. There was a squeal of rubber and the van lurched wildly before making a screeching left-hand-turn. Though some speed had bled off thanks to the unexpected blockage, the van still had a good deal of forward momentum when it entered the exit ramp traveling in the wrong direction.

Chapter 43

Sun was glinting off the windows running the length of the van's passenger side. Below the windows, *Giovonni's Catering* was emblazoned in cursive, the gold-leaf lettering reflecting the sun as well.

Tara saw the driver's face. It was a mask of terror. Surely the flight part of her prehistoric fight-or-flight instinct had won out over the former.

Next to the middle-aged driver, dainty hands partially covering her eyes, was a girl of about ten.

As the driver braked at the bottom of the ramp and began hauling the oversize steering wheel hard right, Tara got a clear look into the rear of the van. Packed in tight were a number of adults and kids. Because of the distance, seventy feet give or take, Tara could only count heads, not determine much more in the way of detail. And if her hasty tally of the silhouettes was correct, there were an additional eight people crammed in back.

Reacting to the sudden maneuver, the sergeant aimed her M4 at the Ford Econoline and bellowed "Halt" in a voice Riker could have never envisioned coming from the young woman.

Jaw falling open, Tara tracked the van as it continued the right turn onto Interstate 69 North and proceeded to speed in her direction.

The van was a green blur swerving and bouncing on worn suspension as it sped by right to left. A half-beat after finally wrestling the van into the center lane twenty feet beyond the Suburban, the driver must have spotted the Jersey barriers, armed soldiers, and armored vehicles in the shadow of the overpass.

"Better stop," said Riker.

As if heeding Riker's order, the van's brake lights flared red and it came to a slow-rolling stop.

Seeing the driver throw off her shoulder belt and her door suddenly pop open caused the tension in Riker's neck and shoulders to ratchet up. The nub where his lower left leg used to be attached was also beginning to throb.

This wasn't a Jersey barrier chute outside the Green Zone in Iraq, but the emotion he was feeling for the people in the van was taking him back. Forcing him to relive the carnage vehicle-born IEDs wrought on soldiers and Marines manning those checkpoints outside the walled city on seemingly a daily basis.

The van rocked forward on its suspension, then leveled out. A tick after the brake lights went dark, the rear doors swung open and people were spilling out.

Like a scene ripped straight from the San Diego/Tijuana border crossing, those people, women and kids mostly, made a desperate dash toward the roadblock and the perceived safety beyond it.

Harboring a sick, sinking feeling of what was to come next, Riker watched Sergeant Burkhoff lower her carbine and sprint to put the Suburban between her and the drama occurring less than a hundred feet to her fore.

Moving much slower than the others, a man tumbled from the van and rose shakily to his feet. Lower left leg swathed in a blood-sullied bandage, he ambled past the van's yawning rear doors and then began to lope toward the phalanx of Jersey barriers. In the blink of an eye, the lope became a fast jog. Arms coming up level with the road, the man vectored straight for the gap in the barriers Burkhoff had come through.

Contradicting his gut feeling, Riker saw the Guard soldiers lowering their weapons.

The crimson-soaked bandage came unfurled as the man broke into a head-down sprint. If Riker was a betting man, his money would be on the man overtaking the women and children before any of them reached the barrier. Just when he thought the situation was going to end with a positive outcome—the innocents making it to safety, and the injured man getting the medical attention he needed—a half-dozen armed men wearing black uniforms stepped forward and aimed their rifles at the approaching people.

"You don't want to watch this, Sis," said Riker.

"The injured guy is moving like a Bolt," she replied.

Riker watched her fish the iPhone from a pocket. She thumbed it on and hit the camera icon. Bringing the phone's camera lens level with the lip of the dash, she said, "I don't just want to watch it, I want to record it."

Shaking his head, Riker looked over his shoulder. "You might want to close 'em, Steve-O."

"I'm a grown man," he replied forcefully. "I'll watch if I want."

"Suit yourselves." Though Riker knew he should heed his own advice, the thing inexplicably playing out before his eyes proved to be too alluring. Like coming upon a crash scene on the road complete with bodies shrouded by yellow tarps, he couldn't deny his inner voyeur.

Without warning—shouted or otherwise—the half-dozen black rifles spit orange licks of flame. Strangely, the Bolt didn't immediately fall. In fact, it didn't even jerk from the impact of a single round. It was the women and children whose bodies in motion met the wall of screaming lead. The driver, who'd been first out with the young girl in tow, crumpled forward, landing face down in an uncontrolled slide before turning rag doll and rolling over to end up on her back and staring wide-eyed at the sky.

"No no no," chanted Riker as the girl stopped mid-stride and turned to regard the stricken driver. "Run. Get the eff out of there."

Too late. One of the soldiers clad in black shifted aim and, with no outward sign of remorse on his part, fired a trio of bullets at the girl. The first struck her center-mass, entering her navel, opening her guts up, and starting her to stand up straight, which put her in the worst possible position to absorb the next two rounds.

Bullet number two, moving at nearly three-thousand-feet per second, struck dead center on the girl's breastbone, lifting her up onto her toes and into the path of the final bullet.

The kinetic energy released from a single 5.56 hardball round upon impact, while not as devastating as that of a .45, is sufficient to split a watermelon in two. The damage the third bullet did to the girl's head was something Riker could not unsee. Before the diminutive form was but a corpse on the blacktop, Riker was screaming and cursing and asking Tara if she recorded "that barbaric shit."

"Got it," said Tara, even as she was documenting the executions of the rest of the women and kids.

Ignoring the dead and dying, a pair of the black-clad soldiers moved from behind the barriers. One had a net of some kind in his hands. The second soldier was brandishing what looked like a dog catcher's tool—a long, brushed-metal pole with some kind of sturdy noose on its business end.

"Still getting it?"

"Yep," said Tara. "The fuckers are trying to catch the Bolt. Those bastards in black didn't give two shits about the rest of those people."

Sure enough, the two soldiers were calling out at the top of their voices, trying to lure the Bolt to them.

From her side vision, Tara saw that Burkhoff had moved from cover and was leaning against the rear quarter panel. The M4 was clearly aimed at the road. Her chinstrap was dangling now and she was pressing a gloved hand to her mouth. The look in Burkhoff's eyes spoke volumes. It told Tara she had been caught completely flat-footed by the actions of the black-clad soldiers and wanted nothing to do with this. Said in no uncertain terms what had just happened violated the rules of engagement as she understood them.

Then Burkhoff's gloved hand went to the flesh-colored bud in her ear. After nodding a couple of times and casting a furtive glance in the direction of the MRAP, she swung her gaze back to the Suburban. In the span of a couple of seconds her expression had gone stony.

What kind of information had she just received?

Tara and the others would never find out.

Burkhoff straightened up and made a fanning motion with her free hand while bellowing, "Everyone out! Hands where I can see them!"

Eyes conveying to the soldier she had no intention of complying, Tara shook her head and ordered Riker to drive.

Riker said nothing. He turned the key to the stop and let the big V8's throaty rumble do the talking.

Burkhoff's free hand went to the rifle. In the next beat, the muzzle was swinging left to line up with the idling SUV.

Still staring at Burkhoff, Tara said, "You just let that go, didn't you. Bad decision … you're one of them now." Flipping the sergeant the bird, Tara added, "Shenandoah still rules."

Burkhoff made some kind of a hand gesture toward the roadblock. A tick later she was racking a round into the M4 and throwing the safety off.

Already swinging her gaze to Riker and saying, "You can outrun a helicopter in this, can't you?" Tara missed seeing Burkhoff shoulder her rifle.

Dropping the transmission to Reverse, Riker asked, "*What* helicopter?"

"You didn't see it parked on the interstate behind the MRAPs?"

Tromping the gas and looking over his shoulder, Riker said, "Nope." As he reached for the transmission stock, he glanced sidelong at Tara. "What color was it?"

The Suburban was now moving about thirty miles per hour in reverse. A humming noise from the transmission was sounding loudly inside.

"Black … maybe dark green," answered Tara. She made a face and her hand shot up for the grab bar above her head as Riker spun the wheel counterclockwise. She was drawing in a deep breath as the SUV slowed a bit and, acting on Riker's steering input, the front end slewed around violently left to right.

Army, thought Riker. Seatbelt holding him in place, he spun the steering wheel back to center and worked the brakes to arrest the spin.

Steve-O was occupying the center of the back seat, holding on to both headrests, and struggling hard against the mounting centrifugal force.

Upper body tensing against the coming whip-like effect, Riker jammed his left knee hard to the door to compensate for his missing lower leg. "How many rotors did it have?" he asked, the words coming out as a gasp.

Busy bracing a hand on the dash, Tara exhaled, then answered, "One on top and a smaller thingy out back."

Once the landscape stopped whipping by the windshield and the Suburban was facing due south, Riker lifted off the brake pedal and quickly rolled the transmission into Drive. With the SUV doing a slow roll forward and still shimmying from the abrupt bootlegger's reverse, he flicked his eyes to the mirror and asked, "Was the front of the helicopter pointy or rounded?"

"Does it matter?" asked Tara.

In the wing mirror Riker saw a black-clad soldier squaring up beside Burkhoff. Though he couldn't be sure, he thought the man's rifle was being trained on the big black target the SUV represented. In his mind's eye he saw the gunners atop the Humvees readying their .50 caliber Browning heavy machine guns to fire.

"I saw the helicopter," said Steve-O. "It was like T.C.'s chopper."

"T.C. from Magnum P.I.?" probed Riker.

"Yep," declared Steve-O rather proudly. "But it wasn't painted pretty colors."

Hughes 500, thought Riker. "That's a little bird," he said. "No way we're outrunning that." In the rearview he saw the guard soldiers gathering around the fallen, while the black forms sprinted toward the nearest Hummer. Turning his eyes forward, he saw smoke rising far off in the distance. A few seconds later he detected the faint horizontal line of the last overpass they'd driven under prior to coming up against the roadblock.

With no clear idea of how to outrun a radio let alone an agile helo capable of high-speed low-level flight, he tromped the gas. The engine responded with a whoosh, the added torque causing the chassis underneath them to shimmy as if the motor was about to launch from its mounts.

"How long before they get that thing into the air?"

Riker looked at Tara. "A couple of minutes. Why? You have a plan?"

She nodded.

He drove on, the overpass looming larger with each passing second.

"Take the next left," she ordered. "Then cross back over the 69 and keep going west."

Riker said, "That's taking us away from where we need to be. Mom was explicit in her instructions." Dumbstruck that bullets weren't yet slapping the sheet metal, punching little shiny craters into the black finish, he jogged the rig into the left lane. Still expecting some kind of a response from the soldiers, he made himself small in his seat. He'd seen what a mad minute of small arms fire could do to an unarmored vehicle. It was not pretty. On the bright side, the big SUV was likely out of the carbines' effective range. However, *out of the pan and into the fire* came to mind, because the vehicle-mounted heavy machine guns were about to become the soldiers' next best option at stopping the fleeing vehicle.

Tara wiped a stray tear from her eye. "That was murder back there."

"I agree," said Riker. "But I think there's more to it. When we get to cell service I wouldn't be surprised to learn this thing has gone sideways on whomever is responsible."

"The government?"

Riker said nothing.

"Who then?" Tara shot a furtive glance at the NRA bag resting nearly forgotten on the back seat beside Steve-O. "Damn it, Lee. If you won't tell me what you think is going on, at least tell me where we're taking Mom. It's gotta be one of the *Great Lakes*, right? At least that's a long way from this bullshit."

When the fist-sized holes made by phantom .50 caliber slugs didn't materialize, Riker's mind moved on to the next threat, imagining the little bird's turbines spooling up to full power. By now he guessed the rotor blades were showing as a solid black disc above the egg-shaped cabin, the five-passenger helo already going light on its skids. Ignoring Tara's query, he asked, "Where the eff are we gonna hide this thing?"

Still frowning from being ignored, Tara said, "I know a place." She pointed to the northbound on-ramp closing rapidly with them. "Take that. We can be there in two minutes."

Riker nodded, but his attention was elsewhere. Never in his wildest dreams did he figure he'd be driving the wrong way on the freeway. But he was. This day had started off strange and was quickly turning into one from his nightmares. So damn if he didn't make the most of it, quickly milking the Chevy's powerplant of every last ounce of power. *Go big or go home,* he thought as the narrow gray strip of on-ramp winding off to the left came upon them at a dizzying pace.

Chapter 44

After nearly overshooting the inbound ramp, Riker wrestled the wheel to get the swaying SUV back on line. Simultaneously, as the intersection with dead traffic control lights loomed, he tromped the brake pedal and, leaning his body hard to the right to counter the building g-forces, spun the steering wheel furiously clockwise.

Riker had found earlier that when it came to stopping power, this Suburban was *nothing* like the up-armored Suburbans, Land Cruisers, and Range Rovers he'd driven in the Sandbox over a decade ago. And as the tires squealed and the shocks and sway bars fought to keep the rig from overturning, he learned his purloined ride's factory suspension was also far from tuned.

With a whip-like snap, the SUV's rear end came around to match the trajectory of the front wheels. In just a couple of minutes they had gone from a dead stop with a platoon of soldiers their biggest worry, to driving across a barren overpass under threat of what could be a heavily armed military helicopter spotting them and giving chase.

Riker looked sidelong at Tara. "See any movement?"

"I bet I see the same thing as you."

After jinking hard to avoid running up on the low median splitting the overpass down the center, Riker said, "Enlighten me, Sis."

"I see something blurry."

The black rotor cone, thought Riker. "They're going to run us down," is what he said.

"Why would they?" said Tara. "We're going back *into* the quarantine zone."

"Because of what we witnessed, Tara. That atrocity you recorded back there on your fancy phone. It gets out and a lot of heads will roll. High-up heads."

Tara said nothing.

Steve-O said, "You need to show that to the police."

Riker said, "If the National Guard couldn't stop that from happening, the local police aren't going to be able to help us."

"You have a point," agreed Tara.

"So we'll go with the assumption they are going to give chase?"

Tara bit her lip. Eyes locked on a point far off in the distance—thousand-yard stare is what Riker saw it as—she nodded and wiped away more tears.

"Where's the elusive hiding spot you spoke of?"

Tara scrunched up her face. "I think we're getting close." She panned her head, scanning the road ahead of them. After they had covered another couple of blocks west, she said, "Two blocks ahead, turn right."

Shaking his head, Riker shot, "But that'll *really* take us back in the direction of the roadblock."

Channeling Phil Knight, Tara growled, "Just do it."

The two blocks blipped by in a flash. At the indicated corner Riker replicated the last hard right. There was the same squeal of tires. The same terrible chassis roll. And another smoke cloud filled the rearview as the hind end broke free and Riker drifted the Chevy around the corner.

A pair of cars passed going the other direction. When Riker glanced at the wing mirror, he saw them plowing through the drifting smoke, their brake lights blazing and throwing off a ghostly red glow.

"After a quarter mile or so on the left you'll see a big sign announcing a pumpkin patch."

Riker's knuckles had gone white from gripping the wheel. Eyes narrowed, he was leaning forward and scanning the left side of the county road. "How's a flat plat of land going to help hide this thing?"

"You'll see," answered Tara. She looked sidelong at him and asked, "Since we're on the subject of seeing. When's the last time you had your eyes checked, Lee?"

"When I turned thirty."

"You really couldn't see that helicopter beyond the overpass?"

"Thought it was a paddy wagon or something. In my defense, it *was* a little bird. It's the smallest helicopter in the inventory, as far as I know."

"I saw it," said Steve-O. He immediately began to hum the up-tempo Magnum P.I. intro.

"Aren't we supposed to be on the same team?" said Riker, turning around to glare at the older man. "You know, the *dude* team."

Shaking his head, Steve-O replied, "Mom said don't take sides unless you know *everything* about both people."

Tara clicked off her belt, turned around in her seat, and sat on her knees facing Steve-O. "So you're saying you like *me* more." It was more statement than question.

Steve-O said, "If I could mimic Roy Orbison I'd sing one of his songs."

Tara saw he was blushing. She said, "Which song? Pretty Lady?"

Steve-O's ears were turning the same shade as his cheeks. Smiling wide, he nodded.

"That's sweet of you, Steve-O. I must say, you're pretty easy on the eyes yourself."

"That's another thing Mom always said to me." He grinned, then went on. "Mom also told me I can do anything I put my mind to."

"I gotta hand it to you, Steve-O … you've got game." Riker paused and looked skyward as the noise of whirring rotors came in through his partially open window.

"If you had an ounce of what he has," ribbed Tara, "you'd be married by now and I'd have a niece or nephew to dote on."

"First Mom starts banging that tired drum. Now you have to go there?" The knotted muscles in his neck and shoulders were now causing a dull ache to radiate down his back and along both arms.

"Someone's got to spur these things along before it's too late," said Tara, a conspiratorial smile on her face. "And while we're on the subject of plumbing … aren't you due for the dreaded—" She pressed the first two fingers on her left hand together, held them vertical and made an upward stabbing motion toward the moonroof.

"Hell," he said. "If the powers that be don't get this cannibal outbreak thing contained, I won't ever have to bend over and get the old two-finger oil check."

"They said my bum is fine," offered Steve-O out of the blue. "Exam didn't hurt so much. Nothing like a shot."

Tara pointed at a driveway coming up on the left. She looked back at Steve-O. "Did your mom and dad set up all your appointments? Or did the people at the assisted living place?"

"I did it myself."

Beginning to feather the brakes, Riker asked, "You weren't at all scared?"

Steve-O shook his head. "No way," he said. "Cancer scares me way more than a finger up the butt."

"There you have it," said Tara. "You need to schedule your exam Monday, *Leland*."

If there is a Monday, thought Riker as he hauled the wheel over and nosed the SUV onto a dirt and gravel road wide enough for two eighteen-wheelers to pass at the same time.

Chapter 45

Riker wheeled the SUV under a sign arching high over the gravel feeder road. *Peter's Pumpkins and Maze 'O' Horror* was emblazoned in red two-foot-tall letters on the sign's face. Affixed to one massive beam supporting the overhead signage was a separate **CLOSED** sign. Taped below the closed sign was a sheet of paper on which the words **Until Further Notice** were scrawled big and bold in black ink.

Riker said, "Peter's throwing a ton of loot out the window by closing shop on the weekend this near to Halloween."

Tara shot a furtive glance at the tan haze lifting off the road behind them. "Peter must know something we don't." She tried the radio again. Still nothing.

Gravel crunched under the Suburban's tires and pinged off the undercarriage as the rig thundered down the road. The plume of dust continued to rise and swirled in their wake until the radials bumped up onto the smooth surface of a huge paved parking lot that looked capable of accommodating a hundred or more vehicles. At the moment there were exactly two triple-axle flatbed trucks sitting on lined spaces at the lot's far southwest corner. Beyond the lot to the left of the work trucks was the two-story farmhouse and pair of red barns where most of the holiday commerce occurred.

Flanking the closed barn doors were chest-high wooden boxes brimming with pre-harvested pumpkins and gourds. Beyond the house and barns, spreading out west and south, was a vast sea of brown earth spotted orange and green and white with pumpkins of all different shapes and sizes. Taking up the entire northwest corner of the property was the Maze 'O' Horror. Though it was October, the field of corn was verdant, the stalks standing tall. But not nearly tall enough to swallow up a vehicle whose billiard-table-sized roof topped out at six feet and change.

"Shit," said Tara. "I was hoping the corn would be taller. At least taller than you, Lee."

"Tara owes the swear jar a quarter," blurted Steve-O as he pulsed his window down. "Hear that?"

Tara powered down her window. Cocked an ear and immediately started a slow nod. "Yes, Steve-O, I hear it, too. And it's coming from somewhere north of us."

The little bird, thought Riker. Simultaneously, he stabbed a finger on the window button by his elbow, spun the wheel hard left, and fed the V8 some gas. "Does what you're both hearing remind you of a box fan set to *high*?"

"Yep," confirmed Steve-O.

Tara said, "The dust we kicked up coming in isn't dissipating fast enough. No way they'll miss *that* from the air." She spun around to face front. Voice rising an octave, she added, "What now, Lee?"

Through clenched teeth, Riker said, "Plan B." He was cutting the SUV across a pedestrian walk, clipping a bale of hay in the process. With the wide double-doors of the barn closest to the feeder road looming large, he backed off the accelerator and slowed the Chevy to walking-speed. After negotiating parallel rows of hay bales he suspected were stacked where they were to act as a sort of chute to lead customers toward the products for sale, he steered straight for the vertical seam between the red and white doors, along the way passing garishly painted plywood signs of ghouls and ghosts advertising *Hot Spiced Cider, Candied Apples, Salted and Roasted Pumpkin Seeds* and all other manner of fall holiday fare.

"Just going to crash through the doors?" Tara asked as her mirror nearly decapitated a sign cut into the shape of a mummy. It was posed arms outstretched and trailing real strips of fabric that flapped in the passing SUV's slipstream.

"How will we close the doors behind us if I destroy them, Tara?"

Nodding in agreement, Tara said, "Hear that, though?"

"Yeppers. T.C. is coming," said Steve-O.

Sure enough, the noise entering Riker's window *was* growing louder, changing from a subtle hiss in the distance to a harmonic whirring clearly mechanical in nature.

Addressing Tara, Riker said, "When I stop, jump out and open the doors. If they're locked, jump right back in." He stopped the Suburban a truck-length from the right-side door.

Steve-O's door opened first and he was through before Riker or Tara could stop him. Legs and arms pumping, he bypassed Tara's door mid-swing, rounded the front quarter of the still-moving SUV, and made a bee line for the doors. He was extremely fast given his shorter stature. Skidding to a stop on the gravel, his hands went immediately to the pair of wrought iron pulls.

"All right then," said Tara. She stayed in her seat, holding her door partway open, and watched Steve-O jiggling the handles. After a few seconds of this, Steve-O turned toward the SUV, defeat showing on his face.

"Move aside," bellowed Riker.

Steve-O backed away and took up station next to a cutout of a green goblin advertising a staggering selection of specialty coffee drinks available inside the barn. Tara noticed that sans Stetson, Steve-O gave up a few inches to the grinning caricature.

Riker's actions failed to match his temperament. Instead of trapping the pedal to the floor and crashing through the door ala the Duke Boys as his shouted words had suggested, he let the idling engine drag the SUV forward until the solid *thunk* of its bumper announced contact with the massive set of doors.

"The concussion thing affecting you?"

He shook his head as he goosed the engine. "CTE. Yep. I have a real bad headache. Seems like every muscle from my chest on up is on fire."

"You going to be okay?"

The SUV's rear wheels spun, spitting a rooster tail of gravel. Though the doors bowed inward in the center, they didn't budge an inch overhead or on the sides by the large steel hinges.

"I'm on the right side of the dirt," Riker replied. "All I can ask for." He shifted the automatic transmission into its lowest gearing and tried again.

There was a keening as properties of metal were irrevocably altered. Then there came a sharp crack as the thick wood beam supporting the right door splintered vertically, a lightning bolt running from floor to ceiling appearing near instantly.

Still, the doors retained their integrity.

"Probably a tractor parked against them on the inside," mused Riker. "Just my effin luck." He selected Reverse on the tree and looked skyward to where he thought the rotor noise was coming from. "They'll likely be searching the ground in a grid pattern. Right now we're sitting ducks. So let's hope they're on a leg that's taking them away from here."

Tara looked a question at her brother.

He said nothing. Just rubbed his neck and drummed the wheel.

"The corn field," she pressed. "It's all we have."

Riker nodded and gripped the wheel two-handed.

Tara waved at Steve-O. "Get in," she hollered, hooking a thumb over her shoulder as she slammed her own door shut.

A solid thunk sounded as Steve-O clambered back into the rig and closed the door at his back. Words dripping with disappointment, he said, "I'm sorry, guys. I tried my best."

Riker draped his right arm over the seat and looked over his shoulder, past Steve-O and out the back window which was filled up with all of the obstacles he had so delicately avoided on the way in. "Yes you did," he said. "Everyone hold on."

Tara's hands flashed to the grab bar by her head.

There was a solid *click* as Steve-O fastened his seatbelt.

Chapter 46

Drive it like you stole it was going through Riker's head as he worked the gas and brakes and steering wheel in unison. He knew that even one bale of hay broken and spread about would be akin to spray painting on the lot WE ARE HERE along with a giant neon arrow for the helicopter pilots to follow. So he kicked out the negative thoughts and drove like he'd been taught during the comprehensive three-day class in the desert.

Passing by outside the windows, the bales were a blur of muted yellows.

The cutout Halloween characters were reduced to technicolor forms leering in the windows as Riker expertly whipped the SUV through the gauntlet in reverse.

"Just good 'ol boys," crooned Steve-O.

"Great Waylon you got there," Riker said as he stood on the brakes and spun the steering wheel hard to the left, whipping them around in their second bootlegger's reverse of the day.

This time there was no tail of dust to give the SUV away as Riker straightened the wheel and cut a laser-straight tack north across the paved lot.

They passed the flatbed work trucks first off. Up ahead on the left was a garishly painted building made of plywood. Roughly the size of a Winnebago, the building was adorned with a sign featuring ears of corn and pumpkins. The vegetables were wide-eyed characters sprouting stick-thin arms and legs and wearing wide, toothy grins. The top edge of the sign was irregular because of the smiling characters and rose seven or eight feet above a sliding window. A six-foot-long shelf jutted out a foot or more below the lip of the window. To the right of the window, painted on the outside wall, was a basic menu containing ten items at most. Just beyond the snack shack, maybe a hundred feet or so, two wide chasms had been cut into the corn. Both entrances led west into the maze. Riker guessed one was for participants entering the maze. The other he figured was where the cornfield conquerors would emerge victorious and wanting a steaming libation or sticky sweet.

Driving by what looked to him like one of the plywood fruit stands ubiquitous to any rural road in middle America, Riker slowed the Chevy to walking-speed. Roughly fifty feet beyond the snack shack, he steered the SUV into the maze entrance. Once the Chevy had penetrated a dozen feet into the maze, he steered hard left into the wall of corn. Instantly, the stalks parted. As Riker applied more gas, the stalks bent and disappeared underneath the front end. There was a continuous barrage of noise, the screeching and slapping of corn against sheet metal echoing inside the cab as they cut a southbound path just inside the corn and parallel with the parking lot's frost-heaved outer edge. The cacophony continued for a few seconds until Riker brought the SUV to a stop broadside to the RV-sized snack shack.

Steve-O stopped singing when Riker cut the engine.

Remaining tight-lipped, Tara tilted her head back and stared up through the moonroof's smoked glass.

Riker swung his gaze between the side mirrors and saw that some of the corn in the SUV's wake was slowly returning to attention. He reveled in the relative silence and cocked an ear toward his open window. Rotor blades were still churning air up there somewhere off the left front fender. Thankful the truck's panels were no longer ringing with the nails-on-chalkboard keen from corn raking against them, he relaxed his body for the first time in a long time. Felt the tension between his shoulder blades beginning to abate. The wickedly painful drumbeat behind his eyes was lessening in tempo and intensity. He rubbed his temples and stared into the mirror where he saw an obviously terrified Steve-O—jaw clenched, lips pursed, and head on a swivel— slowly becoming one with the upholstery.

"Fishing for coins back there, Steve-O?" joked Riker.

"I saw children in the corn," was what he got in response.

"They're the least of our worries," Tara said. She clicked out of her belt and spun to face Steve-O. "You must watch a lot of television."

He nodded.

"There's no children in this corn," she insisted. "They're make-believe. A byproduct of a guy named Stephen King's twisted imagination."

"I saw them," he insisted.

Face upturned to the mostly pewter sky, Riker suddenly found himself on the receiving end of a cyclonic blast of warm air carrying with it a hint of kerosene.

"They've made us," said Riker, shouting to be heard over the turbine whine and rotor chop. A half-beat after stating the obvious, the corn stalks for a dozen feet all around the SUV bent and swayed and then remained supplicant as the vicious down-blast of rotor wash held them near horizontal to the dirt. Louder than ever, the noise of corn stalks battering the truck's slab sides was back.

The helicopter was painted a shade of matte green that looked black in the flat light of early autumn, that much was clear as it hovered a dozen feet above the Suburban. What really struck Riker as odd was that it was unarmed and bore no markings to distinguish it as belonging to any branch of service. The American flag that should have been stenciled somewhere on the fuselage was also missing.

Visible through the chin bubble, the right seater's boots were at work on the pair of pedals there, sending minute adjustments to the tail rotor. As small and nimble as the Hughes 500 was, it still cast an imposing figure—and shadow—as it hovered with the narrow skids dancing just a few yards overhead.

"Who are they and what are they trying to accomplish?" asked Tara.

"Good question. They're not Army or National Guard. I figure they're trying to intimidate us so we'll come out with our hands up."

Steve-O said, "Why? What the heck did we do to them?"

"It's not personal," replied Riker. "Assuming it's one of ours"—which he was beginning to doubt—"they're just following orders. Which aren't always the best. Especially if the politicians are the ones calling the shots."

"Were the soldiers in black *following orders?*" spat Tara.

Riker didn't have time to formulate an answer, let alone come up with a calming word or two, because an amplified male voice rose over the cacophony of rustling corn and mechanical din of the chopper. The orders were clear: *"Throw out any weapons and exit the vehicle with your hands up."* However, the man issuing commands threw another piece of information into the mix by indicating there was a squad of soldiers en route that would let them all go free as soon as they relinquished any and all recording devices.

Tara shuddered at the thought of the consequences they'd face should they not comply.

Sensing his sister's unease, Riker put a hand on her shoulder and opened his mouth to put into words what the gesture could not wholly convey.

When Tara diverted her gaze from the helicopter to acknowledge the gentle pressure on her shoulder, a whole lot of things registered simultaneously.

Two closely spaced gunshots rang out off her right shoulder.

Immediately the turbine noise increased overhead and the chopper, now belching smoke, tilted sideways and dipped its nose in the direction of the parking lot. As the craft Lee had called a "little bird" was in the midst of the evasive maneuver, a man-sized form with arms outstretched was filling up her side vision.

"Malachai!" cried Steve-O as he fell away from the window and drew his legs up onto his seat.

Turning toward the window, Tara heard another gunshot and witnessed the figure's pallid face and right hand dissolve into a multicolored spritz of dermis, muscle, and bone all traveling faster than her eye could follow.

It was instantly clear to Tara the zombie-looking man had come through a nearby break in the corn. And judging by the ringing in her right ear and gore deposited on her wing mirror, the lick of flame responsible for its destruction had come from the right, near the SUV's wide B-pillar, the same direction Tara's attention was naturally drawn by the dual blasts preceding the chopper's hasty departure.

Her eyes focused on the circular opening at the end of a gun barrel. From less than a foot away it was impossibly large.

Licks of smoke spilling from the dark muzzle curled lazily skyward.

Beating Tara to the punch, Riker said, "Now I really wish I had taken the Beretta."

From the back, Steve-O said, "I told you I saw children in the corn."

"I thought you were talking about the movie, Steve-O," admitted Tara. "I owe you an apology."

The gun barrel was tapping lightly on her window. The smoke was gone. The menace the gaping muzzle represented was not.

Tara walked her gaze the weapon's entire length, past the abbreviated black forestock, over the split and wrinkled knuckles of the pale hand clutching it, to the face of the man brandishing what she guessed was a shotgun. The only thing she knew of that could blast skin and flesh and everything else off a person's skull like that.

The gunman's face was as craggy and lined as his hands. As beat up, too. There was a goose egg on his forehead. An inch-long horizontal gash wrapped the bridge of his nose, which was clearly broken, the narrow, vein-addled tip making a sudden and unnatural right turn. Tara was no good at telling people's ages. So, considering he was likely a farmer and hadn't aged well due to all the early rising and days full of hard work, she placed him somewhere between fifty and sixty-five. A boomer, she'd heard people her mom's age called.

And hell if he hadn't lived up to that explosive generational title.

Keeping both hands on the wheel where the man with the weapon could see them, Riker looked sidelong at Tara. In a low voice, he said slowly, "Sis. Might be wise to run down your window." Then, turning toward Steve-O, he assured the man for the umpteenth time in a very short while that everything was going to be okay.

Chapter 47

Heeding her brother's advice, Tara feigned a smile as she looked the grizzled gunman up and down. She noted the mud on his boots first. Then she saw the spattered blood on his shirtsleeves. Finally, her gaze settled on the boxy pistol in the holster on his right hip. Not wanting to argue with one gun, let alone two, she hit the button to start her window buzzing down, then placed her hands on the dash.

At once, easily overpowering the earthy smell of mineral-rich soil recently churned by the SUV's tires, the metallic stink of spilt blood invaded the cab.

"A couple of shotgun blasts at close range sure can do a ton of damage to a whirlybird," said the man, barrel unwavering. He looked to the sky. "I don't reckon they'll be back any time soon. But you can bet friends in Humvees and MRAPs will." He stepped to his right. The gun barrel followed his gaze as he scanned the corn for more threats. Back facing Tara's open window, he added, "And when they do come, there'll be no stopping them."

Tara asked, "They … the Guardsmen, I mean. They did that to your face?"

The man shook his head as he turned to face the Suburban. "Wasn't the Guard that did this to me."

She saw bruises beginning to form under both of his slate-gray eyes.

"I went to the roadblock over on the county road. Parked my Jeep broadside to the barriers they had just put up and started asking questions. I was real calm. Just being inquisitive. Then a fella dressed in all black fatigues comes over"—he cast a furtive glance at the corn. Held it there for a beat, listening, then turned back—"this man in black tells me he has the authority from the highest levels in government to close any roads he needs to in order to contain the *'threat'* ... which I guess is mil-speak for the bug or virus or whatever it was that created these things wandering my corn field."

"Man in black," Steve-O said, then started singing a lyric from Folsom Prison Blues.

Leaning forward, Riker looked past Tara and locked eyes with the older man. "You must be Peter."

The man nodded. "This is my farm. You can call me Pete, though."

Riker introduced himself first, then the others.

Eyes actively scanning the corn, Peter nodded and indicated he wished they were meeting under better circumstances.

Like you in the window of that snack shack and pouring me a hot cider, thought Tara as another hard shiver wracked her small frame.

"Pleasure," said Riker. "I appreciate you running off the contractors in the 500."

"After what they did to my face," said the man, "the pleasure was all mine."

Back to the business at hand, Riker asked, "You said 'things' ... plural. You mean there's more like the one you just shot out there in your corn?"

"Been coming in from the road since morning. First one or two at a time. Had a group of four wander onto the lot an hour ago. Something or someone had gotten to all of them. Hunks of flesh missing here and there. Obvious bite marks on most. Hell, a couple were dang near disemboweled. Had their guts eaten right out of 'em." He braced on the Suburban and rolled the corpse at his feet over with the toe of one boot. "This one got it on the back of the arm." He bent close and rolled the arm back and forth, inspecting it. "Yep," he went on. "A human mouth did this one, too."

Though he thought he already knew the answer, Riker asked, "So how do they die? I mean ... dead for good?"

Shifting from foot to foot, Peter said, "I learned by trial and error that they don't die from normal stuff that'll kill you or me." *Like being gutted*, thought Riker. "Once they go cold like this slogger here, they *do not* bleed out and die. Hell, they don't bleed at all. Even if you sever an arm or shoot 'em in the chest. Tells me their hearts ain't beating in there. So I figured you treat them like a snake and go for the head." His head jerked around in response to a rustling in the corn.

Riker thumbed the door lock button just in case. Hearing a solid and satisfying *thunk*, he asked, "Where'd you put the bodies, Pete?"

"In the barn, for now. I kept a couple alive just to prove I'm no stone cold murderer."

Tara said, "*Alive?*"

"Don't know what else to call it. The soldier in black didn't offer any answers. Lord knows I pried. Tried to get him to tell me something. Got me the rifle buttstock to the face treatment as a reward."

Eyeing the fleshless skull staring up at her, Tara said, "The *things* are still in the barn?"

"Yes," replied Peter. "But not the one you all were trying to hide in. I locked a pair of the them in the barn by the house. Damned if they didn't worm in with the chickens and kill and try and eat every last one of them." He shook his head. "Feathers everywhere."

Still staring groundward, Tara asked, "Did the chickens turn into one of these?"

"What was left of 'em stayed dead."

Riker told Peter about their run-in with the soldiers in black on I-69. He held nothing back and finished by asking, "Any idea who they are?"

Before Peter could answer, Tara interrupted. "And why the ones who beat you had no interest in the sloggers in your barn? Surely someone from the CDC or something like that would want to study them."

"I'm guessing the men in black are mercenaries, so to speak." He went on to detail how his son did two deployments to

Afghanistan. How he rotated out and immediately attached himself to Blackwater for six figures a year. "Contrary to what you hear from the media, those Blackwater boys ... my boy ... were doing a great thing. Especially considering the politicians were juggling the issue like a hot rock. As for the ones we tangled with. Today, things are real different. Folks aren't allegiant to flag and country any longer. It's this side or that." He went quiet for a beat. "Whoever is in power holds the cards and deals the money out to the highest bidder willing to do their dirty work."

Riker's brow furrowed. He said, "And you figure these ones are working for the current administration."

"Affirmative," said Peter. "But unfortunately, I have a sinking feeling this thing is so out of hand that we're looking at more than just a CYA operation."

"CYA?" said Tara. "Cover your ass?"

"Quarter for the swear jar," shot Steve-O.

Tara wanted to frown but couldn't. Instead, she kept her eyes locked with Peter's.

Peter went on, "I was fiddlin' with my HAM set and talking with a fella in Maine. He says one of the shiny new towers that replaced the ones taken down in Manhattan on nine eleven is burning."

Riker asked, "Terrorism?"

Peter shrugged. "I'm not so sure about the cause. Nobody is. There's other problems, though." He turned an oblique angle to the corn. Leveled the stubby pump gun at a spot a dozen feet beyond the SUV's right front fender. A second or two passed before the corn parted and a disheveled elderly man staggered into the open. He stood there amidst the recovering stalks, wavering to and fro. A fist-sized flap of pale skin and shiny, purple-red muscle hung down the side of his face. It looked as if it had been torn away from the cheekbone with brute force. Dual pickets of poorly cared-for teeth were clearly visible as its jaw pistoned up and down.

Riker couldn't help but think the oldster was somehow convinced he was chewing a mouthful of Filet Mignon.

Showing no fear, Peter stalked toward the geriatric interloper.

Closer to fifty, thought Tara, as the shotgun came up and roared again.

And still a boomer.

"Let's go," Tara said, looking Riker square in the eye. She was visibly shaking.

"I want to ask him about the roadblock he came upon. Maybe we can avoid it."

No longer singing, Steve-O sat back in his seat and in a low voice said, "I shot a man in Reno—"

Averting her eyes so as not to see the latest destruction wrought by Peter's shotgun, Tara interrupted Steve-O mid-sentence. "You *shot* a man?" she asked, the words dripping with incredulity.

Riker said, "It's from a song, Tara. However"—he looked ahead to see Peter trudging back to the SUV—"we may be doing some shooting of our own before all is said and done. Why don't you try and sweet talk one of those weapons out of Ol' Pete's possession." He dug in his pocket and dragged out the wallet. Fished out his remaining cash—less than a hundred dollars—and handed it over.

A spent shell trailing smoke cut the air when Peter racked the shotgun's slide. Eyes narrowed and jaw set firm, he came to a halt beside the Suburban and stared into Tara's window. It looked as if he had come to some sort of a decision. One unforeseen even a minute ago.

Abruptly, Peter said, "You need to go now." He leaned in and instructed Riker to drive due west through the maze until they saw daylight. He then mentioned a dirt road that ran along the west edge of the farm. "Go north there," he said. He went on with the history of the road, saying how it was decades old and snaked through several different generationally held properties cordoned off by barbed wire and secured with gates and padlocks.

Apparently, the interconnected network of feeder roads and dirt ruts cutting across pastures had been used by generations of farmers as a way to circumvent county roads and the revenue hungry officers who used to patrol them.

Riker turned the motor over. "What are you going to do when they come back?" he asked Peter. "You planning some kind of a last stand or something?"

Peter smiled and patted the shotgun. "I'm going to block the road with my trucks. The rest will be determined by the deportment of our black-clad mercs."

Tara showed the meager wad of cash. "Will you sell us the shotgun?"

"And some shells," added Steve-O. "Slugs, preferably."

Peter considered this for a second. "I'm a civilian tester for Mossberg. She's not my only boomstick. And it's hard to say no to a pretty lady"—Here comes the *but*, thought Tara. —"but I won't take your money. Just try and get word out about what's really going on here." He turned away and cleared the chamber. After checking that the safety was on, he passed the pistol-gripped pump gun through the window. He then emptied his pockets of shells and handed them over, too. "Slugs and shot," he said, singling out Steve-O. "You seem to know your stuff. But I'd still suggest alternating them. You need to breach a door or make a whirlybird go away, no problem with a slug. You need to reach out and touch someone with a big fat spread of pellets, you got a shot shell next in line. Keep her away from your face and your hand in the strap when she goes *boom*."

"Solid advice," admitted Steve-O. "Dad kept a shotgun for home defense."

"And damn good for it," said Riker. "Thank you, Pete. We'll be coming into some inheritance money real soon. When my chunk hits my account I'm buying you an honest to God big-bucks Ithaca. Gonna hand deliver it to you if I can."

Peter said, "Think nothing of it. You carry yourself like my son. Well, like he did before—" He tugged the semiautomatic from its holster and checked that there was a round in the chamber. After dragging a sleeve across his eyes, he removed his worn John Deere cap and pointed west with it.

Message received. Riker nodded, dropped the transmission into gear, and nosed the SUV into the corn.

Chapter 48

While the doors to the barn had been a formidable foe to the Suburban's stock bumper, breaching rural gates mounted to decades-old posts and secured with civilian padlocks and rusting lengths of chain posed no challenge.

Two hours after leaving Peter standing alone in his corn field, Riker was steering the black SUV off the last of the dirt roads and onto a no-name two-lane road a dozen miles north by west of the roadblock the pumpkin proprietor had insisted was on the outer reaches of what could only be described as some kind of hastily established perimeter.

Dusk was fast approaching. To the west the sky was a jumble of dark clouds, the billowy edges atop them glowing red and orange from the glancing blow of the sun's fading rays.

East of the county road the sky was cloudless and beginning to morph from red and orange to a deep shade of purple.

Due north a fast-moving cloud band was dumping rain in gauzy gray sheets across the flat countryside.

While Riker couldn't be sure they had actually bypassed the roadblock, he had no reason to doubt Peter's directions. The man had taken a helluva beating for asking a few questions. No way he was on the side of whomever the soldiers in black were allegiant to.

"Left or right?" asked Riker.

A gleam in her eye, Tara asked, "Where are we going?"

"We're going north and east of Chicago."

"That rules out Lake Michigan. Any of the other Great Lakes on the itinerary?"

Riker shook his head. "We're not stopping at any of them. Erie will be off our left shoulder for a stretch. You should get a peek at it."

"Go right, then go north whenever it pleases you," she shot. "As long as you're being a vague dick about our final destination, I'll be a vague bitch about doling out directions."

He waited for oncoming traffic to pass. From the back seat Steve-O said, "More money for the swear jar." Then, after a soft chuckle, added, "I like the Bears. What's your team?"

"Bears," said Riker. "Been a fan since I was a kid."

"Our mom started us liking the Bears," said Tara. "Will you please pass her forward."

There was no immediate response from Steve-O.

Tara said, "She's just ashes. She won't bite."

"*Can't* bite, is what she means," said Riker. Instantly disappointed at how totally out of line his response had been, he shook his head. No reason to say *anything* that might cause Steve-O to remember the things he'd just been exposed to. Plus, inadvertently, Riker had dredged up from his memory a macabre image of the elderly homeowner being disemboweled in front of his dying wife and burning home.

"It's okay," said Steve-O. "I'm a survivor. At least that's what my mom always told people."

Riker didn't know what to say to that. So he turned right in a break in the traffic. People were driving as if this was just another weekend night in rural Indiana. As if they were just shuttling back and forth between the Walmart and home. Nothing he saw suggested they knew anything about what was really happening in Middletown and, apparently, spreading from that epicenter at a dizzying pace.

The road was a two-lane affair, just the kind of place Riker envisioned roadside stands selling seasonal fruits and vegetables to be located. A minivan full of high-school-aged kids came up fast on the Suburban and passed on the left when a dashed yellow presented itself.

Flanking the county road here and there were farmhouses set back from the road and surrounded by barns and swaybacked out buildings. As signs began to indicate the interstate was drawing near, the rural feel disappeared and convenience stores, block-long strip malls, and chain eateries became the norm.

Steve-O reached forward and set the bag containing the urn on the console lid between the front seats.

"Keep your eyes peeled for the law," said Riker, already practicing what he preached, his eyes constantly flicking to the mirrors.

Tara placed the bag on her lap and ran her hands over the outline of the item inside. Continuing to caress the urn through course nylon, she said, "Sure would suck to get pulled over and have them find a recently fired gun with a couple of bodies on it in our possession." She glanced at Riker then flicked her gaze toward the back seat. "Not to mention, we're transporting what a prosecutor would likely argue is a recently kidnapped person."

Steve-O was between the seatbacks again. His hands were flexing, opening and closing with a steady rhythm. After staring at Tara for a long two-count, he said, "I'm a grown man. Please don't call me kid."

Taken aback, Tara apologized and began to explain what kidnapped meant but was quickly cut short.

After doing a mental fist pump upon hearing Steve-O assert himself, Riker said, "Yeah, Sis. Steve-O here is a grown *ass* man. From here on out do not treat him any differently. He *chose* to come with us, not the other way around. Isn't that right, Steve-O?"

Nodding, Steve-O curled his right hand into a fist and offered it to Riker.

Contorting his arm, Riker bumped knuckles with the back seat passenger. "Damn straight," he said. Letting Tara off the hook, he changed the subject. "Sis, where to now?"

"Back onto the 69 north if it's not blocked."

Détente, thought Riker, as he slowed and scanned ahead for any sign of a roadblock.

***

From a quarter-mile out it looked to be business as usual at the interchange with Interstate 69. Thankfully, nothing pointed to the quarantine having reached beyond the three-mile buffer north of Peter's Maze 'O' Horror—which had truly lived up to its name. Riker shivered again at the recollection. Sure, he'd seen mangled bodies—some recently deceased, most dead for days and dry as mummies from baking under the harsh sun. But he'd never seen so much death up close and personal. And it had all happened in such a compacted time frame that his mind was having trouble processing it all. A good night's sleep was what he needed. Take eight hundred milligrams of Ibuprofen to dull the aches and pains his body was prone to. Maybe even pop a couple of melatonin and call it a day.

What he really hoped was to wake up from said siesta and find that this all had been a bad dream. That he was still in the back of the cab on the way to Sis's apartment and had simply dozed off. *Vee are ear. Dis your stop, mista* sure would be a welcome voice to wake up to. Hell, if it reversed everything that had happened the past twenty-four hours, he'd even be content to come to on the Greyhound bus with the Cat Lady bitching and moaning and spewing bourbon breath a half-foot from his ear.

An eighth of a mile from the interchange the sight of a pair of Black Hawk helicopters cutting the air left-to-right a few miles east drew Riker back to reality. The helicopters were illuminated like a pair of road flares, the light from the westering sun sparkling orange off their west-facing glass. Moving at a very fast clip and descending rapidly, the helos were soon lost from view amid the darkening backdrop.

"*Not* T.C.'s chopper," observed Riker.

"Whose then?"

"No idea," admitted Riker. "But look where they're headed."

"Toward Middletown."

"Correct," said Riker. "What time does it get dark around here, Sis?"

"We've got another hour or two."

Noticing the fuel gauge needle hovering on *E*, Riker said, "We need to fill up."

"And I'm hungry," added Steve-O

As she fiddled with the navigation unit, Tara said, "Me, too. And I'm also going to need to find someplace to get a pair of shoes."

Riker stopped them at the traffic signal a block west of the I-69 interchange. He glanced at Tara's bare feet, then leveled his gaze at the navigation unit. "That magic box still acting up?"

"It's still stuck all zoomed out." She pressed on the screen to no great effect. Next, she thumbed her iPhone on. Saw it was still registering zero bars and slapped it down hard on her thigh. "Phone's still down, too. We're just going to have to navigate from memory."

When the light changed, Riker looked both ways, then accelerated through the intersection. Up ahead a number of vehicles were loitering in a neat line on the right shoulder. Though he couldn't be sure, it appeared as if they were patiently awaiting a red light to change.

As they drew nearer to the stoppage, it became clear there was no red light holding them at bay.

A pair of Jersey barriers had been placed by the on-ramp to I-69 South. The concrete slabs stood hood-high to the Subaru heading up the line. A van with a boom and attached satellite dish extended over its roof was to the left of the barriers. And dwarfing the van was an electronic reader board on wheels whose constantly changing message was not quite yet legible to Riker.

From the back seat, Steve-O said, "I know the cities and states like the back of my hand. We got Fort Wayne next. Then Toledo and next comes Detroit ... *Motown* ... *Motor City.*"

Half-expecting Steve-O to launch into a Jackson Five ditty, Riker said, "You a Motown fan, Steve-O?"

"The real Motown," he said with conviction. "I don't like the new sound. The robot talkers."

The light cycled to green. Riker said, "What's that called? I hear a lot of it up and down the radio dial."

"Robots talking," repeated Steve-O

Tara said, "It's called Auto-Tune. I hate it, too. Didn't even like it when Tupac and Dre used it on a song."

"Not to worry, kids. We're not going to Detroit or through Detroit. I've been there. It's on the mend, but nowhere Mom would want her ashes spread."

"I am not a *kid*," said Steve-O. This time he didn't launch forward. He remained seated and buckled in. "That's your only warning, Leland."

"Figure of speech," muttered Riker.

Tara took her eyes from the electronic reader board, shot her brother a quick glare, then turned to face the back seat. "You're not a kid in my book, Steve-O. You're a vast wealth of knowledge." She stated this calmly even as her stomach was sinking due to what she'd just read off the giant screen at the head of the line of cars. It was totally blocking the freeway entrance, its lit-up facade bathing the WANE 15 remote-news van sidled up to it with a soft buttery glow. Standing by the multi-colored sliding side-door of the van was a rotund middle-aged man with a boxy video camera perched on one shoulder. Awash in the harsh artificial light thrown from the camera, a perfectly coiffed male reporter seemed to be in the middle of a live on-the-scene report. Mouth moving with an economical rhythm, the rigid thirty-something reminded her more of one of those animatronics at Disneyland than a caring human being relaying information as dire as that splashed across the board behind him.

Tara read the words scrolling across the sign out loud. "No access allowed. Radiological accident seventeen miles ahead. Daleville under travel advisory. Middletown quarantined. Emergency personnel only beyond this point." Then, she amended the message with an imagined warning of her own. "And if you proceed past this point, eventually, men in black will kill you."

"Doubt if that would keep these people from wanting to go wherever they need to be," observed Riker.

"I'm still seething at what they did to the people from the catering van," she said forcefully. Then, softer, she added, "There were at least three women my age. And the kids ... that woman's little girl. All of them gone in the blink of an eye."

Riker had already mourned the dead. As Tara spoke, he was thinking about the Bolt. How the injured man had gone after the people whom just moments earlier he had been sharing space with in the van. How the numerous bullets striking him center of mass didn't slow him. Didn't really seem to faze him at all until one of them split his head in two like an overripe melon.

"That's no radiation accident," proffered Steve-O. "It's a monster accident."

Riker steered around the vehicles waiting to go southbound. Once on the overpass, he said, "I agree wholeheartedly, Steve-O. Now where to gas up and get a bite?"

Chapter 49

On the opposite side of the overpass from the reader board, sprawling across three blocks north by east, was a PETRO SHELL truck stop. The canopied fueling islands set aside for automobiles were nearest to Interstate 69. Next came the IRON PAN restaurant, which, judging by the artfully drawn steak and baked potato gracing the sign, likely served hearty fare in large portions. Just the thing Riker needed. Stomach growling with approval, he looked beyond the restaurant, marveling at the dozens of gleaming eighteen-wheelers sitting idle east of the massive canopied fueling islands dedicated solely to them.

He waited for a beat-up pickup going the opposite direction to pass, then turned into the Shell station. Slid the Suburban up to the nearest island, keeping the yellow and red pumps on his side.

Tara asked, "How'd you know which side the fuel door is on?"

Steve-O said, "Every car has an arrow by the fuel gauge that points in the direction of the gas tank door."

Shrugging, Riker said, "I just took a wild guess. Fifty fifty is pretty good odds." He slouched down, squinted, and peered at the gauge cluster. "Well I'll be damned, Steve-O. There *is* a little orange arrow." He tapped the clear plastic fronting the gauge. "Right damn there. And damn if it isn't pointing left, too."

"Seventy-five cents for the swear jar, sir."

Riker cut the engine. Reached down and popped open the fuel door. "At this rate, Steve-O, you're going to be a rich man before we get to where we're going."

Tara unbuckled. "Never know when to quit, do you, Lee? Keep teasing me and you're really going to regret it."

After shouldering open his door, Riker leaned back inside and said, "Do you really want me to tell you prematurely where Mom wants us to take her? You want to carry that kind of guilt around for the rest of your days?"

"She's dead, Lee. No way she can cut you out of the will, no matter how bad you eff up."

Steve-O said, "Close call, pretty lady."

Screw your swear jar, crossed Tara's mind. She said, "Let's go, Steve-O. Leave this big brother of mine to pump his own gas."

***

Inside the Shell market, Tara struck off by herself, leaving Steve-O to chart his own course. She grabbed a basket then went to the coolers in back and loaded up on waters and Diet Cokes. She stopped on one aisle, took an Emory board off the wall, and selected a black pair of Croc knock-offs that fit her. On the way back toward the counter an assortment of candy bars and chips somehow found their way into the basket.

Even with two cash registers manned by a pair of no-nonsense-looking men, the line was barely moving. A couple of minutes passed before Steve-O formed up next to Tara. Ignoring the sour look on the trucker's face he'd just cut, he displayed a handful of pepperoni sticks and asked for an advance on the swear jar money to pay for them.

With a tilt to her head, Tara said, "Only if you let me and Lee buy you an early dinner at the Iron Pan next door."

"Next," said the cashier, a man in his late fifties sporting a wide handlebar mustache and wearing a hat designating him as a Marine Veteran of *Operation Desert Storm.*

Steve-O nodded and displayed the foot-long sticks of spiced beef.

Tara placed her haul on the worn counter and dug into her wallet for her debit card. Just as she placed the plastic on the counter, a calloused hand came down atop hers and a folded-up wad of bills was taking the debit card's place.

Looking up to meet Riker's gaze, the cashier said, "What's your problem, buddy?"

"My sister's money is no good," said Riker. He looked at the cash register's green digital readout and peeled off enough cash from the wad to cover the tendered amount. Then he added three twenties to the mix. "That's for fifteen gallons of regular off of pump number four."

"You're supposed to pay *before* you pump," said the Marine veteran.

Shrugging, Riker said, "I couldn't find my own card. And with this leg of mine"—he hiked up his pant leg to show off the aluminum and carbon fiber prosthesis—"the less I walk, the better I sleep at night."

The cashier's expression changed.

Riker noticed the man's eyes roaming his face. No doubt he was wondering how the scar tissue stippling the skin around his left eye had come to be.

After staring for a long two-count, the cashier said, "You left a piece of yourself over there, eh?"

Riker nodded. "Brought some dark shit home with me as well."

"Sorry I jumped your shit, brother." The cashier offered his hand.

As Riker reciprocated, his attention was drawn to the small television atop the counter behind the cashier. On the screen a multi-faceted skyscraper wrapped in mirrored glass was on fire. From roughly two-thirds of the way up from street level, smoke billowed from the windows facing camera right. Licks of flame danced behind many of the windows already blown out by the intense heat or some kind of an explosion, whichever the case, Riker hadn't a clue.

Noticing Riker's interest in the television, the cashier said, "That's Four World Trade in Manhattan. She's still cooking off. Been going gangbusters for a few hours now."

Having already removed the tags and slipped on the wannabe Crocs, Tara called to Riker from the store's entry. "Let's go, Lee."

Voice full of twang, the man in line behind Riker said, "Yeah, jabber jaw. Why don't you listen to the lady and get a move on."

Ignoring the quip even as his neck and ears flushed hot, Riker said, "What started the fire?"

The cashier twirled his mustache. "Not an airplane this time. Still, you and me both know who did this. It's so *hard* for the media to call a spade a spade."

Again the voice at Riker's back. "Meter's running."

Feeling a wave of tension ascend from his lower back to his neck, Riker turned and found himself looking nearly eye-to-eye with a cleanshaven thirty-something wearing a San Francisco Giants ball cap. Aside from the MLB lid, the man's ensemble— denim from head to toe, big turquoise and silver belt buckle, and black boots with lug soles—all but screamed over-the-road trucker.

Decision time. Riker craned and saw Tara and Steve-O between fuel islands and scanning for cross traffic. Discretion winning out over valor, he stepped aside and tipped his Braves hat to the Giants fan. "Good luck this year."

The trucker set his coffee and can of Red Bull on the counter. "Thanks. Considering the odd-year curse is still alive and well, we're going to need it."

Riker parted the doors and strode off toward the Suburban. Along the way he could feel his muscles slowly uncoiling. And as a perfect metaphor for this thing he'd brought back from the Sandbox, in his mind's eye he saw a King Cobra slinking slowly back down into its basket.

Returning to the SUV, Riker saw that Tara was behind the wheel and Steve-O had already commandeered the passenger seat. Before taking his spot in the second row, he spent a moment squeegeeing the residue from the trip through the corn off the windshield and back window. The human detritus on the passenger side would have to remain. No telling if he could contract the virus or whatever it was by coming into contact with it. Better safe than sorry was a good a policy as any, Riker figured.

Finished, Riker slid in the back on Tara's side and was surprised to find that with her seat run forward in its track he was left with ample leg room. So much so that his knees didn't touch the seatback in front of him, a rarity in nearly every vehicle he had ever ridden in. He also noticed that either Tara or Steve-O (likely the latter) had placed the pack containing Mom's ashes on the seat next to him.

Tara adjusted the mirrors and fired the engine over. Flicking her gaze to the rearview, she asked, "Iron Pan?"

Riker said, "The reader board says their chicken fried steak is on offer for $12.99." He raised his hand so Tara could see it. "I vote yes on Iron Pan. Steve-O?"

"How much is in the swear jar?"

Tara steered away from the fueling islands, looped around behind the Shell market, and slid into a diagonal space a dozen feet left of the restaurant's front doors.

Throwing his door open, Riker said, "We've got your meal covered, Steve-O." Before stepping onto the blacktop, he reached across the seat and grabbed the NRA bag by its straps.

Tara killed the engine. "Lee," she said, catching him before he closed his door. "Why didn't you want me to use my card?"

Riker stuffed the stubby shotgun in the bag diagonally, then threw it over one shoulder.

"Is it because our names may be on a log in the coach's office?"

He nodded. "They had our IDs all night long. We may also be listed on a BOLO ... *be on the lookout*, in layman's terms."

She made a face then said, "How are we going to pay for our meals?"

Riker closed his door. "I've got eighteen bucks left."

Tara actuated the alarm with the key in the lock. "That'll do if we're eating toast and drinking water."

"I'll use my card. It's got about seventy or eighty bucks on it."

She shifted from foot to foot. "How is that any different than me paying for the cokes and stuff in the store with *my* card?"

"Because," he said, "we'll be leaving immediately after we pay, not loitering around for an hour while we eat."

"How do you propose we pay for lodging tonight? They take the card and authorize it for a nominal amount before we even check in. That'll give anyone looking for us plenty of time to track us down. All damn night, actually."

"While I'm paying for the meal, you go to the ATM and take out as much as it will allow you to."

A knowing look crossed Tara's face as she nodded in understanding.

"By the way," said Riker. "Those rubber shoes are awesome."

"Don't blow smoke, Lee. They're butt ugly."

Riker chuckled. "At least now they'll let you in the restaurant."

Throughout the entire conversation, which lasted a minute or two, tops, Steve-O's head had been panning back and forth as if he was spectating an Olympic-caliber ping-pong match. When the siblings finally paused to draw a breath, Steve-O nodded toward the restaurant and reminded them both of how hungry he was. Then he showed them his left hand and rubbed his thumb and pointing finger together—universal semaphore for *you owe me money*. "D-A-M-N is still a bad word," he added. "And that'll be one more quarter for the curse jar, pretty lady."

Tara smiled as she followed her brother and their new friend into the restaurant. Seeing a waitress acknowledge them with a nod, she went to her tiptoes and spoke into her brother's ear. "Maybe I should have bought a bar of soap in the store. Wash both of our mouths out, Lee."

Chapter 50

Being the dead zone of time sandwiched between lunch and dinner, they were seated immediately at a corner booth overlooking the road fronting the truck stop. Kitty-corner from the Iron Pan, south by west, was the closed stretch of I-69. Flanked by low bushes, it was barely visible as it shot off due south from the nearby overpass. There were a few vehicles, mostly passenger cars, heading north. Not a single vehicle was moving south. Which struck Riker as strange. Even this far removed from Middletown and the supposed shooting-cum-biological-incident that was now being augmented by a radiological incident. He'd already stopped obsessing over the former correlated happenings of the day before. Hell, he'd had hours to think about all of that as he stared at the ceiling in the high school basement and was still unsure of what had really happened.

This new red herring, though, was pure bullshit in his opinion. By all rights there should be emergency vehicles passing through. If the people responsible for the ongoing nuclear incident charade really wanted to cover up the ghastly nature of the biological outbreak and had half of a brain, they'd run a couple of NEST (Nuclear Emergency Search Team) trucks down the freeway, lights ablaze and sirens wailing. Let the WANE 15 cameraman and Harry Hairdo get a whiff of it and go all breathless and broadcast it live to every television in a hundred-mile radius. That would certainly seal the deal on the cause du-jour for any fence sitters. It would also likely serve to deter the random Curious George or those striving to become "YouTube famous" from disregarding the electronic reader boards Riker was certain were deployed on every access point to major routes of transit well beyond the original quarantine zone.

The waitress who seated them returned with a stainless Bunn urn and poured coffee all around.

"You're having coffee?" said Riker as he slid his menu aside.

"Barista's gotta stay awake, too." Tara regarded the well-proportioned (34-26-34 sprang to mind) forty-something with a smile and thanked her.

The waitress, whose nametag read CHLOE, set the coffee urn on the edge of the table. "Everyone decided?" she asked, a pen and rumpled pad of paper appearing in her hands.

"The reader board outside sold me," said Riker. "Chicken fried steak, extra gravy. Eggs over easy, sourdough toast, and hash browns with Frank's Red Hot."

Chloe tucked a stray blonde curl behind her ear. Licking the pen, she said, "I like a man who's ready and knows exactly what he wants. The Frank's *sold* me."

Riker removed his Braves hat and smiled. "I put that shit on everything, Chloe."

Chloe seemed to melt for a second but composed herself marvelously. Giving Steve-O her undivided attention, she nodded and held the pad aloft with the pen poised and ready to go.

"The same," said Steve-O, placing his menu atop the rest. He looked to Riker. "And you, Mister *Red Hot*, owe the swear jar another quarter."

Riker sipped his coffee and looked toward the interstate. Same view, except the light spill from the WANE van was more pronounced.

Still nothing going south.

Tara removed her stocking cap. Under Steve-O's watchful eye, she ran a hand over her short braids, checked the dozen or so rubber bands, then quickly donned the hat and tucked it all away again. "Don't worry about getting paid for us being a couple of pottymouths," she said to him. "We're good for it."

"Or will be real soon," added Riker with a sly grin.

Chloe delivered the food and they ate in silence. Scarfed down their food was more like it.

Holding it angled like a snowplow's blade, Riker ran his last piece of toast across the plate. Moving the spilled yolk and sausage gravy remnants to one side, he scooped it all up, folded the triangle of toast over on itself, and downed it in one bite like a tiny, finger sandwich.

"Going to lick the plate, too?" ribbed Tara.

Riker glanced at Steve-O's half-full plate, then stared at Tara's vegetarian skillet, only partially consumed and still steaming. "I'm going to the bathroom. Be right back."

***

The restaurant was full of mostly truckers and locals, the latter sitting in a couple of tables pushed together and jawing lightheartedly with one another. The former seemed a diametrically opposed group, sullen and stiff and eating by themselves though they were seated along a bar on round stools and nearly elbow-to-elbow with each other. A half-dozen men and a couple of women all silently ruminating on how and when the loads languishing in their trailers would get delivered.

The Iron Pan's walls were decorated with oil paintings of farm equipment and old trucks sitting in weeds and going back to nature. There were a few that depicted various wild animals in their natural habitat, none of it close to the Iron Pan. All of the pictures were for sale. Even if he wanted to know the price, the numbers were too small for Riker to see without donning a pair of magnified readers.

Bypassing the restrooms whose doors were labeled BUCKS and DOES, Riker parted a pair of saloon-style swinging doors and found himself inside a wide-open low-ceilinged bar. It was dark inside, most of the light coming from the illuminated bottles behind the distant mirrored back bar and pair of flat panel televisions flanking it.

In a few long strides, Riker covered the distance to the bar. Like the breakfast counter behind him, the men bellied up to the polished slab of wood here were wearing mesh trucker's hats and stooped over in silent repose. One man lazily stirred his cocktail with a straw. Another hoisted a longneck beer as he stared straight ahead at the mirror, surreptitiously sizing up Riker.

To a man, the bar patrons were fixated on the televisions. Filling up the screen left of the bar was the same burning building. Same channel: Fox. Same crawl at the bottom. Thanks to the size and placement of the screen, the font was large enough for Riker to read.

"Need a drink?" asked the redheaded bartender. She had paused and looked over her shoulder only long enough to make the offer, then turned back to face the television to her right.

"No thanks," replied Riker. "Got coffee cooling at my table."

He squinted and read the crawl long enough to see a story about a man attacking kids in a SoHo preschool come back around on a second pass. Strangely, not a single word about what was happening in Middletown, Indiana merited a mention. There was nothing about the supposed bus shooter's foray into the MU biology lab. Nothing concerning the mass casualties outside of the MU atrium. It was clear nothing was more important than traffic being at an hours-long standstill in lower Manhattan. Not even a radiological mishap in Middle America that would normally set reporters' tongues a wagging on both coasts. As far as the cable news network was concerned, Middletown and the broad swath of quarantined real estate surrounding it had been swallowed up by a black hole.

The television the bartender was fixated on was still broadcasting from a live remote somewhere near Daleville, the town the reader board had indicated was under a travel advisory, whatever in the hell that meant.

The crawl on the screen below the female reporter was mostly doom and gloom. A few words scrolled by indicating the roads in and out of Middletown were expected to be closed for forty-eight hours while the hazardous material response crews made the area safe for travel.

The omission of a couple of things stood out. First, there was no mention of bereavement counselors for the families of victims and surviving witnesses. Not a phone number or email address. Nothing. Second, and this one truly unnerved him, was the fact that there wasn't a list of evacuation or decontamination sites. Nor was there a single instruction as to what one should do if they feared they'd been exposed to radiation. Surely a mishap with the severity to effectively seal off a town of several thousand residents from the outside world would have officials doing everything in their power to let the local population know how and where they could find the necessary help.

Everything he had seen so far on the two televisions started him to think the two incidents were somehow connected. And all of those same things had also led him to believe the government at every level from the top on down didn't want that connection to be known.

Riker tore his eyes away from the televisions and retraced his steps back to his table.

Chapter 51

Riker sat down and described what was on the televisions in the bar.

"We better get going, then," said Tara, craning to find their server.

Chloe showed up a few seconds later with the check and Tara's card in one hand and a large take-out cup in the other. Judging by the steam wafting from the lid and recycled paper sleeve wrapping the cup, he guessed he was about to be the recipient of a fresh cup of java.

My kind of woman, he thought as he slid in next to Steve-O, who had just wiped his mustache and was in the act of throwing the proverbial towel in on a plate well-cleaned.

Wearing a big smile, Chloe handed Riker the coffee, brushing his hand with hers in the process. "Here you go, sweetie. And you take it black just like my daddy."

Riker smiled and thanked the buxom woman.

Steve-O said, "I think she has the *red hots* for you, Lee Riker."

"Your friend is very perceptive," Chloe said before walking away with an exaggerated sway to her well-rounded hips.

Tara signed the slip and pocketed the card. "She was way out of your league, Bro." She craned to find the ATM. "How long do you figure we have before our whereabouts are detected by me using my card?"

"*If* they are even looking for us and happen to be in the area, And that's a big *if.*" He paused for a beat. "I imagine they'd be here real quick, if that were the case."

Steve-O said, "What if someone sees us get in the truck? And then says something to the police?"

"I doubt if the BOLO is attached to the vehicle," said Riker. "But just to be safe"—he regarded Steve-O—"seeing as how you and I stick out like sore thumbs, let's have Tara sneak to the truck and pick us up around back. That way there'll be less of a chance of someone seeing us pile into that big black beast."

Smiling at the prospect of maybe getting to practice a little subterfuge, Steve-O briskly rubbed his hands together.

Tara returned carrying a wad of bills.

Rising up from the booth, Riker leaned close to Tara. In a near whisper, he asked, "Has the money hit your account yet?"

Shaking her head, she fanned the crisp hundreds out on the table.

After a quick count, Riker said, "Fifteen hundred dollars?"

"I'm a student living on a barista's income."

"What about your tips?"

"I only grabbed this week's. Last week's are at home in my underwear drawer."

Riker saw Steve-O turn away. From his vantage nearly two heads above the older man, it was clear a touch of color was rising up his neck and beginning to migrate to his cheeks.

"And you didn't bring them, why?"

"You were rushing me, Lee. That's why."

Riker told Tara his plan, shouldered his bag, then set off towards the saloon doors with Steve-O on his heels.

"What's the plan, Stan?" asked Steve-O.

"Just follow me," said Riker. "I've already reconnoitered our egress."

"What?"

"I know where the back door is. And there's no windows in the bar."

"Good thinking," said Steve-O as he raised an arm to parry the swinging doors and followed Riker into the gloom.

The back door was near the pair of bathrooms exclusive to the bar patrons. Boxes filled with empty longneck bottles were stacked beside the door, their folded-over tops nearly reaching to the panic bar. Riker was still processing what he'd just seen on the televisions when he pushed through the back door. As he stood there walking his gaze around the lot filled mostly with big rigs, he realized that what troubled him the most about Fox's coverage of the disaster was how the shiny tower still burned and the camera recording the conflagration was doing so from the same distance and angle as it had been during his first foray into the bar. Hell, on 9/11 the footage was coming in live almost instantly from news crews aloft in helicopters as well as numerous teams set up on the ground around Manhattan. The stations even cut to different feeds and, as hard as it was to wrap one's mind around the happenings of that awful day, did their best to describe what they were seeing. So if this *was* terrorism, why such a dearth of live coverage?

They didn't have to wait long for Tara to pull up in the SUV. Riker couldn't help but chuckle. Tara looked like a twelve-year-old perched up there behind the steering wheel. He opened the front passenger door. With a sweep of one arm and a slight dip, he offered shotgun to Steve-O.

"Nope," said Steve-O, "I enjoy being chamfered." He smiled and impersonated Riker. Though the move looked more like a curtsy than an act of chivalry, Riker took him up on the offer, swinging his bionic in first, then climbing the rest of the way in with the aid of the pair of grab bars. He closed the door and felt the rig begin to move before he could go for the belt. As he got ahold of the buckle, inexplicably all forward momentum ceased and Tara was rolling the transmission into Park.

Riker regarded her with a stunned expression. "Want me to drive?" he asked.

"Don't patronize me, Lee. I'm driving until we turn in for the night."

He scanned the surroundings. They were parked in the shadow of a dark brown Volvo tractor hooked to a tandem trailer emblazoned with the brown and gold UPS logo and sporting the tagline: *What can Brown do for you?*

Dead ahead was the Iron Pan, only they were viewing it from the east. Both the double-doors out front and the single windowless door out back were visible from the hide. They'd be able to see any vehicles rolling in off the frontage road as well as anyone going in or coming out of the building.

"What's going on then?" queried Riker.

"Just like you went into the bar on a little unannounced recon trip"—Riker slowly panned left and fixed Steve-O with a blank stare—"I'm taking it upon myself to see if we have just gained a tail."

"Someone's been watching reruns of *24*. Newsflash, Tara. I'm no Jack Bauer and you're about as far from his sidekick Chloe as our aptly named waitress."

"That show was very intense," said Steve-O.

Riker nodded in agreement.

Tara smiled and said, "I'm all you got Mr. *I carry an old-ass flip-phone*. Take me or leave me."

"Swear jar."

In unison, Riker and Tara told Steve-O to butt out so they could get this out of their system.

"Thank God I'm an only," said Steve-O. "While you two fight, I'll keep an eye out for Johnny."

The Riker siblings went quiet for a second.

Riker asked, "Johnny?"

"That's what I'm calling the soldiers in black."

Riker shrugged his wide, sloping shoulders. "Very fitting."

Tara said, "We'll just give the recon a few minutes, okay? I want to know either way."

Riker said, "Remember how well our recon of the high school went?"

"That's different," remarked Tara. "We were going to them. And we had no idea men with guns were waiting."

"You have a point, Sis. However, this won't be definitive either way if they don't show. Then it'll be in the back of our minds pecking away like a bird after suet." He paused for a second. "On the other hand—"

Tara said, "What's on your mind?"

"There's at least twenty pissed-off truckers in there who aren't getting to go where they need to. Some of them are drinking. Might be fun seeing the Feds or whoever shows up looking for us run into that kind of meat grinder." He flashed a lopsided smile.

Steve-O said, "My money is on the truckers. Anyone seen B.J. and the Bear?"

Riker and Tara shook their heads.

"Trucker and a monkey," said Steve-O. "Nice truck, too."

Riker regarded Tara. After a short pause during which he was staring at the truck stop restaurant, he tapped a finger on the clock in the dash. "You have fifteen minutes, Sis."

"Thirty," she countered.

"Twenty."

"Okay, okay, hard-ass. Twenty it is."

He nodded. "And not a minute longer."

Chapter 52

"Your twenty minutes is up," said Riker. "Let's go."

"I'm sorry," she said. "I thought it'd be like the movies. They'd come swooping in lights a blazing."

"Better that than what I was thinking," said Riker. "I was afraid black helicopters would fast rope a cleanup crew of specialists. Hood all of us up and take us to a CIA black site."

"Really?"

"No. Just pulling your leg. The way the Johnnies opened fire on the people in the van says more than you may know. Pandora's Box is wide open. They're no longer in containment mode. That back there ... *that* was an act of survival. Those Johnnies were in self-preservation mode. I've seen civilians packed into passenger cars speed toward a checkpoint and not stop even after warning shots were fired. Left the guards no choice but to light them up. 'Us or them' is the attitude you adopt real quickly once you're dropped into a war zone."

Tara asked, "The civilians?"

"Every one of them died. Nine, I believe. They were running from Saddam's former henchmen."

"Baathists," said Steve-O. "Bad hombres. Newsflash ... I like the History Channel, too."

"Correct. Later it was Sunni killing Shia and vice versa. Amidst all that Al Qaeda was going nuts with their bombing campaigns." He rubbed his temples. The fire was back and spreading to his shoulders. "Their civil war was hell to be around."

Envisioning another team of Johnnies manning a roadblock somewhere along their eventual path to wherever Lee was taking them—*No, wherever Mom is taking us*—Tara fixed a watery gaze on her brother. "I lied," she said. "I'd feel better if you drove."

"You sure?"

"Positive." She opened her door, letting in the caustic nose of diesel exhaust hanging in the air. On the way out the door, she said, "I just want to navigate from now on."

Riker didn't want to allow her any time to change her mind, a thing she was wont to do at the drop of a hat. So he shouldered open his door and clambered out.

They met near the tailgate and exchanged a quick hug and a second round of heartfelt apologies.

Riker wasted no time getting them moving north again. Instead of backtracking the short distance to the interstate, he turned onto the frontage road heading back toward I-69 and then hung a sharp right on the first county road he came to. They stayed to the county road northbound for several miles, seeing the paralleling interstate now and again through breaks in the trees.

Closing fast with a four-way crossing, Riker asked Tara to check the navigation unit again. At about the same time Tara leaned over to press the appropriate pixelated button on the control unit, a series of instantly recognizable tones sounded from within one of her pockets.

Ignoring her iPhone's Siren's call, Tara brought the map up on the display. When she depressed the + icon a half-dozen times, the map of the surrounding area recalculated for the first time since they took the Suburban from the high school parking lot hours ago.

"We've got GPS coverage now," she crowed. "And my phone just received a shit-ton of updates."

Riker said, "That's what those sounds were, huh. I thought maybe the navigation unit was dying entirely."

"Nope. It's working now." She looked away from the display. Fingers poised over a QWERTY keyboard rendered digitally on the screen, she said, "Okay. Hit me with the city and state we're taking Mom."

"Good try," said Steve-O. "I saw that one coming from Albuquerque." Voice an octave higher, he added, "Swear jar needs to be fed."

Tara turned toward the back seat and stuck her tongue stuck out at Steve-O.

"You almost had me," said Riker.

"Really?"

Laughing, Riker shook his head. "Not even close."

Back to fiddling with the nav-unit, Tara said, "Go left here. It'll connect up with the interstate." She hit the − key until the interstate was a thick green line cutting the rectangular screen in half vertically. "If we're to believe the color code, I-69 is lightly traveled right now."

"Smooth sailing, then," said Riker. "Let's hope it's accurate." He steered left, then took a hand off the wheel long enough to jab a finger at the smartphone balanced on Tara's thigh. "Anything from the lawyer hit your inbox?"

She thumbed the screen for a moment. When she looked up, the expression she wore was not what Riker wanted to see.

"Relax, Lee. I bet we'll get the confirmation emails tomorrow. Banks keep banker's hours. Always have, always will."

Fishing his phone from a pocket, Riker said, "I want you to check mine."

She took the phone, flipped it open, and peered down at the screen.

Seeing this, Steve-O said, "My dad had one of those. *Ten* years ago."

"That's about how old it is," replied Riker. He craned and saw that the navigation computer had correctly gauged the flow of traffic. It was very light moving north, with maybe one or two vehicles flitting by every few seconds.

The traffic light gods were smiling on them and Riker cruised through on a green and took the on-ramp to merge onto I-69 North. He slid the black SUV behind a white minivan, quickly matched its speed, then transitioned to the fast lane, his eyes taking a half-second inventory of the vehicles reflected back at him in the rearview mirror. Save for a white SUV in his lane a third of a mile back, there seemed to be nothing to worry about. The gold Prius one lane over and ten car lengths back was not the kind of ride he'd expect to see one of the men in black choosing to use as a pursuit vehicle. No range and no get up and go.

"Now that you got that thing working," said Riker, "why don't you plug in Akron as our destination."

The mere mention of the birthplace of Alcoholics Anonymous made Tara sit up straight. Fixing Riker with a side-eyed look, she said, "Are we driving all the way to New York and spreading Mom's ashes at Stepping Stones?"

Riker kept his eyes on the road and made no reply.

"Dad was the alcoholic, not her. Makes no sense to me at all." Tara went quiet for a beat, hand poised near the colorful display. Finally she made a face and said, "Why would she want her last earthly remains to be there for all of eternity?"

"Dad was a brilliant man, Tara. Sure, he had his problems with the drink—"

"You can't argue the fact that Dad did his best work after he got sober. I guess Stepping Stones makes sense now that I think about it. Hell, A.A. saved his life. Saved Mom's, too, in a roundabout way."

Sort of saved mine, too, thought Riker, as he looked up and noticed the white SUV had halved the distance to his bumper rather quickly. He was about to inform Tara that his decision to go to Akron was purely one of economics, because surely a night's lodging for three would be much easier on the wallet there than in Cleveland, when red and blue lights behind the SUV's black grill suddenly lit up behind them.

"We may not even make it to Akron," said Riker. "Make sure the pump gun is loaded and hand it over."

"How exactly do I do that, Lee?"

"The handle up front is attached to the pump. Should be a slide release. Some kind of button behind the trigger guard you'll need to press to get it moving. Keeping your finger *away* from the trigger, push the button and slowly pull the pump toward you. There's a rectangular window on one side where the spent shells are ejected. When that window is open, you'll either see a shell in there or you'll see an empty chamber."

She took the gun from the bag. Looked it over for a brief second. Satisfied she had her bearings, she placed her left hand atop the gun near the rear sight, depressed the nub by the trigger guard, and racked the pump back a couple of inches.

Riker checked the mirror. The SUV was now only two car lengths back.

"What do you see?" he asked.

"It's empty."

"Then jack a round into the chamber."

Apparently *jack* had a universal meaning to the Riker siblings. No need on his part to elaborate, because Tara pulled back hard on the pump and slammed it forward with authority.

She handed the Mossberg over butt first, keeping the barrel aimed at the floorboards. "You're going to blow a cop away?"

"Only if they're in bed with the Johnnies."

"What about the Guard soldier at the high school? You let him live."

The white SUV was now on the Suburban's bumper. The Prius had fallen back and was growing smaller in the wing mirror as it came to a stop in the breakdown lane.

"Better to be judged by twelve, than carried by six."

"I don't even know what that's supposed to mean, Lee." She glanced at Steve-O in the back seat. He had somehow acquired the iPod Tara had lifted from the kid at the shelter. A pair of earbuds were jammed in his ears and his head was bobbing to a beat she couldn't hear. Parking her gaze on Riker, she said, "You better do something. That truck is about to drive up your tailpipe."

"And the butt jokes keep a comin'," said Riker as he bumped the signal stalk up and slowly drifted them out of the fast lane. In the rearview he saw Steve-O look up from the tiny screen for a second, flick his eyes to the road ahead, then go back to whatever he was doing.

As the white SUV overtook them, the less than aerodynamic Suburban was buffeted by the wall of wind pushing ahead of what Riker guessed was a Chevrolet Tahoe.

Head facing forward, hands gripping the wheel white-knuckle-tight at the proper ten and two, Riker did all he could to appear uninterested while scrutinizing the vehicle filling up his left-side peripheral vision. First thing he noted was the yard-long *Department of Homeland Security* decal gracing the right-front fender. As the Tahoe crept forward, Riker's eye was drawn to the cobalt blue stripe cutting its rear flank diagonally. Then, as the vehicle slowed to match the Suburban's speed, Riker recognized that the passenger was a woman in uniform. And that she was shaking her head side to side and looking in his direction. He saw from the corner of his eye a glimmer of movement he knew was her mouthing something completely unintelligible to him due to the oblique viewing angle.

The Homeland rig kept pace for a long three-count, during which both vehicles traveled several hundred feet of I-69. A full second of the woman's eyes boring holes into his head was all Riker could take before his gaze was drawn to her face. Then, as if a puppet master was behind the curtain and working unseen strings, his head was swiveling left and he was staring her square in the face.

In the end Riker was glad his resolve had crumbled. Because instead of comprehending those mouthed words as *Pull over, now* or *Yes, I'm certain it's them* he actually understood what she was saying word for word as she continued berating him across the four-foot divide.

"Eff off, lady. I'm not driving like a grandpa," is what he mouthed back as the Homeland vehicle pulled away.

Brake lights flared red as the sparse traffic ahead noted the strobing grill lights and began to congregate in the right lanes.

Once the Tahoe was nearly lost to the horizon, Riker steered into the fast lane and matted the accelerator. His lone goal: Keep the retreating flashers in sight.

Chapter 53

Twenty minutes removed from the ten-second encounter with Homeland Security, Riker's nerves were no longer sparking like live-wires on a wet street, the tightness in his shoulders and neck had slackened, and his laser-like focus on the speeding SUV was waning.

"Lee. Lee," said Tara. She was pointing at the Tahoe. Its right rear blinker was flashing amber, the brake lights flaring red.

A quick speedometer check told Riker they were traveling the interstate a tad north of ninety. Not quite scratching the bucket list itch, but getting close. When he looked up, he saw they were rapidly closing with their quarry.

"They're pulling off," said Tara.

"I see that." Riker eased off the gas and took his eyes from the road only long enough to glance at the squiggly multi-colored lines crisscrossing the navigation screen. "Where are we now?"

"Van Buren is up ahead a mile or two."

"Where do you think the Homeland folks are going in such a damn hurry? The supposed radiological spill, incident, whatever the hell they're using as an excuse is the other way."

Tara was listening but not actually looking at her brother. Instead she was focused on a point in the distance where the Tahoe seemed to be headed. She saw the broadside of the vehicle as it took an off-ramp and crossed over right to left. She found herself again staring at the flashing grill lights as the Homeland SUV doubled back and raced down an elevated road paralleling the interstate.

"I may be mistaken," she said, "but it appears they're meeting up with those vehicles by that RV dealership."

Riker looked off to the left, squinting to see what Tara was talking about. Only things readily discernable to him were the stringers of colorful flags popping in the wind above dozens of train-car-sized rectangles sporting shiny chrome bumpers and two-tone paintjobs. He only categorized them as RVs because of Tara's mention of the dealership.

Panning left of the fleet of RVs, Riker spotted what at first blush struck him as a field filled with Indiana Department of Transportation vehicles: asphalt pavers, graders, dozers, back loaders, and all of the accoutrements necessary to efficiently execute a lengthy repave job.

By the time the distance to the off-ramp was halved, both literally and figuratively, several things became clear to Riker. What he'd pegged as INDOT machinery was in fact a smattering of MRAP armored vehicles wearing the tan paint schemes ubiquitous to both theaters of war in the Middle East. He stopped counting at two dozen. Though he didn't know the specific models, from the multiple different profiles standing out against the setting sun, it looked as if both Oshkosh and MaxxPro's offerings were accounted for. And mixed in with the bulky armored wheeled vehicles were at least a dozen slightly smaller armored vehicles outfitted with low-profile turrets and riding on four wheels versus the eight or ten of the MRAPs.

Back when Riker was employed and had kept an apartment and could afford basic cable, he'd seen prototypes of the smaller Mine Resistant Ambush Protected All-Terrain Vehicle, or M-ATV for short, profiled on the Military Channel. They were fast and agile and could pack a punch with its Special Forces operators able to acquire and engage targets with the roof-mounted Crew Remotely Operated Weapons System. The CROWs system, which he'd learned was basically a remotely operated turret, could be fitted with M240 or M2 belt-fed machine guns, 40mm grenade launchers, or, for use against tanks and other armor pieces, the BGM-71 TOW missile launcher.

Soldiers in full battle rattle milled about among the vehicles. Others were scurrying on and around the MRAPs and

M-ATVs, likely dogging down hatches and securing spare parts and personal gear to the angular armor plating.

Light flared off the south-facing plates of green glass as the Suburban came even with the unlikely assemblage.

Tara scrutinized the static vehicles until the overpass shadow washed over the Suburban and the concrete structure was behind them and blocking her view. "What did we just see?"

"Looks like a rallying point for some kind of major joint operation. Pretty sure I saw Homeland, Army, and National Guard vehicles staged together."

"For a training operation, right?"

Riker signaled and moved over to the center lane. *Always more options there.* Glancing at Tara, he said, "Don't be naive, Sis. The noose is *not* tightening around Middletown. I'm afraid the exact opposite is true."

As if to add an exclamation point to Riker's statement, four U.S. Army Chinook helicopters painted in Woodland Desert Sage thundered low and fast overhead. Though he couldn't see them in the rearview, judging by their southwest heading they were likely going to put down in the vast fields south of Liberty Recreation's sales lots. The same mostly flat parcels of crushed-down grass where a pair of fuel bowsers, mobile generators, and multiple telescoping light standards had been pre-positioned.

"I'm not naïve, Lee. I'm trying to be optimistic. That was more of the MRAP things, wasn't it?"

"Correct."

"What were the smaller vehicles? The SUV-looking things with guns on their roofs?"

"L-ATVs. Baby brother to the M-ATVs. They're a few tons lighter and can get into tighter areas. They're also employed by our Special Forces."

"You drove those?"

"Nope. They're pretty new to the inventory." Riker reached down to scratch an itch on his stump. Dug around under the cup for a second, in the process causing the metal of the prosthetic to clank against the Mossberg. "Take this back," he said, returning the shotgun to Tara in a safe manner. "And plot us a course to a seedy motel somewhere near Akron."

Queens, New York

When Tony woke, several hours had passed, his head was throbbing, and his tee shirt was damp with sweat. Strangely, the street outside his Queens apartment, usually bustling with activity on a Sunday evening, was deathly quiet. Through the vertical seam in the curtains he saw that the flat light of autumn had been supplanted by a dull gray sky quickly turning to black.

The power-saving feature on the flat-panel television had taken over and turned the Samsung off for him, leaving his tiny front room quiet and a profound sense of loneliness building within him.

Powering the television back on, he flipped to the local news channel and saw that 4WTC was *still* burning. A cold shiver wracked his body when he realized the upper twenty stories were now fully engulfed, some of the metal beams seemingly aglow.

As he watched the flames licking up the mirrored surface, beads of sweat formed on his forehead which he found hot to the touch.

Tearing his eyes from the surreal sight, he focused his attention on the crawl at the bottom of the screen, quickly learning that a person dubbed the Central Park Biter had struck again, upping his total number of victims to six in the last fifteen minutes. Then a petite female reporter was on, describing similar "copycat" attacks occurring inside emergency rooms at Lower Manhattan Hospital, Gouverneur Health, and NYU Langone Medical Center on Manhattan's Upper East Side.

As a story about a Norovirus outbreak in Middletown, Indiana usurped the 4WTC coverage, Tony grabbed the fifth bottle and poured himself another three fingers of Old Crow. Changing the channel to CNN, he saw a wide panorama of Manhattan, likely taken from a helicopter hovering somewhere south of Battery Park. Lights in the skyscrapers were winking on as day slipped away. Slowly defining their outlines, the lights strung on the bridges were becoming visible against the dark waters of the Hudson and East River. And as the camera panned right to left and zoomed in, the Washington Bridge filled up the screen. A number of police vehicles were positioned at each end, their red and blue lights strobing hypnotically.

To validate what he was seeing, the crawl on CNN began listing closures of bridges and tunnels all leading in and out of Manhattan.

Tony was pouring himself a third drink when the words *Manhattan Island Under Quarantine* appeared on the crawl. Before he could process what that had to do with a biter in the park and a brand new skyscraper catching fire or the bridges and tunnels connecting the island with the other boroughs and New Jersey being declared off limits, air raid sirens began to wail, their high-pitched warble fake-sounding coming through the television's tiny speakers.

Almost immediately the Manhattan sirens were joined by others close by. Faint at first, their undulating peals soon rose to an ear-splitting crescendo. There was nothing "fake-sounding" about these. Even through the double-glazed windows in his efficiency apartment, though he didn't know their significance, there was no mistaking them for what they were—a portent of bad things to come.

Chapter 54

Four hours had slipped into the past and the corn maze lay roughly two hundred and seventy-five miles behind the Suburban when darkness fell and the sky decided to open up on them. Rain pummeled the Suburban and lightning forked in the distance over Akron, Ohio as the wipers struggled to keep up with the deluge.

The traffic that had picked up east of Fort Wayne where US-24 became US-30 had stayed steady until they crossed the Indiana/Ohio state line. Their entire time spent driving in Ohio, Riker had stayed to the fast lane and made good time, only seeing two patrol cars the entire way, both charging westbound on US-30 and lit up like Christmas trees.

Their only stop between the Iron Pan Restaurant and their current location on I-76 a few miles southwest of Akron was a much-needed fuel and bathroom break at a Speedway station in Mansfield, some sixty miles behind them.

***

Seeing a sign indicating Akron lay a scant eight miles ahead, Riker slowed to five above the posted limit and slipped over to the center lane. A short while later I-76 swung around east and became Vietnam Veterans Memorial Highway from which downtown Akron presented as a bright bubble of light looming large on the horizon.

"Steve-O," said Riker, eyes flicking to the rearview. "You've been quiet as a ninja back there. Whatcha got on rotation on that iPod now?"

Nothing.

In the passenger seat Tara didn't look up. She was busy running the Emory board over the badly mangled nail on her left middle finger. She'd split it in two places helping her brother to close the door against the weight of the Bolt back at the high school.

Riker adjusted the rearview mirror down with one hand but saw no movement in the gloom behind his seat. Raising his voice to override whatever country crooner currently had Steve-O's ear, he said, "You still with us, buddy?"

Still no response. There was only the steady hiss of radials cutting the slop on the road and a metronomic *scritch, scritch, scritch* made by the tool in Tara's hand as she went about reshaping the nail.

Slowing to the speed limit, Riker cast a quick glance over his shoulder. Got eyes on Steve-O. He was back there all right but was sound asleep. The white earbuds were still in place, the wires snaking to the lit-up iPod which was on his lap and illuminating his upper torso. His plastic-framed glasses were folded and sitting beside the iPod. Next to him on the seat was the perfectly shaped Stetson.

A rope of drool stretched from the corner of his lip to the lap belt where a dark stain had already formed on the black nylon. Judging by the angle of Steve-O's neck, he was going to have one hell of a crick in it once he awoke.

As Riker swung his gaze around, he glimpsed a lake gliding by on the right. Its surface was black as obsidian and reflected the halide lights ringing its shore. Again focused solely on the three-lane awash in twin cones of light thrown from the Suburban's headlights, he said, "Steve-O's sound asleep. How are you doing?"

Tara kicked off the fake Crocs and put her feet on the dash. "This is nothing like I envisioned it being," she said, her voice betraying a hint of sadness. "This trip to scatter Mom's ashes is supposed to be a celebration of her life. We should be enjoying ourselves like Carrie and the Bandit. Or Thelma and Louise. *Not* hiding from helicopters in corn fields and looking over our shoulders for tails."

Trees and cement noise-abatement panels lining both sides of the highway blipped by as a minute ticked into the past.

Finally Riker shifted in his seat, cleared his throat, and said, "Who am I supposed to be?"

A rare smile curling her lip, Tara said, "The Bandit, of course."

Riker's brows hitched as he shot her a questioning look. "Thelma or Louise?" he said, gruffly.

She checked on Steve-O. Saw that he was still out cold. So she asked, "Which one got boned by Brad Pitt?"

"Thelma, I think," said Riker. "And J.D. was the name of the character played by Pitt."

"Well then," she said dreamily, "J.D. better be at the motel bar when we get there."

"That movie came out a long time ago, you know. You were about to be born ... or just had been. How do you know about those old movies, anyway?"

"I fall asleep with the boob tube on. Usually to Turner Classics. Living alone, I like my background noise."

Now Riker was smiling. And looking at her. He said, "You do know that Brad Pitt is like fifty years old now, don't you?"

"Thanks a lot. You just ruined my *only* sexual fantasy."

Squinting against the oncoming string of headlights, Riker said, "Just saving you from yourself, Sis."

***

Ten minutes of silence ensued after Riker's parting quip. As he was slowing to take the ramp off of I-77, he couldn't help but pick up right where he had left off.

Voice dripping with incredulity, he said, "*Only* sexual fantasy? Man, Sis, you need to broaden your horizons. Maybe pick up a copy of Fifty Shades or something."

Steve-O made a snorting noise and was suddenly bolt upright and jamming his glasses onto his face. In the next beat, his wisps of reddish-blond hair were hidden underneath the white cowboy hat. "Where are we?" he asked.

"We're looking for a place to stay the night. And when we get there, Tara will be going straight to the bar"—Riker snorted, choking back laughter—"and what she finds there will determine how many rooms we get."

"S … e… x," said Steve-O. He grinned and ran his sleeve across his mouth.

Riker imagined Tara next to him in the cab turning several shades of red. That it was dark and he didn't want to leer meant he couldn't confirm his suspicion. So he chalked it up as fact and went on, "We're in Akron, Ohio. Figure we get some shut eye, then wake up at the butt crack of dawn and get going."

"Good," said Steve-O. "I'm tired and my neck hurts. Maybe there's tickling fingers in the bed."

Tara looked at Riker, who merely shrugged and began scanning the road ahead for any kind of sign offering Clean Rooms or Free HBO or the availability of a Hot Tub and Heated Pool. The latter amenities of which he would definitely take advantage of. The repercussions from the fast and furious scrum with the Bolt in the school tunnel were beginning to manifest in the way of a soreness running up both sides of his ribcage. Then there was the driving. Ever since the IED explosion, sitting behind the wheel of anything for prolonged periods of time did a number on his lower back and left arm.

As for Steve-O and his "tickling fingers"—whatever in the hell they were—he was going to let good ol' fate determine their availability.

Queens

The biggest thing Jillian Delinford hated about being on-premise manager for the Waverly Heights apartments was confronting a tenant about any transgression unbecoming of a grown adult. Though disturbances here were few and far between, she abhorred having to play policeman—especially when the one who needed policing knew a thing or two about it.

She clomped up to the third-floor landing, cursing and muttering the whole way. She turned toward the door to Unit 6, keys in hand and a monumental resentment filling the small landing alongside her.

"Tony," she cawed. "Are you drunk again?"

Nothing.

Jillian jingled the keys once.

Silence.

"I heard you banging around in there, Tony. If you're going to cook after you've had a few, please use the microwave."

There was a low rumble from behind the door. Sounded a lot like a heavy piece of furniture being forced across bare floor.

Jillian thought about announcing herself again but decided against it. Instead, she dragged out her portable phone and hit redial.

A phone rang somewhere deep inside Unit 6. It jangled on for fifteen seconds.

"I know you're in there, you old sot." She stabbed a finger at the phone and instantly the ringing ceased. "Coming in."

It took Jillian a moment to throw all three locks with her master key. Finished, she slipped the keys and phone in the deep pocket of her floral-print housecoat.

"Tony?" She pushed the door inward to the sound of glass breaking somewhere down the hall.

Once the door reached the wall and hit with a soft *thunk*, she looked past the jamb and took a step inside.

"Tony? You okay?"

A guttural growl answered. Then footfalls, heavy and deliberate, sounded from within.

Jillian turned to close the door at her back and was hit broadside by two-hundred-plus pounds of lumbering flesh. She went to her knees and felt the bones in her shoulder snap like twigs as her attacker drove her to the floor.

A scream was just forming in Jillian's throat when she was hit full on with the sour stink of some kind of whisky. In the next beat, as the howl brought on by the pain from a hundred shards of crushed clavicle and ribs piercing flesh and lung crossed over her lips, the sweet stink of flesh just beginning to decay supplanted the waft of booze,

Jillian didn't feel the added pain of her assailant's incisors rending meat from her neck. The hot, sticky blood matting her hair to the floor barely registered as her eyelids fluttered once and the shock from the attack and vicious takedown graced her with the sweet oblivion of unconciousness.

Chapter 55

The *King's Court* marquee rose up beside a rambling two-level motor court set a dozen yards off a busy, oil-streaked stretch of four-lane shooting north into the heart of Akron. Glowing red and reflecting off the Suburban's glossy black hood, the neon sign was mated to a white reader board announcing that the *King* offered *Free Wi-Fi, Clean king and queen beds,* and *free HBO,* the latter statement assuring Tara that basic cable was part of the deal as well. Truth was, she didn't care a lick about HBO. She wanted to park herself on the end of the bed and surf every available news channel until she gleaned all she could about the happenings in Middletown and beyond. She figured the information would be sanitized and limited. So first things first: There was a list of things she needed to procure to avail her to dig deeper for more intel than the local channels and cable were allowed to divulge. Some electronic items that an out of the way two-star roach motel simply didn't offer.

Checking for her wallet, Tara said, "Pull up to the office and let me out."

Complying with the curt request, Riker rolled up the drive and hung a wide U-turn and parked under a portico a half-dozen feet from the office door. There was a sign reading VACANCY in the fogged-up front window. After slipping the ignition into Park, he said, "Sure this is the one? It's just a few minutes past seven. We still have time to find a better deal."

Again with a clipped response. "This'll do."

Something must really be eating at her, thought Riker. He said, "How are we paying for this?"

She held up a white card embossed with numbers and sporting the *VISA* logo.

"They can trace it if you use it. Then they'll come a knocking in the dead of night," he said, not so sure he was correct but still wanting to be a little more cautious than they'd been at the truck stop. "Do you want to wake up with a gun pointing in your face?"

"You're overthinking this one, Lee." She smiled. Second time in an hour. "I got this from the Speedway when we gassed up. It's a hundred-dollar-denomination gift card. 'Good anywhere,' the clerk said."

"You're still going to have to show your driver's license," proffered Steve-O.

Riker nodded agreeably. "Steve-O's right. What are you going to do if they insist on a credit card with your name on it?"

"If it's a guy, flash him my tits and bat my eyes. If it's a woman—" She paused for a second.

Steve-O said, "Show *her* your boobs," and burst out laughing.

Tara tried real hard to not join in. Her resolve lasted a few seconds. Soon they were all laughing and the windows were steaming up.

Tara dabbed at her eyes with a sleeve. After looking at her face in the flip-down vanity mirror, she declared herself "Okay to face the world" and shouldered open her door.

Riker watched Tara disappear through the single door, then let his gaze roam the building and grounds. Save for its name and earth-tone paint scheme decorating the two-level affair, the King was no different than the dozens of motor inns he had had the displeasure of patronizing during his thirty-eight years on Planet Earth. The parking lot was a vast sea of rippled asphalt with dull yellow lines denoting parking spaces. From the entrance off the boulevard, the King wrapped around the lot clockwise and was capped off at the end by a tarpaulin-covered in-ground swimming pool. A half-dozen vehicles were nosed in to spots lining up with red doors bearing cheap looking NO SMOKING plaques and six-inch-tall room numbers made of stamped brass.

Riker tried the radio again and found much of the same. If something untoward was happening in Ohio or the bordering states, the disc jockeys either weren't in the know, or were under strict order to keep quiet about it.

The rain ceased just as the door to the office swung open and Tara emerged. She wore a half-smile as she flashed a thumb up and displayed a plastic key tag for all to see.

Mission accomplished, thought Riker as his industrious sibling climbed into the SUV.

"How'd it go?" asked Riker as he pulled another U-turn and let the idling engine drag the SUV in the direction of the pool at a walking speed.

The dashboard clock read 7:09 when he slid the Suburban into the parking spot fronting the door to Unit 13. He left the engine run and turned to Tara. "So ... how'd you pull it off?"

Steve-O interrupted. "Did you have to show him your—"

Cutting Steve-O's comment short with a harsh look, she said, "I put the prepaid Visa on the counter and specifically asked the clerk for a room at the rear of the building. 'So I don't have to listen to freeway noise' is what I told him. When he asked for a license and a different credit card with my name on it, I told him my abusive boyfriend is a pledge at the university and is looking for me. Told him his dad is a cop and has access to databases and such." She smirked. "Then I showed him my knuckles and the split nail. That seemed to soften him up. When he persisted—."

Steve-O chuckled. "No, I didn't do that. I let Andrew Jackson do the talking for me."

Steve-O was having a hard time containing his laughter. His cheeks were red and he was clamping a hand over his mouth.

Throwing a quick glance over her shoulder, Tara said, "Let's get one thing clear, gentlemen: I am not that kind of girl. So both of you, stifle it." Regarding Riker, she added, "Take Mom and the gun inside with you. I've got some shopping to do."

Riker looked a question at her.

She handed over the key. "The clerk was a young guy. Probably a student moonlighting here to make ends meet. We're very lucky it wasn't a bifocal-wearing oldster behind that counter."

Riker shouldered the pack containing the urn. "What difference does it make?"

She held up the sheet containing the Wi-Fi login and password. "He urged me to get dirt on my ex to get even with him. Then he told me how to use this to get onto sites I didn't know existed and where to go to get the dirt. But I have other plans for it. So don't lose it."

Riker glanced at the sheet. "Who's going to forget Graceland in all caps as the login?" After dragging the sheet closer to his face to see the password which was scrawled much smaller below the login, he added, "You can't remember Elvis123?"

"I got it," replied Steve-O confidently.

She glanced at the clock. "I gotta go. Thirty minutes to get to the Chapel Hill part of town." She began inputting the address into the navigation unit.

"What's in Chapel Hill that you can't get at a store nearby?"

"You tell me where we're taking Mom and I'll—"

Riker put a hand up to stop her. "I keep forgetting you're a grown ass woman. Just keep your phone turned on. I'll do the same."

She frowned, then nodded.

Riker hauled his left leg out and planted the boot on his prosthetic directly into an inches-deep puddle. *Not going to feel that,* he thought, smiling to himself at one of the few advantages the lack of a lower leg afforded.

Clambering out with a bag of snacks and the iPod trailing white buds, Steve-O called to Tara, telling her to be careful out there.

She was climbing over the center console and paused to say: "I will, Sir Galahad. I have my phone and will use it if I have to."

He smiled and tapped the side of the SUV before turning and following Riker through the door to room 13.

Chapter 56

Riker let Steve-O pass him, then closed them both inside the dimly lit room. He breathed deeply, detecting the faint nose of bleach with some kind of fragrance added to it. Fresh Spring, Ocean Surf, maybe Mountain Dew? It was something with a catchy name, though not the latter he decided after laughing inwardly. Mountain Dew was that neon-green soda whose maker sponsored the X-Games.

Riker flicked on the overhead.

No roaches scurried under the bed.

"What do you think?" he asked.

Steve-O plopped down on the bed nearest the open bathroom door. He examined the nightstand wedged between the pair of queen beds. Ran a hand over the pressed-wood headboard. Finally, face conveying a measure of disappointment, he replied, "No tickler fingers."

"We'll live. They do have HBO, though."

"Game of Thrones is over until forever," said Steve-O soberly.

"I picked up one of the books overseas. Couldn't get into it," admitted Riker. He squeezed past the dresser at the foot of the bed nearest the door and grabbed the remote from the desk at the foot of Steve-O's bed. Aiming it at the flat panel atop the dresser, he thumbed the power button and watched while the screen flared to life.

The television was already tuned to a local channel. A female anchor sat behind a polished glass desk, her shapely legs crossed casually under the see-through knee-well. *Who needs a miniskirt and four-inch heels to relay facts?* thought Riker as he sat on the corner of the bed opposite Steve-O.

"You make a better door than a window."

Catching the hint, Riker pushed off the bed and relocated to the one nearest the door, compressing the mattress and box springs as he settled back down on the corner facing the television.

Behind the blonde anchor on the television was a wall comprised of interconnected displays. The one to her right was showing a handful of static military vehicles with men and women milling around them. The tag at the bottom of that screen read STAGING GROUNDS FOR AS YET TO BE NAMED JOINT SERVICES OPERATION. Basing his assumption on the backdrop comprised of dozens of recreational vehicles, he figured he was looking at the same staging area they had passed earlier in the day. However, due to artificial lighting and the limited focal length of the camera lens, he was left with the impression he was looking at only a small contingent of National Guard troops. Maybe it was by design, he mused. Keep the public in the dark.

Suddenly the image on the flat panel was split down the middle. The left half was filled up by a reporter dispatched from Cleveland. He wore light-gray raingear and a navy ball cap sporting a FOX 8 logo.

The female anchor loomed large now on the right side of the screen. She displayed a wan smile, greeted the at-large reporter, then promptly launched into a series of probing questions.

After the barrage ceased, the at-large reporter greeted and thanked the anchor then delved right into the questions, answering them in the order posed.

"In light of the unprecedented dual calamities in Middletown and Daleville, both small Indiana towns, the Indiana and Ohio National Guard are using the biological and nuclear accidents as a reason to conduct a hastily thrown-together joint training operation I overheard being called—." He paused and began to search his pockets for something.

Waxing poetic, the blonde anchor interjected, saying, "You know, Kyle, it takes a special kind of commitment to answer the call on such short notice." She pursed her lips and shook her head. Looking straight into the camera, she added, "All of you at home should applaud these troops for their dedication to flag and country. These men and women are your neighbors. They might own the store down the block. And they all dropped what they were doing and put the uniform on to proudly represent Ohio."

"You've got that right, Susan," replied the reporter. "And from what I've overheard, they're all being tested fully tonight."

"Can you elaborate, Kyle? Maybe tell us what you're seeing. What's the mood among the troops on the ground?"

Kyle opened his mouth, then closed it and looked to his left. Focused intently on something off screen, he pressed a hand to the flesh-colored bud in his right ear.

Susan's brow furrowed. It looked to Riker as if the anchor thought the feed's audio was dropping off.

"Susan. Are you there?" said the reporter just as the bass-heavy rumble of an engine made him wince and turn a one-eighty.

The anchor responded with a simple "Yes, Kyle," then repeated her questions concerning what he was seeing and the morale of the soldiers.

"Well, Susan," said Kyle. "It appears that the RMT … Real Military Training joint exercise I overheard being called"— he paused to consult a square of paper palmed in his off-hand— "Romeo Victor is growing larger as we speak. A contingent representing the Illinois National Guard just rolled by on my left. I see Humvees and armored vehicles … a Bradley or two, I think. And from what I've heard the soldiers saying, Susan, they're all about to be mobilized to begin a march south."

The blonde anchor asked a couple of inane questions that caused Riker to change the channel to CNN where he found the young President just wrapping up an address to the nation.

The President's closing words seemed off the cuff and sincere. It was basically a plea for all Americans to come together and remain vigilant in the wake of the worst act of homegrown terror the nation had ever seen.

Riker tried to recall how many died at the hands of McVeigh when he bombed the Alfred P. Murrah Federal building in Oklahoma City. Somewhere around three hundred was what he came up with off the top of his head. This tower fire must have taken a turn for the worse from where it was at when he saw it on the television in the Iron Pan bar.

Without warning, Steve-O stood up and high-tailed it to the bathroom—covering all five feet to the door in three purposeful strides.

Exhausted, Riker pulled his pant's leg up, removed his prosthesis, and stowed it beside the bed. Seeing a commercial touting the benefits of gold ownership come on the television, he laid down diagonally across the bed he'd been sitting on. He parked his gaze on a grapefruit-sized water mark marring the popcorn ceiling and began to work over a problem that had been troubling him since he heard the words Romeo Victor spoken by the FOX 8 reporter.

While the Department of Defense did have a penchant for naming every action it took in a military capacity with randomly generated monikers, Romeo Victor struck him as odd—especially for an impromptu call-up and deployment of men and women who, when not on overseas deployment, usually only donned the uniform for one weekend a month and a couple of weeks during the year for extended in-the-field training. Sure, it was feasible the words overheard by the anchor, words that just so happened to be designators for the letters R and V in the NATO phonetic alphabet, *could* have been chosen at random. However, as Riker thought about it, he started to believe Romeo Victor to be an acronym for something else. Maybe something sinister, considering that he'd recently witnessed soldiers in black shooting civilians in cold blood.

"Romeo Victor," he said under his breath. *Rings nothing like Operation Iraqi Freedom*, the action in which he'd lost his lower left leg and, for a long while after, a great deal of his sanity.

He continued to stare at the ceiling and mulled over in his head the names of other operations he could remember from past history: *Operation Desert Storm*, the first war in the desert. *Operation Just Cause* was what Reagan called his invasion of Panama during which four Navy SEALs died tightening the noose on the despotic President of Panama, General Manuel Noriega. There was *Enduring Freedom*, the name bestowed upon America's invasion of Afghanistan and ongoing combat action against the Taliban—all in direct response to the 9/11 attacks. *Operation Red Wing* was the infamous *Lone Survivor* rescue operation that unfolded in the mountains of Afghanistan and cost eight Navy SEALs and eight Night Stalker pilots of the famed Special Operations Aviation Regiment their lives. Finally there was *Operation Jade Helm 15*, the most recent and by far pertinent RMT (Real Military Training) exercise Riker could remember. Conducted in the Southwest in 2015, Jade Helm succeeded in getting a lot of conspiracy theorists riled up. Some speculated it was conducted to condition civilians to the sight of armed troops in American cities, thus rendering the population lax when the actual roundup of Americans' guns commenced.

If Romeo Victor was indeed an RMT, why the nonsense name? And why hadn't any of the previous operations' names contained a single word from the NATO alphabet?

The longer Riker thought about it, the more convinced he became of his acronym theory.

Drawing a blank as to what R and V might correspond with, Riker sat up and stared at the television.

When the latest string of panic commercials selling gold, food dehydrators, and "Same as those used by Navy SEALs" high-intensity flashlights finished playing on the television, two things happened back to back, First, the bathroom door swung open, releasing an invisible cloud of stench that to Riker smelled like beef jerky dipped in dog shit. Then, on the heels of Steve-O exiting the tiny bathroom amidst his eye-watering handiwork, the wash of blue-white light rippled across the threadbare burgundy curtains and a vehicle pulled into the unit's parking space.

Chapter 57

As quickly as the vehicle had pulled up in front of the window to room 13, the engine cut out and the headlights were extinguished.

With spots still dancing before his eyes, Riker fixed Steve-O with a look borne of equal parts wonder and incredulity. "What the eff crawled up inside you and died?" He covered his nose and mouth with one hand. With the other he pointed at the door— universal semaphore for *You gonna get that?*

Steve-O said nothing. Nor did he acknowledge the engine rumble or intrusive glare from the Suburban's Zenon bulbs as they swept the picture window. He was standing rigid in front of the television and staring down at the pale nub protruding over the end of the bed. He seemed especially interested in the pink scarring where skin overlapped bone.

Riker said, "The pretty lady is back."

No effect.

Steve-O walked his gaze up Riker's leg, locked eyes with him, then asked, "What happened?"

"A roadside bomb happened," replied Riker nonchalantly.

Steve-O was rubbing the red stubble on his chin absentmindedly. He asked, "When did it happen?" He flicked his eyes back to the stump. "And where did it happen?"

There was a pair of bass-heavy thumps on the door. Down low near the floor. As if Tara was kicking at it instead of knocking to get their attention.

"Lost it in 2005 on Route Irish outside of the Green Zone in Baghdad, Iraq."

A second barrage of urgent-sounding thumps rattled the hollow-core door against its hinges. Voice muffled, Tara called, "Open the *damn* door. My hands are full."

Still studying Riker's stump, Steve-O called, "Coming." Hesitantly, he tore his eyes away, walked over and opened the door.

Tara was standing on the concrete walk. Her stocking cap was soaked and listing to one side. Water dripped from the small eave overhead, further wetting her hat and face and beading up on her red North Face jacket. She shook some of the water off then bugged her eyes. "Before we have a Jinga moment, will one of you strapping gentlemen take some of this crap off my hands?"

The handles of two overstuffed plastic shopping bags were looped over each arm. Said arms were curled up in front of her bosom and struggling to keep hold of the rectangular cardboard box balanced there.

Riker craned to see past Steve-O. Once eye contact was made with Tara, he pointed to his stump to let her know he was in one-legged mode.

Without a word, Steve-O grabbed the box and placed it on the bed next to Riker.

"Better grab her a towel," said Riker as he picked the box up and placed it across his legs. The rain-dampened box was three feet end to end, nearly two front to back, and four inches tall. Scrawled in Sharpie across the lid were the words *Open Box Return*. There was a sticker on the side, but the size of the font made it impossible for Riker to read. Looking up, he asked, "The suspense is killing me. May I open it?"

Tara had already shrugged the bags off her arms and was dabbing at her face with a hand towel Steve-O had brought her. "Be my guest." She tossed the towel aside and turned the flimsy bags inside out, depositing their contents on the floor in a wide spray from end to end. She kicked off the fake Crocs and slipped on a fresh pair of socks. Over those she laced up a new pair of Merrell hikers. Finished, she tossed a package of white tube socks and men's boxer shorts onto the bed next to her brother. Steve-

O's socks and boxers, she took from the Target sack and hand-delivered.

Addressing Riker, who was just working the tape off the end of the box, Tara said, "Both are extra-large. And if they don't fit, tough shit." She smiled and regarded Steve-O. "I know, feed the swear jar."

Steve-O smiled and rubbed a thumb and forefinger together. "Pay up," he said, smile broadening.

"You have nothing to worry about," she said. "Because if things work out tomorrow the way I think they're going to, I could channel a salty Merchant Marine sailor and curse for an entire year and still not run out of cash for your imaginary jar."

Steve-O reached for the dresser and took a wrapped plastic cup off a tray home to an empty ice bucket, a single-serve Keurig coffee maker, and all of its accoutrements. He slipped the cup from the plastic slowly and set it upright next to the television.

Removing her new coat, Tara said, "I'm good for it, Steve-O," then looked to Riker. "What do you think of the purchase?"

"The coat, boots, undergarments, or computer?"

She pointed at the shiny black laptop.

Turning the DELL over in his hands, Riker said, "Why do we need a computer?"

"Let me tell you. How long do you have?" Suddenly, as if a light switch had been flicked, Tara's eyes narrowed and she clamped a hand over her mouth and nose. "What is that smell?"

Without missing a beat, Steve-O said, "Lee's been farting."

Tara slowly panned her head and fixed Riker with a sour look. "Really, Lee? You couldn't go in the bathroom and do that?"

Again Riker pointed to his stump. "No crutches, Sis." Then he looked to Steve-O. He was wearing the best poker face Riker had ever seen. After staring at the older man for a beat, Riker received a conspiratorial wink.

Gasping for air, Tara started for the front door but paused midstep. Remembering the face-shot slogger from the corn maze near Daleville, she decided rather than cracking the door to ease the bathroom fan's work load, she'd open the bathroom window a few inches instead.

"This computer," pressed Riker. He had it hinged open and powered on. "Why do we really need it? And how did you afford it? You only took out fifteen hundred dollars at the Iron Pan."

"We need it to see what's really going on out there," she replied. "I could afford it because it was a returned item and only a fraction of the cost of a new one. I figured it'd be easier for you to access your bank account on that than on my tiny phone screen. Besides, if the previous owners set it up already, it won't be connected to either of us."

Wearing a knowing look, Riker nodded. "No way for the MIBs to track us."

"Exactly." She removed her damp hat and donned Riker's Braves cap. She waggled her fingers at the computer in a *give it here* manner then sat on the bed opposite her brother.

After passing the computer over, Riker said, "I don't even do the computer banking thing." He glanced at the window. Steve-O was peering out between the curtains. Addressing Tara, he went on, "I call the bank because I'd rather try to understand a person in a call center in India than try to get a robot to understand me."

"We're in." Smile quickly disappearing, she added, "But it's wiped. The Geek Crew kid warned me that it probably had already gone through their re-shelving procedures."

"What do we do then?"

"Make shit up."

"Swear cup," called Steve-O.

Riker asked, "What do you see out there?"

"Rain," said Steve-O." And some lightning up by Lake Erie."

Riker said, "No monsters?"

"Negative, Ghost Rider."

Tara said, "Keep us informed."

Steve-O didn't reply.

Tara whipped through the setup process.

"Minnie Mouse … really?"

Tara chuckled. "I live on Disney Lane, too."

"You already said the social media sites are probably scrubbing any video proof or news segments before they post."

She nodded.

"How are you going to get around that?"

"Same way I'm going to share my video: The Deep Web."

Deep web sounded ominous, to Riker. Like somewhere Indiana Jones might reside if he was an avatar. He opened his mouth, then closed it without asking about it.

Anticipating the question, Tara said, "The Geek Crew kid was more than eager to help direct me there." She pulled up *Wi-Fi* in *Windows Settings*.

Abruptly, Steve-O stood up from the bed and declared himself "Bushed." He stretched, shucked off his Wrangler's, and laid them on the chair between the bed and wall. While they didn't quite *stand up on their cuffs* as Riker had predicted when he'd first met Steve-O, they still retained most of their form. In fact, as they settled in the chair, it almost seemed as if they were actually taking a load off.

Tara said, "I bought you a toothbrush and toothpaste. They're in the Rite Aid bag with the thumb drives and charging cables I bought for our devices."

"Thanks," said Steve-O. "I brush in the morning." He removed his glasses and set them on the nightstand beside the digital clock. His Stetson went atop his jeans and he unbuttoned his shirt, taking care to snap the pearlescent buttons before carefully placing the denim number over the chair back. Without another word, he crawled between the sheets and rolled over to face the clothes-laden chair.

Riker shrugged. Then he looked at the bed and walked his eyes to the plush chair beside the window.

Sensing her brother's unease, Tara moved over to the chair, computer in hand, and told him to take the bed. "I don't plan on sleeping anyway." She nudged the NRA bag under the table with the toe of her hiker. "And if I get lonely, I've got Mom to keep me company."

Riker propped the shotgun muzzle down against the headboard. Since he was in trustworthy company, he left the prosthesis on the nightstand, standing up and ready to be thrown on in a moment's notice. Lastly, he recapped to Tara everything he'd seen on television while she was gone, making a point to mention his problem with Romeo Victor as well as just how oddly calm he felt the President had come across in his speech given the ramifications of another terrorist attack in Manhattan. Finished, he pulled a Steve-O and abruptly shucked his pants and sweatshirt, leaving the twin pools of fabric where they had come to rest on the floor. Wearing only boxer briefs and a worn gray tee shirt, he took station between the sheets dead center on the bed closest to the front door.

Tara set the Dell on the small oval table in front of the window and started tapping away at the keyboard.

Propped up on one elbow and watching over his sister's shoulder, Riker said, "How'd you get so good at typing? That's got to be way more than thirty words per minute."

"Sixty or so," replied Tara proudly

"Where'd you learn that?"

"I'm younger than you, Lee. For as long as I can remember, *everything* electronic has had a real or virtual keyboard."

He watched as she entered the Elvis-inspired login and password on the King's Court Wi-Fi launch page. She consulted a piece of paper with the Best Buy logo as masthead. Copied the string of letters written in pen into the web browser bar.

"Yeah. I just hunt and peck," admitted Riker.

Tara didn't seem to hear that. The address she had just inputed landed her on a site with instructions on how to download something called a TOR browser. After jumping through the hoops and waiting a couple of minutes for the new browser to come online, she typed in the browser's bar the next provided address. It took less than a second for a dog breeder's web page to fill the screen. The thing was plain and looked to have been designed by an amateur. Splashed haphazardly on a black background were pictures of different breeds of dogs standing stiffly in show-pose positions meant to show off their proportion and lines. The aquamarine text was small and hard to make out despite its stark contrast against the background.

Tara scrolled down to the bottom of the home page where a number of colorful badges suggested the breeder was in good standing with the American Kennel Club, Golden State Breeder's Association, Silicone Valley Humane Society, and the Cupertino Chamber of Commerce. She enlarged the screen and positioned the arrow pointer over a blue dot wedged in the lower right corner.

Riker heard a click and saw the screen go dark.

"You killed it, Sis."

"Nope," she said. "I just accessed the Deep Web." No sooner had she turned back to the computer screen than it flared bright blue. Dead center on the field of cobalt was a rectangular white box. Inside the box, in bold black *Times New Roman* font, the words **Who Are You?** flashed incessantly.

Tara consulted the Best Buy stationary as she typed a new string of letters and numbers into the box.

The blue screen became black again. Hovering in the center was a logo eerily similarly to YouTube's iconic red and white *Play* button floating on a white background.

"That Geek Crew kid … did you have to—"

"No," shot Tara. "No skin was exposed."

A stifled laugh sounded in the back of the room.

Ignoring Steve-O, who was obviously not asleep yet, Tara clicked on the arrow, bringing up a number of panes stacked in a vertical column. The clips were ranked from top to bottom, with the most viewed at the very top.

"Twenty-two thousand views," said Tara as she clicked on the top pane.

The pane grew to fill the screen. The beginning of the clip had a jittery *Blair Witch* feel to it. It was dusk and the shooter was breathing hard while apparently backpedaling. Then Riker saw a blurry image in the distance take on human form. As the blob drew nearer, the camera's autofocus feature began to catch up with it. At the three-second mark of the eight-second piece of footage, a piercing scream rang out and the advancing form launched itself at the person holding the camera. As the shooter pitched backward, she brought her arms up defensively, crossing them in front of her chest just as the violent impact with the ground stole her wind and sent the recording device flying from her grasp. As the device tumbled end-over-end, the image on the laptop screen matched its rotation while still catching snippets of the woman's demise.

Exhaling sharply, Tara scrolled the footage back a few frames to the point in the camera's rotation when it recorded the attacker's face.

Riker asked, "Can you enlarge that?"

"Let me see." Tara moved the pointer to the taskbar and clicked repeatedly. Once the image of a sneering, blood-streaked face filled up the screen, she leaned back and rotated the laptop left a few degrees.

Riker said, "That's a Bolt. And like the others, it's a younger male."

Tara said, "Scary thing is"—she paused to take a breath—"it's tagged Cannibal Killer."

"Where was it shot?"

Tara exhaled sharply. Swallowed hard, then said, "Fort Wayne."

"It's jumped their perimeter." Riker tossed the extra pillow aside and lay back. Staring at the ceiling, he said soberly, "So much for Romeo Victor."

Tara said nothing. She spun the laptop so it was facing her, donned Steve-O's earbuds, and plugged the jack into the computer.

The box spring squeaked as Riker rolled over and closed his eyes against the strobe effect of the footage playing on the screen. He was asleep in less than two minutes, entirely unaware of the morbid sights and sounds Tara was experiencing after having nudged that first domino the clip from Fort Wayne represented.

Chapter 58

Dawn didn't break over Akron, it crept in from the east gray and heavy, like a fogbank at sea, but on a much grander scale. Riker had slept fitfully until four in the morning when he jolted awake sweaty and tense. He had remained prone and watched silently over Tara's shoulder as she pulled up video clips from a Deep Web site, watched them, and moved on. For a full hour, during which the rising sun illuminated the gun-metal-gray clouds ever so slightly, he was bombarded with images similar to the ones that had come in the night. Things that he couldn't unsee.

***

The dull ache culminating from the nightmare and exacerbated from him craning his neck to see the computer screen was still with Riker two hours later when he sat up and plucked his prosthesis from the bed stand.

Startled, Tara came off the chair and closed the screen partway. "Damn, Lee. I thought you were Steve-O. There's shit on here he shouldn't see."

"I know. I've been watching over your shoulder for awhile now," admitted Riker. "How do you know he hasn't already seen it all. He was in the school basement, too."

Tara removed the Atlanta Braves cap, leaned back in the chair, and stretched her arms toward the ceiling.

Riker said, "He's a grown ass man, remember?"

Tara tossed the cap on the bed, looked to the ceiling, and began to worry her braids. After a few seconds in the same pose, she leaned forward. "I've got something you need to see." She plugged a thumb drive into a port on the side of the computer. Tapped a few keys and brought up the video player. Without letting on what was about to play, she tapped the touch pad and started the clip rolling.

On the screen was a twenty-something woman with a blonde bob hairdo being interviewed by a male reporter. Microphone inches from her lips, the woman shared her version of what went on inside the Middletown University foyer directly behind her. Stabbing a thumb in the direction of the blurred elevator bank, she implied she was making a pumpkin spice latte for a customer when the bus shooter entered from the hallway next to the elevators and "Just started spraying bullets." She went on to say it was her first day working the kiosk and she had never seen the shooter before. When pressed by the reporter whether she thought the shooter was a student, she confidently dismissed it as "Crazy. Because dude was old. And white. Fit the profile of those mass shooter types. Probably an NRA member, too."

Once the camera swung a one-eighty, Tara paused the video with a stainless-steel kiosk dead center. It was wedged against a cement planter with a wall of windows behind it.

Riker noted that the windows in the frame were all intact. Not a bullet hole punched through that he could see.

"Is that MU?"

"Yep. That's *my* kiosk, too."

"And she's a coworker of yours?"

Tara shook her head.

"Never seen her?"

"Nope," said Tara, her hands beginning to shake. "Never."

"Crisis actors," said Riker. "I thought that was all a bunch of tinfoil hat bullcrap."

Tara looked a question his way.

"There are conspiracy theorists out there who think that several events ... that big school shooting, the Boston bombing, the Orlando nightclub, are all false flag events orchestrated by our shadow government. They supposedly use crisis actors and film them in ways that will evoke emotion when plastered all over the newspapers, cable, and social media."

Tara's brow furrowed. "Why?"

"It's a sick way for them to nudge public sentiment one way or the other at a time of their choosing."

"Crisis actor or not," said Tara, "that bitch is full of shit."

"I have a feeling this is their last gasp at keeping this thing in-house," said Riker.

Tara glanced at the digital alarm clock.

"Think the transfer's going to come through today? It's almost eight," said Riker. "Don't most of them open at eight?"

Tara shook her head. "Bankers' hours are usually nine-to-five." She smiled knowingly.

"What aren't you telling me?"

"I have a feeling the transfer went through at midnight."

"How much?"

"Scout's honor. I didn't look."

"Why? You always peeked at your Christmas presents early."

"I was waiting for you to wake up, Lee."

"Must have been difficult."

"Not really. You know how Mom operates. We could be getting a dollar, a thousand dollars, or a hundred thousand each."

"But Dad had all those patents." Riker leaned over and scooped his clothes from the floor. "She sold them all, didn't she?"

"She alluded to it," answered Tara. "This is just another one of her games. Sure you don't want to tell me where we're going today?"

Riker shook his head. "I can't. But I do want to know what our inheritance looks like."

She turned back to the computer and pulled up the CHASE bank home page. "What's your login and password?"

"I just call and use the automated thingy."

"Really, Lee? I bet you still write checks at the grocery store."

"Chase gives me free checking," he said sheepishly.

"Tell you what. So as to keep the suspense, you get dressed and go outside and check with your phone. While you're out there, I'll check mine on the computer. We'll do it at the same time and then compare notes."

"Mom would approve." Riker shrugged on his sweatshirt and donned his cap.

From across the room there came a snort. Then the box springs squeaked and Steve-O sat bolt upright with a *where the hell am I* look on his face.

"Morning, Steve-O. Want some coffee?"

Steve-O grunted something that sounded like yes, swung his legs off the bed, scooped his clothes up off the chair, and charged into the bathroom.

"Clearly, our friend Steve-O is *not* a morning person," quipped Riker. Forgoing the fresh underwear and socks, he pulled on his jeans and cinched the belt tight. Under Tara's watchful eye, he slipped his good wheel into his boot and laced it tight. Next, he smoothed out the liner meant to keep chafing on the residual limb inside the carbon fiber socket to a minimum, maneuvered the prosthesis into place, and stood on it to achieve suction. After making sure the bionic was going nowhere barring an unforeseen Chuck Norris leg sweep, he leaned over and tightened the laces on the boot.

Tara sat forward in the chair. "Why bother with the laces?"

"Because I won't feel it if the boot starts working loose. You think getting a flat tire where you can feel the shoe coming off your heel is bad, try it happening when you can't. Results in me falling on my face, usually. Doing this daily is one of the first tricks I learned after the long rehab process."

The shower cut on. Then the singing commenced. And it was damn good. Something by Willy Nelson about mommas and letting their babies to grow up to be cowboys. *Fitting*, thought Riker as he edged past Tara and slipped out the front door.

Inside, Tara reopened the Edge browser and pulled up her bank's website. A few keystrokes later she was in and clicking a dropdown menu. She paused, letting the white arrow hover over the Checking Balance option for a three-count. Finally, she drew a deep breath and brought her finger down on the touch pad.

Outside, Riker was shivering against the morning chill. The neon No Vacancy sign was casting an eerie red pool on the damp parking lot entrance. From a distance it looked like lava encroaching on the office door. *Sure would suck to die doing that job,* thought Riker as he flipped open his phone and thumbed it on.

Casting a furtive glance at the seam in the blinds, he saw Tara at the laptop. As he looked to the keypad, from the corner of his eye he saw her go rigid and an expression he couldn't decipher ghosted across her face.

Riker dialed up his bank. Once the feminine robotic voice answered and started rattling off the prompts, he thumbed in his PIN and waited to hear what digit on the keypad he needed to press to let him hear his checking balance.

"Come on, come on," he said aloud as the tinny voice droned on.

Through the curtain seam he spied Tara cradling her face in her hands. Her eyes were now wide open, the image from the computer screen reflecting off of them.

For your checking balance, press six, said the bank's unpaid help.

Riker thumbed the appropriate key, replaced the phone to his ear, and turned toward the window.

The robot voice emanating from the phone's earpiece recited the balance to Riker then offered some options. Hand shaking, he took the phone from his ear and punched the star key to listen to his balance again.

As he stood there with the phone to his ear and heard the balance repeated, he saw his own reflection in the window to his fore. And when he heard the amount in his ear, he witnessed an expression identical to the one that had crossed Tara's face appear on his and stay there for a beat.

Riker stood there for a moment with a million thoughts racing through his mind. Heart racing, he dug his wallet out and retrieved the dog-eared business card from inside. Holding the card in one hand, he punched in the number on the back, area code first.

A person picked up on the other end after two rings and with a pronounced drawl said, "Whatcha need?"

Riker held a lengthy conversation with the man, dropping somewhere in the middle that Jack "Chaos" Ross had given him the card and urged him to call if he needed anything. After going over times and places related to the surprise Riker was setting into motion, he accepted the price quoted and memorized a phone number recited to him by the voice on the other end. Finally, to ensure everything would go smoothly, Riker paid in advance with his check card and then greased the skids by adding an extra thousand-dollar tip on top of the included gratuity.

I've always wanted to be able do that, thought Riker as he closed his phone slowly and slipped it into his pocket. Experiencing a strange out-of-body kind of feeling, all the while fighting the urge to belt out a war whoop, he pushed through the door, eyes ahead and mouth shut, and closed it covertly behind him.

Riker met Tara's gaze immediately. She was standing between the bed and table with a pinch-me look of astonishment parked on her face.

He blinked first.

Then the door to the bathroom swung outward and a fully dressed Steve-O broke the plane amidst a roiling cloud of steam.

Tara screamed. Not a shred of terror in it.

Near simultaneously, Riker let go a throaty, Tarzan-like howl complete with a few chest thumps.

Ala Buckwheat in nearly every Little Rascals episode, Steve-O's eyes bugged from his skull and a 7.0 tremor transited his body head to toe, causing him to drop an armful of underclothes and the Stetson to slide off his head. "Buttholes," he blurted. Then, softer, he said, "You scared the bejeezus out of me."

In unison, Tara and Riker faced Steve-O and said, "Swear cup."

Chapter 59

"You first," prompted Riker.

"Six zeros," replied Tara.

Riker looked at the ceiling, a smile creasing his face. "Me, too," he said, leveling his gaze on her. "What number is in front of yours?"

She looked him in the eye and held contact.

Having calmed down, Steve-O retrieved his hat from the floor and snugged it back on his head. He stared at them in the mirror as he straightened and leveled the brim. "What's wrong with you two?" he finally asked. "You look like crazy people. Or cousins about to kiss."

Suppressing a smile, Riker said, "You mean *kissing cousins*, right?"

"No, Lee. I say what I mean and mean what I say." He turned from the mirror and fixed them with those watery blue eyes. "Quit breaking my balls."

Hands up in mock surrender, Riker said, "That was *not* my intention." Changing the subject, he asked, "Where to for breakfast?"

Tara looked a question at Riker.

He held up both hands, made fists, then flashed them open and closed twice.

"Twenty?" mouthed Tara.

Shaking his head, Riker smiled and said, "I *was* breaking your balls." He revised his count by holding up both hands palms facing her and slowly making a peace sign with one of them.

"Seven?"

He nodded.

A look of relief flashed across Tara's features. "Me too," she said. "I was hoping Mom wouldn't play favorites with one of us. Drive a wedge from the grave."

"She already has," replied Riker.

Tara looked to Riker's bag. "Does that mean you're going to tell me where we're going today? Remove the wedge, so to speak."

"It doesn't bother me that you don't know."

"You little shit."

"Lee is not little," remarked Steve-O. "I bet he can touch the ceiling with both hands."

Riker reached up and placed both palms flat on the ceiling. "Steve-O wins. Pay up, Sis."

Tara was already packing up the computer. Finished stowing the cables in the box, she policed up the trash and tossed it into the wastebasket. She donned her new coat, trapped the computer box under one arm, and scooped a stack of envelopes off the table. They all bulged slightly and bore a couple of bucks worth of Forever Stamps emblazoned with Old Glory.

Riker shouldered the bag containing the urn and gun and plucked the key fob off the dresser top. Pausing by the door, he asked, "What's with the outgoing mail?"

"I downloaded some of the footage from the Deep Web and copied it and the roadblock attack video from my phone onto six thumb drives." She held up the uneven stack of envelopes. "These are getting mailed to a number of different news outlets."

"Why not just post it on social media? Cut out the middleman?"

"I tried."

"Denied?"

She nodded.

"I'm starving," said Steve-O. "Can we go?"

Tara tore the tags from a pair of all-black Columbia jackets and passed them to Riker. "Double XL is yours. Steve-O gets the medium."

"Perfect color," noted Riker.

"Perfect color," declared Steve-O. "Thank you, Tara."

"Figured it would float both your boats. You're welcome."

Room 13 was a mess when they left. So Tara turned back, peeled a hundred from the diminishing wad in her pocket, and flipped it onto the table before closing the door behind her.

At Steve-O's behest, they hit a fast food drive-thru and ordered breakfast sandwiches.

Protesting on the grounds of cruel and unusual punishment, Riker decided to fast until they stopped for lunch.

At the first window Riker paid the teenage worker and was told to pass the second window and pull into the parking spot designated specifically for customers waiting on drive-thru orders to be filled. When the Suburban came to a halt, Tara said, "Be right back," and jumped from the truck. Envelopes containing the thumb drives tucked under one arm, she dashed across the wet parking lot to a big blue U.S. Postal Service mailbox on a nearby corner and dropped them inside.

As Riker sat there waiting for Tara to return, he caught sight of the fast food joint's flagpole. Old Glory was at half-staff and popping and snapping before a glass cube home to a pit of colorful balls and two stories of playground equipment. The sight of a kid moving between platforms in a see-through tube reminded him of a gerbil scurrying through a Habitrail.

Tara's return coincided with the food being delivered to Riker's window. A beat later he was pulling from the lot and hanging a right with the noise of wrappers crinkling and lips smacking filling the cab.

Traffic was lighter than Riker figured it would be as they left South Akron. Much lighter than it should have been on a Monday during rush hour, he noted, as he circumvented the downtown core by sticking to Interstate 76 east.

I-76 became I-80 forty miles east of Akron. After transiting ten more miles of laser-straight freeway, Riker exited at Girard and stopped at a Shell station visible from the tangle of elevated ramps where I-80 merged with Ohio State Route 11.

Figuring that if the MIBs *were* chasing them, their Monday morning would have already started with a broken motel door, cordite-reeking gun barrels poking in their faces, and culminated with biting zip ties being cinched around their wrists, Riker threw caution to the wind and paid for a tank of gas, a six pack of Diet Coke, and eight pieces of greasy fried chicken with his debit card.

As soon as Riker returned to the rig, Tara pulled a pair of drumsticks and a wing from the sack. She passed a leg to Steve-O, then dangled the other one in front of her brother. "You didn't ask for my prepaid. You're not worried about us being followed anymore?"

He took the leg and shook his head. "The quarantine is blown up. You watched more videos than me. What's your assessment of the situation?"

"I want to get as far away as possible." Mimicking Riker, in a deep voice, she added, "That's my assessment of the situation."

Riker nodded agreeably. As he devoured the savory skin and substantial chunks of dark meat from the leg, he imagined a map of Illinois, Indiana, and Ohio. On the map he plotted the cities and townships from which the Deep Web videos shot over the last forty-eight hours had emerged.

It was one hell of a large footprint.

Thousands of square miles, he surmised, sucking the last morsels of flesh from the drumstick. Needles in a haystack were what he and Tara and Steve-O amounted to. And it heartened him.

Addressing Riker, Steve-O said, "Yesterday, you said I would be able to see Lake Erie from the road. Where is it?"

Riker tossed the bone in the bag. He reversed from the parking spot and nosed them onto the street and toward the runout feeding the Route 11 on-ramp. Once he merged in behind a sleek red import and accelerated to make room for the big rig coming up fast on the Suburban's bumper, he leaned onto the center console and pointed out over the hood. "Somewhere beyond those clouds is the lake, Steve-O."

Tara tossed the remnants of the wing in the bag and licked the grease from her fingers. "Let me see what the navigation thingy has to say." Tapping lightly on the touchscreen, she zoomed the map out and manipulated the image until the pixelated length of SR-11 North stretching from Girard to the lake's southern shore was centered on the display. At the bottom, Girard was a tan irregular shape crisscrossed by a mishmash of streets and freeways. A horizontal blue blob representing Lake Erie dominated the top edge of the rectangular display.

SR-11 was a straight run between the two for most of the way until it took a gradual jog left and merged with I-90 a couple of miles before reaching the Great Lake.

After comparing the green line with the inches-to-miles conversion key, Tara said, "One inch equals twenty-five miles. Looks like two inches of Route 11 to me." She regarded Riker and asked him for his take.

A quick glance at the navigation screen had Riker agreeing with her assessment.

"Looks like fifty miles or so, Steve-O," Tara said as she leaned over the console and noted the needle was pegged on seventy-five. After quickly working the equation in her head, she added, "We should see Erie filling up the windshield in about forty minutes."

"Can't wait," replied Steve-O. He rolled the chicken bone up in his McMuffin wrapper and fished the last sandwich from the bag. He held the item up so Riker could see it. "You going to eat this?" he asked.

Riker took another leg from the bag. "I'm good."

***

Tara's estimate of forty minutes didn't hold true. An hour had slipped into the past by the time they came upon a road sign with three different entries listed one atop the other.

Astabula 8 and a white reflective arrow pointing straight capped off the stack. Below that was *Cleveland 60* and a white left-turn arrow with the blue and red I-90 W shield next to it. The bottom entry read *Erie, Pennsylvania 50*. Beside it was a white right-turn arrow and the same blue and red shield labeled I-90 E.

Riker pointed to the map scrolling slowly top to bottom on the navigation screen and let Tara know they were going east at the cloverleaf a few miles north of them.

"What landmark is east of there?" said Tara in a voice that made Riker think of someone mulling over a geography question on a Trivial Pursuit card.

"Mum's the word. Besides, what makes you certain we're going to continue east?"

"Bastard," she said playfully.

Riker reached across and patted the bag on the floor by Tara's feet. "Mom would disagree with that statement."

Tara said nothing to that. She turned her attention to the colorful landscape outside her window. Fall was in full swing here, that was for sure. The groves of trees scrolling by off to the right were ablaze in yellows and reds. Closer in, the expanse of grass flanking the freeway was beaten down by recent rains and home to shimmering pools of standing water.

***

Ninety seconds after passing the ODOT sign, Mother Nature made a liar out of Riker. Though they were within spitting distance of Lake Erie and the series of piers Astabula was known for when they came upon the city limit, all that was visible to the north from the cloverleaf's elevated ramp was an impenetrable veil of clouds and sheeting rain.

Riker said, "I lied to you yesterday, Steve-O. I'm no weatherman. Hope you find it within yourself to forgive me." The last part was delivered in a joking manner as he flicked on the wipers and prepared for the merge with I-90 East.

"No problem," said Steve-O. "The lake isn't going anywhere."

Chapter 60

The convoy of desert-tan and army-green vehicles stretched for as far back as Riker could see. Behind the half-dozen Ohio National Guard Humvees that had suddenly materialized in the Suburban's blind spot as he steered from the ramp and onto I-90 were at least a dozen tractor trailers hauling Jersey barriers, mobile electronic signage, boxy MRAPs, Humvees configured for command and control, and pieces of tracked armor Riker recognized as Bradley Fighting Vehicles. Behind the loaded-down tractor trailer rigs was a trio of tan, low-slung multi-wheeled vehicles. Even viewed in the tiny side mirror and through eyes charting way less than 20/20, Riker had them pegged as Oshkosh Defense fuel servicing trucks.

"More Army trucks," said Steve-O as he buzzed his window half of the way down and flashed the soldiers staring back at him a double thumbs up.

"So-called Operation Romeo Victor is in full swing on day two," proffered Riker. "I know exactly where this element is going, and from the looks of the fuel trucks bringing up the rear, they're definitely planning on an extended mission profile." Out of the corner of his eye Riker saw a grim-faced soldier steal a glance at him, then promptly return his attention to the road ahead.

First impressions being what they are—*everything* in Riker's opinion—he concluded the young twenty-something was scared shitless and carrying some kind of an unwanted responsibility on his wide shoulders.

Tara sat up straight in her seat. Craning hard to get a look at the lead Humvee keeping pace with them, she asked, "What does all of that mean?"

Riker glanced at the speedometer and saw the needle slowly creeping toward fifty. "First off," he said, matting the accelerator, "some of these guys are heading for the Pennsylvania border."

There was a mechanical whirring, then a period of relative silence after Steve-O's window sucked shut.

"How do you know all of this, Lee? You have a crystal ball or something?"

Steve-O answered for him. "Those cement things and big electric signs are the same that were put up at the roadblock."

"Ding … ding … ding," said Riker. "Somebody is paying attention, boys and girls. And the gender pronoun just so happens to be '*he*.'"

Tara looked to Riker. "What are those cement thingies called?"

Like a pounced-on fighter jock trying to get eyes on the bandits, Riker leaned toward the steering wheel and whipped his head to the left to see over his shoulder. "Jersey barriers," he answered as he jinked the SUV into the fast lane, cutting off the Humvee full of helmeted soldiers.

"They're not happy," noted Steve-O. "I think one of them is telling us to pull over."

Sweeping his gaze to the rearview mirror, Riker was afforded a frontal view of the driver and passenger. The latter was clearly mouthing "Give to" and gesturing toward the slow lane with a gloved hand. *Give the fella a pair of orange-tipped batons,* thought Riker, *and he may as well be working the flight deck on an aircraft carrier.*

"Stick it," muttered Riker. He ordered everyone to check their seatbelts, then tromped the gas. It took a second or two for the engine to spool up, but once the *whoosh* of the power plant sucking air to convert to horsepower subsided, the bulky SUV was pushing ninety and quickly distancing them from the military convoy.

***

The Ohio/Pennsylvania border lay halfway between Ashtabula and Erie. The twenty-five miles from the I-90 off-ramp where they first encountered the convoy to the border between the two states dissolved in a little under seventeen minutes.

All that marked the crossing was a trio of signs. The largest of the three announced to anyone paying attention that they were entering the *Keystone State*. The second was a public service announcement warning against drinking and driving and declaring a fine of up to five thousand dollars could be levied on the offending party upon conviction. Lastly, a bit smaller than the others and affixed lowest on the post was a sign with a picture of a cell phone on it. Below the handset was the admonishment: *Hang Up And Drive!*

"What's a Keystone?" asked Tara.

"What are those white things up ahead?" responded Riker. He took a hand off the wheel long enough to point out the objects pushing up against the thickets of trees flanking both sides of the four-lane interstate.

"Tents, I think."

"Confirms my suspicion that the state line is where the convoy is headed," declared Riker.

"Why is the Ohio Guard setting up *inside* of Pennsylvania?"

"Maybe the Pennsylvania Guard is operating in support of"—he took both hands off the wheel and made air quotes—"*Operation Romeo Victor*." He quickly rehashed his theory that Romeo Victor was actually an acronym that had something to do with what had happened in Middletown.

Tara said, "I think *Victor* is code for *virus*. It's gotta be."

Riker nodded but said nothing. He was focused on the half-dozen bio-hazard-suited figures positioning barriers on the westbound lanes of I-90. The suits were bright yellow and not at all easy on the eyes. Black masks covered their faces. What looked to be small scuba tanks hung off their backs, the black shoulder straps clearly visible against the loud suits.

Here the stretch of I-90 was comprised of four lanes, two going in either direction. A thirty-foot-wide grass and dirt median home to trash and marshy-looking puddles ran down the center. Hemming the interstate in to the north and south were narrow breakdown lanes. Beyond the westbound breakdown lane was a ten- to fifteen-foot-wide strip of ankle-high grass. Rising up next to the grassy area and completely denying drivers any chance of viewing Lake Erie was a picket of mature trees that ran for miles in either direction.

Parked on the grass and partially straddling the westbound breakdown lane was a pair of white Tahoe SUVs bearing government plates.

Noting how the landscape here provided a natural chokepoint with ample flat ground on the Pennsylvania side to erect tents on and stage vehicles from, Riker said, "Whoever ordered this roadblock couldn't have picked a better place for it."

At about the same time Riker voiced his observation, the brake lights on the minivan in his lane a dozen car lengths ahead lit up red and it began to fishtail and bleed off speed. Simultaneously, a pair of westbound vehicles were coming to a slow-rolling stop before the pair of suited forms manning newly erected barriers beyond the median.

No sooner had the westbound lanes filled up three vehicles deep than a man jumped out of a pickup with colorful leaves in its bed and bristling with gardening tools. He was short and stocky and wearing orange raingear. Mouth moving a mile a minute and gesticulating wildly, the landscaper stalked toward the barricades.

While one of the hazmat-suited forms seemed to be addressing the unhappy motorists, two more yellow-suited figures began dragging a head-high traffic barrier through the median grass.

Strangling the wheel in a two-handed grip, Riker scanned the road ahead and triaged the situation.

Snugging her lap belt tighter, Tara asked, "What are we going to do, Lee?"

One of the suited forms looked up from the task at hand, pointed toward the speeding Suburban, and then repeatedly performed a patting motion toward the ground with both hands that Riker understood to mean *slow down*.

"Not stop here, that's for sure," called Steve-O from the back seat.

Through gritted teeth, Riker said, "Last thing I'm going to do."

Watching through the fingers of one hand, Tara said, "Better gun it then, Thelma."

The hazmat-suited figure nearest to the eastbound lane reacted decisively. The driver of the minivan in Riker's lane did not. While the former ceased the *slow down* gesture, bent over, scooped up something two-handed and began dragging it toward the eastbound lanes, the minivan driver was slaloming left and right, obviously unsure of what to do.

With fifty feet separating the Suburban's grill from the action taking place on the median, the minivan came to a complete stop in the left lane with a third of its squared-off rear end jutting into the right lane.

Having barely a second to commit, Riker jerked the steering wheel right, taking the speeding SUV around the minivan and onto the shoulder where the passenger's side tires sent a spray of wet grass and gravel airborne. Feeling the rear tires begin to break from the slick pavement, Riker steered toward the slide and got a good look at the person in yellow struggling to get what appeared to be a set of spike strips deployed across his lane.

The SUV was travelling a hair over seventy when Riker issued yet another course correction, just a little twitch to the left, which straightened out the previous slide and caused two things to happen simultaneously. First, after nearly being decapitated by a wing mirror the size of a boxing glove scything the air an inch from his face, the man in the suit went wide-eyed, let go of the spike strips, and launched himself backward.

From the back seat, with only the glass and barely a yard separating them, Steve-O engaged in a split-second staring match with the luckiest man on earth.

"That was close," said Steve-O. "The way his eyes were bugging out of his head made me think of SpongeBob."

Riker said, "SquarePants?"

"No. SpongeBob the Barbarian," quipped Tara. "You know … the dude who lives in the *castle* under the sea."

"Pineapple," corrected Steve-O.

Riker flicked his gaze to the side mirror. "That was *after* my time."

Taking into consideration the road condition, their high rate of speed, and the snappy back-to-back course corrections Riker had just put the big SUV through, this nearly became his *time*. They were *all* lucky to not be weightless and staring at the horizon from an entirely different perspective with gravity and inertia and Newton's Law conspiring to crush the SUV with them inside it.

In fact, having been in one rollover accident in his youth, Riker knew how deadly they could be. Twenty years removed, the memory of the sky and road trading places way too fast for him to keep track of was as vivid as if it had taken place yesterday. He recalled the glass spider webbing as his head impacted the window, giving him his first of many concussions. Heard again in his head the cacophony a dozen recently drained beer cans tumbling around inside the car had made. Then the split-second moment of silence that followed the startled yelp and single sharp cough his buddy from high school had made when the air left his lungs as he was ejected through the glass moonroof on that first revolution.

Being belted in and upside down and listening to the creaking of metal and soft rush of hot coolant draining from ruptured hoses while being unable to do anything but call for help was the second worst day of his life.

These were all things he would take to the grave with him.

Now, as the adrenaline dump from nearly repeating it all over again was flooding his system, his entire body began to shake.

Seeing the tremor, Tara reached over to comfort him. "Thinking of Ricky?"

Riker said nothing. His attention was drawn to a rapidly approaching billboard on which a happy couple was smiling and toasting to something with their half-filled wine glasses.

Chapter 61

A mile east of the state line roadblock, the steady rain turned to a light mist.

The roadblock was two miles back when the rain ceased and Riker silenced the wipers. A short while later he relaxed his grip on the steering wheel and regarded the map scrolling slowly down the dash-mounted display. Lake Erie was on the left side now with virtual I-90 a vertical green line dutifully following the curving tan shoreline.

After curling gently to the right, the quickly drying four-lane again went die-straight on Riker. As the interstate lanced through miles of treed countryside, it remained strangely free of traffic. Frequent glances at the rearview revealed no white SUVs with headlights ablaze bearing down on them from out of the curtain of gray hanging over Ohio.

The real congestion was near Erie where nearly every exit off the freeway was backing up. They bypassed Erie without seeing any police cruisers or military vehicles or SUVs with government plates.

Just outside of Erie, one of those ping-pong-table-sized electronic reader boards was all lit up and sitting on the right shoulder of I-90. It was unattended, which prompted Riker to want to stop and change the message on it from **MANDATORY CHECKPOINT — PENNSYLVANIA/NEW YORK STATE LINE — 15 MILES AHEAD** to **WHAT IN THE HELL DOES ROMEO VICTOR REALLY MEAN?**

He doubted anyone would get the cryptic nature of his query if he did. So he headed off the question he knew was coming by asking Tara and Steve-O to be on the lookout for Exit 41.

Still, the barrage of questions came.

"Is that in New York?" asked Tara. "If it is, how are we going to explain this truck?" She glanced at the bag by her feet. "Then there's the problem of the shotgun. Just having it in New York probably breaks a couple of laws."

"We're not crossing into New York at the roadblock," replied Riker.

"Are we going to the lake, then?" queried Steve-O.

"Go fish," said Riker.

"Does the exit have to do with where we're taking Mom?"

"Getting warm," said Riker.

"I'm getting hungry," said Steve-O. "Will there be somewhere to eat lunch near Exit 41?"

"Let me ask the Magic Eight Ball." Abruptly Riker went quiet and he stuck his hand in the air, fingers curled as if cupping an invisible orb. "Magic Eight Ball," he said while pretending to shake said imaginary orb, "will there be a place for Steve-O to eat near Exit 41?"

Steve-O had hooked his elbows over the seatbacks and was directing a skeptical look at Riker.

In the passenger seat, Tara was looking at the headliner and shaking her head.

Riker pantomimed bringing the phantom object to below eye level and peered down into it.

Calling Riker on his bullshit, Tara said, "Well, Mr. Fortune Teller ... Whatcha got?"

"Outlook is good," replied Riker, cracking a smile as he pulsed his window down and pretended to toss the orb away.

Steve-O pumped a fist. "Yesssss."

"No fast food," begged Tara. "That breakfast sandwich reset my digestive system."

"No Golden Arches," said Riker. "You have my word."

***

Exit 41 lay just seven miles west of the Pennsylvania/New York border. The PENNDOT sign announcing the exit was a massive thing emblazoned with the names of places to find food, gas, and lodging in *North East, Pennsylvania - Pop. 4,294.*

The off-ramp meandered to the right then quickly curled back around on itself before ending at a T where PA-89 shot off to the left and right, the former going to Greenfield Township, while the latter disappeared under the interstate then fed into the Borough of North East, Pennsylvania.

"How about the Freeport Restaurant?" said Tara, consulting the list of services splashed on the panel beside the map. "It's on Lake Road north of us." She adjusted the map on the navigation display. "And it's right by the lake. Looks like it's only three miles or so from here."

"Sounds good," replied Riker. "But I already have a place in mind where we can kill two birds with one stone."

"I'm calling PETA," said Steve-O ahead of a wicked laugh.

"I'm beginning to like how you think," said Riker as the light changed to green and he maneuvered the SUV onto 89 North.

Coming out from under the freeway, the land fell away gradually toward outer North East. Close in, the landscape was made up of mainly tilled fields and a smattering of one- and two-story homes. Farther out, abutting the fields, were a number of subdivisions consisting of dozens of single-family homes separated by narrow tracts of sparsely treed land.

Some of the services indicated on the exit sign were clustered around the interchange. There was a multi-story Holiday Inn Express & Suites off to their left. On the right, surrounded by a sea of gray asphalt, was a Shell station that looked woefully under-patronized. Parked beside the Shell market was a pair of flatbed trailers. Positioned side by side and facing the interstate, both flatbeds carried the same load: dozens of Jersey barriers and a single black fuel-filled bladder that looked to be larger than Tara's precious Smart car.

Riker slowed and craned as they transited the cross street. Behind the market a pair of light-tan Humvees were stopped behind a pickup truck, hemming the late model Chevy in against the cinderblock structure. Four airmen wearing ACUs in the Air Force's blue and gray camouflage scheme were in the process of dismounting from the Humvees.

Riker slow-rolled the Suburban to the curb and started the hazard lights flashing.

Sitting in the cab of the jacked up 4x4, their hands thrust in the air, was what looked to Riker to be a family of three. Stuck between the male driver and female passenger was a grade-school-aged girl complete with pigtails and rosy cheeks.

As the dismounts surrounded the pickup with black rifles held at a low-ready, muzzles pointing groundward, the girl let out a piercing scream that may have been heard two states over.

Recoiling from the sound, Tara said, "What's that all about?"

"That is *not* part of a joint exercise," said Riker. And the reason he knew this was because the girl was not acting. She appeared genuinely scared—terrified, actually—and was beginning to cry.

While part of the Special Forces training was a hyper-realistic exercise called Robin Sage, all of those involved—Green Beret candidates, SOCOM instructors, and the local indigenous population—were in the *know*. To ensure the exercise mirrored real-world scenarios while keeping in mind the safety of said civilians, everyone had scripted roles they were ordered to stick to.

Riker saw the man and woman being questioned. They were both visibly upset. Apparently the questions weren't answered to the satisfaction of the airman asking them, because the man was taken from the pickup against his will and forced at gunpoint to undress completely.

Passing vehicles were slowing as drivers began to rubberneck.

"He's butt naked," said Steve-O.

"Drive, Lee," said Tara through clenched teeth. "That heavy-handed crap makes my skin crawl."

Riker pulled from the curb and stole a final quick peek at the man's pasty white body. As one of the soldiers motioned with his rifle and the man began a slow pirouette, it became clear to Riker the blood-soaked bandage encircling his bicep had something to do with the encounter.

As Riker gunned it to catch the next light on the green, Tara tore her gaze from the action taking place. "When the soldiers saw the bandage they all backed off a few paces and pointed their rifles at the man."

"I blame good old Romeo Victor," said Riker. "Whatever in the hell that is."

***

Three minutes after leaving the interstate behind they were cutting through the heart of North East on South Lake Street, where the main point of interest advertised on a roadside sign was Lake Shore Railway Museum. The blocks surrounding the intersection with Main Street, where South Lake became North Lake, were home to a United States Post Office, McCord Memorial Public Library, cross-competing pizza joints, the Boston Bean Café, and Johnny B's Restaurant, the latter of which had an empty lot. Not a good sign so close to noon.

Pointing out a green and red sign affixed to a single-story building's faux brick façade, Steve-O said, "Anyone feel like having pizza for lunch?"

"We're dining at a four-star joint today, Steve-O. And we're almost there."

"I haven't seen you playing with the navigation unit since we left King's Court. How do you even know about this place, Lee?"

"Patience is a virtue, Sis."

***

After traveling a few blocks north, the downtown core gave way to residential. Shortly thereafter, fields and treed lots dominated and North Lake Street became Freeport. As the intersection with east/west-running Lake Road came into view, so did Lake Erie. Only it wasn't quite defined yet. It presented as a bright blue haze that dominated the horizon from left to right for as far as the eye could see.

Riker said, "Your wish has been granted, Steve-O."

326

Steve-O was still parked between the front seat with his elbows braced on the headrests. "That's Lake Erie?"

"The weather is breaking," noted Tara. She looked out Riker's window and saw the gray smudge hovering over northwestern Pennsylvania. Swiveling her head right, she saw blue sky dotted with fast-moving clouds.

"Looks like the system is moving south by west."

"Which is in our favor," said Riker as he waited for a motor coach to pass by on the aptly named Lake Road.

He turned right and they followed the tour bus along a windy two-lane with the lake keeping company off to their left.

Seeing a large sign advertising a nearby vineyard, Tara said, "Lake View Winery. I didn't realize Pennsylvania was the right climate for growing wine."

"My mom and dad didn't like wine," asserted Steve-O, his voice trailing off at the end.

Riker and Tara exchanged glances. "Wish I could say the same," admitted Riker.

"Mom could open a bottle and have one glass and that was it," said Tara.

"Dad was the exact opposite," added Riker. "He'd drink everything in the house. Nothing was safe … not even Mom's weeks-old wine. Turning to vinegar or not, Dad would drink it."

"People thought we were religious or something," said Steve-O.

Three car-lengths ahead, the tour bus braked and it signaled a right turn. Less of a turn, really; Lake Road basically split in two, with it continuing on along the shore, and the new two-lane vectoring off to the right at a shallow angle.

Without signaling, Riker followed the Coastal Tours motor coach onto Vineyard Drive, staying close as the smooth paved road cut through acres of rolling land covered with row after row of symmetrically aligned grape vines.

"We are not scattering Mom's ashes at a vineyard, Lee."

Riker smiled. "Go fish."

Chapter 62

The road to the vineyard rose and fell for a mile or so, then made a sweeping right before angling in from the south. There was a sign with the vineyard's name arching twenty-five feet over the feeder road where it spilled onto an enormous paved parking lot. Dead ahead was Lake View Vineyard's sprawling chalet. To the left, parked in neat rows, were a handful of motor coaches. To the right the yellow-lined spaces accommodated a smattering of cars, trucks, and SUVs.

The chalet was a three-story stone and hewn-timber structure. The multi-pitched roof was shingled with interlocking red tiles trimmed with polished copper busy throwing the emerging sun in all directions. And here and there, home to multi-paned windows, shuttered gables jutted from the upper story.

The tour bus went straight for the chalet and drove onto a brick drive leading to a portico constructed of the same honey-colored timbers as the chalet. The angled six by eights were held together at the joints by oil-rubbed bronze plates shot through with massive carriage bolts.

The tour bus came to a halt with an angry pneumatic hiss adjacent to the chalet's towering entry, its door hinged opened, and geriatrics began to waddle out.

Riker steered the Suburban toward the tour bus's bumper and was greeted just outside the portico by a young man snappily dressed in black slacks, gun-metal-gray silk vest, and starched white oxford dress shirt, the sleeves of which were rolled up to mid-forearm on him.

"Going to let him valet this beast?"

Riker nodded as the valet reached for Tara's door handle. "Grab the bag."

Tara said, "The shotgun is still inside."

"I know," said Riker through clenched teeth as he flashed the valet a half-smile. "Just grab it and pretend it's not. Bring the laptop, too."

After getting the door for Tara and Steve-O, the valet looped around and did the same for Riker.

Riker planted his bionic on the pavers and, with a little help from the grab bar near his head, hauled his two hundred and forty pound frame out of the idling SUV.

Still smiling and holding onto the open door, the valet stood rooted and shot a quick glance at Riker's empty hands.

"Oh, shit," blurted Riker. "I'm not used to all this." Wearing a sheepish expression, he checked his wallet and patted his pockets. "I don't have any cash."

Riker looked to Tara, who was slowly shaking her head side to side.

The valet's smile wavered.

Seeing this, Riker said, "Don't worry ... I'll find a way to take care of you."

"Come on," called Steve-O. "I'm starved."

Walking away from the disappointed valet, Riker said, "Keep your pants on, Steve-O."

A young guy dressed similarly to the valet held the oak doors open as Tara and Steve-O climbed the front steps. Riker watched from midway up the run as the Suburban driven by the valet edged past the motor coach and continued on toward a separate lot hemmed in by two metal-roofed buildings he guessed were used to store the wine while it aged. The distant structures were the size of airplane hangars with the same type of rollaway doors.

Riker caught up with the others at a podium serving as the host stand for the restaurant aptly named *Panorama*. The stand was positioned directly underneath a chandelier made of antlers and acted as a barrier of sorts between the lobby and restaurant entrance. He looked over the top of Steve-O's balding head and saw that a chest-high wall ran the length of the restaurant, separating the bar on the left from the dining area on the right. The abbreviated wall ended at a wide bank of floor-to-ceiling picture windows affording a panoramic view of Lake Erie. Perched atop the alabaster wall was an unbroken chain of meticulously pruned plants.

A woman, middle forties, guessed Riker, caught his eye from a distance. She wore her hair in a bun. The bifocals hanging on a gold chain swayed back and forth as she hustled back from seating the last of the geriatrics, some of whom were wearing surgical masks. She smiled, put her glasses on, then asked Riker if he had a reservation.

Riker's shoulders slumped. "No," he said. "Can you seat the three of us anyway?"

She consulted an iPad-looking thing lying flat on the podium. It had a to-scale diagram of the restaurant which included the wall, picture window, and bar area, complete with tables—all of them lit up red. She tapped the screen a couple of times, likely for show, thought Riker, then shook her head.

"Two tour buses from New York came in unannounced in just the last thirty minutes." She glanced at her watch, a platinum ladies Rolex from the looks of it. "It's almost noon," she said. "I've got full books and locals coming in." She paused for a moment. "I can put you at the bar."

Waiting patiently, Stetson in hand, Steve-O glanced over his shoulder at Riker and shrugged indifferently.

Tara turned back and said, "I'm okay with it if you are."

Riker looked down at the hostess. "*At* the bar ... or ... *in* the bar?"

For a long two-count she stared at Riker as if he'd been speaking Klingon when he posed the question. "I said *at* the bar," she finally replied. "The lounge tables are reserved as well."

"Just my luck," complained Riker. "I finally come into some money, go to take my mom to a fancy restaurant, and get offered the least desirable place to sit."

The woman shot a confused look over the top of her bifocals. Her gaze ranged from Riker to Steve-O to Tara then stayed locked on the younger woman. "So there's four of you now?"

Smiling, Tara said, "It's complicated."

The hostess grabbed four menus off a pile. "Follow me," she said, striking off for the bar.

At the bar Riker took the urn from the bag and put the laptop in its place. He set the urn on the bar top before an empty stool, then sat on the stool to its immediate right.

"Where are your manners?" asked Steve-O. He plopped his Stetson on the empty stool and pulled the one to its left out for Tara.

"Chivalry is not dead," remarked Tara.

Jabbing a stubby finger at his own balding head, Steve-O addressed Riker. "Hats off."

"You wore yours in the Speedway minimart."

"That's a deli. This is a fancy restaurant."

Point taken, thought Riker as he removed his Braves hat and placed it on the stool with the Stetson.

The bartender was nothing like the clean-cut valet and doorman. About the same age, mid-twenties or so, but with a full black beard a pirate would be proud of and the earrings to match. His unruly mop of hair was barely constrained by what Riker could only think to call a top-knot. First thing that came to mind when the hostess called the bartender by name to get his attention was how much the two of them looked alike. Same angular face and narrow nose. While the bartender was at least two decades younger than the hostess, he had the same dark eyes and easy smile.

Joey greeted them warmly and threw paper beverage napkins onto the bar with all the flair of a Vegas card dealer. He asked, "What are you drinking?"

Riker rubbed his bald head, turned the menu over, then looked Joey square in the eye. "Bottle of your best champagne and four glasses."

"One bottle of Louis Roederer Cristal and"—he paused to count heads—"*three* ... flutes."

Riker said, "Four. It's complicated." As Joey left, he looked to Tara. "Flutes?"

"Fancy name for champagne glasses."

"I'm having a bacon cheeseburger with extra bacon and no onions," said Steve-O.

"Sure you don't want a steak? I'm buying."

"No, Lee. I'm a simple man. A bacon cheeseburger will do."

Riker said, "Hey everyone … Ronnie Van Zant here is having a cheeseburger in a four-star joint."

Joey came back and set out the flutes. He went over the specials as he popped the cork.

While Joey was filling her flute, Tara looked to Riker and said, "Ronnie Van who?"

"He's in the band Lynyrd Skynyrd. Sings a song called Simple Man," replied Steve-O, placing a hand over his champagne glass. "Coke for me," he whispered to Joey.

"Definitely trivia someone my age shouldn't be expected to know," shot Tara.

Riker covered his flute and pointed to the empty one sitting near the urn. "Fill Mom's to the top."

Joey didn't hesitate. He filled both flutes and placed the bottle in an ice bucket. "What's for lunch?"

Tara ordered light: a Caesar salad with chicken and a cup of tomato basil soup.

Holding true to his word, Steve-O went with the bacon cheeseburger. "Soup in place of fries," he added.

Riker chose the prime ribeye and fries.

Joey asked, "How do you like your steak?"

Stealing his late grandfather's line, Riker said, "Knock its horns off and bring it to me mooing."

"Pittsburgh rare it is," said Joey as he collected the menus.

Riker leaned in. "What's with the masks the honored citizens are wearing?"

Joey stole a peek at the oldsters. "Some kind of bug going around Queens and Manhattan. Making people real sick, I guess.

Can't really blame them, though. Hell, they're one foot in the grave already."

Riker was about to dress down Joey for the remark when his attention was drawn to the windows. He was experiencing a familiar sensation in his gut. A tremor caused by something mechanical in nature and still out of sight.

At the far edge of the football-field-sized swathe of lawn outside the windows was a white gazebo. Behind it was a vineyard that fell away toward the glittering lake. Planted around the gazebo was an assemblage of red, yellow, and white flowers, their colors vibrant against the dark background.

As Riker remained fixated on the gazebo, the flowers encircling it began to dance and whip about. A tick later, Joey came from stage left and dropped off the soups. Then a helicopter flew in fast and low out of the east, flared hard over the vineyard, spun a ninety-degree turn so that its aerodynamic nose faced the windows, then lit nimbly on the grass a few yards left of the gazebo.

Acting as if a helicopter landing on the premises was no big affair, Joey produced a peppermill the size of a marching baton. Waved off by both Tara and Steve-O, he went on to explain how Lake View Vineyards was a popular destination for weddings and family reunions. "Cheaper than the Hamptons or Martha's Vineyard," he noted. "Bigwigs charter helicopters to pick them up here, take them to Niagara Falls for wedding photos, then bring them back here for the ceremony."

"Is the hostess family?" asked Riker.

Joey nodded. "My mom."

"She's the owner, too, isn't she?"

"Guilty as charged," answered Joey.

"I saw the resemblance."

Tara asked, "Who's the helicopter here for?"

Joey shrugged. "Mom didn't mention it." Hand going to the pager-looking thing on his belt, he said, "Your lunch just hit the window."

Chapter 63

Riker ignored the fries and tore into the steak. He didn't realize how hungry he was until the sizzling hunk of meat hit the bar in front of him. As he sliced thin pieces of meat off and savored the cool, smooth texture of the high-grade beef, he kept one eye on the chopper and the other on the television mounted high up near the ceiling in a corner behind the bar.

On the television, the feed was alternating between the 4 World Trade Center building—still smoldering internally, judging by the smoke trickling from many of the lower floor windows—to scenes from various staging areas scattered over half a dozen states.

Joey said, "This joint operation sure makes that one they held out west look like a Boy Scout outing."

Riker looked to Tara and Steve-O before responding. The former was picking at her salad and seemed to be staring at a galaxy-shaped knot on the wooden bar top, while the latter was down to three fries and cleaning the plate of ketchup with them.

"Jade Helm 15," said Riker. "Those were not Boy Scouts—"

"Oh, I know," interrupted Joey. "I was meaning scale-wise it seems as if this Romeo whatever it's called is way more involved. I don't remember there being one story about Jade Helm on the news until it was over and done with."

"That was a Special Forces joint op. Those guys usually never divulge what they're doing. At all. Only reason they did in that instance was to placate the tin-foil-hat crowd who were claiming Jade Helm was providing cover so the United Nations could take all our guns. Hell, you had fringe groups thinking Helm was to get the population used to seeing military vehicles on the streets so it'd be easy pickings when the powers that be let Chinese forces loose on their own population."

Joey took Steve-O's sparkling clean plate. "Hated it, eh?"

"Best four-star burger ever," replied Steve-O.

"I'm not hungry anymore," stated Tara, pushing her plate forward. She finished the Cristal in her flute, then refilled it herself while Joey was gone with the plates. She was tipping back the fresh champagne and staring out the window at the helicopter when a door on the side facing her hinged open.

"Lee," she said, pointing at the window with her pinky finger. "Looks like he's just flown in for lunch. The steak that good?"

Riker nudged the bone around on his plate with his fork. There was nothing left clinging to it. He finally said, "I don't know about all that. It was one hell of a good steak, though." He watched the pilot step from the helicopter, close the right-side door behind him, and begin walking in the direction of the restaurant.

The man wasn't short or tall. He carried his weight proportionately. Riker had never seen an obese aviator. Figured he never would. On the other hand, crew chiefs and loadmasters, virtually one and the same in Riker's book, came in all shapes and sizes.

Riker nudged his plate forward.

Joey went to take it away.

Riker asked for the check.

"Not having dessert?"

Tara perked up. "Do you have anything chocolate?"

"We gotta go," said Riker. He grabbed his hat and hauled the bag up and placed it on his lap.

Tara's shoulders slumped. "You sure, Lee? Steve-O … dessert?"

Joey's eyes were dancing back and forth over the trio bellied up to his bar.

"Positive," said Riker. He fished his wallet from his pocket and retrieved his Chase Debit card.

It wasn't a dream, he told himself as he tossed what now amounted to a seven million dollar gift card onto the bar.

Joey picked up the card. Tapped it twice on the bar and said, "Okay. I'll call the valet. Have them bring your car around."

"It's a black Suburban," said Steve-O

"Don't bother, Joey," said Riker. "Just hurry back with the check."

***

Joey was back in thirty seconds with a check presenter bulging with a gold pen and half a dozen thin, foil-wrapped chocolates.

Tara smiled and passed a couple of chocolates to Steve-O. As she peeled the foil from one, her eyes were drawn to the television and her jaw dropped.

Riker added a thousand-dollar tip to the four-hundred-and-fifty-dollar lunch.

Palms on the bar top and leaning close, Joey said, "That's not necessary, sir."

"It's Lee. And, yes, it's very necessary. Mom enjoyed the view and the service." He put the urn in the bag and zipped it closed.

"Give the doorman and valet a hundred each, please. I'm sure you'll figure a way to take care of whoever cooked our meal."

Joey nodded. "I'll give them a couple of hundred to spread around amongst themselves. Money has a way of telling the back of the house crew they did good work."

"Lee," called Tara. She was fixated on the television. The camera covering the fire was now zooming in on tiny forms hanging from broken windows halfway up 4WTC. Every now and again one would jump and the camera would pan down and follow them all the way to the ground.

Steve-O was paying attention too. He said, "Damn terrorists. Not again." He grabbed his Stetson, put it over his heart, and closed his eyes.

"Motherfuckers," blurted Joey. "I was nine when the towers fell. I remember the jumpers." He shook his head. "Lost an uncle that day, too. He was FDNY. A lifer. His house lost the most men that day."

"I'm sorry," said Riker. "I lost a part of me that day as well. Lost another part later as a result. We'll bounce back."

Joey's mom came into the bar and stood staring at the television.

No sooner had she left her post than the helicopter pilot bypassed the podium, cupped his hands around his mouth and, with a Texas twang seasoning the words, bellowed, "Is there a Lee Riker in the house?"

"Right here, Clark," said Riker, waving the pilot over.

Fielding a confused look from Steve-O, Tara, Joey, and Joey's mom, Riker picked the bag off his lap and slid off the bar stool.

Joey made eye contact with the aviator. "Clark, how you been?"

"Season's hitting the dead spot it always does before the holidays."

"Tell me about it," replied Joey's mom. "If it wasn't for a couple of tour busses full of hungry seniors stopping by unannounced, this place would be half-empty."

Clark smiled at the owner, then entered the bar and approached Riker. Even in combat boots, he only came up to Riker's chin. Maybe he was five-foot-eight, max. Pulled down tight on his head was a faded orange Texas Longhorns ball cap, its bill frayed but perfectly shaped and matching his brow line. Aviator-style sunglasses fronted a wide face bestowed with well-defined features. Instead of the ubiquitous full-body flight suit Riker was used to seeing on Army aviators, Clark wore desert-tan 5.11 tactical pants, the cuffs spilling over black combat boots. A black Arc'teryx vest zipped to the neck rode over a Crye Precision top, the sleeves of which were bunched up mid-forearm on the man. On Clark's left wrist was some kind of a multifunction watch, black in color with a metal case thick enough to stop a bullet.

As Clark drew near to the bar top, the half-smile he wore faded and his lips pressed into a thin line. The quick change in expression Riker chalked up to the tragedy playing out on the television above the bar.

The business card given to Riker by Chaos back in Atlanta listed the pilot's full name as Wade Clark.

Clark stopped a yard from Riker and peeled off the aviator glasses. With a tilt of his chin, he said, "Chaos wasn't lyin' when he said you's a biggun."

All business, Riker said, "I take it the transaction went through okay."

"I'm here, ain't I," drawled Clark. "Funds were in my account an hour after we talked."

Tara said, "When did you two talk?"

"This morning after the inheritance showed up in our accounts. I stayed outside the room and placed the call."

"Sneaky," said Steve-O.

Tara addressed Steve-O. "He's been known to push the envelope on *sneaky*." She regarded the man in question. "Was this"—she pointed to the sleek black and white helicopter crouched on the lawn—"all part of Mom's plan?"

"The helicopter ride, no. Where we're taking her, yes."

For the umpteenth time over the last couple of days, Tara asked, "Where are we going, Lee?"

Sensing the rising tide of emotion, Joey and his mom moved to the side of the bar and turned their attention to the television.

Already briefed on the secretive nature of the charter destination, Clark answered for Riker. "We're going to take your mom on a leisurely tour of the Lake Erie shoreline. Your brother here will have to fill you in on the rest."

"I hate Mom for this," fumed Tara. She made a fist and pounded on the bar.

Enjoying his part in all this not one bit, Riker paid attention to the television and let Tara get it out of her system.

On the screen, orange and red lights strobed all around the building while ant-sized figures in turnout coats and carrying axes and pulling hoses dodged the falling bodies. Streams of water caused puffs of steam to rise intermittently from within the charred facade of the building that the day before was a gleaming testament to New York's ability to rebound after taking a hit.

"We better go before we can't," urged Clark. "By the way ... name's Wade Clark. I prefer Clark."

Servers and cooks and customers from the main dining area had crowded into the bar and were staring expectantly at the television.

Riker urged Clark to lead the way, then let Tara and Steve-O fall in behind. He thanked Joey and his mom one last time, then threaded through the mass of bodies and hustled to catch up with the others.

Chapter 64

During the short walk through the lot and around the restaurant's east side, Clark told them he was ex-Army—"A real hush-hush group"—and had logged a couple of thousand hours of stick time flying everything from Hughes 500 Little Birds to CH-47 Chinooks. He then explained that the Airbus AS365 Dauphin they'd chartered was a civilian version of the helicopter currently in use by the United States Coast Guard. He rattled off the specs, most important of which to Riker was the helo's top speed in knots and their equivalent in kilometers per hour. Once Clark was finished, Riker said, "I know we're close to Canada and all, but what the heck is a hundred and sixty-five knots *slash* three hundred kilometers when converted to *miles*?"

Clark opened the door and held it while Tara and Steve-O climbed into the passenger compartment. "It means we'll be pushing two hundred miles per hour," he said. "And that'll get us to where we're going in two shakes."

Riker took hold of a handle inside the door, planted his bionic on the step, and hesitated in that position for a tick. "What kind of range does she have?"

Clark was caught examining the prosthesis revealed when Riker's pant leg rode up. Looking up at Riker, the forty-something aviator said, "Don't worry, Mr. Riker. We'll only have to stop once to refuel. It'll be on the return flight. Take twenty or thirty minutes, max. And to spare us any hassles, I already charged your card for a full tank of JP at the going rate as per oh nine hundred this morning." He smiled and his face showed off a lifetime's worth of wrinkles likely earned during deployments in deserts and jungles the world over. "I'll have y'all back here before dinner."

Riker said, "Chaos wasn't lying when he said you'd be accommodating." He ducked his head and climbed into the spacious cabin.

He sat in the row to his left where he could see into the cockpit through a small windowless opening. Because his back was against the rear bulkhead and near the turbines and machinery, he was able to stretch his legs out along the helo's center axis.

As Clark closed the door, Riker walked his gaze around the cabin. To his fore, in an aft-facing captain's chair, Steve-O was already buckled in, hat on lap and smiling wide.

After having helped Steve-O with the complicated safety belt, Tara had claimed an identical chair across the narrow aisle from him. Like nearly every surface in the helicopter's passenger compartment, the chairs were wrapped in supple cream-colored leather and trimmed with polished walnut.

"Fancy shmancy," remarked Tara. "Feels like I'm in a limousine."

"I've never been in a limo," admitted Steve-O.

"This is pretty much the same," said Riker. "Except we'll be hundreds of feet in the air and this limo is costing me an arm and both legs."

Voice filtering through the pass-through, Clark said, "You'll find headsets in the compartments on the sides of the aft-facing chairs. Mr. Riker, yours is in the starboard-side armrest. Adjust the boom microphones so that the foam piece sits a couple of inches from your mouths." As he flipped switches and the turbine engines whined to life in the background, he explained that the headsets were Bluetooth and interconnected so that everyone could communicate with him so long as they didn't all attempt to talk at once.

Clark finished by reminding them a little bit of volume in the voice went a long way when speaking over the shared connection.

Riker adjusted his hat, then donned his headset and powered it on under Steve-O's watchful eye.

After collapsing her headset to the smallest possible position, Tara snugged it on. "Like this?"

"Perfect fit," said Riker. He leaned forward and adjusted her boom microphone. "Now you're good to go." He regarded Steve-O, saw his headset was squared away, and flashed the man an enthusiastic thumbs up.

"Comms check," said Clark.

One at a time, beginning with Riker and ending with Steve-O, the passengers confirmed verbally that they could hear the pilot.

"Hot damn," said Clark. "First time's the charm." He held a gloved hand up in the pass-through for all to see. "Wheels up in five."

He began the countdown and a sensation Riker could only describe as pure power caressed the Airbus's airframe.

At "Four," Riker heard the turbines spool up exponentially; however, thanks to the noise-cancelling properties of the Bose headset, he wasn't being subjected to the full range of their high-pitched whine.

At "Three" the helicopter went light on its tricycle-style landing gear.

Getting to "Two," Clark was proven to be a man who liked to jump the gun, because Riker's stomach and the pound of prime ribeye inside were instantly ambushed by positive Gs when the helicopter rocketed from the vineyard lawn.

As the helicopter pitched nose down and the gazebo and flowers flashed by the starboard side in a technicolor blur, Riker detected the sound of the landing gear seating home. He exchanged a quick glance with Tara, whose face had gone pale. Seeing the death grip she was putting on the leather armrests, he met her gaze and mouthed, "It'll be okay. Just relax and enjoy the ride."

Across the aisle from Tara, as the Airbus leveled out over open water and accelerated briskly, Steve-O let out a war whoop and pumped his fist.

All at once, the deep waters of Lake Erie, dark and foreboding, dominated the ship's port-side windows.

Five hundred feet below the Airbus on the starboard-side, the lake's shoreline snaked by. At speed, the strip of clay and sand presented as a tan ripple sandwiched between lapping water and shocks of brown and green grass. Now and then lakefront homes and piers with watercraft tied to them flitted by.

Seconds after going airborne, a golf course with its narrow fairways, white-sand hazards, and vibrantly hued undulating greens dominated the shoreline. A beat later the Airbus slowed considerably and Clark directed all eyes to the Pennsylvania/New York state line where an inordinate amount of tan military vehicles were parked in two large clusters on both sides of Interstate 90.

The fields of grass on either side of the four-lane as well as the grass-covered center median bore dark brown gashes from the passage of tons of machinery. By Riker's estimation, two dozen Humvees and half as many MRAPs were divided equally between the two massive motor pools. Interspersed among what had to be a good chunk of the New York National Guard's northern contingent were dozens of white SUVs.

"This multi-state joint exercise seems to be expanding," proffered Clark.

"I concur," said Riker. A part of him wanted to tell Clark all that he'd seen and been through the last couple of days. Instead, hoping to get the aviator's unbiased take on the events here and in Manhattan, he merely mentioned watching the live television feed beamed from the RV lot and then stressed how he was skeptical anyone had actually named the operation Romeo Victor.

"More likely," suggested Riker, "is that reporter who'd admitted on the air to overhearing the op called Romeo Victor was making one hell of an assumption about what the soldiers had been talking about."

"No way *anyone* who's been through basic training would bestow an operation of this scale and scope with a name containing one, let alone two of the most commonly used monikers in the NATO phonetic alphabet," said Clark.

"Communicating on any net at any level would be nothing less than a monumental goat rope if in fact they did."

"I concur," said Riker. "My money says the reporter merely overheard a couple of weekend warriors discussing the focus of the exercise in code."

This time, Clark was the one who said, "I concur." But he took it a step further, adding, "Something big is afoot. I think the moment the reporter assumed Romeo Victor as the op's name and reported on it, whoever is heading it up, Joint Chiefs or someone at the battalion level, decided to let it grow legs and run."

Riker said nothing.

***

Ten minutes after wheels up, Clark directed their attention to the starboard windows. "Dunkirk, New York. Population eleven thousand and change as of the last time I visited. Know that the drive was not worth it. Judge didn't see fit to lower the bail on my speeding ticket."

Riker laughed.

"How fast were you going?" asked Steve-O.

"Hundred or so in a fifty-five," answered Clark.

"Any relation to Sammy Hagar?" asked Riker.

"Likely Tom Cruise," said Clark. "Because I always feel the *need for speed.*"

"Is that why you're not flying for the 'hush hush' unit any longer?"

"No, Mr. Riker," replied Clark. "I pranged a bird during a very important op."

"Call me Lee. Did you *prang* said chopper anywhere near Islamabad?"

"If I tell you, I would have to kill you," said Clark. "Since we're taking a stroll down memory lane … wanna tell me about that leg of yours?"

A tensing of the muscles began the inevitable slow crawl up Riker's back. "Left it in Iraq," he admitted. "Somehow a sweep missed an IED penetrator set up beside Route Irish."

"Everyone get out alive?"

"*Nobody* got out alive."

Riker felt something land on his stump and a tremor shot through his body. Looking down, he saw Tara's hand. Meeting her gaze, he saw empathy.

Clark said, "I'm sorry to hear that, Lee." Then, all business, he announced they were "Feet wet" and would be over open water until entering Buffalo's airspace.

***

Eighteen minutes into the flight, Clark was talking to a tower controller at Buffalo International. In less than a minute the controller was back with a new heading for Clark and granted him permission to enter Buffalo airspace.

"Sure, Mom used to like to stop at the Anchor Bar for authentic buffalo wings," said Tara, peering down on the city's southwest suburbs. "Doesn't mean she'd want to be crop-dusted over top of it."

Riker remained stoic, staring at the ceiling as the helicopter banked hard to port.

"You know the '*secret*'"— she made air quotes— "ingredient in their wings is Frank's Red Hot?"

Beating Riker to the punchline, Steve-O said, "I put that shit on everything."

Stifling a laugh, Riker closed his eyes and buried his face in his hands.

Tara said, "Swear jar, buddy."

"For what it's worth. It's what I make my wings with on Super Bowl Sunday," Clark drawled over the shared comms. Then, without missing a beat, he added, "We'll be eyes on our destination in twenty mikes."

"The suspense is killing me," said Tara.

"Sit back and close your eyes."

She did.

"Keep them closed," said Riker as he unzipped the bag and removed the urn. "No peeking until I say so." He placed the urn gently in Tara's lap.

Instinctively, Tara wrapped the vessel containing her mom in a loving embrace.

Listening in to the exchange, Clark held up a thumb to indicate he knew Riker was calling the ball from here on out.

Still enamored by his first "limo" ride, Steve-O craned toward the window, taking it all in as they thundered north.

Eyes still closed, Tara's jaw took a granite set.

Chapter 65

As the Airbus slowed and leveled off, Riker said, "Okay, Tara, you may look now."

Tara remained in the same repose as she'd been for the better part of twenty minutes: legs crossed underneath her on the plush chair, arms wrapped around the urn. She stayed unmoving until the helicopter was still, finally opening her eyes when Steve-O said, "That's beautiful."

Upon opening her eyes, Tara looked out the window to her right. At first all she saw was a voluminous white cloud. It was roiling and rising and dancing as if alive. Sunlight played at the base of the mist plume, refracting violet and blue and red as the aerated water whirled about in the disturbed air.

Still not saying anything, she leaned forward to see through the larger window inset into the cabin door.

She let out a pained groan and shook her head back and forth, a frown forming where once there had been bliss.

She looked at the urn, then regarded Riker. "You kidding me? Here?"

"Yep."

Her grip tightened on the urn. "Bullshit, Lee! No effin way Mom would want her ashes churning around Niagara Falls for all of eternity. She always said how much she loathed this tourist trap. The boat rides that made her seasick. And she hated wearing one of those stupid plastic coats she put on all of us even more than she hated getting wet by that drifting mist. 'Drowning by eyedropper' is how she described it once."

The helicopter drifted left and rotated to give them a view of a small island below.

"Did you like coming here as a kid?"

Tara nodded. "I loved it. I always looked forward to coming here. Winter ... spring, summer, didn't matter." She smiled and tears welled in her eyes. "The caramel apples. I can smell them now." She locked her gaze on the raging river.

"So can I, Sis. This place evokes all the good memories of our childhood. Mom knew that." He went quiet and took a deep breath. "It was *our* Disneyland, Tara. The Riker family Disneyland. She wanted us to be happy and be with her—feel her presence—whenever we visited here. On the phone when she was giving me my marching orders, she said to me how one day she expected us to bring our kids here to meet her."

Steve-O took his eyes off the water churning below and fished a napkin from a pocket. He put a hand on Tara's shoulder and offered it to her.

She dabbed at her eyes and blew her nose. After thanking Steve-O, she said, "Let's do this," and forced a half-smile.

"The slider will only open a few inches," said Clark over the shared comms. "Underneath Lee's seat is a funnel."

Riker snaked an arm under his seat and felt around blindly. Feeling his fingers brush the wide end of the cylindrical device, he found purchase and dragged it out.

The funnel was red and made of the type of hard plastic that leached that *Made in China* odor. It was free of oil residue and still bore the instruction and warning stickers. The same kind of generic item could be had at every truck stop and gas station Riker had ever set foot in.

Riker took the urn from Tara. He pried off the top, then removed the softball-sized box from the base.

The box was wrapped in a small plastic bag, which Riker slipped off and stowed in his pocket. There was a strip of tape securing the box top. He peeled off the tape and opened the cardboard cube. Inside was another plastic bag, its contents light gray and malleable through the plastic.

"It's like opening a Russian nesting doll," joked Tara.

Steve-O was watching intently. He said, "That's all that's left of her?"

Riker handed the empty box to him. "Yep, Steve-O. The human body is mostly water."

As Riker slid the window open, a blast of rotor wash found its way inside. It was cold and carried with it a dampness and an underlying odor of kerosene-tinged exhaust.

"You get honors," said Riker. "Mom insists." He handed Tara the bag of ashes then threaded the funnel's flexible nozzle through the window opening.

Holding hands, brother and sister recited the Lord's prayer.

Finished saying a short eulogy for their mother, Tara held the bag in both hands and poured while Riker steadied the funnel. "Ashes to ashes, dust to dust," he said as the last of the gray powder trickled into the funnel and the bag sucked in on itself.

Crossing himself, Steve-O said, "Rest in peace, Rita."

Tara gasped as she took her eyes off the spot in the water that had just swallowed up the last of the ashes and regarded Steve-O.

Riker's head snapped in Steve-O's direction. "How'd you know her name?" he demanded.

Steve-O upended the box. "It's written right here."

Sure enough, her name was scrawled there in black ink.

Suppressing a grin, Riker said, "That it is."

"Let me have that," said Tara. She took the box, stuffed the bag inside, and put it in with the reassembled urn.

"Thank you, Clark," said Riker. "We're done here." He stowed the funnel, then reclaimed his seat and buckled in.

"Always a pleasure," replied the pilot. Then, voice going soft, he added, "My condolences. Sounds like Rita was a helluva lady with a good head on her shoulders. Pretty good combination, if you ask me."

"That she was," said Riker agreeably. "She and Dad are together now."

"Are we continuing on to destination number two?"

"Yes, sir," said Riker.

349

There was no acknowledgement from Clark. He simply banked the helicopter to starboard and set them out on a mostly southbound heading.

Tara looked a question at Riker.

He said, "No more secrets. We're going to see the Big Apple."

"New York City?"

"As close as we can get."

"Right now Manhattan airspace is closed," said Clark. "But I'll get you as close to Ground Zero as I can."

Chapter 66

Riker spent the first hour of the flight observing the goings on down below through the Steiners. From an altitude that varied between three and five thousand feet, save for seeing a couple of military convoys heading in the same general direction as the Dauphin, it looked like business as usual.

Across the aisle from Riker, Tara was all but swallowed up by her seat. Listing to the left, head pressed against the window, her eyes had been locked on the landscape below since they left the airspace over Niagara Falls.

Steve-O had lost all interest in the sprawl of towns and their car-choked thoroughfares ten minutes into the flight. He had managed to get his chair reclined and had removed the headset and kicked off his boots shortly thereafter. Now he was fully stretched out with his tube-sock-clad feet crossed and the Stetson balanced on his upturned face.

"Steve-O's sound asleep, Sis. Anything *we* need to discuss?"

She sat up in her seat and stretched and yawned. "For the record," she said in a low voice. "I'm not mad at you for—"

"For what ... honoring Mom's wishes?"

"I was over that the moment you told me why Mom chose Niagara. I'm talking about the whole secret helicopter trip and now this little sojourn to New York. I was pretty pissed up until about ten minutes ago."

"What changed?"

"It's more a question of what's *changing*. What do I have to go back to in Middletown? My car? My apartment and the second-hand-store furnishings? My wardrobe that fits in one drawer and on two dozen plastic hangars?"

"Now you're sounding like me, Tara. Restless. Irritable. Discontented. One or all of those things rearing its ugly head is all it takes to make me want to pick up and relocate. As a matter of fact, I've had a habit of falling prey to it and moving on every few months."

"So what are *we* doing after *we* check this next item off your bucket list?"

"I think we owe it to Steve-O to see what he has in mind. If he doesn't want to go back to Middletown, we can all come up with a couple of alternate destinations and put it to a vote."

The helicopter slowed considerably and began to descend. Clark came on over the comms and said he had just received clearance to land and refuel at Wilkes-Barre International in Scranton, Pennsylvania. He wasn't sure how long airspace would remain open over the southern half of New York and didn't want to get caught light on fuel.

Riker flashed a thumbs up as the distinct sound of the landing gear deploying made its way into the cabin.

"We'll be back on track in thirty minutes," Clark promised.

***

Twenty minutes after the bowser hooked up and started transferring fuel, it was driving away and Clark was going through his pre-flight and awaiting the all clear from the tower.

***

They sat there with the rotor spinning over their heads for another fifteen minutes as a trio of commercial jetliners taxied one at a time to the runway, burned a minute or two each waiting for their clearance, then thundered into the pale blue sky, off to their next destination.

Finally clearance to launch came from a male air traffic controller in the tower.

Riker found it humorous how Clark instantly switched into professional mode and his voice lost some of its twang as he spoke to the controller. Riker also noted how Clark's launch from the tarmac under the watchful eye of the tower personnel was nothing like that at the vineyard.

The liftoff was smooth and measured and likely barely perceptible unless one was watching the horizon. Only after the helicopter had gained a considerable bit of altitude did Clark stow the gear. Then, instead of pouring on the power and dumping the stick forward and closing the gear doors on the fly as he had back at the vineyard, he gave the doors ample time to close, rotated the craft clockwise on a flat plane until its nose pointed south, and then slipped away slow and steady. It wasn't until the Dauphin was well clear of the airport's fenced perimeter that Clark spooled up the turbines and the ground below began to blur and fall away.

For the remainder of the flight Clark pushed the Dauphin hard, keeping her charging southeast just a few knots shy of the manufacturer's recommended top speed.

"Twenty miles out," called Clark. "We'll be following the Hudson in and the East River out. Get your cameras and binoculars ready. We're only going to get one pass."

Tara leaned across the cabin and gently nudged Steve-O awake. Once he removed the Stetson from his face and brought his seatback up, she explained to him where they were.

Twenty miles. Riker did the math in his head. Came to the conclusion that Lady Liberty would be outside the windows in seven or eight short minutes. Wanting a preview of things to come, he steadied his elbows on his knees and pressed the Steiners to his face.

Aiming down the center axis of the helicopter allowed Riker to see through the cockpit glass the plume of pale gray smoke rising into the cobalt sky. *Just like 9/11*, he thought. *The extremists raising another middle finger to the Great Satan.*

***

Barely two minutes had elapsed when Clark was back on and directing all eyes to port. As he slowed the craft, he said, "Some kind of mass exodus happening. That's Riverside Park there. The Hudson Greenway is next." He whistled. A long drawn-out and mournful sound. "Look at those lines at Convention Pier."

Peering out his window at the gridlocked vehicles choking nearly every arterial in and out of the city core, Steve-O said, "Looks like rush hour down there."

"And then some," remarked Tara.

"Bridges and tunnels have been closed since last night," added Clark. "Manhattan's locked down. I have contacts at Logan International in Boston who tell me some of the terrorists were taken care of yesterday. There's a big manhunt underway for the rest here in Manhattan. Likely why it's all choked up."

On the greenspaces below, Riker saw thousands of people milling about. There didn't appear to be any order. There were no lines here. If there was any attempt being undertaken by government officials to check IDs prior to the boarding of the myriad watercraft waiting to ferry people across the Hudson, Riker didn't see them.

"Lady Liberty," said Clark. "And out the port windows is 4 World Trade Center. She's still burning internally."

The airspace over Battery Park as well as a good deal of that on the Manhattan side of the Hudson was home to a half-dozen news helicopters as well as a trio of Black Hawks moving out eastbound fast and low. The civilian birds were mostly hovering in place, no doubt waiting like mechanical vultures for the other shoe to drop.

Tara unbuckled and wormed in between Steve-O and Riker and pressed both hands to the window. "Think it's going to come down?"

"Not likely," said Riker. "They designed the hell out of this one. So much so that it would hold up to a fuel-laden airliner hitting it."

Tara said, "I read on the television in the vineyard bar that they think the fire suppression systems were sabotaged before some type of incendiary bombs were detonated."

"I'm not surprised they struck again. But I am baffled as to why they left the Freedom Tower alone. This one though, it'll burn itself out before it collapses," said Riker, voice filled with confidence.

"Those black squares—" began Tara.

"That's where the towers used to stand," finished Riker. He pointed out the building twisting its way skyward kitty corner to the 9/11 Memorial. "And there's its replacement. The Freedom Tower is the tallest building on the island."

The middle of the Freedom Tower was at eye level with the helicopter as it curled around the tip of Manhattan. The distant landscape was reflected back at them in the mirrored glass. And as the angle changed, they caught a glimpse of the back side of 4 World Trade Center in the larger building's southeast-facing windows. And strangely, it looked untouched.

It wasn't until Clark brought them around to the East River side of Manhattan Island that they saw the true scope of the disaster. It was nothing like what they saw three hours ago on television. The top two-thirds of the structure was listing. Captured by the mirrored glass in the windows of the lower floors were the constantly strobing lights of dozens of first response vehicles. Parked on the east side of the building were a trio of ladder trucks. White horsetails of water under pressure arced from nozzles in the extended ladders.

Nearby it looked as if a skirmish had broken out. Six deep and growing, a crush of bodies pressed against chest-high metal barriers erected around the ladder trucks. On the opposite side of the fencing two dozen people in black, wielding body-length shields and black batons, were giving the nearest of the rioters a vicious beating.

"The water isn't reaching the fire," said Steve-O.

"I'm afraid you're right," said Riker.

Tara stabbed a finger at the glass. "What kind of dicks would attack firefighters?"

"The world is full of dicks," replied Riker. "I'm sure reinforcements are on the way."

On the tail end of Riker's response, a whole bunch of things happened one right after the other.

From the point where the building began its lean right on up to the top stories, a ripple pulsed through the intact windows. In the next instant, mirrored glass was raining down ahead of a tsunami of debris being jettisoned through the newly created openings.

As glass and insulation and papers rained down on the streets and vehicles below, the top two-thirds of 4 World Trade Center slipped away from the rest of the building. While the weakening of the building's core structure took forty-eight hours, its final act happened incredibly fast.

When the helicopter banked hard to starboard—surely an instinctual maneuver on Clark's part—Riker was afforded a panoramic view of the breadth of Battery Park. What he initially thought were people waiting to board ferries to take them across to the New Jersey side were suddenly revealed for what they truly were: thousands upon thousands of mindless automatons, their pale faces turned up, dead eyes gazing expectantly skyward. Though they were ant-like from this distance, he knew they were no different than the creatures prowling the streets of Middletown, the ones on the cannibal attack videos playing on the Deep Web site, or the ones coming through Peter's corn maze.

Hands pressed to his face, Steve-O said, "No … this can't be happening again!"

Voice unwavering, Clark said, "This is not good."

On the tail end of Clark's statement, the comms came alive and a tower controller at John F. Kennedy International began to address all Eastern Seaboard air traffic.

Waiting for the controller to finish the preamble to the emergency mandate and get to the meat of the order, Riker cocked his head dog-like.

The meat never reached Riker's ears. Instead, he was cut out of the comms and had to resort to watching Clark's mouth move during the five long seconds of silence.

When Clark finally opened up the channel, the controller was finished relaying the emergency declaration, and all that was coming through was what sounded like the pilot drawing some calming breaths.

Riker was watching some kind of a melee taking place on the upper deck of the Staten Island Ferry. There were a dozen people in a scrum with a handful of attackers. In a matter of seconds the attackers had overtaken the larger crowd and freshly spilled blood was being smeared across the wooden deck planks.

Directly below the ferry's port side, seven or eight people were huddled in a small pocket created where a gore-streaked ambulance was backed in against the sloping gangway and chest-high cement seawall.

On an electronic reader board nearby an appeal for calm and maintaining orderly lines was still being broadcast.

As the helicopter passed over the group behind the ambulance, one of their own was yanked forcibly underneath the rear wheels and disappeared into the crazed throng pressing in from all directions. The last thing that registered with Riker was the half-dozen faces looking expectantly skyward.

Tearing his eyes from the carnage, Riker looked straight ahead and out the cockpit glass. Having come to a decision, he rattled off everything he knew about the things Tara was calling zombies.

Soberly, Clark said, "I saw what you saw down there. Good enough name for them as any."

Relieved the aviator didn't call him crazy, Riker asked, "What was the emergency declaration?"

"The entire Eastern Seaboard has been declared a no-fly zone," answered Clark. "I'm not going to be able to finish the tour, let alone return you to the vineyard."

"Where do we go from here?"

"I've been ordered by JFK Control to immediately land at the nearest airport."

"Why ground all flights?" asked Tara. "A plane did not do that to the tower."

"You're right," replied Clark. "This order has nothing to do with that building coming down. And if we're comparing events … the FAA let the news choppers own the airspace up here after the towers came down." He went silent for a beat. When he came back on the comms he made it known that he was convinced the grounding order was a direct result of the madness happening at Battery Park.

Tara put a hand on Steve-O's shoulder and shot her brother a worried look. "What do we do now, Lee?"

Riker covered the boom mic and mouthed, "I'm thinking."

Steve-O wiped a tear. Looking Riker in the eye, he said, "The world just changed again, didn't it?"

For the first time since he met Steve-O, Riker was certain the man wasn't voicing a lyric from a country and western song. Another thing Riker was certain of after seeing Battery Park teeming with things whose existence defied all logic was that Steve-O's statement was directed at the wrong threat. Terrorists, homegrown or otherwise, were the least of their worries. Riker feared that what he was seeing now and what he had witnessed the day before in Middletown was but the tip of the proverbial iceberg.

With the memory of their escape from Shenandoah High fresh on his mind, Riker took his hand off the microphone. "Clark," he blurted. "Can you put us down anywhere *but* an airport? Like maybe a high school field or abandoned lot?"

Clark was quiet for a moment as he navigated the busy airspace. Once he had the Dauphin running back up the Hudson, he let Riker know he had just the place in mind.

"Where?" asked Riker.

"Your turn to be in the dark," said Clark cryptically. "And there's no need for any of you to worry. I can land this old girl on a pinhead in the dark of night. Stow your tray tables in the upright position and gather your gear. We'll be wheels down in five."

Chapter 67

Trying to purge the memory of the tower sliding toward the ground, Riker focused on the Statue of Liberty filling up the port-side windows. From up close her copper skin looked to have grown a sheen of mold. And Lady Liberty surely wasn't as attractive at eye level and from a hundred feet distant as she was on currency.

Tara zipped her coat to her neck. "Where do we go after Clark drops us off?"

Riker shrugged. "We have money. Lots of it, too. I say we get some new wheels and get the hell out of Dodge." He looked to Steve-O. "Any ideas, pal?"

"Somewhere warm." Taking a cue from Tara, he zipped his coat to his neck.

"Almost there," said Clark. "When I set down, Riker's in charge of the door. Get out quick and move away with your heads down. And remember to hold onto your hats."

"Thanks for the lift," said Riker. "Be sure to tack on an extra thirty percent as a thank you from all of us."

"That's damn near six grand," replied Clark. "You sure about that?"

Tara broke in. "It's my brother's money we're spending. I'm cool with it."

Riker said nothing. He motioned for the others to remove their headsets.

"Feet dry," said Clark as the river was replaced by an area of New Jersey home to wharfs and piers. The boardwalk was deserted and nearly all of the slips empty.

Seeing Tara and Steve-O stowing their headsets, Riker said, "Worth every penny, Clark. I have your card. We may be repeat customers."

Clark flashed a thumbs up and said, "Two minutes out."

Riker shed his headset and put it away in its cubby. Looking out the window, he was surprised to learn they were coming in fast and low over a boulevard lined with strip malls and crisscrossed by arterial streets bustling with traffic.

It wasn't until a stand of mature trees flashed underneath the bird that he saw the fairway and sand traps and he knew what Clark had in mind.

The landing was nothing like the takeoff from Milton Barre in Scranton. Clark brought the Dauphin in fast and steep, flaring and deploying the gear just feet over an immense and seemingly flat green.

Outside Riker's window, the herald on the flagstick was whipped hard by the rotor down-blast. Bag in hand, he threw open the door. Only when Tara and Steve-O were out the door and hustling away from the helicopter with heads down and hair whipping did Riker slide the door shut and tap twice on the fuselage.

Before he could take a step toward the far edge of the green where the others were already waiting, the turbines howled and the Dauphin launched skyward.

By the time Riker turned and waved at the ascending chopper, the air around him was calming and he could hear traffic sounds from the nearby boulevard.

Epilogue

Bell Ford was basically a trio of gleaming glass cubes built side by side with the cube in the center dwarfing the pair bookending it.

A phalanx of shiny new Fords with window stickers and dealer promo plates stood between the grass strip bordering the boulevard and Bell Ford's geometrically inspired front elevation.

When Riker set foot inside the showroom, there was still mud on his boots from the trek through the greenspace separating the golf course from the dealership's side lot.

"I'm going to the bathroom," said Tara. "All that flowing water at the Falls started it. Damn near pissed myself when the building came down."

"Go ahead," said Riker. "I'm going to start the process."

"I have to go, too," said Steve-O.

Tara paused mid-step. "Good," she said. "You can help me find them."

"I'm a human compass," said Steve-O with a smile. His boots clomped on the tiles and mud calved from them as he hustled to catch up.

Riker watched the two wend between a pair of new electric econoboxes parked grill to grill near a partition fronting what he guessed to be the sales managers' domain. Seeing streaks of brown and bits of mud and grass they were leaving in their wake, he thought to himself: *They're going to have no problem finding their way back.*

Riker stood there for a short while surveying the place. The air in here smelled of floor wax and new tire rubber. To his left, past the pair of hybrid cars and sales managers' area, was a customer waiting area comprised of an assortment of stuffed leather chairs and sofas. Stationed here and there were a handful of metal and glass end tables all home to magazines and customers' soda cans and paper coffee cups.

Everything was arranged in a U-shape. At the open end of the U was a television that had to be eighty-inches diagonal if it was a foot. It was huge. And had a vivid screen showing the news of the day. Which wasn't good by any stretch.

There wasn't a soul utilizing the plush furnishings inside the U. They were all standing in a rough semicircle before the humongous flat screen television.

There was maybe a dozen people of varying ages and genders crowded real close to the television. Riker had them pegged as customers waiting for oil to be changed or scheduled maintenance to be concluded.

Another dozen people stood off to the side at an oblique angle to the screen. Not quite in the waiting area. But not quite disassociated from it either. A good mix of men and women. Some wore shirts and ties. Others wore slick-looking gray jackets emblazoned with the blue Ford oval. Riker guessed they were employees not selling cars or trucks at the moment.

Everyone was watching the demise of 4WTC being replayed by a local channel.

A salesman dressed in shirt and tie and nearly a head taller than the others looked away from the television.

Riker waved and caught his eye.

The man stood his ground but regarded Riker for a long three-count.

Riker got the impression the salesman was sizing him up. Some kind of a decision was being made. The correct decision was going to result in a commission going in the human string bean's pocket. The incorrect would see Riker strolling over there and calling him out in front of the sales managers currently standing around inside their glassed-in area, no doubt watching a television exclusive to them.

The tall salesman's decision favored Riker. He threaded his way through his fellows, walked in front of the television, then parted the customers and approached Riker.

From a dozen feet away Riker caught the man looking down at the mud streaked across the floor. At six feet out the salesman's gaze dropped to Riker's muddy boots, hung there for a beat, then flicked up and leveled on his face. At arm's length the salesman's right hand shot out and he was smiling big and introducing himself as "Chad" and apologizing for the lack of help on the floor.

"Name's Lee," said Riker. "No worries. I've got nothing but time on my hands."

"Did you know Building Four just fell?"

Jaw going rigid, Riker nodded. "I watched it from a thousand feet over the Hudson."

Chad did a double take.

"In the air?"

"No," said Riker. "In a helicopter. Pilot just let us out on the golf course beside your place."

Dumbfounded, Chad craned and looked in the general direction Riker and the others had come in from. "Colonia? The country club?"

Riker nodded. "How my boots got muddy."

Chad shook his head slowly side to side.

Riker figured the man thought he was being put on. Like one of those gotcha-style hidden video shows.

"What are you looking to get into?" asked Chad, his gaze settling momentarily on the distant television.

"I want a truck. F-150, preferably. That's what I had before."

Chad's smile drooped a little. "New or pre-owned?"

"New," said Riker.

Chad's smile was back full force and cheesy as ever.

Riker was expecting the old *What's your price range?* query. Instead, Chad asked what he needed in his truck.

Ticking the items off on his fingers, Riker said, "Moonroof, four doors, four-wheel-drive, big engine, and automatic transmission ... 'cause clutches and me don't get along."

"Premium stereo?"

"Radio in my last truck didn't work."

Chad's smile was back to half-staff. "Do you want to lease or finance your new truck?"

"Paying in full. You take a debit card?"

Now Chad's mouth didn't appear to know what to do. His lips were pressed into a thin white line as he mulled over Riker's question.

"We can call your bank and work out a money transfer."

"Whatever works," said Riker. "What do you have on the lot in the way of F-150s?" Before Chad answered, Riker looked past his head and saw Tara and Steve-O emerge from behind the television viewing area.

"Our base F-150 is—"

Riker interrupted Chad by stabbing a thumb toward the ceiling.

"Next model up is the—"

Again, Riker did the thing with the thumb.

"There's the Platinum, but it's nearly the same price as the Raptor. Now that's a beast of a truck. Five hundred plus horses. It'll go *anywhere*."

"What color do you have in stock?"

Chad seemed to deflate. He began worrying his tie. "We're between model years on the Raptor. They're bringing an all-new one out next year. Aluminum body. Twin turbo V6."

"Riker frowned. "V6? Do you have anything similar to the V8 Raptor on the lot?"

Chad's eyes went wide and swiveled to the left. "We do. Follow me, Lee."

Tara and Steve-O showed up next to the customer waiting area, totally blocking Chad's path in the process.

"What's up, Bro?"

"Chad's going to show me …" He looked to Chad. "What's it called?"

"Shelby Baja 700," said Chad. "It'll blow the doors off the Raptor Lee came looking for."

Tara shot Riker a look of approval.

Riker said, "Where is she?"

"Right this way." Chad was smiling coyly at his coworkers as he led Riker, Tara, and Steve-O past the television where they took a left.

After filing into a smaller cube-shaped building, they came upon a raised platform textured to resemble a gently sloped field of rock or maybe scree, which one Riker couldn't decide. Parked on the platform at an angle so as to partially show off the undercarriage was a cobalt-blue pickup standing tall on big tires and lifted by factory off-road suspension.

At once Riker was smitten.

Steve-O said, "Wow," and began to circle the display like a shark would an injured seal pup.

Tara stared for a long three-count, after which she said, "You need it, Lee. I *love* the white stripes. And those light bars up front. Wow!"

Not one to let a golden opportunity go to waste, Chad opened the door and ushered Riker behind the wheel.

Staring down from the driver's seat and basking in the rich smell of new leather, Riker said, "It's damn comfortable. And roomy." He was subconsciously massaging the leather-wrapped steering wheel.

"Pop the hood," said Chad. "It's got the big V8 with a Whipple supercharger. She's pushing over seven-hundred horsepower."

Riker said, "No need," and climbed down from the big truck. "You had me at seven-hundred horsepower. Let's get 'er done."

Pausing with one hand still on the door, Chad leaned in close and said, "She's one of fifty made. We just got her in. The owner insisted we put a big premium on her. Always does that to see if he can get a whale to bite."

Tara said, "A whale?"

"Someone in Vegas with money to burn," answered Steve-O. "Learned that from the Kardashians."

Riker said, "Never say that name in my presence again, Steve-O. Guilt by association and all that." He turned back to

Chad. Speaking slowly, not that it really mattered to him, he asked, "How much is she?"

"A hundred and fifty thousand."

"I'll take it with one condition, Chad."

Chad was already looking toward the sales managers' office. He swiveled his head back around. Regarded Riker and swallowed hard. Dry lips making a strange sound when they parted, he asked, "What is it?"

Riker looked to his boots, then pointed at Tara and Steve-O's boots. "Throw in some all-weather floor mats."

"And free undercoating," added Tara.

Not wanting to be left out, Steve-O said, "And a pine tree for the mirror."

Chad said, "Done" and took Riker's driver's license and bank card. Then, as Riker recited them from memory, Chad wrote down the routing number to his Chase checking account.

Riker scooped up the NRA bag and led Tara and Steve-O to a nearby table to wait.

***

Chad was back in twenty minutes with a folder clamped under one arm, the keys to the Shelby Baja in one hand, and a large plastic sack stuffed to brimming with the set of black all-weather floor mats, complete with the white Ford Shelby logo.

Riker said, "Bank didn't hassle you?"

"On the contrary," said Chad. "They bent over backwards to make the deal happen. All you have to do is sign and drive."

As Riker added his John Hancock to what seemed like half a ream of paper, Chad went over the truck's various safety features. He also presented the owner's manual and mentioned that all routine service was on Bell Ford for the first two years.

"Don't think I'll be back this way," said Riker.

"Where are you headed?" asked Chad.

"I'm not sure." He looked to Tara, then Steve-O. Both were wearing toothy grins. Which seemed strange considering the things over at Battery Park and the stuff still playing out on the television behind them.

"What?" said Riker.

"You'll see," said Tara.

"We already booked the place," added Steve-O.

Riker's brow furrowed. "A hotel?"

"No, a mansion. It's an Airbnb," said Tara.

"Air what?"

"Never mind," she said with a sly grin. "Me and Steve-O are the cruise directors on this one."

"Tell me," insisted Riker. "Someplace warm and zombie free, I trust."

Chad pushed the keys across the table to Riker. "Did you say *zombie* free?"

"Inside joke," said Tara.

"Come on, Sis."

Tara rose from her seat. "Karma is a bitch," she said, shouldering the duffel containing the urn and shotgun. "Take the keys. Let's go."

The Riker siblings and Steve-O will be back in Book 2 of Riker's Apocalypse in late 2018.

Thanks for reading! Reviews help. Please consider leaving yours at the place of purchase. Please feel free to Friend Shawn Chesser on Facebook. To receive the latest information on upcoming releases first, please join my mailing list at ShawnChesser.com. Find all of my books on my Amazon Author Page.

RIKER'S APOCALYPSE (THE PROMISE)

Also by Shawn Chesser

Surviving the Zombie Apocalypse

TRUDGE

SOLDIER ON

IN HARM'S WAY

A POUND OF FLESH

ALLEGIANCE

MORTAL

WARPATH

GHOSTS

FRAYED

DRAWL: DUNCAN'S STORY

DISTRICT

ABYSS

CUSTOMERS ALSO PURCHASED:

JOHN O'BRIEN
NEW WORLD
SERIES

JAMES N. COOK
SURVIVING THE DEAD
SERIES

MARK TUFO
ZOMBIE FALLOUT
SERIES

ARMAND
ROSAMILLIA
DYING DAYS
SERIES

HEATH STALLCUP
THE MONSTER
SQUAD

www.ingramcontent.com/pod-product-compliance
Lightning Source LLC
Chambersburg PA
CBHW060153260626
47160CB00001B/252